THE
BROOD
OF
NIGHTMARE

ALSO BY BETHANY HELWIG

International Monster Slayers:
The Curse of Moose Lake
The Bite of Winter
The Ghosts of Yesteryear
The Dark Whisper

∼

Darkest Light

INTERNATIONAL MONSTER SLAYERS
BOOK FOUR

THE BROOD OF NIGHTMARE

BETHANY HELWIG

BRIGHTWAY BOOKS

This is a work of fiction. Names, characters, places, and incidents either are the product of the author's imagination or are used fictitiously. Where real-life historical or public figures appear, the situations, incidents, and dialogues concerning those persons are entirely fictional and are not intended to depict actual events or to change the entirely fictional nature of the work. In all other respects, any resemblance to actual persons, living or dead, or events is entirely coincidental.

Copyright © 2018 by Bethany Helwig
Published by Brightway Books, LLC

THE BROOD OF NIGHTMARE, characters, names and related indicia are trademarks of and © Bethany Helwig.

Cover Illustration: Bethany Helwig

All rights reserved.

First Edition: October 2018

ISBN-10: 1-946639-00-1
ISBN-13: 978-1-946639-00-4

For people who like longer books.
(Sorry, I couldn't help myself.)

P.S. (Not actually sorry.)

Werewolf Containment Site
Maison Bêtes de Gévaudan

Agent Pierre Moreau shines his flashlight into the gaping hole in the prison cell floor with a sigh. The jagged opening leads into one of the storm sewers beneath the Maison Bêtes de Gévaudan. His light reflects off rusty pipes, dripping water, and a layer of filth on the tunnel floor. In the gloom he can barely make out claw marks and footprints. One of the rougarous must have made the hole to escape. It wouldn't be the first time. They've been making holes for centuries—the prison is pockmarked with their attempts to flee—but they never make it past the guardians in the tunnels. Ten years of guarding rougarous and more than half of his time is spent chasing after them in these damned tunnels. He hasn't had a decent night's sleep in ages and it seems tonight he will fare no better.

Clicking on his radio, Pierre contacts the watchtower to let them know what he's found and that he's going in after an inmate that's decided to make a run for it.

"*Bonne chance,*" the watchtower responds.

Pierre grumbles under his breath, tugs on a pair of latex

gloves, and lowers himself down into the hole. His heavy boots splash in the filth, acquiring a new layer of rat poop and whatever other feces are left behind by the critters below. He grimaces and holds his flashlight aloft. At least his bite-resistant uniform withstands the filth and it slides off the bottom of his pants as he marches into the eerie depths of the tunnel.

The trail of human footprints eventually becomes paw prints that widen out. The rougarou must have started running once he tasted freedom—or so he thought. Pierre chuckles to himself. Never has one managed to slip past the gargouilles in the passages beneath the prison, the guardians of stone that no rougarou can take down with their deadly bite. Many have either ended up crushed at the hands of the gargouilles or dragged back with broken bones. Pierre's job here is only to convince these runaways to return before they end up as tenderized meat.

He steps over the skeleton of an imbécile who never saw daylight and never returned to his cell either. Pierre laughs at the stupidity of the prisoners, the ones that howl at the moon, the ones that beg for mercy, the ones who deny any wrongdoing. But their very existence is a menace and one that must always be contained no matter how much they plead their innocence.

The horrid smells of the tunnel don't faze Pierre anymore. He's grown used to the stench of rotten things. Although, he does pull his mask up over the lower half of his face to make sure he doesn't ingest the mold fibers and worse things lingering in the air.

His flashlight catches on fur held down by a fist of stone. He radios the watchtower with his find and a promise he'll be bringing back another prisoner—alive or dead is yet to be seen.

"*Bonjour!*" he calls and flicks the flashlight to catch the gargouille's attention. "*Pris une autre?*"

The guardian doesn't move. Pierre shouts at it again. "*Oi!*"

He stops five feet short of the stone giant and its unmoving wolfish prey. The girth of it blocks half the tunnel and he has to shuffle up on the rounded edge of the floor to get around it to see what's going on. When he rounds to the other side, his meager light reveals the left side of the gargouille is gone. From its beastly head, down its torso, and to the remnants of its leg, it looks melted as if it were made of hot wax, not magical stone.

"*Que se passe-t-il?*" he exclaims under his breath and bends closer to examine its body.

The rougarou that had tried to escape lies flattened under the intact gargouille's right fist, its back broken and lifeless. More than that, half of the flesh on its face has melted away just like the left half of the gargouille. What on earth happened here?

Pierre steps forward and part of the floor gives way into a gaping void beneath his feet. With a yell he leaps out of the way and shines his light into the abyss. It opens up directly where the gargouille's body melted as if whatever had done this had taken away part of the ground as well.

Breathing hard and pressed up against the side of the tunnel, Pierre fumbles with the radio clipped to his shoulder.

"*Tour de guet,*" he says but the watchtower doesn't answer. "*Entrez, tour de guet.*"

Static and then nothing. Pierre clicks the button again and again but no one answers.

Something slithers in the darkness. Whatever it is, it shouldn't be down here. Calling upon his agent training, Pierre moves carefully backwards and keeps a hand over his light. He needs to get back to the hole and into the safety of the prison. Taking careful steps, he inches back down the tunnel as fast as he dares.

The slithering draws closer followed by a low rumbling growl.

Pierre, distracted by the noise, glances over his shoulder and trips over a loose stone to fall noisily into the filth lining the tunnel. He scrambles to his feet and whips the light about to face the blackness behind him.

The pursuing growl vanishes.

To be replaced by the sound of water dripping and ending with a nasty hiss.

He freezes where he crouches low in the tunnel, the hole too far away to run to. He draws up his bio-mech gun as shadows snake into the beam of his flashlight.

Drip, *hissss*.

Drip, *hissss*.

A droplet falls from above the breadth of his light and touches the floor of the tunnel, hissing as it eats through the filth and forms a hole in the stone. Another droplet follows with the same effect.

Not water. Acid.

Hands shaking, Pierre guides the beam of the light up to the source of the drip.

The scream building in his throat dies as a set of powerful, acid dripping jaws clamp around his neck.

1

Hawk

I have never been a fan of Murphy's Law. Anything that can go wrong, will go wrong. Murphy must have been a real hoot at parties.

And yet my life finds new ways to find irony and laugh along with Murphy as the proudest moment of my life is quickly followed and overrun by one of the worst moments of my life.

This is supposed to be my day of crowning achievement. Despite all the horrible things that have happened—losing my parents, becoming a werewolf, doing unthinkable things I wish I could forget—I've managed to make it to this moment.

Spartan Knox gives me a proud smile as he pins the inverted V over my heart on my new uniform.

"Congratulations, Spartan Hawk Mason," he says.

Spartan Hawk Mason.

Six months of a brutal boot camp followed by another six months of extensive specialized training has led to this moment. I conquered the odds. I've earned the pin on my chest and can wear it proudly.

I think Mary and Robin Mason would be proud of their son.

The smile on my face grows and grows as I swivel my head to follow Spartan Knox—coolest person on the planet—as he proceeds to my sister.

"Congratulations, Spartan Phoenix Mason."

She has her hair tightly tucked into a bun—a change from the wild mane she used to favor before training—and sports the same uniform. Matching uniforms, matching hair color—my twin. I see my own giddiness mirrored in her face as she accepts her pin but there's more beneath the smile and crinkles around her eyes that I've seen grow over the last year. She wears her determination and anger like a shadow. She doesn't laugh quite so much as she used to and she's likely to be staring off into space—contemplating something dark and serious, I'm sure—when she thinks no one's looking. There are walls built around her that never used to exist. But I know.

What happened in Underground a year ago has changed her in more ways than one. But I think we've both earned a bit of happiness and should be allowed to enjoy this moment. At least, optimistically that's how the world ought to work.

We stand at attention in an orderly row as each person from our class that made it through training is awarded their Spartan insignia. There's Amanda Fry, the hothead who turned out to not be as big a weasel as we first thought. Then there's Newton—a.k.a. Newt—the boy able to lift things with the power of his mind. Man, I wish I had that ability. Charlie Jaeger stands further down the line and sticks out a bit since he's the tallest of our graduating class. Charlie, Phoenix, and I have certainly developed a strong camaraderie after fighting vampires, lamia, and drill instructors together—and to think he despised us when we first met. Now he's one of our best friends. The rest of our classmates fill out the line, people we struggled through the hardships of boot camp with and learned that true teamwork comes out of adversity. I've made my share of friends here. The future is bright. Things can only look up from here, right?

The pinning ceremony ends and Spartan Knox leads us in a chant of "molon labe," the Spartan's motto. *Come and take them.* It's our cheer of defiance against the monsters that seek to rip our world from us. We are the guardians. We are the shield and the sword.

We're just *awesome*.

The packed stadium in Underground thunders with applause and we exit in an orderly fashion. Phoenix and I find each other like magnets through the crowd and Charlie joins us a second later, teleporting to my sister's side. We're all smiles and laughter. People we've known for years in Underground come to congratulate us as we gather in the faun and giant fields for a celebration bash. Our faun guardian Celina finds us, blubbering with tears cutting down her velvety cheeks. She wraps us both in a hug and tells us how proud she is of us. Doocan the giant stands as a shadow behind her. It feels like years since I've seen either of them. They're sort of our surrogate family, what with Celina taking us under her wing when we first came to Underground as kids and Doocan always in her shadow like an extremely tall, shy uncle. It's strange meeting them again after everything that's happened while they've been gone, as if we've all become completely different people in the meantime.

The last time I saw them was before everything changed.

"I only just got back," she manages to choke out past her proud tears. "I knew I couldn't miss this."

Phoenix goes in for another hug. "I'm so glad to see you again. How are you?"

"It's been . . . I'm—well, don't worry about me, dear. I want to hear everything about you two, and don't you dare leave a detail to the void!"

She looks to me and I give her my warmest smile. Celina has always been a bright, bubbly personality full of compassion, but there's something wane about her face. Her fur isn't as shiny as it once was and her ears stay low as a sign of stress. Phoenix's question about her state seems to have distracted Celina from the festivities around us. I can't blame her.

The world's been thrown into chaos. After the attacks on major hidden sanctuaries, things have only gotten worse for the legendary community. I heard talk that there have been a record number of code black calls in the last year and that number is steadily increasing. The forces of both Echidna and Dasc have been active, waging battles against each other and the IMS directly.

I push aside a rising memory of Genna at the thought and keep my smile intact, threading my arm through Celina's. I pick up the conversation and steer it away from sour thoughts or what it must have been like in Faunus where she's been for the last year or so tending to her family and those who lost loved ones. I don't fail to notice Phoenix and Charlie take a step back and follow in our shadow as they walk side by side. We've become a tight knit group but I'll leave the introverts to their comfort zone.

I lead the way to one of the banquet tables setup to enjoy the meal prepared for us. Once we're seated and the food is dispersed, the others seem to relax. Some of our classmates join us and before long we're roaring with laughter, swapping jokes, and daring each other to sing at the mic left open before the live band for free-for-all karaoke.

In the midst of egging on stone-faced Charlie to give it a go, I notice Phoenix slip away into the crowd gathered around the dancers. While Newt tries to give Charlie a mind nudge towards the band, I excuse myself with a smile—somewhat sad I'm going to miss that battle of wills.

People and creatures move aside for me as I give my winning smile and a polite "excuse me." Some people might not be able to notice the difference between those that move out of respect or politeness and those because of stigma or fear. But I can tell.

The word "werewolf" has grown to be said with more fear than it used to. I can thank Dasc for that—and Genna.

That tight leash I keep on the angry beast inside me snaps if only for an instant. There's a deadly sort of rush through my veins before the pendant around my neck grows warm and that bloodlust abates. I don't let my face give any sign of the momentary lapse or change in demeanor as I edge through the crowd and into the clear street. After nearly sixteen years of practice, my disguises hardly ever fail to hide what lurks beneath.

I catch sight of my sister passing around the corner of the last of the apartment buildings, heading towards IMS headquarters. I tuck my hands into my pockets and whistle as I follow my twin's footsteps.

The city looks good as new after our long hiatus away. While we've been off training, they've completely restored the cement ceilings, the damage to headquarters, and breach in the lower levels.

My whistling dies in my throat. I never saw it coming. Genna's betrayal, Witty's betrayal, the grandiose escape, and then Phoenix grabbing onto the magic of that portal—pure majestic dragon strength magic—and pulling it to Scholar so she could escape. While getting clobbered by that lamia, Epsilon, I could see it—the shimmer of magic, the warping of space as the magic moved in time with Phoenix drawing back her fists. It was incredible. It was terrifying. It was... more than what I can comprehend.

Ahead of me, Phoenix slips into headquarters. By the time I enter, she's already vanished down a hallway but I know where she's going. I pass the receptionist with a friendly greeting and take the familiar pathway to the communications room on the first level on the left. I halt inside the open doorway and lean against the frame, crossing one foot over the other.

The walls of the room are packed from one end to the other with telephones, computers, and radios. If any message comes in or out of Underground, it's through this room. A number of agents operate the lines, sending out messages to people in the city, or having administrative assistants rush out with important information to someone in headquarters. I tuck up out of the way as a pair of them goes running out the door with memos clutched in their hands and a desperate look in their eyes. It's not good, whatever's going on. That's sort of been the running theme though lately so it's nothing new.

I find Phoenix talking with her favorite operator near the middle of the room. After a brief conversation, she turns away disappointed. When she spots me, she doesn't look surprised. She gestures to me as she exits the room and we walk step in step until we reach a series of windows overlooking the portal arch.

Phoenix crosses her arms and stands with the rigidness we've both obtained from months of being chewed out by our drill instructor for bad posture.

"I thought he'd be here," she says quietly, eyes glued to that arch where she did the impossible.

"No word then I take it?"

"No. I thought he'd leave a message at least but . . . nothing."

"I'm sure there's a good reason. He could still be on his way—stuck in traffic maybe, wrestling a troll, stopping to chew out some teenagers for wearing their pants too low or something."

She snorts a laugh. "He would."

It's always been this way between us. Phoenix worries too much. I have freak accidents. But we balance each other out in the end. Things have gotten . . . tense between us at times, more so lately than before. We've each been grappling with who we really are. At least I can proudly say we've never come to blows—which is good because, as much as I hate to admit it, Phoenix would win that fight.

"Well, are we going to stand around here staring into

space wondering about our place in the universe?" I ask. "Or are we going to get Charlie to sing 'Eye of the Tiger' before he teleports out of here?"

She shakes her head with a faint smile. "Oh, we're definitely going to discover Charlie's got golden pipes that he's been hiding."

"That's the spirit."

I sling an arm around her shoulders and we march out of headquarters together. I make easy conversation to get her to loosen up and forget about that certain very important person that's missing from our very important celebration. I miss him too, but he's been a hard man to reach for the last year. Not that we've been super available to chat by phone either, what with Spartan training, but Phoenix has made an effort and he's done what he can when he can.

We take a meandering detour through the colonnade, arms linked and walking in sync side to side because we get goofy when we're together. The water sprites laugh with bubbly sounds from their shallow pools and the air sprites whizz by overhead rattling the cherry tree blossoms. We're about to turn left on the path that'll take us back to the celebrations when fast approaching footsteps cause us both to pause.

A familiar figure jogs up the lane between the trees. And by familiar, I mean, I know the guy, but wow, has he changed. He's nothing like the man we first met in Moose Lake nearly two years ago. Our mentor—and in some ways crabby uncle—looks nothing like the woodsy hick that had trained us. No longer scruffy with a Santa beard and plaid shirt, he's got a military crewcut, just a five o'clock shadow, and a seriously impressive leather-slash-canvas jacket that would make a Spartan proud. I'd say he's also lost a lot of the flub and replaced it all with muscle.

"Jefferson!" Phoenix exclaims and jogs to meet him halfway.

He doesn't exactly *smile*—it's more like a grimace aiming for more in its life—and says in his usual gruff way, "Hey, kid."

They hug and Jefferson gives her two solid pats on the back. I jog to catch up and am greeted in the same fashion. When I pull back, I give his bicep a solid squeeze.

"Geez, when did you become the terminator, Jefferson?" I ask.

"You should've seen me in my prime." He claps a heavy hand on both of our shoulders. "It's good to see you two."

"I didn't think you were going to make it," Phoenix says. "You weren't at the ceremony, and you didn't leave a message . . ."

"Sorry, I got into a bit of a jam."

I raise an eyebrow at my sister as a "told you so" and she rolls her eyes.

"Look, I'm proud of you two," he says and bends a bit so he's at our eye level. "You've gone through a lot of crap in your lives, and I'm glad to see you making the most it."

"Why do I feel like there's a 'but' coming along?" Phoenix says.

Jefferson lets loose a sigh. "I wish I had good news for you, I really do. I didn't want to come running in here ruining your big day."

"You make it sound like we're getting married," I quip.

Ah. There's that classic Jefferson scowl I've been missing.

Then I realize his focus is staying on me. Well, that's never good. Phoenix seems to notice too and her face falls into a troubled frown.

"Okay, don't look at me like that, Jefferson," I say. "You'll make me nervous."

He releases his grip on our shoulders and gives a forced smile. "You know what? It can wait. We should just . . . well, whatever you kids do to celebrate."

Giving the dark moment an opportunity to pass, I shake his shoulder and say, "Then I guess you're up next on the mic! Come on!"

"Wait, what?"

"How's your tenor?"

I drag him along and we make our way to the fields. Phoenix's eyes remain glued to Jefferson, clearly unwilling to let his bad news stay quiet for now. But I'm certainly willing. I'd love to never hear bad news ever again. Let me be blissfully ignorant for the remainder of this day. Just one day. That's all I want. Then I can go off and fight the bad guys as Spartan Hawk Mason.

I like the sound of that.

Spartan Hawk Mason.

Legendary hero *Spartan* Hawk Mason.

When we get back to the celebrations, I notice a couple of the messengers from the communications room talking in whispers to several important people, like Director Knox, Spartan Knox, and one of the council members. Great.

Ignore it. This day is mine. It does not belong to bad news.

Celina comes round when she spots Jefferson and they take a seat at the banquet table while Phoenix goes to save Charlie from Newt trying to drag him to the mic by the band. Without giving a thought to the director and Spartan Knox hurrying away from the celebrations, I stride up to the mic before anyone else can reach it.

"Queue up 'Thriller' for me, fellas," I say to the band. The elf on the electric piano chuckles and turns up his speaker system. The others get ready, and when the song starts, it blares through the field.

My perfect afternoon begins with my rendition of "Thriller" by Michael Jackson while Phoenix leads a group to the dance moves, even trying to get Charlie to join in before he vanishes. After my song and my lead, others give the karaoke a try while Phoenix and I dance in front of the band. Charlie eventually comes back and does his very safe and easy side-to-side step in his usual serious fashion.

The party goes into the night and at the end of it we crash at our apartment for the last time with Jefferson, Charlie, and Celina to swap stories. In the morning we'll be receiving our assignments and joining our Spartan teams for the first time. I'm excited but I can tell Phoenix is nervous. Whatever happens, we'll be out there making a difference. And who knows? Maybe I'll even come across Genna out in the field and get some real answers for once.

Phoenix nudges me in the ribs as we sit out on the balcony while the others head out, except for Charlie who's claimed the couch.

"You've got that dreamy-eyed look again," she whispers.

"I'm just thinking about kittens and rainbows." I give a comical love-struck sigh.

"Hey, Hawk?"

"Yeah?"

"Do you think they're going to split us up?"

Clearly something that's been on her mind—and mine—a lot lately. "We always knew it was going to be a possibility. But who knows. Maybe they'll realize the dream team needs to stick together."

"Yeah. Maybe."

"Gee, Phoenix, I've always been a fan of your optimism."

"Har-har."

Turning serious, I say, "Whatever happens, we'll be okay. Okay?"

She swallows and gives a half-hearted nod. Seeing her obvious distress, I fling my arms around her and give her a tight hug while fake crying.

"Come here, Fifi!" I say dramatically and blubber onto her shoulder.

Phoenix eventually laughs and wraps her arms around me in turn but she holds on too tight, too long to be playful. But I hold on too, knowing that tomorrow could change everything.

When the following day eventually does come after a fitful night's sleep, I wake and dress as professionally as I might. For once I take my time combing my hair. This is it. One way or another, I'm heading out into the field to take on code black emergency cases. This is what I've been training for my whole life.

Time to make my parents proud.

Phoenix meets me in the kitchen and we exchange a low-five before scarfing down eggs and bacon.

"We ready?" Phoenix asks once I've cleaned up the rest of the bacon.

"I was *born* ready."

"Pssh." She waves an absent hand and makes for the door. "You were born drooling on a pillow and asking for five more minutes."

Well, she's in a good enough mood if she's cracking a joke.

I catch up to her at the top of the stairs. "Let's do this."

The walk to headquarters is both incredibly long and far too short at the same time. It takes a lot to get me nervous but this is doing the trick. I mimic Phoenix's breathing pattern that she uses to calm herself down. We fall in sync and I wink at her out of the corner of my eye which earns me a smile. Charlie teleports out of nowhere and our trio walks to our future together.

We join the rest of our classmates inside of headquarters waiting in the hallway on the second floor. There's a flurry of messengers and agents this morning that puts us all on edge. Something's going on. Does it have to do with the ominous news Jefferson came to deliver yesterday? He's not an agent anymore but he's been conducting his own investigation and shares any critical news he comes across. He remains "in the know" even if he doesn't carry a badge anymore.

One by one, we're summoned into the director's office by Spartan Knox. We're called out of alphabetical order so I have no idea when my name will be next. Phoenix is one of those to go first and is quickly escorted out again away from me and the others. She casts a glance over her shoulder before following an aide to the level below. We better get an opportunity to say goodbye if it comes to that. The remaining crowd thins, Charlie disappears too, and I realize the only ones remaining are werewolves. There are only three of us but the coincidence is too obvious, too disconcerting. Why are we last?

Spartan Knox comes out of the director's office and waves to us. "Spartans, follow me."

Not just one of us. All of us. Everyone else has gone in alone.

The creature lurking underneath my skin growls at what I fear is coming next.

We file into the director's office and stand at attention before the desk as Spartan Knox shuts the door behind us.

Director Knox rises from his chair slowly as if a heavy weight rests on his shoulders. He draws in a breath to bring up his shoulders and clasps his hands behind his back.

"First off, I want to congratulate each of you on such a hard-earned accomplishment. Your efforts have not gone unnoticed and the pin on your chest is yours by right." He pauses and looks to his brother behind us. I feel a "but" coming on like some kind of joke. Because it would have to be a joke, right? "The International Council has adopted a new policy going into effect today in response to the latest attacks by forces we believe are led by the werewolf alpha."

Dasc. A continual pain in my side. So what's this new policy to thwart Dasc?

"Effective immediately, all agents infected with the werewolf disease are being pulled from active field duty."

I fight the urge to shake my head and get rid of the water in my ears because I must have water in my ears. This is a mistake. I didn't hear right. They wouldn't. They can't do this.

"That leaves me with the unfortunate responsibility of informing you that none of you will be assigned to the Spartan teams."

I listen in a daze as a crushing weight fills my lungs and that creature in my chest lets out a steady growl of anger.

"Each of you will be transferred to non-combative positions. I have your assignments here." The director passes out folders to each of us. I take mine numbly. The others immediately open theirs but I stare at the ugly manila in my hand, feel the sharp edges of this desk job death hiding inside. "This change is to ensure that no more agents in the field are subjected to compulsions that may cause them to attack their fellow agents."

My eyes snap up. So that's what this is about. I heard a rumor a couple of days ago that a field agent in Chicago turned against his own team and then absconded with top secret data. Maybe that was Jefferson's news yesterday. He knew this was going to happen.

He shifts his jaw as if what he's about to say next really frustrates him. "And more than that, they are making probation rings mandatory for all werewolves as a precaution to prevent unauthorized shifting."

My heart stops.

A probation ring—meaning they'll be able to tell if I'm taking the serum or not. Meaning I have to take the serum again. The very same serum that, the last time I had to take it, nearly drove me to insanity.

"We will end this," the director says and sounds truly angered by the situation. Good. I am too. "Our best agents are looking for the alpha. As soon as this crisis is over, you'll be assigned to where you're supposed to be. You're excellent agents, all of you, but this decision is to ensure the integrity of this agency. You're dismissed."

We exit the room numbly. I clutch the dreaded folder in my hand and walk until I reach the window overlooking the black arch in the center of headquarters. The impossible happened down there. Maybe, somehow, the impossible can happen again and Dasc will be captured and this policy overturned that's about to jeopardize my very life.

Moments later I find Spartan Knox standing beside me.

"Sir," I say automatically.

"This is for the best."

"I assume this policy includes you as well, sir?"

"It does."

I shake my head. What a supreme waste. Spartan Knox is a Spartan commander and a living legend. How can they pull him from the field?

"Shake it off, Spartan. We have work to do."

Spartan Hawk Mason. What a lie.

With the monster clawing up my throat and the pendant growing hot against my sternum, I open that blasted manila folder to discover exactly where this miserable turn of events is sending me.

2

Phoenix

It makes sense now why they shuffled me out of headquarters as fast as they could. If I had known what they were about to tell my brother, what they were going to make him do, I would have marched into the director's office and given him a piece of my mind. I think Hawk knew as much too so he didn't tell me about it when we packed our bags, headed to the airport, and said our goodbyes. All I knew was that they were sending Hawk off to Seattle to sit behind a desk doing paperwork where he's going to be absolutely miserable.

No, he decided to tell me about the probation ring policy and taking the serum in a note he left in my bag. A *note*. Because he knew what I would do, what I still want to do. But storming into the director's office or taking Hawk and making a run for it are impractical at the moment as I wait along the runway at Camp Ripley with Charlie for our assigned Spartan team to fly in. The note is a crumpled mess in my hand and I keep wringing the life out of it as if I can magically make the words disappear and become untrue.

"You seem agitated," Charlie says dully with his nose in a book. "Could you stop pacing? You keep blocking my light."

I gesture angrily to the sky. "It's the *sun*. You can literally sit anywhere else."

"And you can pace anywhere else. I'm comfortable here."

I make a sudden move to yank the book out of his hands, ready to toss it a mile over the military base, but Charlie must sense I'm about to do something rash. He—along with his oh so precious book—disappears only to reappear five feet further away sitting cross-legged on the tarmac. With a sigh he sticks an old receipt as a bookmark in the pages, carefully closes whatever fantasy story he's into, and stretches his legs out before him, bracing his arms behind.

"Well, aren't you in a particularly fine mood today." He cocks his head. "This is about the new werewolf policy, isn't it?"

I swivel about on him. "You knew about it?"

"I hear things."

"Then why didn't I know about it until right now!" I shout and wave Hawk's crumpled ball of a note at him.

"Probably because Hawk—who I'm assuming that note is from—knew that my book you were about to destroy out of anger would have been somebody's head if he told you while we were still in Underground."

"This—" I wave the note angrily some more before shoving it back into my bag. "—is ridiculous!"

"Phoenix, the only reason you think that is because Hawk is affected by it. You know as well as I do why they made that policy. We both know what happened in Chicago."

I blow out a sharp breath. Over in Illinois, a team stationed at a suburban field office with a werewolf agent was attacked, and in the midst of the fight the werewolf turned on his team. It hasn't been the first time in recent months that IMS agents have been used like puppets against their friends. Dasc's doing. When in close proximity his compulsions are hopeless to resist. I know from experience—he nearly had Hawk kill me before. As soon as I heard about it, I sent a message to Jefferson to let him know, but neither he nor the IMS managed to find Dasc.

"I get this isn't ideal," Charlie continues. "I know sending Hawk to a desk is a waste of talent, but this isn't forever. We just need to find the alpha, that's all."

He says it like it's so simple and that it's some random "alpha" out there. This isn't as personal for him as it is for me. Dasc is on the loose and wreaking havoc because I wasn't able to stop him—the werewolf who killed my parents, who made Hawk a monster, who turned Witty into a traitor, who stole back Genna.

And I'm standing here on the edge of a runway waiting and waiting and waiting some more. Useless.

I stand rigid with my arms crossed and squint against the brilliant summer sky, letting the hot air wash over my face. Come on, where's our team? I'm ready to get out there and start knocking some heads already and hunt Dasc down. Although, I don't actually know what I'll be doing.

All my assignment said was to meet my team here to receive further instructions. I'll be joining up with Spartan Team Sierra. Most of the Spartan teams handle code black emergencies but some are tasked with highly secretive missions. I can only hope I land on one hunting for Dasc. There are some wrongs that I need to fix and it starts and ends with him.

I make out the faint chop of helicopter blades in the distance. I shade my eyes and watch as an aircraft approaches. The twin rotor engines are at a slight tilt as it eases down like a plane but with the rotor blades safe away from the ground to land. I imagined it'd be louder but even when it reaches the tarmac and rolls along the runway, the noise isn't nearly as deafening as I remember it being the last time I was around an Osprey aircraft, the choice mode of transportation for the Spartan teams.

"Time to go," Charlie says and tucks his book into his duffle which he then slings over his shoulder. I follow suit and we trek down the runway to the massive hangar bay where the Osprey goes to park as it were.

The hangar bay is a scene of well-organized chaos. Technicians check on planes, jets, helicopters, and a pair of Ospreys while the one that just landed is guided into the hangar by a pushback vehicle to make way for another one about to depart. National Guard and military share in the duties while a group of police officers jog past the massive open doors in a block formation. For all intents and purposes, we and the Spartans we're about to meet are a special ops team currently using Camp Ripley as a way station. Beyond that, very few know that we're really elite monster hunters preparing for an emergency call to come in.

Charlie and I march through the workers and officers in our black uniforms and tactical boots to the newly docked Osprey, duffles over our shoulders like soldiers heading out to war.

A twinge of anxiety makes the muscles in my shoulders tense as we wait for the ramp to drop and meet our new team. The ramp doesn't immediately go down but the rotors fold, the propellers realign, the wing swivels on the head of the aircraft, and once the wing and propellers are in line with the body, the flaps drop so it's all tucked in and tidy for storage in the hangar. Dang, that's awesome.

Only once the Osprey is securely stationed does the ramp descend. Surprisingly, the first ones to come out are two air sprites that dart away like ghostly birds and disappear before anyone else can see them. The breeze from their passing smells of oil and metal.

Before I can see anyone, I hear a voice exclaim from within, "Look! Fresh meat!"

"Here we go," Charlie grumbles under his breath beside me.

In unison we drop our bags and stand ready with feet spread apart and hands clasped behind our backs.

The first face that comes out to greet us is so charming and smiley that I feel like this can't possibly be a hardened Spartan—except he's in matte black armor and has a high-powered sniper rifle resting across his shoulders. His face is vaguely familiar and it takes me a few seconds before I realize he's one of the Spartans that saved our butts in Moose Lake a year ago—when some of Dasc's misguided werewolves almost killed Jefferson. Is that the team we've been assigned to and I didn't even realize it? While balancing the weapon across his shoulders, the Spartan trots down the ramp, that smile of his never fading, and he stretches out a hand to me first.

"Hey, Red! It's a pleasure."

While going straight for a nickname usually doesn't do it for me, there's something about the way he embraces my hand like an old friend and his very relaxed demeanor that makes me feel comfortable, at ease. He's one of those naturally gifted people persons. He's also rather good looking—the infectious smile helps—with warm caramel skin, a neatly trimmed beard, and energetic eyes.

However, since I find myself so focused on identifying my new teammates, my language skills are flimsy at best.

"Right. Hello. I'm Phoenix. Phoenix Mason."

"Of course you are!" That smile of his only grows and he turns to Charlie next to shake his hand as well.

"Spartan Charlie Jaeger," Charlie says stiffly. I guess we're both pretty awkward at fresh introductions. Neither of us was actually introduced to the team members keeping guard when we were stuck in the hospital. I'm nervous but Charlie tends to be more off-putting.

This man—who's name I've yet to discover—gives Charlie a mock salute with a heavy dose of grandiose and sarcasm. "*Yes, sir,*" he replies an octave lower.

When Charlie's expression goes flat, I can tell he's already revving up to be terribly unpleasant like he was when I first met him. Keeping people at arm's length as usual. I can't blame him. I feel more cautious towards new people ever since the last friend I made ended up setting my parents' murderer free and nearly drowning me in a river. I clench my jaw and redirect my focus elsewhere as bitterness gnaws at me.

"The name's Theo Benoit, at your service." He gives a dramatic bow and then sweeps an arm behind him—one still lazily holding the sniper rifle in place across his shoulders—as the rest of his team disembarks. "May I present her royal majesty, Melody Boyd."

"Melody?" Charlie gasps as our familiar blonde friend comes into the light with a mischievous smile. She's a Spartan now? When did that happen? Last I knew, she was still running the field office in Duluth.

"Did you miss me?" she says, her British accent a friendly and welcome tune.

As she reaches us wearing the same uniform as Theo and gives us both one-armed hugs, Theo continues his lavish introductions for the rest of the team.

"Next, I am proud to present the shadow of the skies, the queen of ravens, Alona Ravenspell, pilot and communications officer extraordinaire."

"Good job, Theo. You remembered it correctly this time," quips a young woman I also recognize that comes down next. She has gorgeous hair black as—well, a raven—and when she unfurls it from its tight braid at the nape of her neck, it reaches her waist. She carries herself with the swagger I can only associate with a top gun fighter pilot from the movies.

"And last but not least," Theo continues and turns to stiffly salute the last to disembark. "Our commander in chief, the man whom even the majestics fear, who single-handedly saved Canada, invented toaster strudel—"

"Theo," a voice scolds from inside the aircraft.

"Spartan Leader John Kessler! ATTEEEEEENTION!"

The others instantly drop what they're carrying to create a line alongside Theo to salute as their leader steps down with a duffle slung over his shoulders.

I know him. He's the team leader. The one who didn't push for answers about Scholar even though she left obvious clues behind. Soft-spoken, silver haired, tall as Charlie but brawnier, and a ragged scar down the side of his face. He joins the rest of his team who lower their salutes and face us together. In their black combat gear, they make an impressive and imposing unit. I try not to swallow to show any sign of intimidation.

I fought Dasc and won. I slew my fair share of vampires and walked away. I battled a pair of lamia and managed to survive. I've gone through the rigors of Spartan training and achieved top marks. I have power in my veins that's still growing, becoming more powerful by the day. I manipulated a majestic's portal with my strength of will alone.

And yet I feel like any one of the Spartans standing before me could kick my butt. Hardened by trials I have yet to experience, I know I'm going to have to prove myself to them. Charlie and I, despite our training and own harrowing ordeals, are the newbies.

"God, they look so green," Alona the pilot says.

Theo scrunches up his face and holds his hands under his chin as if he's adoring a newborn baby. "Oh, look at them! That porcelain smooth skin!"

I have absolutely no idea how to respond but Charlie stiffens beside me, clearly agitated.

Their leader—*our* leader—John Kessler scoffs and shakes his head as he starts to move past us with his duffle bag. "I think you missed the scars on their necks," he says and keeps moving. "They're not that green."

Theo comes in exceptionally close to squint at the faded scars on my neck where both lamia and vampires had gotten their teeth into me. I automatically backup from his intrusion into my personal space.

"Don't worry," Melody offers in her usual comforting way. "You'll get used to him."

Alona shrugs past us, giving us a cold up and down. "I bet they don't last a month."

"And don't mind her," Melody says quietly before gesturing for us to follow. We snatch up our bags and jog after.

I feel ambushed and overwhelmed so words are difficult to form. I've got a thousand questions, both curious and professional. Then there's that other part of my brain assessing my environment, the people around me, my teammates walking ahead towards the barracks. That part of me, whether through training or my own experience, has lost a touch of its innocent curiosity to be replaced by distrust and wariness. I know it. There's no denying it. The girl that once would wonder what kind of music the strangers around her might listen to has been replaced by the woman who weighs their weaknesses, eyes their strengths, and focuses on potential threats. Maybe if that girl had been more careful, she would have seen the betrayals coming and saved herself the pain of their cruel barbs.

My mind drifts into a dark cloud of anger and malice. It's the sort of mindset that gives me a killing calm. I'm not afraid to hunt monsters anymore. I'm eager to.

I also don't fail to notice the side-eye glance I get from Charlie. For someone who pretends to be oblivious to the feelings and moods of others, he's gotten good at detecting my own.

As a way of distraction, I'm sure, he asks Melody, "How's it feel being back with the Spartans?"

"It's been good," she says lightly. "I needed the time away . . . after things happened but it feels good to be back where I'm the most useful."

That bright sense of curiosity strikes me before darker questions rise. I don't know the story of why Melody took leave of the Spartans for a time to work as a field agent. Clearly she *was* a Spartan before if she's now back with them. Who knew? Well, Charlie I guess but . . . Why did she leave? Was she forced out? What are these "things" that happened? Did she do something wrong? Could she not be trusted, relied on?

What do I really know about Melody Boyd?

"So, what can we expect?" Charlie asks.

"We'll all be briefed in a moment by John. He'll give you the lay of the land." She offers us both a smile but its warmth doesn't quite reach me. I remain silent. "What about you two? How have you been? I'm sorry I missed your graduation ceremony. We were handling a code black in Grand Marais that took a while. We just got back in actually."

"What happened?" I ask, finally stirred out of my reverie.

She clears her throat. "Werewolves."

"Okay . . . but what *happened*?"

"Their field office was attacked directly. Two of the agents stationed there were werewolves. They turned on their team."

My footsteps falter for only a moment before I catch up again. "Any sign of Dasc?"

"Not that we could find."

Grand Marais. That's way up the shore of Lake Superior edging near Canada. Minnesota *is* considered werewolf territory. Maybe Dasc is hiding in a state where he feels the safest protected by his pack. But if that's true, why attack a field office directly and bring attention to himself? It doesn't make any sense. Dasc's presence is the only way those agents would have turned on their own team though . . . isn't it?

"What about the team?" Charlie asks quietly.

"One was infected. The other was hospitalized. The two werewolves were brought to a secure site. I guess it was the straw that broke the camel's back so to speak and drove that new policy."

I guess "secure site" is code for the void where bad werewolves go to disappear. The very same place I've been trying to protect Hawk from all this time. If they find out he hasn't been taking the serum, or about his physical reaction when he does, they'd toss him in along with the rest.

My chest constricts and even though I'm surrounded by people, without my twin nearby, I feel alone.

This is going to be our first true test of separation. Sure, there was that month I spent in Scotland, but he had been in a place I consider safe, with a pendant of my blood keeping him in control, and friends to back him up. Now, he's been shipped off to a place we've never been, to a city he won't know, taking the serum that drives him mad, and having to keep control of himself under the watchful sensors of a probation ring. My blood boils with anger yet freezes in fear at the thought of it.

I'm not afraid of much anymore, but I will always fear for my brother.

We at last reach the barracks, maneuver around a group of National Guardsmen, and make for a row of bunks on the right wall. The others immediately stake out their beds, tossing their bags onto the thin cots to lay their claim. Charlie and I follow suit for the last set of bunkbeds next to the others. I've grown accustomed to coed living situations—with people other than my brother—since Spartan training. After a year of using a coed barracks at the remote training facility in the Boundary Waters and then at various other training sites, it's become a nonissue. But as my training has advanced, so has my appreciation for IMS ethics and especially the mindset of the Spartans. Men and women are treated equally as they were back in the days of the first Spartans. We're all warriors. In fact, some monsters can only be killed by women so it would be stupid not to include them.

"Newbies! Heads up!" Theo practically shouts to get our attention.

He points and we turn to meet a gangly man carrying two black packages each the size of a file box. One gets handed to me and the other to Charlie before the man leaves again without a word.

Our leader gestures to the packages in our arms then jerks his head to the restroom facilities at the back of the barracks. "Your new uniforms from the Tailor. Go try 'em on."

My extra sensory perception detects the smallest trace of magic within the package. I've been looking forward to this for some time ever since we got our measurements taken by a rather peculiar noble class dragon that everyone calls the Tailor. When you join the elite ranks of the Spartans, you get your own tactical gear specifically tailored to suit your needs. I've been itching to see what they look like, feel like. Some of the Spartans I trained under said they're like a second skin.

Charlie and I march off with our packages and separate at the segregated bathrooms. There are a couple of women in here taking showers behind semi private screens. Tucking away into the corner of any empty shower, I ease open the package and let out an appreciative murmur as I inspect what's inside.

I eagerly strip out of my standard field agent uniform and slip into the most *awesome* thing I've ever worn in my life. The first layer is almost like some kind of wetsuit but thinner and more breathable. The material is also made of sterner stuff that feels like it could hold up against a knife or sharp claws, making it ideal for close combat. Next comes the flex-weave pants and shirt with pockets galore, and adjustable straps for the arms and legs to keep them tight. On top of those go molded armor pieces to offer greater protection that are connected by ligaments of Kevlar. After I adjust the pieces for a secure fit, I strap on the supple boots, holsters, and utility belt.

A helmet comes next that looks like it came right out of a sci-fi movie, all slick curves and dark matte finish and yet similar enough to a SWAT helmet to fit in. I flip it over to try it on but find a pair of gloves stuffed inside with a note attached. I tug them out and find the source of magic I felt earlier. There's some kind of energy threaded through the fabric of the gloves with molded plates over the knuckles.

I unravel the small note.

Protect your hands and your secrets, dear.
- Your Librarian

I flip the note over but there's nothing on the back.

Your Librarian. I smile at that. There's only one person who could have made these gloves imbued with magic. We haven't had an opportunity to talk for a year even if I did manage to sneak updates on her from the selkies in Scotland via Spartan McDonnell. I shake my head. I don't know how Terra a/k/a Scholar managed to smuggle these gloves to me among the armaments from the Tailor, especially since she's in hiding from Draco and his scouts. Even dealing with that, she managed to make and deliver a pair of special gloves. She's one of the few people I trust in this lousy world and I can't even send her a proper thank you for this.

Tugging the gloves on, I find they have the same texture as my under layer—light yet durable. I flex my fingers and curl them into a fist. I nudge that bit of magic covering my hands and it reacts—just like Scholar's trinkets when she was training me. But instead of giving a mere glow like those trinkets, a shimmer of a dragon's barrier activates like a shield fit to the contours of my hand.

"You clever dragon," I murmur and uncurl my fingers. The barrier vanishes and the gloves look ordinary again. I'm going to have fun seeing what I can do with these.

I shred the note into tiny pieces and inspect what's left in the box. A metal container fills up the bottom with an array of weapons and gadgets that go with my combat uniform—a bio-mech gun, rappel gun, two retractable blades, a compact first aid kit, general antidotes, mini flares, a dagger inlaid with various types of metal, collapsible eye gear, and a sleek breathing mask. All the things a growing Spartan needs.

Taking out each piece one at a time, I fill up the pockets and holsters of my uniform until everything is in its proper place. I stand and pat each pocket, quickly memorizing where each thing is, tuck the helmet into the crook of my elbow, grab the empty box with one hand, and move to one of the bathroom mirrors.

I know what I looked like in the junior agent uniform, then the agent uniform, and the Spartan training attire. I always looked like me albeit more tough. I don't see that girl in the mirror.

The woman staring back at me is a warrior—a lethal, powerful warrior.

Pixies, I'm giddy at the sight. And proud.

But mostly giddy.

I bite my lip against a high-pitched, excited giggle that somehow manages to escape me. I hear the two women behind me pause as they dry off so I clear my throat, roll back my shoulders, and march out of the bathroom.

Charlie is waiting for me outside in his own uniform. I stumble to a stop and blink at him. He's in the middle of readjusting the cuff of his sleeve but stops and looks up.

"What?"

And I thought he was good looking before. "Nothing."

"Well, you took your time."

"Not all of us can fall out of bed gorgeous, Charlie. It takes time to achieve this." I make a circle motion about my face with a smile.

He chuckles and peers at me. "You're in a good mood all of a sudden."

"Is there a reason I shouldn't be? Have you seen what we look like?"

He shakes his head. "Come on, *Fifi*."

One word.

One word is all it takes to break my giddy spell and send me crashing back into dark reality. Fifi is my brother's nickname for me. He's the only one that calls me that. Like a blow to the chest, I feel the absence of my brother so strongly it hurts. He should be here with me, sharing in my giddiness over our new uniforms that make us look like our favorite action stars. I get to see my hard work realized. Hawk gets to see the inside of a cubicle somewhere on the other side of the country while being monitored like a criminal.

It's with a dour mood that I rejoin the rest of my team. I try to keep my face neutral and not reveal the frustration beneath but I've never been good at hiding my emotions from others. Whether they notice or not, they don't mention it.

Our leader guides us out of the barracks and to a building next door that houses the nerve center of the base. As we walk, I try not to focus on Hawk's current predicament and instead work on memorizing the names of my comrades—Theo Benoit, Alona Ravenspell, John Kessler. At least I already know Melody and Charlie.

We walk in silent single file through the hallways until we reach a briefing room with a large conference table. John shuts the door and locks it behind us. None of the team sits so I remain standing as well around the table, one hand resting on the bulky side pocket of my utility belt.

John joins us and plants both hands flat on the tabletop to make a very serious figure. The overhead lights turn his silver hair brilliant.

"We're a new team today," he begins. "We've got fresh blood that needs to integrate."

"Fresh blood," Theo whispers in a rather creepy, dramatic voice.

John ignores him and turns his gaze to Charlie and me. "But we aren't just a team. We're family. There are no secrets here. If you have a problem, you tell someone—family trouble, something eating at you, whatever—you tell your teammates. We need to have each other's backs. Spartans depend on trust. If we don't have trust, then we crumble. And for starters, we need to know exactly what everyone around this table is capable of magic-wise."

I do my best not to make any indication of fear or anxiety. I've been practicing but I'm not sure how effective I am.

John gestures to Charlie. After he clears his throat, Charlie explains his teleportation ability and includes the part about being able to port past dragon's barriers. He describes the pain for other people he brings along and gives me a sideways glance before he says, "Well, everyone except her."

My eyes narrow on him but he doesn't recoil. The team's focus shifts to me expectantly. I can see the curiosity but not the kind that broods on hostility like I imagine Draco's expression would be if he knew what I was capable of.

Seeing as how the pixie is out of the bag, I heave a sigh and say, "It's true. As far as we know, I'm the only one that isn't affected adversely when he teleports."

Melody tilts her head and her eyes shift mischievously between me and Charlie. I don't know what she's thinking but I don't think I'm a fan of it, whatever it is.

"That wasn't in the report I received," John says. "Why not?"

"Because we never told anyone about it," I say and, to spare Charlie, add, "It was my idea. I told him not to tell."

"Why?"

Because a majestic dragon currently in hiding from the leader of the IMS told me not to. Do I start off my time with my team on lies? But I can't trust them with this. No one is supposed to know there's more to my magic than every other Blessed out there.

"I didn't think it mattered," I say calmly. "But I guess it does now."

"It sure does." I don't think he sounds angry that we hid it, but he's not exactly thrilled about it either. "Any other special abilities we ought to know about?"

"I'm strong."

"Freakishly strong I hear," Alona says and her dark eyes study me. I don't know what to make of her yet. "You managed to close the flood doors against the Mississippi River."

A muscle in my jaw twitches as I remember it. It was either let Dasc go and close the doors, or go after Dasc and let Underground drown.

"Yes, I did that."

"I think we'll be able to work that into our tactics along with Charlie's ability." John rubs his square chin in thought. "As for the rest of the team, Theo and I are ordinaries. Alona is a spirit walker. Melody is a hollow."

My jaw drops for a moment before I regain myself and snap my mouth shut. First, I trip over spirit walker as I recall the spirit walker raven that guided me to Scholar a year ago. I never knew who the raven was. Could it be this Alona?

Then Melody is a *hollow*? Hollows are rare—extremely rare. They're beings or people that used to possess magic but then were stripped of it. It's such an unusual thing to happen that hollows are practically nonexistent. I focus in on Melody beside me and feel for the presence of magic. I can sense Charlie's beside me and Alona's earthy aura across the table, but where Melody stands, it's like there's a void. It's not the same as John and Theo, born ordinary humans without magic in their blood. No, with Melody I can feel the absence. It's easy to miss if I'm not looking for it. If no one had ever said anything, I'm not sure I would have ever figured it out by myself.

"Melody . . ." And there I stop. How can I possibly ask her what happened? Every variation of the question I form in my mind sounds impossibly rude. People can't just be stripped of their magic. The only ways possible are vile and traumatizing which is why I suspect I never knew of it until now.

She gives me a sad smile as if she knows exactly what I'm thinking and doesn't want me to feel too badly about it. Always the peacemaker.

"We can save that for another time," John says to break

the tension. "Now, we'll be stationed here for a week to practice some drills and get a feel for each other. Two other Spartan teams, Tango and Foxtrot, will be meeting us to initiate some of their own members as well. At the end of the week, we head out on special assignment." He looks each one of us in the eye as if to make sure he has our full attention before he says, "We're going to end this werewolf problem once and for all."

3

Hawk

I do my best to suppress the shakes in my hand as I press the serum injector to the crook of my arm. I wince against the sharp sting of pain at the needle and then the acid creeping through my veins. Setting the injector aside, I brace both hands on the sink and take measured breaths.

I can do this. I'm stronger than the serum. I have to be.

The pendant resting against my sternum grows warm as the two parts of magic—one part werewolf disease and the other serum—battle each other inside me. Like some vigilant peacekeeper, the warmth of the pendant soothes the pain but doesn't make it go away entirely. It keeps it tolerable. Instead of acid burning through me, I feel like I've got fever sensitivity in my limbs. It's annoying and draining but it won't kill me.

This is the one time I want to be alone, right when I take the injection. Of course, as my life seems to go at the moment, the one time alone is the only time I get any company around this place. Spartan Knox walks in along with three other men to use the restroom. I hastily scoop up my injector, slip it into my pocket, and give a brief nod of acknowledgement to my fellow Spartan who's also cooped up in this paper-laden hell hole.

It's barely been a week and I already feel my constant ebb of energy fading. I like people. I like interacting and cracking jokes and finding out new things about my coworkers. Their energy gives me energy. So after being stuck in a cubicle where the only other person around doesn't even remotely want to talk, I can feel myself wilting like a flower in a cave. Because let's face it—this place is a cave. And not a cool cave with bioluminescence, bats, blind little salamanders, or even little dudes swapping riddles over a ring. No, this is where the cheery go to die beneath paper and boredom.

Pixies, I'm so bored. The most exciting things that happen around here are paper cuts and donuts appearing in the break room. Wow. How exhilarating.

And I thought nothing could be worse than the serum.

Banging my head against a wall would be more fun.

I maneuver through the rows of cubicles and remember a time when I had been in such a building under the false pretense of being an FDA agent doing a random check. That building was *much* more exciting.

I wave to my fellow hunkered coworkers as I pass but hardly anyone even acknowledges me. It's like some kind of desperately unhappy library—with no dragon librarians either. There's only murmured chitchat here and there but everyone's too involved in their mindless work. It's not my kind of crowd at all.

Deciding to take my sweet time getting back to my own secluded corner of misery, I stop in the break room and snag a cup of coffee. After being heavy-handed with the sugar, I simply stand there and soak in the aroma. It brings me back to Java Jitters in Moose Lake, to days working probation rounds with the werewolves, to werewolf games, to pranks on my sister and Jefferson, to bringing iced coffee to Genna while she was working in her gardens . . .

Genna.

This coffee almost matches the color of her eyes.

"Mason?" That voice has come to be known to me as the death of happiness.

I don't even look up but mumble, "Spartan Mason."

"Did you finish that report?"

The death-of-happiness waits in the doorway tapping one foot on the floor. Knowing that there's no way out of the room except through him, I meet his gaze with a smile that doesn't reach my eyes.

"Almost done," I say with all the false cheeriness I can muster.

I don't think anyone's gotten on my nerves as quickly and violently as Milton has. The head baboon in this circus, the grammar hag, the office Nazi. I want to shove those stupid link cuffs down his stupid throat.

Oh, pixies. I'm starting to sound like Phoenix. I can't tell if that's because of the serum bringing out my inner rage monster or if it's just Milton.

He taps the thick watch on his wrist. "Less breaks, more work."

"It's at the top of my list. I'll get it done immediately." I'll say anything to make him go away.

Thankfully it works and he disappears, his stubby legs sort of shuffling along. I think he does it on purpose to build up electrostatic. I swear, every time he touches me on the shoulder or arm to get my attention when I'm thundering music in my headphones, he gives me a painful static shock. It's intentional, I just know it.

Coffee in hand, I trudge down the hallways to my cubicle waaaaaaaay back in the corner. I'm stuffed behind a couple rows of filing cabinets and a noisy copier. No divider separates my desk from Doug, the most silent person on the planet who I think actually *enjoys* being here. He's a werewolf same as me but prefers his desk, his paper, his . . . boringness.

"Hey, Doug," I say even though I know my greeting will receive no response. It's like talking to a brick wall—one which I am determined to prod at until it does something.

"You know, I was just thinking about when my sister and I infiltrated Werevine Pharmaceutical. Did you ever hear about that?" I sit in my swivel chair and lean back as far as it'll let me as I cradle that cup of coffee. Doug gives me a blank stare, the most acknowledgment I'm bound to get, before he goes back to highlighting phrases on a long document. "I can tell you're real curious about what happened, Doug."

Nothing. Not a peep or grunt of annoyance.

"Yeah, Phoenix and I—well, mostly Phoenix—sort of set fire to the top floor. She blew out a window and we rode a window washer's scaffold to the parking garage to escape. Man, that was awesome."

Doug doesn't even look my way.

"Then we came across some unicorns and they gave us a

ride to Underground. Once we got there, I bet Draco I could beat him in an arm wrestling match. I won—naturally—and as part of our bet, he made me director of Minneapolis Division." I twist the cup in my hands waiting for Doug to roll his eyes or laugh. You know, a normal human reaction. Nothing. I purse my lips and stare into the steaming dark coffee. "But in the end I gave up my mantle to become a wandering wizard and somehow ended up in a parallel universe where no one laughs."

He finishes highlighting the page with intense precision and moves onto the next.

I heave a sigh and mumble, "And where no one cares."

The report Milton left for me glares at me from the center of my paper-strewn desk. It's a mess and I haven't bothered to organize. I haven't even touched the report in contradiction to what I told Milton. I'm supposed to be grammar and typo checking before it gets put in the file to be closed. I don't know what the point of this job is but it's made me realize something—it's absolutely useless.

The coffee doesn't last long. I guzzle it as the serum wraps its hypersensitive fingers around me and the ticking clock on the wall feels like hammer strokes against my patience. At least I finish Milton's report and am able to hand it in error-free at the end of the day. I join the throng marching out of the building like complacent ants.

Spartan Knox appears directly behind me. "Another day in paradise."

"Yeah, I just love the smell of depression."

"It's hard not being in the field. I understand that. We aren't meant for this, but it's only temporary, Spartan."

He claps a heavy hand on my shoulder and we part

ways at the glass exit door. From the outside, the building looks like some bland paper company but it's just a front for the IMS report processing station upstairs. It sounds so much more exciting than it really is.

I take a moment to breathe in the fresh air once I'm free. It's overcast, but then again, it's always overcast here in Seattle. The weather's fair but average. Nothing crazy. Nothing too exciting.

It's not a long walk to my new apartment. The accommodations were made specifically for IMS agents working at the processing center. The complex is only a few blocks away and shaded by a stilted group of trees that look as hopeless as I'm starting to feel.

Come on, Hawk, old boy. Chin up.

But my inner pep talks aren't working as well as they used to.

I trudge to the second floor and enter my reasonable apartment. There's nothing on the walls except a photo I stapled of Phoenix, Jefferson, Genna, and I grouped together in the cabin. The place came furnished so the only things here that belong to me are my big duffle bag and that photo. The rest of the place just feels so . . . empty.

Now comes the usual time in my day when I stare longingly at that photo and decide I don't want to sit around here by myself being all mopey and pathetic. Gathering up my exercise clothes into a small gym bag, I move right back out of that empty apartment and walk through the muggy evening air to a local gym I located almost immediately after I arrived. Spartan Knox recommended it actually. I think he knew I needed to get the edge off and to live up to the Spartan credo—sweat more in practice, bleed less in war. Not that I'll have any opportunities to bleed unless I get a paper cut. But I'll keep myself ready in case things magically get better. And since magic is real, you never know.

I'm halfway to the gym when a tall shadow falls over me.

"Great minds think alike," Spartan Knox says with his own bag in tow.

"I guess so. I really need to go a few rounds on that punching bag."

"Milton?"

"Milton."

"Same." He rolls his shoulders. He's an impressive figure and I adjust my posture slightly to match his. Spartan Knox has been my hero forever and only became more so when I trained under him. He's a force to be reckoned with and seems to have absolutely no trouble whatsoever with his animal side. I've tried to glean as many pointers from him as I can.

We enter the gym and find several other IMS agents from the report processing center joining us. However, no one apart from Spartan Knox cares to chat. Most of the other workers aren't werewolves and the only ones that are were sent here just like Spartan Knox and me. I guess the point was to get us as far away from the action as possible and into a state not deemed "werewolf territory" lest we get any ideas. I push that to the back of my mind as I work through the aches in my body and keep pace with Spartan Knox as he does a circuit through the gym. At the end of it, my limbs are shaking not from the exertion—I got plenty used to this during training—but the toll of the serum fighting against me.

Unfortunately, Knox notices. "You feeling all right?"

I run a hand through my hair and offer a generous smile. "I'm just tired. I haven't been sleeping well. The apartment's too . . ."

I swallow and don't say the rest as we walk back to the locker area. I don't want to say "lonely" or "empty" or something as equally melodramatic—not to Knox anyway.

"It'll get better," is all he says and drops it.

After a quick shower, I bag up my sweaty things and walk with Knox out the doors. Instead of heading towards the apartments where we both live, I wave him off with the excuse that I need some more fresh air. I mean, it is true, but I don't plan on lingering outside.

Taking the familiar route deeper into the city, I stroll to a small cafe I had the pleasure of discovering a few days ago when out looking for a distraction. It's a quaint little place that's run by a local family. A bell chimes when I walk in and take my usual spot at the counter. The daughter of the family, Daisy—a rather pretty girl—trots over with her apron and a pad of paper in her hand. Her smile is infectious.

"You're becoming quite the regular," she says and whips out a pencil ready to take my order.

"This place has just the sort of charm I need in my life. And pie."

She laughs and the sound eases the ache in my joints. "The pie *is* good. What'll it be?"

"Oh, I don't know." I purse my lips at the menu, making a ham of myself, before saying, "Surprise me."

"Are you sure?"

"I trust your judgment."

She turns away into the kitchen with a spring in her step. Well, glad to know I can still happily interact with people even if most of my coworkers refuse to acknowledge my presence at work. I wait at the counter, donning a casual smile at other patrons that enter. I absently spin the probation ring around my finger on my right hand. Genna had referred to hers as a shackle before. I can't say I disagree with that assessment. The IMS has updated the specs of the rings to wirelessly transmit data to keep a better eye on the werewolves. If I stopped taking the serum or went off the rails, they would know immediately. I wouldn't be surprised if the GPS is activated too. You think the IMS could conjure up a little more faith in their own agents, even if they are werewolves.

"That some kind of promise ring?"

Daisy slides a plate of eggs, bacon, and pancakes in front of me but keeps her eyes on the probation ring.

"Of a sort."

"Does that mean . . . you have a girlfriend?"

I can't help but chuckle. "No. The last girl I liked ran off with an older man."

"That's too bad." But from the twinkle in her eye, Daisy makes it sound like anything but a bad thing. "I hope you enjoy those pancakes."

She walks away to help another customer. I smirk as I look down at the pancakes and realize she made a smiley face with the syrup.

I take my time eating and watch the other customers ordering their own dinners. There's a comfortable atmosphere here. People laugh and chat with friends. Whenever Daisy is free, she comes over to talk. It puts a spark of life back in my veins and my energy returns despite having been drained from work. I find out she's been living here since she was a little girl. Her father founded the restaurant. He died a few years back—may he rest in peace—so she and her mother run the place now.

"So what about you?" she says and rests her elbows on the counter as the dinner crowd starts to thin. "Last time you were here you said you moved because of your job?"

"Yeah. It's terribly boring. Minnesota was much more exciting."

"Really?" She crinkles her nose which happens to be very cute.

"I know, I know, but it's the truth."

"You have any family back home?"

A knot forms in my stomach. "Yeah. My twin sister. She . . ." I roll my lips as I feel the emptiness of that apartment creeping up on me again like a dark cloud that refuses to go away. We've shared a few phone calls but there hasn't been much to say except promising everything is fine. I don't want her messing up her own career as a Spartan to baby me. I'm a big boy. I can handle the serum by myself. She doesn't need to rush to Seattle to hold my hand.

And yet there's that small part of me that wishes she would.

"You okay?" Daisy asks.

"Yeah, I'm fine." I dissuade her worry with a practiced smile. "I just miss her, that's all. We've hardly ever been apart our whole lives. This is a big change."

"You know what I think will help?"

"What?"

"A piece of pie."

I fake a gasp of surprise. "Daisy, I think you're a genius."

"I know." She laughs and disappears into the kitchen.

She returns with a piece of blueberry pie and I take my sweet time finishing it off. I hover a while longer, probably longer than Daisy's mother likes judging by her narrow-eyed gaze from the kitchen. Daisy is happy enough to keep me entertained with stories of other customers and I enjoy listening until twilight comes and it's time to go.

As I walk to my apartment under the streetlights that blink on as dusk settles in, the hairs on the back of my neck stand on end. I stop and inspect my surroundings. I don't see anything, but that doesn't mean there isn't someone there. I stall my breathing in order for my hearing to work its best. There's nothing odd to pick out between the wind rustling the grass and litter and cars driving past. Switching senses, I take a deep whiff and close my eyes. There's a familiar scent mixed in with the car exhaust, fries from a nearby fast food joint, and a touch of fragrance from a garden somewhere close.

I continue on but I can't shake the feeling that I'm being watched. I make it back to the apartment without incident but I linger outside the doors for a minute just to see if anything happens. When the growing night remains calm, I heave a sigh and make for that void of emptiness on the second floor.

It turns out to be one of the bad nights. Restless, aching, and not quite able to fall asleep, I move from the bed to the couch and stay up late into the night watching whatever's on TV until I lapse into an uneasy slumber.

Mornings are always tough but this one feels especially rude. Who in their right mind wants to wake up this early? I don't care to make myself breakfast or go out and get it. I'm in an irritable mood that I can't bounce out of as I get to work, steal whatever coffee is available along with a donut, and shuffle to my little dungeon in the back.

The day passes in a daze just like all the others except I can't take my mind off the aching. Doug is no help as a distraction as usual. I bump into Spartan Knox and he gives me a pep talk and encouraging phrase. I nod as if he's changed my view on the world but it's a lie. It's all a lie. The smiles, the friendly greetings, the casual chit-chat in the break room. I want to punch something, rip out of my body, make this all stop—

I tip back in my swivel chair and take a great, labored breath. My fingers automatically clutch the warm pendant beneath my shirt and I close my eyes, focusing on it.

I can't let myself deteriorate this quickly.

A minute passes, maybe two, before I open my eyes and sit up straight once more only to find Doug eyeing me with suspicion. Sure, now he decides to be interested in what's going on around him.

"Cat nap," I say casually and press a finger to my lips. "Shsssh. Don't tell anyone."

He returns to his work like the robot he is.

Paperwork, bathroom break, more paperwork, lunch—oh, yay, more donuts—paperwork, an actual nap, another round of paperwork, then out the door, to the gym, and round and round we go. Is this what normal people do every day? The same boring thing over and over again? No magic, no monsters, no supernatural creatures. It's so *boring*.

I don't take my usual spot at the counter when I reach the cafe. The aching has only been made worse by my intense workout so I slide into a booth and keep my head down. Daisy comes by and asks what's wrong. A cold or maybe even the flu, I say. She offers to get me tea like the kind person she is. I don't bother with small talk today.

I don't feel like me. I don't feel right. A week. It's only been a week and it's already this bad. Pixies, how am I supposed to hang on for the rest of my miserable time here?

Something's broken in me and there's no magic that can make me right.

A girl slides into the booth opposite me and I startle.

"You look awful, Hawk."

Blonde tresses trail in soft curls nearly to her elbows. Her eyes hide behind dark sunglasses. She doesn't smile. Her clothes are colorful and bright. All these things are obvious attempts to hide what is familiar—because I know her. Beneath the wig, the clothes, the sunglasses, *I know her*. And that smell of overturned earth and fragrance of flowers I smelled last night wasn't from some garden. It was *her*. She must have been following me.

She takes off those ridiculous sunglasses to reveal her coffee brown eyes I had been thinking about earlier. Every part of me is simultaneously full of anger and joy, suspicion and relief. She's not dead. That's great. But she also betrayed me, betrayed Phoenix, swayed Witty to the dark side, and released the powerful monster that cursed my life and killed my parents.

Genna.

4

Phoenix

I've been over the same reports at least a dozen times but I still can't see the pattern. None of this makes sense.

Our team received a detailed briefing on all of the known "werewolf disruption" attacks that have occurred since Dasc's escape from Underground. Each night after training, when the equipment has been stowed, the gear tucked away, and everyone hits the bunk, I find myself up late on Melody's personal tablet combing through the data. Today we finished our training drills early so I sit in the mess hall reading, the frustration of not being able to figure this out eating away at me.

The werewolf attacks are random. They've attacked seemingly useless targets and also high-security complexes. The number of attackers changes. Their methods change. Their apparent objective changes.

The attacks where IMS agents turn on their own have troubled me the most. Every time it happens, the anti-werewolf movement grows. Hawk and I were lucky. We spent most of the last year tucked away at Spartan training. We knew what was going on out in the world but it didn't reach us where we were. With Spartan Knox at the helm, there was little to no discrimination against Hawk for what he was.

And now...

Agitated by the reports, I pull out my phone and dial Hawk. I want to hear how he's doing. From our last conversation, I could tell he was putting on a brave face and trying to hide just how miserable he is. It rings and rings and then goes to his voice mail.

I sigh and wait for the beep. "Hey, it's me. Just checking in. Training finished today so we're heading out tomorrow. Not sure where. We're on special assignment like I said. I'll let you know more when I can. I love you, dog breath. Hang in there. Call me, okay?"

I tuck my phone away and worry my lower lip. I haven't told him the whole truth about what our special assignment is. I don't want him to know that we're going to be "ending the werewolf problem." I still don't even know what that entails. It makes me so incredibly uneasy that it's been a real trial trying to integrate with my team. Are we going out to slaughter the werewolves or help them?

A breeze tickles my skin and I look up to find Charlie sitting across from me. His teleportation doesn't faze me in the least anymore. Sometimes he's there and sometimes he isn't. It just is what it is.

"You look far too serious over here by yourself," he says and clasps his hands together on the tabletop. "You reviewing the brief again?"

I turn the tablet off and massage the bridge of my nose. "Can you make sense out of any of this? Why? How? To what end?"

"Well, that's what we're going to figure out."

"Is it?" I mumble.

He's silent for a long time—so long it starts to make me feel uncomfortable. Eventually, he says, "What are you afraid of, Phoenix?"

As my usual instinct, I deflect and reply, "Clowns."

"Well, obviously. They're terrifying," he says, completely unfazed. I think he's become far too accustomed to my sense of humor. "But I meant about this assignment. Are you afraid you're not going to find answers? Or that you are?"

I level a glare at him. "What's that supposed to mean?"

"I know this is personal for you. All I'm saying is that maybe you need to look at this with a wide angle lens and not tunnel vision."

"Thank you for that bit of advice, Mr. Wizard."

"You know, increased levels of sarcasm are a sure sign of stress."

I'm not sure if he's trying to tease me or not. He's so good at the straight face that it's difficult to judge him at times.

"I read that sarcasm correlates to superior intelligence," I say.

"Then I'm surprised you haven't cured cancer yet."

He grins so I grin. Somehow, in our own strange way, our battle of wits and words has become a comforting thing. We're not afraid to rebuff each other but, you know, in a way to show that we care.

I fold my hands on top of the tablet and tilt my head to study him the way he tends to study me. He seems relaxed, but I know him well enough now to notice the slight crinkle at the edges of his eyes and the rigidness of his jaw that shows up when he's stressed.

"And what about you?" I ask.

"What about me?"

"I'm not the only one that's been on edge since we got that brief. It wouldn't have anything to do with who wrote it, does it?"

He presses his tongue against his cheek and stares down at his hands. Yup. He's definitely agitated and I know exactly why. Well, part of it anyway. The name at the top of each report compiled in the brief lists Specialist Laurence Jaeger as the investigating agent—the Hunter as he's commonly known as, and less commonly known as Charlie's uncle. Every mention of his uncle puts Charlie on edge. There's some nasty history there but I don't know any of the details. He doesn't speak about it and attempting to bring it up only makes him defensive and angry. It wasn't until recently that I found out his uncle's specialty was werewolf hunting.

Despite not knowing anything about the man himself, I can't help but dislike him.

Charlie starts tracing invisible circles on the table. "I haven't seen him in two years. I was hoping not to break that streak, but I don't doubt we'll be running into him shortly on this special assignment of ours."

"Do you want to talk about it?"

"Not yet."

Well, that's not a no. It's progress.

A shadow falls over me. "You guys look *way* too serious."

I spin around in my seat to find Theo standing behind me. He looks particularly odd with a flour dusted apron over his Spartan gear. His sleeves are rolled up to his elbows and he holds a plate in either hand bearing a slice of chocolate cake and fork.

"Let them eat cake!" he announces and proceeds to place the plates in front of Charlie and me.

"Did you just make this?" Charlie asks.

"Yup! Family recipe."

I shake my head. "We finished training like forty minutes ago. So you went and whipped up a cake?"

"Obviously."

He slips away in a rush back towards the kitchens. Charlie raises his eyebrows, shrugs, and picks up his fork. "Well, can't let it go to waste."

"*Obviously*," I quip.

The cake is really good. I guess Theo's an excellent cook as well as a marksman. He keeps saying he is but I'll admit I was skeptical. There aren't any doubts now.

The rest of the team converges around us with slices of their own. Despite the cake and the fair evening, everyone's quiet as they eat, dour even. Charlie and I take our cue from them and remain silent. My eyes automatically draw to Alona sitting down from Charlie. During our training exercises, she's revealed that her spirit walker form is a raven and I can't help but wonder if she's the same spirit walker that had been working with Scholar. Is Alona the majestic's hidden friend? I can't come straight out and ask, though, in case she isn't.

Theo takes the seat on my left and whispers to the pair of us, "Chocolate cake is tradition before we head out on assignment."

"What, like some kind of last meal?" Charlie asks.

In the most serious tone he's used since I've met him, Theo says, "Exactly."

That's when it really hits me. After today, it's not training anymore. It's the real deal. I've been in nasty situations before during my time as a junior agent, but as a Spartan, I'll be seeking out the most dangerous foes every day. We're the shield, we're the sword, the first into the fire, and the last to leave.

When the plates are clean and the forks set down, John is the first to stand. "Hit the hay. We leave at 0500 tomorrow morning. Molon labe."

The rest of us chant back, "Molon labe."

Everyone disperses. Alona goes to check on the air sprites hiding in the Osprey, Melody says she's going to take a swim at the pool before bed, and Theo challenges me to an arm wrestle which I politely refuse before heading to bed. Charlie follows in my wake. I don't change immediately but stretch out on my bed with that tablet to go through the reports once more as Charlie settles in with a book in the bunk beneath me. The rest of the team files in one at a time as they prep for tomorrow and settle in to sleep early.

John comes in last and I'm about to put the tablet away when an alarm blares through the camp with a high-pitched two-twang repetition. That's no ordinary alarm. It's a signal that all IMS agents know. The call to arms against monstrous things.

"Guess we're not getting sleep tonight," Theo says without a shred of anxiety despite that adrenaline-inducing alarm. "They're playing our song."

"Sierra Team!" John shouts, the loudest he's ever raised his voice in my presence. "Dust up in two minutes. Let's go!"

My heart pounds as that alarm floods my ears and I launch into action along with the rest of my team. This isn't practice anymore. I'm thankful I didn't change out of my gear yet. Theo took off half of his things but manages to smoothly slip everything on as we run for the hangar bay. The rest of the base has come alive around us. Workers have already started moving our Osprey out to the runway while other personnel check the inside of the craft to make sure everything is ready for take off.

Alona's the first one in. She slips up front and with practiced efficiency gets the wings rotating into flight position. The rest of us pile in, inspecting our gear with cries of "check!" to each other. Seats are folded down, we strap in, and within two minutes the Osprey lifts off. Once we're in the air, John moves to the front to get on the horn and receive our orders. I can feel when we've reached the proper altitude and the rotors tilt to change the Osprey from helicopter mode to airplane mode and we pick up speed.

A couple of minutes into flight, the tremendous noise of the aircraft dims to a bearable hum. That's curious.

Theo, the ever helpful guide, must take notice of my strange look to the side of the aircraft and points to where the rotors are outside. "Fart and Flitter just got into position."

"Excuse me?"

Melody laughs opposite me. "He means our air sprites. They're able to make us go faster and redirect the sound of the engines so we can come in much quieter."

"But . . ." Charlie says with a quizzical brow. "Fart and Flitter? Please explain."

Theo leans forward in his seat to better see Charlie past me. "Fart is whichever one isn't behaving."

"That seems pretty rude," I say.

He grins. "Neither one of them wants to be Fart so they always do their best to outdo each other. They're the most efficient pair of air sprites the Spartans have ever had!"

"You can thank Theo for that bit of ingenious mischief," Melody says.

He presses a hand to his heart and gives her doe eyes. "Anything to impress you, m'lady."

She shakes her head. I haven't failed to pick up on Theo's nicknames for Melody. They always have something to do with royalty or the like—princess, your majesty, m'lady, queen of hearts. I've also noticed he tends to base his nicknames on traits, not random flights of fancy. I'm Red. Charlie's been Cranky, Tight-shirt, and Hunturd. Is Melody some kind of royalty? The fact that she's a hollow hasn't come up again. I try to put two and two together but I don't come up with anything. Who is Melody really?

As intriguing as it is, that train of thought only distracts me for so long. I wait anxiously for John to come back with information on where we're headed. Another minute or so passes before he walks back and takes a seat next to Melody.

"Here's what we know," he begins and we're all ears. "Ten minutes ago a distress beacon was activated by a specialist in the field."

Wow. That's pretty unusual. The distress beacon is a subdural implant given only to specialists who operate alone on dangerous missions. It's the very last thing they go for when all other options fail.

"What specialist?" Charlie asks.

John levels a meaningful look at him. "Specialist Laurence Jaeger. Your uncle."

Charlie's throat bobs and he stares darkly at the floor.

"All we know is that the location of the beacon is the field office for the Paul Bunyan State Forest. Dispatch has tried raising the office but there's no response. We have no idea what the situation is or what hostiles we'll encounter so we're going in stealth to get the lay of the land."

I look to the others. Not one looks uneasy—apart from Charlie who looks queasy, but I think that has more to do with the fact that he's about to meet his uncle again.

"What we *do* know," John continues, "is that Specialist Jaeger was there investigating a possible lead on the werewolf situation. Apparently one of the agents at that field office is a werewolf still waiting for his replacement to arrive so there's no telling what we're about to head into."

So will that mean the agent has turned on his fellow agents? Will I sense Dasc's presence nearby when we reach our destination?

The intercom to the cabin from the cockpit activates and Alona announces, "ETA five minutes."

For the next several minutes, John goes over our plan of action. Before I know it, the Osprey slows and I feel our inertia change. John raps three times on the metal hull and at his signal, all sound of the engines vanishes. Without focusing on speeding us along, the air sprites can focus on making our approach silent. In fact, everything goes silent inside the aircraft. It's an odd sensation as if I've suddenly gone deaf because I can still feel the thrum of the engines and shifting of my seat but I can't hear any of it.

The team switches to nonverbal signals. John motions for us to put on our masks before he hits the lighted sign to the cockpit and the bay door opens. Wind gusts inside the bay and I'm glad of the mask and goggles protecting my face. Theo's the first to go. He connects his line to a carabiner above the door then rappels down into the night. John holds onto his line and when he receives the two tugs as the sign Theo has made it to the ground safely, the line is winched up in a snap and we move on.

The next time we hover, Charlie and I step up to the ramp and secure our own lines. At John's wordless gesture, we leap backwards off the edge of the ramp and rapidly descend into darkness. I keep my eyes down to spot my landing with my night-vision goggles in place. I increase the tension on my line moments before I touch the ground in order to slow my descent and bend my knees to absorb the impact. With quick, efficient motions, we unhook and give our lines a tug. A few seconds pass and then John and Melody join us on the ground.

The sounds of the forest surround us as we leave the vacuum of the Osprey created by the air sprites.

First thing we do is check our surroundings. We're in the middle of a forest filled with the croaking of frogs, buzz of insects, and chorus of crickets. My back touches Charlie's as we sweep the landscape for threats before we position ourselves into a slight crouch. We nod to each other and the others to signal the all clear.

John says ever so quietly into his headset, "We're clear. Winch the lines and move on, Alona."

A second later, the lines whip up into the Osprey and the inky blot of the aircraft against the sky moves silently away. As a group we move beneath the trees to the faint light in the distance coming from our target—the field office. Our footsteps are careful yet sure, unhurried yet purposeful. Hardly a sound is made at our passage.

"I'm in position," Theo says through our headsets. "I've got eyes on the field office. Most of the windows are covered."

"Can you see anything?" John asks.

"Yeah, one of the curtains is ripped. Two males, one is tied to a chair. It's Specialist Jaeger. He doesn't look so good. The other's in a park ranger uniform . . . I think he's the field agent."

Alona speaks up. "I just ran past with thermal. There are only two people in the building and one is registering slightly hotter. I'm thinking werewolf."

The field office is in sight. With most of the windows covered, it'll make our job of sneaking up easier. The woods come up close to the building as well to provide additional cover.

"Guys," Theo says in a warning tone. "You better get a move on. Our park ranger just pulled out a saw and is moving for our specialist. Do I take the shot?"

John swivels to me and Charlie. "Go for emergency breach."

As we've been practicing for the last week, I place my hand on Charlie's shoulder with my sights on the way behind us. In a disorienting instant, we disappear from the woods and appear directly beside one of the windows. Through a rip in the fabric I can see what Theo saw. I keep my hand on Charlie's shoulder as we take three seconds to assess the room before we make our next move.

It's a small cabin eerily similar to the field office in Moose Lake except it's a single open room. A bed is tucked against the far wall, a small kitchen fills up the space next to it, there's a couch and television for the living room, and a door to what I assume is the bathroom. In the very middle of the space is a man tied to a chair with blood running down his face. A park ranger stands before him brandishing a handheld saw and reaches for Specialist Jaeger's hand. There's no question of what he's about to do next.

I give Charlie's shoulder a squeeze.

We reappear beneath the yellow lights inside the cabin directly beside the two men as if we had been there all along. I snatch the man's hand holding the saw and wrench him backwards away from his hostage. In a fluid movement I swivel my body into his and then fling him full force over my shoulder onto his back. Charlie disappears and reappears as he makes sure the rest of the room is clear. Five seconds later, Melody and John burst through the door.

"All clear," Charlie announces.

Clean and efficient.

I keep the man pinned to the floor and knock the saw under the couch. Charlie comes round with handcuffs to help me. His gaze seems to veer purposefully away from the man strapped to the chair.

"As Spartan response time goes," Specialist Jaeger says with a bored drawl, "that wasn't terrible."

Theo's voice whispers through the headset. "He sounds like a super swell guy."

65

I haul my prisoner to his feet, keeping a hand on his shoulder and the other gripped tightly on his arm to make sure he doesn't try to run. When I straighten, I finally get a good look at Charlie's uncle.

If I want to know what Charlie will look like in twenty some years, the answer is before me. His uncle is an eerie spitting image of him except with a full beard, more wrinkles from age, and a touch of gray at his temples. At the moment he's also sporting a black eye, a cut above his eyebrow that's dripping blood down his face, and abrasions on his hands. His plaid shirt is rumpled and his workman boots scuffed with mud. Despite the situation he's in, he looks merely bored that he was seconds away from having his fingers sawed off.

Melody cuts away his restraints and he rubs his wrists.

"Anything worse than that cut and your hands?" she asks as he gets to his feet. He's just as tall as Charlie too. What, is Charlie a clone from his DNA? Good grief.

Specialist Jaeger actually laughs. "I'm fine."

He ignores Melody attempting to inspect his forehead, takes the bandage right out of her hands, and dabs at the cut himself as if simply drying off his face. His eyes sweep over the rest of us then land on Charlie.

"It's been a while CJ," he says. "Still hand washing your shirts in the evening?"

The temperature in the stuffy room drops about ten degrees and even the crickets outside quiet their chirping. Ice could have formed between the frosty gazes uncle and nephew give each other. Whatever history is between them, it's clearly left a jagged mark on them both.

"It's Spartan Jaeger," Charlie says and turns a cold shoulder to face me instead. "We should check the perimeter."

"Yes, you go do that," his uncle says sarcastically.

My hand tightens unconsciously on my prisoner's arm to the point he actually lets out a yelp. John motions to me and we switch places. The second I'm free of my obligation, Charlie grips my shoulder almost painfully and we vanish out of the cabin. Before I can say anything, Charlie shakes his head. It's obvious he doesn't want to talk about the elephant in the room. I respect his silence. We all have things we'd rather not talk about. When he does want to tell me about it, I'll be here.

Alona's voice comes over our headsets. "I've swept the area with thermal. I'm only picking up wildlife as far as I can tell."

"We'll see if we can find any tracks," I say.

"I'm coming in," Theo says. "There's nothing up this way."

Charlie and I hunt in a pattern around the cabin for signs of any other creature or monster in the area. We walk through dense brush that turns into prickly bushes rising out of a swamp. We pick our way carefully through but can't avoid stepping into the murky water. As background noise, John and Melody start questioning the werewolf field agent who sounds disoriented and confused. If he was acting under a compulsion by Dasc, that would make sense.

I try to stretch out my own senses. Charlie stands out like a beacon beside me of pure magic. The werewolf at the field office is an acrid smoke behind me. Melody's presence is that odd void. Apart from that, I don't sense anything, but my range of perception might not reach far enough. We still don't know the distance Dasc's persuasion ability covers. Maybe it's a hundred feet. Maybe it's miles.

The only tracks either of us comes across are human footprints to and from the cabin leading to an ATV. There's nothing here. *Pixies.*

We return to the cabin just as Theo reaches the door. We walk in together—Charlie coming in last after he pauses to take a deep breath—and find Melody and John guarding the werewolf who's now sitting on the couch. Specialist Jaeger lingers in the background patching himself up.

"I told you, I don't know what he's talking about!" the agent says desperately, flinging a hand towards Charlie's uncle.

"You don't remember torturing him for the location of the Fields?" John asks sternly, one hand resting on the gun at his waist.

The Fields? What on earth is that?

He shakes his head. "Why would I do that?"

"Why indeed," Specialist Jaeger says and walks forward with a confident swagger to tower over our captive agent. "Why would a werewolf hold hostage and interrogate one of the few people that knows the location of the werewolf rehabilitation center?"

I'm careful not to make any sudden movements, any shifts in stance or expression. I've known werewolves that have vanished to some secretive black site. I've heard the rumors that they never come back. But there's not one report, not one mention of the site in any of the IMS news feeds or anywhere I can find. No one wants to acknowledge its existence. I've hunted for answers about it myself to find where a few of the werewolves from Moose Lake disappeared to after being taken into IMS custody.

And it seems I'm not the only one who's been looking into it.

Charlie speaks up from his spot by the door, arms crossed and as far away from his uncle as he can get. "Why were you even here in the first place?"

His uncle gives him a haughty look. "I was setting a trap to see if there was a werewolf conspirator in this office."

"Well, that backfired."

"Actually, I would say it worked perfectly."

I put two and two together. "You wanted him to take you hostage."

He smiles but it carries none of the warmth when Charlie does the same in my direction. It's smugly cruel. "People reveal the most when they think they have the upper hand. And speaking of revelations . . ." He steps around the others to stand directly before me—a little too close for comfort—with that smile still in place. "I'd love to have a word with the girl so near and dear to Dasc's heart. And to think you're a Constantine."

"Excuse me?"

He studies me, eyes flicking up and down. "You don't know, do you?"

My hackles rise. "Don't know what?"

"I knew your mother."

All brain function comes to a halt at those words and I wait stunned for him to continue.

"Before she was Mary Mason, she was Mary Constantine. A werewolf hunter."

5

Hawk

I wish my food had arrived already because then at least I would have a fork or something for a weapon. I mean, anything can be used as a weapon but there's not much in reach in case Genna decides to, you know, kill me or something. Then again, it wouldn't make sense for her to attack me now. She's been following me so she would know I'm most vulnerable on my walk home when I'm alone and away from the apartment complex where other agents live. Going for me in the middle of a cafe during the dinner rush would be stupid. Genna may be many things but she's definitely not stupid.

"Is this the part where you threaten me?" I ask.

"I'm not going to threaten you."

"Threaten to hurt someone else if I don't do as you say?"

"I'm not going to threaten anyone."

I wet my lips as I consider why on earth she'd come

here of all places. "Did you leave a shirt behind when you fled and want it back? *Why are you here, Genna?*"

"I'm sorry," she says quietly.

I almost laugh. "Oh! You came here to apologize. I should have known. Well, now that that's been taken care of, would you like a cup of coffee? Some tea? A pardon from the IMS, perhaps?"

A crease forms between her eyebrows, the first indication of any emotion whatsoever—like one of Dasc's werewolf robots.

"I'm not apologizing for what I did," she says. "I'm apologizing for hurting you and Phoenix. That wasn't supposed to happen."

It's difficult to keep my tone even and calm when I want to shout. The serum boiling in my blood in no way helps with my rising temper. I'm usually better at holding myself together than this. "What exactly did you think was going to happen? And not just to us but all those people that *died* that day. Did you really think bringing a horde of monsters to our doorstep was going to end well? I watched a man get cut down right in front of me. You don't get to say you're sorry for that and expect to be forgiven."

"I don't expect that," she says quietly. Her dark eyes glimmer from the last rays of light piercing through the window blinds as the sun sets. It makes her look more beautiful—and more dangerous. "I know what I am. I know what I've done. I also know that one day I'm going to pay for all of it, but I'm willing to pay that price if it means I can do this one good thing."

My eyes narrow. "What are you talking about?"

Before she can answer, Daisy appears with my plate of ham and eggs. She sets it before me rather stiffly.

"I'm sorry. I didn't realize you were having company today," she says and looks to Genna. "Can I get you anything?"

Genna doesn't even turn her head in Daisy's direction. "No, thank you."

"Let me know if you change your mind." She moves away but throws a curious look at us over her shoulder.

"Well, I'm glad you didn't flirt with her this time," Genna says flatly. "I just about threw up in my mouth the other day."

I blink and rally a solid defense of deflective sarcasm. "Why flirt when I know you're right here and not spying on me in the background? That takes the fun out of it." I lean forward and set my arms on the table beside my plate—one arm casually resting atop the dull knife Daisy left for me. "Why are you here? You didn't come all this way just to apologize when the whole of the IMS is looking for you and Dasc."

She's silent for a long moment as if weighing her words carefully and folds her hands in her lap. "I need your help."

I laugh—a big, obnoxious laugh that probably draws more attention than prudent—at the absurdity of it. Then I keep on laughing and wipe at the fake tears at the corners of my eyes for dramatic effect to really hit my point home.

"Whew!" I say loudly, give my eyes one last wipe, tuck my napkin into the collar of my shirt, pick up my silverware, and proceed to delicately cut my ham. "That's hilarious."

"I know what you must think of me."

If my eyes could burn holes with a glare, that's what would be happening right now. "I really don't think you do."

"See me as a monster, your worst nightmare, a conniving fiend—whatever makes you happy, Hawk—but don't let that stop you from seeing the truth."

"And the truth is what exactly?"

She uncoils her hands and slides a slip of paper across the table. I weigh my options—more sarcasm, indifference, rejection—and decide I'm too curious to do anything except take the piece of paper and unfold it to see what's inside.

"This is an IMS case file number," I mumble as I recognize the arrangement of letters and numbers. "Where did you get this?" I clap a hand to my forehead. "Oh, wait. Never mind. Witty. *Of course*, you would have gotten this from Witty. You're both 'conniving fiends' now."

"Aaron is the most selfless person I've ever known. Certainly more than you or Phoenix."

"Excuse me?"

"Read the file. I know you have access at your new job."

I stuff the paper into my pocket. "And what if I decide to call Spartan Knox instead and tell him exactly where you are?"

She smiles. "By the time you dial him on your cell phone, I'll be long gone. Read the file. If after that you still want to sic the Spartans on me, then I'll be here this time tomorrow. If instead you think better of things, I'll be in this booth ready to explain everything. Until then . . ." She rises and puts her sunglasses back on. "Enjoy your ham."

I watch as she exits the cafe, turns the corner outside, and disappears. I don't move. I *ought* to move. I should pull out my cell phone and call in a code black to have the area shut down and Genna found.

But I don't.

"Are you okay?"

I look up to find Daisy hovering beside me with a pot of coffee in her hands. The rest of the world comes crashing back into focus and I blink a few times as if to remove the haze of Genna's presence from my mind.

"Yeah, I'm fine," I say.

"You look like you've seen a ghost."

I swallow and stare at my uneaten meal. "Can I get this to go?"

"Um, sure. I'll go get you a box."

Thirty seconds later, I walk at a rapid pace through downtown with a warm box of eggs and ham in hand. I pass the apartment building, walk a few more blocks, and reach the IMS processing center. Still in my sweats from working out, I march up to the front desk and badge the security guard.

"I wasn't expecting to see you," Jerry says and straightens his uniform. I don't miss the casual resting of his hand closer to the gun on his belt.

"Is Vicky still in?" I ask and lean an arm on the security counter.

"Yeah, she's in her office."

I do my best at a shy smile. "She's always working so hard, I thought I'd bring her supper. You know how she forgets to eat sometimes." I wiggle the box in my hands for emphasis.

Jerry nods and gestures to the staircase. "It'd make her evening. Good luck."

"Thanks."

I jog to the steps and take them as quickly as I dare without arousing suspicion. Once I reach the elevators, I slide my card and hit the button for the restricted floors.

It's a good thing I've made an effort to make friends here even if no one really cares to be friends. I know Jerry's an old gossip and expects that I'm probably making a move on Vicky by bringing her dinner. It won't be suspicious to him. I also happen to know that Vicky—Milton's right hand around the office—is a workaholic and usually stays a couple hours after the day is over to meticulously organize her paperwork. Combine the two together and I get a perfectly reasonable and thoroughly unsuspicious reason for returning to work after hours when I'm pretty sure everyone knows I hate it here.

The elevator dings and I step out onto my floor. It's oddly quiet here. I'm used to there being a constant buzz of phones, shuffling of papers, and bubbling from the coffee pot. Without anyone here and most of the lights off, it's eerie. Box in hand, I move silently down the stretch of cubicles to where Vicky is at the far end. The light's on and I can hear her sipping at a can of Coke. The second that drink's gone, she'll be heading home. That's my time limit.

Going as quietly as I can, I make for my desk at the opposite end of the floor. Despite the appearance of the rest of the floor being deserted, I make a quick sweep just to make sure someone isn't going to stumble upon me accidentally.

It isn't until I'm sitting at my desk and logging in that I wonder what on earth I'm doing. I should have gone straight to Spartan Knox. Genna's here. This is probably the first time anyone's had a lead on her since she disappeared with Dasc a year ago. She could have information on the werewolf attacks. She probably knows where Dasc is. I'm getting played again, aren't I? Stupid me.

And yet with all that floating around in my mind, I unfold the piece of paper she gave me and search for the file number in the system. Two seconds later, it opens up.

2011-W4-01377. Jason Marsden.

Jason. As in the Jason I went to school with in Moose Lake, the one that bit Phoenix, that had the same reaction I did to the serum, and then was summarily hauled away because of it. I never heard what happened to him after that. He vanished—like all the other horror stories of werewolves being thrown into a black hole never to be heard from again.

Why give me his file number? What is Genna up to? What could possibly be so dire in this report that she would show up and slip me the information, despite the huge risk?

When I try to access it, a prompt comes up requesting higher clearance credentials. Taking a chance, I enter Jefferson's information and password. I picked it up a long while back when he had activated the GPS tracking on Genna's probation ring in Moose Lake. The man types like a t-rex on sleeping pills. It wasn't hard to memorize his password from watching him. I figured it was information worth remembering.

With fingers crossed, I hit enter. The spinning circle of loading drives me crazy for about four seconds before the report comes up and I heave a breath. They still haven't suspended Jefferson's account in the system. Maybe Director Knox has kept it open in the hopes that Jefferson would return to being an official IMS agent again. Lucky me.

The first section of the report is Jefferson's account of that night when Jason slipped his probation ring and made a break for Ashley's house where Phoenix had conveniently been at the time. He talks about Jason's "complications" and "adverse reaction to the serum." He recommends closely monitored treatment and relocation for the time being until a more permanent solution can be assessed for Jason's condition.

A part of me is irked by Jefferson's treatment. He knows about me and my "complications" but he let me be because of Phoenix. Couldn't he have done something more for Jason? Could I have?

Jefferson's report ends and documentation follows with Jason's relocation. He's sent to some place code-named "The Fields," whatever that is. The actual location of the facility is redacted which is all sorts of suspicious. If it's blacked out, it means it's dangerous and that's saying something considering what our agency does.

After he's relocated, there's a bunch of medical documentation as he underwent physicals and examinations and testing to figure out what went wrong with Jason Marsden.

Then I come across another report—an interrogation—by Specialist Laurence Jaeger.

Jaeger? Could it be Charlie's uncle? I remember he's supposed to have some jerkwad uncle. Phoenix got all prickly when she couldn't wring the facts out of Charlie about what their beef was. She gets easily frustrated when she can't satisfy her curiosity—just like me.

As I start to read the report, that slumbering beast inside me bares its teeth. Specialist Jaeger is none too gentle in his questioning of Jason who's in the middle of a psychotic breakdown. He's unfeeling in his report as Jason has violent outbursts that lapse into sessions of weeping. It's clear that Jason is unhinged but Specialist Jaeger seems convinced he has more information on Dasc since Jason was directly involved with what happened in Moose Lake. The interrogation ends with nothing fruitful coming out of it—just Jason being sent to the infirmary for more evaluations and medicine.

I'm angry. There are no two ways about it. I clench my jaw so hard my teeth ache.

But the interrogation isn't the worst of it. The doctor assigned to his care—who appears much more sympathetic to his plight—records his deteriorating condition. Jason's not getting any better, but how can he? He's locked up, stuffed in a room with no handle when he shifts, forced to take varying doses of the serum to see what he can handle, and isn't allowed to make contact with his family.

When I scroll to the last of the documentation, I find a death certificate and a brief report. As the serum drove him to insanity and the facility only made the situation worse, Jason broke. One day when they opened the cell after he had shifted, they found he had committed suicide. I can hardly take in the gruesome details of it, of what he had to do to end his own life alone in that cell. No one had been able to see that he bled to death in the corner as he had curled up into a ball to hide it. They thought he had fallen asleep.

I stare numbly at the screen, unable to move, hardly able to breathe. My hands shake and my chest starts to heave.

Jason had been a version of me without Phoenix there for protection. I tried so hard to help him and give him the support he needed but it wasn't enough. It was never going to be enough.

And now I'm out here all alone, miles away from my sister.

I could become Jason.

I quickly close the report as if it's fire and I don't want to get burned.

"Hawk?"

I startle. Vicky stands over me with a crushed can of Coke in her hand. She looks seriously alarmed—eyes wide, a deep crease between her brows, lips pursed.

"What are you—are you crying? Are you okay?"

Sure enough, when I hastily run the back of my hand under my eyes, they come away wet with tears I didn't even know I had been shedding. News of what happened to Jason has shaken me to my core and my carefully controlled mask that hides the pain begins to break apart.

"I was . . ." My voice cracks so I try again. "I just found out a friend of mine died."

"I'm so sorry. But—but what are you doing here?"

Without much delicacy I shove the box of leftovers into her hands. "This was for you, but when I came in you were busy, and then I got that message . . ."

"Oh, I—" She clears her throat and looks down at the box of food as if I brought her wilted flowers—happy at the effort but disappointed with the end result.

"I should go," I say and quickly rise to my feet, eager to get away from here as soon as possible.

"I'll walk you out," she says and escorts me to the elevator.

The whole ride down I feel like I'm drowning, sinking deeper and deeper into some dark abyss. Vicky doesn't say a word and when we part at the doors I don't even respond to her quiet farewell. It takes me twice as long as usual to return to my apartment. I don't greet the doorman or say hello to anyone in the hallways like I usually do. The second

I reach my empty little square of space, I close and lock the door behind me. I take a seat on the couch and gaze blankly into space.

Jason killed himself. He went to extremes to do it. I had tried everything to help him before he was taken away. Was it always inevitable?

Fear slips its spindly fingers around my spine.

Is it an inevitable outcome for everyone that reacts adversely to the serum?

Twilight passes outside through the window on my right but I don't move from my spot as I contemplate everything I've been through, everything I am, everything I've done. My thoughts gnaw away at me deep into the night.

At one point my thoughts take a turn, that I'm being used again for whatever scheme Genna is hatching. I tug out my cell phone and pull up Knox's number, but that's as far as I get. I ought to call him and tell him where Genna will be tomorrow at dinner time. I *ought* to . . . but I don't.

Genna wanted me to read that file. Why? To what end? What could she gain?

But don't I already have the answer to that? My faith in everything I believe has been shaken. I fear that one more push is all it'll take to send me tumbling over the edge. I've been itching to do something for ages. I've been trapped inside the dangers of my own life for far too long. Maybe it's time for a drastic change. The truth of Jason's fate has opened my eyes more than I would like to admit. He was a victim of his circumstances just as I am. There are injustices that must be righted. But how?

I don't sleep. Night wanes and the sky blooms gold and pink. My phone still rests on my leg but unused. When my alarm goes off, I startle. It's Friday. I'm supposed to go into work. But how can I possibly do that with this burden resting on my shoulders? Yet I'm sure my absence would be noticed—not because anyone would miss me, but because there's no doubt the IMS is keeping a very close eye on their werewolves at the moment. Behavior out of character would be noted by someone and I can't draw any sort of attention. Last night was enough of a risk.

Always living a lie, trading sanity for safety.

At last I rise and take a shower to wake myself up. I get ready and trudge into work amidst the flow of IMS employees. When I pass the security guard, he winks at me and nods his head in Vicky's direction ahead of me. I give him a shy smile and continue on my way.

The day is as tedious as the rest but I don't chip in for small talk around the water cooler or make my usual attempts to have social interaction as I walk between the cubicles to grab jobs off the printer.

Near the end of the day, Spartan Knox comes to me at my desk. "Hawk." He claps a hand on my shoulder and looks to my co-worker. "Doug, take a water break."

Without a word, Doug shuffles away and I realize I'm being cornered. It's just me and Spartan Knox in this obtuse little hideaway where no one else can see us. Does he know I spoke to Genna? Did they find out I used Jefferson's account? It's a matter of practice that I'm able to keep my breathing even and look Knox straight in the eye.

He pulls over Doug's chair and takes a seat. "Are you okay?"

"How do you mean?"

"I heard you lost a friend." He jerks his head towards

the cubicles past the shelves surrounding us. "Office gossip. Can't avoid it apparently."

Is that it? I guess Vicky would have spread the news. Have I been moping without realizing it? Or has being less chatty given myself away? I can only hope Knox is here concerned for my well-being and nothing else. I feel like a traitorous worm living in a man's skin—so, same old thing.

"Yeah," I say quietly. "I did."

"I'm sorry to hear that. You have my condolences."

"Thank you, sir."

"I've lost men before," he says in that low baritone of his and leans forward on his forearms, hands clasped together. "The best we can do is do right by them and honor their memory."

"Right," I say quietly and keep my head bowed.

"If you need to talk, I'm around."

"Thank you."

The Spartan leaves and I'm left pondering his bit of advice. Do right by the dead and honor their memory. How do I do right by Jason who was alone and helpless in the end?

It's a lifetime before the work day ends. I scowl in the direction of the unmoving clock. I want it to speed along to this evening and yet I still don't know what I'm going to do once the time comes. Genna will be at the diner waiting for me. Even if she thinks Jason's fate will have swayed me away from the IMS, does she really think I'm going to join up with Dasc? Having the werewolves as his lackeys isn't exactly a step up in their livelihood.

When the clock strikes five, it's a mad rush out of the building. I take care to move at a normal pace. Now that the time is finally here, my feet feel like lead. I've broken the rules before, sure, but this is something entirely different. But if I go to meet Genna, it's not a true betrayal to the IMS. I'm going to get answers and information. If I don't like what I hear, then I'll tell Knox. Yes, that sounds more like a plan.

A random sneaking thought slips into my brain—what would Jefferson do if he knew I was meeting Genna and didn't tell him? I swallow.

To keep up appearances of everything being an average day, I hit up the gym but my performance is lackluster. Knox gives me another hearty pat on the shoulder and bids me farewell after we clean up.

I walk to the cafe. As I near, I squint to see who's inside but there's no sign of Genna. That doesn't mean she's not around, though.

Daisy greets me with a smile when I enter. "The usual?" she asks.

"Yeah, thanks," I say subdued, distracted.

The booth I had met Genna in before is empty so I snatch it up before it's gone. I keep an eye on the street and front door, appraise each patron that comes in—looking for IMS agents as well as Genna—and fidget as I wait. Daisy brings over my food but then leaves me be. That's good.

For the thousandth time I ask myself what I'm doing. This is Genna I'm dealing with. The girl had me convinced she was on our side and then brought a horde of monsters down on Underground and set my parents' murderer free. *Pixies*, I'm so stupid. Now that I'm here, I'm regretting not saying anything to Knox. He's a good man. We could have brought Genna in quietly. She would have told us where

Dasc is eventually and the situation would be in our control. But like this . . . anything could happen.

I see Genna a second before she enters the cafe. She's wearing that blonde wig again, has a pink purse hanging off her arm and wears bright colored clothes—basically the complete opposite of what some would think a traitor and werewolf might look like. She pauses at the counter before making her way to my booth. I force myself to stop fidgeting and sit straight.

She slides into the seat opposite me. "Is this the part where agents swarm in and arrest me?"

"No."

"You're not wearing a wire?"

"No."

"Then why are you here, Hawk?"

"I don't know," I say quietly. I study her face that has become so familiar to me. It's the same as ever—an expressionless mask to hide what's underneath. But I know what's under there. Joy, pain, determination, strength. At least, that's what I'd like to think and that her true self isn't some cold-blooded monster like everyone else in the IMS believes.

"We were friends, weren't we?" I ask. "That wasn't a lie."

"None of it was a lie," she says.

"If that's true, and if you really hate Dasc as much as you claim, why are you here acting as his Whisper? Why did you free him?"

Her stoic face changes with a glimmer in those dark eyes. "Dasc doesn't know I'm here."

A spark of hope—quickly followed by a wave of wariness and suspicion.

"Remember Phoenix's bargain," she continues. "He can't come after you or try to use you. If I was here under his orders, Phoenix would have felt the life-debt bargain break. And I have a feeling if that happened, she would be calling you in a heartbeat."

That's true. If there's ever a hint I'm in danger, Phoenix comes swooping in like a storm. But she hasn't called. I even press a hand to the phone in my pocket to make sure it's not vibrating with her call right now.

The spark of hope flares.

"If you're not here under his orders, then why are you here? Why have me read Jason's file?"

"So you did."

I swallow. "I did."

"I wanted you to read that file to understand why I had to get Dasc out. I couldn't trust the IMS with the safety of the werewolves. I also couldn't find Dasc's other cells without his help." She leans across the table and speaks in a low conspiratorial tone. "I'm going to save the werewolves, keep them out of the agency's reach, and kill Dasc. But I can't do it alone."

I want to believe her. Oh, I really do. Every part of me can't deny that I savor her vision of a future free not only of Dasc but of the fear of being found out by the IMS, being free of the serum forever. The ache in my bones and the horrible memory of Jason's file make me want to be a part of that utopia.

And she wants my help. Once I go down that road, there will be no turning back. She's not going to fight a war only against Dasc but the IMS itself—*my* agency. Yet it's also the agency I've feared as much as loved since I was four. If it were any other week with Phoenix at my side and my body free of the serum, I think my answer would automatically be no. With the reality of my situation sinking in and the serum chewing me up from the inside, I find my loyalty and certainty tenuous at best, like a castle built on sand. I'll be a traitor if I help Genna with her cause, if I believe what she's saying is true. If she could accomplish it . . .

Just one small problem. It seems impossible.

"That's quite the to-do list," I say. "It sounds like you've got your work cut out for you."

"It's already begun."

6

Phoenix

After spending the night sweeping the Paul Bunyan National Forest for signs of Dasc or his followers, I've only got two things on my mind—sleep and not talking to Specialist Jaeger. So far it hasn't been difficult to avoid his attempts at conversation since I have the excuse of focusing on my job. John cut him off at the first opportunity and ordered us to scour the area while he made the specialist sit in the Osprey with our prisoner. Jaeger obviously did not like being bossed around but Spartans take over authority in code black situations. After no luck in the woods, we put out a warning to nearby field offices to keep an eye out, call in some backup agents to man the office, and then pile into the Osprey to return to base.

When we touch down at Camp Ripley, the Osprey is shuffled off the runway but kept out of the hangar bay and ready for flight if the need arises. I find Specialist Jaeger at my side in an instant but John orders us to hit the hay until we get more information to run down. We enter the barracks as the sun rises, ready our gear for another outing, and then fall into our bunks. I'm certainly tired but my brain continues to buzz for a long time before I eventually fall asleep.

It's part way through the afternoon when I wake at John's sharp whistle.

"Rise and shine," he calls. "Debrief in twenty minutes. Grab some chow and meet me at headquarters."

I sit up and rub at my eyes as the others do the same. It's back to work. We're a quiet bunch as we dress, tie on our boots, and head to the mess hall. We get a special meal for our odd eating hour—pancakes, bacon, and orange slices. When we commandeer a table as our own, I find Theo taking the seat beside me.

"Hey. Did you really not know you're a Constantine?" he says without preamble. He's a bit blunt and I've noticed he has a tendency to say whatever's on his mind without a filter.

"I had no idea," I say quietly. "I guess I don't know much about my parents."

"My family knew them. Pretty sure my mother was friends with a Mary Constantine. I didn't know she was your mother."

My food is quickly forgotten. "She knew my mother?"

"Yeah, the Constantines and the Benoits are old slayer families. We go waaaaaaaay back." He makes a gesture like outlining a rainbow for emphasis. "The Benoits obviously came out of France. We've been hunting vampires since forever. And the Constantines came out of Romania I think."

"Hunting werewolves," I interject.

"Yeah. Back before it was illegal to, before the serum."

That doesn't make me feel much better. "Right."

"They were the pros back in the day before they were wiped out."

"What?"

"Well, they hunted the werewolves so the werewolves hunted them. The whole line of Constantines was picked off one by one until there were just a few stragglers left. I guess the werewolves realized the Constantines were too big of a threat to ignore. The old families always know more than the rest. Speaking of which, did you know that if you jab a vampire in the back of the neck, they go limp for about three seconds?" He puffs up and rolls back his shoulders. "Old family secret."

"Not much of a secret anymore," Alona chimes in.

He squints and points his fork at her. "Eavesdropper. That wasn't meant for *you*."

They bicker back and forth as I retract from the conversation, too absorbed in my own thoughts. The more I think about it, the more it makes sense. I had always wondered why my mother had wolfsbane bullets and where she got them. They're illegal nowadays. But if she was from a long line of ancient werewolf hunters, I'm sure she would've had connections to get them. And she was the one who realized it was Lycaon in Moose Lake back in 1996 causing the werewolves to go crazy. No one else was able to put it together, but she did.

I wonder how Mary Mason would react if she knew her son became a werewolf.

"You should eat something," Melody says to me.

I nod mutely and force myself to eat despite having no

appetite whatsoever. I'm also not the only one. Charlie hasn't spoken a word for a long time and he's barely touched his food. He catches me staring and returns it in kind until I look away. I guess both of us are feeling unsettled.

Within ten minutes we exit as a group and make for headquarters. Charlie and I gravitate to each other's side on the walk there as if unified in our discomfort of facing his uncle again. I desperately want to know more about my mother but at what cost? Learning she killed hundreds of werewolves? Would have been infuriated to find her son turned and her daughter hiding his non-use of the serum?

"Hey," Charlie whispers. He casts his eyes downwards and I realize he's holding out his hand for a low five. That's a first. I hit my palm to his—the symbol Hawk and I always use to let each other know we have one another's back. I guess Charlie picked up on it and is feeling as uneasy as I am.

He takes a deep breath and exhales slowly. A frown forms on his face and he shakes his head. "Nope. Didn't help."

I chuckle. "It's not magic, idiot."

"Well, it always seems to work for you and Hawk to bolster your confidence."

"Yeah, well, maybe we're just idiots."

He laughs and shrugs as if he has no argument with that assessment.

I punch him lightly in the shoulder. "That's where you say 'no, of course you aren't idiots,' you jerk."

"Hey, you said it, not me."

"You're a horrible and vicious person, Charlie."

"Thank you."

"You're welcome."

We exchange smiles and enter headquarters with a little

more gusto to our step. Melody leads the way to the room we had used earlier and find John and Specialist Jaeger already waiting for us. Charlie's uncle doesn't look particularly happy. We gather round to discuss plans. Theo immediately rolls out a chair and props his feet up on the table. Without a frown or even looking in his direction, John motions silently with one hand and Theo removes his feet.

"We may have a lead on what happened to the agent at the field office," John begins. "He still insists he can't remember taking Specialist Jaeger hostage. He says the last thing he does remember is picking up groceries in Bemidji. If that's where the memory lapse started, then that must be where he was triggered."

"Do we know why?" I ask and find all eyes on me. "I mean, why that field office? Why that agent? There must have been a reason."

John nods once to acknowledge my question. "That field office monitors the headwaters of the Mississippi River and a population of trolls in the Paul Bunyan National Forest. It's not of any particular significance."

"Apart from the fact I was there," Specialist Jaeger cuts in. "I had a feeling they'd come for me eventually since I've been investigating this mess."

"Okay." Charlie speaks up from my left. "Then why were you there?"

"I told you. I was—"

"Looking for a conspirator. You said that," Charlie says flatly. "Why that office? What led you to that particular one?"

They stare each other down in some sort of contest for a whole three seconds before Melody clears her throat. "Gentlemen, another time," she says softly.

As if there had been no interruption, Specialist Jaeger says, "It fit the profile of the other locations—had a werewolf agent that typically performs tasks alone for long stretches at a time, in Minnesota—which seems to be a recurring trend—and relatively secluded."

"There must be plenty of locations like that," Alona says. She stands behind Theo with arms crossed and a scowl on her face. At least Charlie and I aren't the only ones having less than friendly feelings towards the specialist.

Charlie's uncle cocks his head, rolls his eyes, and looks to our team leader. "Is your team always this quick to question? Or is this my nephew's influence?"

I become very prickly on Charlie's behalf but I learned more than just how to fight during my Spartan training. It gave me a modicum of patience and control. So, I curl my fists, take a slow breath, and don't let my anger make me do anything stupid.

John remains stoic as he replies, "We like having all of the facts. I won't apologize for my team finding holes in your report. So again, why that field office?"

The rest of us give Specialist Jaeger the intense yet polite look of waiting for him to continue his story. Theo actually props his chin up with both hands, elbows on the table, and stares intently at the specialist with a benign smile on his face. Watching Theo, I can't help but be reminded of my brother. They're both goofy and always ready with a clever quip. Although, Theo is much more carefree—he doesn't carry the burden Hawk does. An ache swells in my chest.

Specialist Jaeger clears his throat and straightens. "I kept knocking on doors. I knew eventually one of them would lead to someone involved in this werewolf conspiracy. I've been visiting likely field offices and agents all over the state. Whatever's going on, there have been more incidents in this state than anywhere else. This is werewolf territory. Dasc is obviously hiding somewhere in the state and using his werewolves to spread chaos."

John gives a single thoughtful nod. "Hmm."

"Hmm? That's it?"

Theo leans back and whispers to Alona, loud enough so we can all still hear. "Wow, this guy is seriously *tense*."

"Theo," John warns. Before Specialist Jaeger can say anything, he continues. "I take it you've read the transcripts of Spartan Mason's interviews with Dasc and her assessment of the attack on Underground?"

I was wondering when I'd be drawn into this.

"Of course I have," Jaeger snaps. "Why do you think I've been wanting to talk with her? And you keep denying me the opportunity."

"She was doing her job. Your questions could wait."

"Oh, is that it?"

"That's exactly it, and I'd appreciate a little more cooperation from you if you plan on working with my team."

No one moves or dares to interrupt except for Theo who mimes eating popcorn and watching the argument with excitement. Alona whacks him upside the head.

"My *point*," John says quietly but in a way that carries force, "is that this Dasc doesn't like to bandy about his resources and people for useless reasons. If he really triggered that agent into doing what he did, then I'd like to think there was a very specific goal in mind."

"We know the goal," Jaeger argues and throws out a hand wide as if the answer is clear. "They wanted to know the location of the Fields and let those deranged werewolves free."

I clench my jaw and study the table before me, doing my best not to imagine pummeling the specialist in the face.

"A rather careless move on his part and I don't think Dasc is careless."

"What are you getting at?"

"We know that Dasc fled Underground with one of our techs who had insider knowledge of how we operate," John says. I swallow and avoid looking at anyone. He's talking about Witty. I find Charlie's hand on my forearm. I glance at him but he isn't even looking at me. "He knew about the subdural implants specialists have. If Dasc was planning on making a move on you and being successful at it, they would have removed that implant and taken you away. Dasc wouldn't have you tied down in an IMS field office and waited for a team of Spartans to arrive."

Well, I'm glad to hear our team leader isn't dead set against werewolves in general. It's a comforting thought, especially when Specialist Jaeger seems keen on just killing them all.

"You're saying he didn't order this attack on me?"

"I'm saying we need to get to Bemidji and retrace that agent's footsteps to find out what's really going on here."

The specialist shakes his head in disbelief. "This is still my operation. You were assigned to help *me*, not the other way around."

"Fantastic," John says in a flat tone. "Are you coming with us or not? Because we're going to Bemidji."

Looking rather incensed, the specialist glares at John

and says, "Then why are we still here?" and marches out of the room.

The rest of us get up, ready to leave as well, but John raises a hand towards us and we still.

"I trust no one is going to have a problem working alongside Specialist Jaeger?" He looks specifically at Charlie and me. Neither of us immediately responds, so he adds, "Spartans work as a team. I don't care about your personal opinions of him. There's no slacking on cooperation. *He* might, but that's not our concern. We do our job and we do it right. Understood?"

"Yes, sir," we say in unison.

"Good. Then everyone change into civies and hit the tarmac. Wheels up in five."

With the order given, we jog out of headquarters and stop at the barracks to change into our civilian clothes but with concealed weapons on our person. It's hot out but I put on jeans, a t-shirt, and a light button-down to help hide the arsenal I'm carrying. I also keep Scholar's gloves in my pockets in case I need to use them. The others dress in similar fashion and we hurry onto the Osprey. Alona's already beaten us onboard and starts up the rotors. Specialist Jaeger comes on last with a scowl and straps in without a word to us. We settle in, the ramp closes, and the aircraft lifts off. We rise and then the momentum shifts as the rotors tilt and we plow along in airplane mode.

John raps twice on the hull of the craft. There's a whoosh around us and suddenly the roar of the engines and wind are merely a hum in the background—certainly quiet enough for us to talk without shouting to be heard. Those two air sprites are brilliant at what they do.

"We'll be landing at the Bemidji airport but we're going in quiet with cover. We don't want to draw too much attention to ourselves, but I want our bird there in case we need it. We'll scout the town, starting at the store where our agent last remembers being. From there, we split into teams of two, one magic to a team. Specialist Jaeger will—"

"I'm better on my own," Jaeger interrupts.

"—stay out of our way, apparently. Stay alert. I'd bet my grandma's shoes that whoever flipped the switch on our agent hasn't stayed around but I'm not too proud to say I could be wrong. Watch yourselves."

With another knock on the hull, the engines and wind roar back to full force so the air sprites can focus on moving us faster instead of manipulating sound.

The ride there feels like forever. Specialist Jaeger sits across from me and seems content to sit there staring at me. Determined not to be utterly annoyed, I ignore him and lean to my right where Charlie has opened up a paperback. The pages are well worn and the edging of the cover looks like it's about to tear apart. I distract myself by reading over his shoulder. He doesn't seem to mind and leans a little more my way as well so I can see better. After half a page, I realize this story is awfully familiar. I grasp the front flap and turn it over so I can read the title. *Pride and Prejudice*.

Well, that's why it's familiar. Melody had us watch the movie adaptation in the hospital after the ambush in Moose Lake a year back. Charlie couldn't stop ridiculing it at the time.

I snort and he glowers at me. With it so loud inside the Osprey, I merely point to the cover, then him, and raise an eyebrow. His response is to jab his finger at Melody—who beams—and returns to reading as if he's been given a school assignment. On Charlie's other side, Theo shakes with laughter.

Eventually the sound quiets in the Osprey again, turning into a vacuum, as we make our silent descent into Bemidji. When at last we touch down and the vibrations from the engines end, the sound of everything comes back in a rush. The ramp lowers and we move out. Someone from the airport comes out to greet us—a civilian IMS contact—who quickly ushers us past security and to the rental car area.

As the guy signs out two black sedans for us, he says, "These aren't going to come back with bullet holes or claw marks are they?" and gives a nervous laugh.

"Bullet holes?" Alona says. "Definitely not."

"But we make no promises about claw marks," Theo adds solemnly.

The man pales but passes over the car keys.

To my surprise, John tosses a set of keys to me. "I'll take shotgun," he says and we pile into the car on the left. Unfortunately, Specialist Jaeger slides into the second row. There's no escaping him, is there?

The others get into the second car and follow my lead out of the airport and into town. We each have small earpieces and check in on our channel to make sure we can all be heard.

"First stop is the local Walmart," John says. "Phoenix and I will go in and review their surveillance video. Hopefully that'll give us a lead on where to head next. In the meantime, the rest of you start a grid canvas of the city. See if anyone saw our agent doing anything suspicious or our alpha werewolf. And do an infrared sweep while you're at it."

"Roger that," Melody responds.

A few minutes later, we pull into the mostly full Walmart parking lot and I manage to grab a spot near the doors. The second we step out, Specialist Jaeger heads in the opposite direction from us.

"I work better on my own," he says without preamble and slips away between the cars.

John doesn't seem surprised in the least and doesn't bother stopping him. He gestures silently to me with two fingers and I follow him into the store. We approach the greeter at the door and John immediately asks for the manager.

"Excuse me?" the scrawny-looking teenager says.

In unison, John and I discreetly show our FBI badges before tucking them away again. The kid's eyes go wide and he stammers some more for us to wait there as he fetches his manager. I suppress a smug smile—that's the first time I've gotten to use my FBI badge. I like the response it gets. Mere moments later, the boy comes rushing back with a man in a blue polo shirt and a manager badge pinned to his chest.

The manager swears full cooperation and leads us to the security office so we can review their surveillance video. We produce a picture of our agent and, with the help of two rather young looking associates, start the hunt. I'm reminded eerily of when Charlie and I were tracking a vampire. I sure hope this hunt ends up better than that one did.

We have a general timeframe—yesterday afternoon around four o'clock is when our agent said he was in town. In the background through my earpiece I can hear the rest of team going around town. They pick up a number of werewolf heat signatures—as they are slightly higher than average—but all of them are known citizens of Bemidji.

It takes a while before we find what we're looking for on surveillance.

"I think I've got him," I say and point to my screen for John's benefit.

He comes around to lean over my shoulder. "That looks like our man. Let's mark the time he enters the store so we can back trace his steps earlier if we need to." I make a small note on a pad of paper beside me and we continue watching.

Will Dasc appear in the footage to mind control our agent? Or was he not close by? Or involved at all? I know that Echidna's forces have setup the werewolves to take the fall for attacks before but not in this way.

We comb through video during and around the time our agent is in the store but there's nothing exciting unless you count him accidentally running into a woman and making her drop a bundle of frozen meats. He acts completely normal the entire time he shops, takes his time deciding between turkey and ham, reads the ingredients on the bottom of the bread bags, picks out an insane amount of seasoning, and then pays for his things before returning to his car and driving away.

After a disappointing showing, we still get copies of the video, thank the employees, and then head out to our car.

"Walmart was a bust," John says over the channel. "Any luck out there? Everyone check in."

"All infrared hot spots have been cleared so far," Alona says.

Melody's wistful British accent comes next. "We've got bupkis, John."

We keep walking towards our car waiting for one final reply but we don't get it. John waits until we're both in the car before prompting a response.

"Specialist Jaeger?" he says.

There's a beat of silence before the specialist replies. "Yeah, I'm here. I don't have anything either."

"Thanks for the update," John says flatly. "Everyone keep checking. We knew this could be a long shot but let's overturn every stone."

We spend the rest of the afternoon canvasing the city. It's not the size of Minneapolis but it's still a big enough city. The day gets on, I get sweaty from walking around under the sun and in the uncomfortable humidity, and eventually the light starts to wane.

"All right, let's pack it in," John says, calling it. "Jaeger, we're coming to pick you up. Where are you?"

Again, he's slow to respond. "I'm near the south bridge. I'll meet you there."

Frustrated with our lack of success, I drive us to the south bridge with a scowl. I hoped we would find something—Dasc or otherwise—but like Melody said, we've got bupkis. As the light dims, I bring the car to a rolling stop at the end of the bridge where the specialist is waiting. He climbs into the second row with a loud exhale.

"We should get moving," he says. "This was a waste of time."

But I don't move to put the car in gear or turn the wheel. I swivel in my seat to be able to look at Specialist Jaeger. He's a regular human, so why is it I can sense magic on him all of a sudden?

He glares at me. "What?"

"Phoenix, take us out," John says.

I concentrate harder to pinpoint that sense of magic. It's odd and faint but it's there, like sticky threads as if he walked through a spider's web.

"Phoenix," John says with more force.

"Something's wrong," I say without taking my eyes off the specialist. I don't know what sort of magic is wrapped around him but it's not pure—it's tainted like the werewolves, like the vampires, like the lamia. I'm not going to turn my back on him.

The specialist continues to glare at me. "Are you deaf? Get us out of here. We're wasting time."

"What do you mean something's wrong?" John asks.

How am I supposed to explain what I sense? That I learned the ability from a dragon that's been in hiding for centuries? That I have a power I'm not supposed to?

"There's something . . . off about him," I say.

Instead of debating with me, John turns in his seat to inspect the specialist as well. Jaeger looks liable to start shouting at us. When he continues to appear the same grouchy person as ever, John slowly turns to me. His stoic gaze cuts through me and I swallow.

"I'm telling you, something's not right," I say in the most serious tone I can muster. "You have to believe me. Call it a—a gut feeling."

His eyes narrow a little but then he faces the specialist again. "Where were you last?"

"Are you kidding me? You're actually listening to her nonsense?" The specialist gestures angrily towards me.

"Where were you last?" John repeats.

"Checking around like the rest of you."

"And more specifically?"

"Nowhere. Just the wastewater treatment plant."

John and I share a look.

"Please believe me," I say quietly.

He contemplates me for a moment before he presses a finger to his ear. "Team, meet us over at the wastewater treatment plant on the southern end of the city near the bridge."

There's a chorus of "check" in reply. I take us off the bridge and to the treatment plant nearby. The whole way, Specialist Jaeger raises a ruckus in the backseat.

"I already told you, the plant is clear! I checked it along with the other shops nearby. Do you really think Dasc is going to be hiding in one of the water tanks? We're wasting time. We should get back to the Osprey and head to Camp Ripley so I can hunt down the next more likely target for a werewolf rogue to appear."

He goes on like this as we pull into the parking lot, step out, flash our badges at some very confused employees, and march inside. The building is made up of pipes, giant water tanks, walkways over the water tanks, and a constant thrum of running machinery. A radio plays in the background with a woman singing. There's a lingering odor of rotten eggs and other subtle things I'd rather not think about. The few workers here look up curiously at their odd visitors before bending their heads back down over their work. As John runs a skeptical eye over the operation, I take a deep breath and push out my feelers for any other strange magic in the area. I find the source of the spiderweb-like magic deep below my feet.

And, to my surprise, find its sticky tethers latched onto every single person inside the plant. Flies caught in a web.

John turns to me and I flinch as I realize whatever's latched onto everyone has somehow gotten on him too.

"I don't think there's anything here," he says. "We should head back to the Osprey."

The hairs on the back of my neck stand on end.

"I really think we should check below," I say.

All of the workers stop what they're doing and face us—no face *me*. Whatever magic has gotten a hold of them, it's taken over John and Jaeger too. But not me.

"False alarm," John says into his earpiece. "Everyone meet back at the Osprey." He gestures to me and starts to walk to the door. "Come on."

For a moment I don't move until I notice that Specialist Jaeger's hand is hovering near his concealed gun at the back of his waistband. I give him a small smile, nod, and move after John. The three of us walk single file along the hallway. I hold the door open for the specialist to let him pass. The second he's past me, I slip back inside, slam the door shut, and lock it.

A second later gunshots shatter the air and glass rains over my head. I hear my teammates call out in alarm over my earpiece as they hear the gunshots through the radio. Hands over my head, I run low back into the building and around a wall for cover.

"Phoenix!" Charlie shouts in my ear. "Talk to us!"

"Yeah, I'd say we came to the right place," I say slightly breathless and turn around to find the plant workers rushing me. "We've got serious problems."

7

Hawk

Genna sits calm and relaxed as if we're talking about the weather over a dinner for two. I can't help remembering all those times we ate meals together at the Moose Lake Field Office—like family.

"You say that none of it was a lie," I say. "Our friendship, your goal of saving all werewolves, and whatever."

Genna gives a single nod. "I never lied to you."

"Okay, then riddle me this." I lean forward with my hands clasped together on top of the table. Before this goes any further, I'm going to cut right through with a knife. "You said Dasc killed James, your friend during the years you were missing. Then before Dasc escaped Underground, he said *you* killed James. You mind explaining that? Or am I going to end up as another James?"

The blood drains out of her face. It's the first time I've ever seen her pale like that, not even when her father was hospitalized. Well, I guess the knife to the heart tactic really worked.

"I said Dasc *had* him killed," she says softly and lowers her eyes to her lap. "I never said he was the one that physically did it."

Part of me wishes she would deny it and say Dasc is a liar.

"You killed him," I say quietly, stunned. "You really killed him."

"I did," she whispers.

I don't know how to respond. For the last year, after Phoenix told me what Dasc revealed when he escaped, I've been thinking up excuses for Genna. She couldn't have killed her best friend. I had been so sure.

"How can I possibly trust you?"

That question sits between us for a long time. Genna ponders the tabletop with a hollow look as if she's left the cafe completely and left her body behind.

"That was the worst thing I've ever done," she says at last. "And I know you have no reason to trust me, but I would ask that you at least give me the opportunity to explain myself."

"Well, I'm here, aren't I?"

She takes a deep breath and folds her hands on top of the table. "Then perhaps we should move somewhere a little more secluded."

I snort. "Where? If I go anywhere suspicious, I'm sure someone will notice." I hold my hand up to display the probation ring.

Her eyes flash. "They've collared the rest of you."

"Like you didn't notice."

She doesn't say anything.

"The IMS felt provoked, what with Dasc having agents turn on their comrades and all," I say testily. "That sort of screwed up my whole plan to be a Spartan."

Her eyes narrow slightly. "That wasn't us."

"That's a little hard to believe."

"And that's exactly the point, isn't it? Echidna knows how to pin the blame and play on the fears of the IMS."

I hold out a hand. "Wait, you're saying she's the one turning agents on each other? How?"

"An excellent question."

I run both hands through my hair, give it a good fluffing and scratch my scalp. "Okay, fine. Those attacks aside, why did you betray us? Why free Dasc? Why turn Witty to the dark side?"

She leans across the table and says quietly, "If you want answers, meet me at the back of the arcade two blocks south in ten minutes."

"No."

She blinks. "Why not? It's not a suspicious place for you to go."

"Because I'm not going to be that sucker that's lured into a dark alleyway by the pretty girl. I've seen those murder mysteries."

"I appreciate that you think I'm pretty."

I glower at her. "That's not what I—"

"If you come, then you'll be able to hear everything from a source I think you may find more trustworthy."

When she begins to exit the booth, I grab her arm to keep her in place. She stiffens and her gray eyes turn dark to pin me where I sit.

"Before I go anywhere, you tell me one thing."

She considers me for a second then bobs her head.

"Why did you kill James?"

A crinkle forms between her eyebrows. "Because he wanted me to."

Then without another word, she slips out of the booth and vanishes from the cafe.

I don't have a clue what to make of that except that I now desperately want to know *why* someone would want to be killed. I growl under my breath and massage my forehead. Meeting her at this place is one thing. Straying out to a place I've never been in order to collude with her is something else. I glance around at everyone in the cafe and those out on the street. There's no sign of any IMS agents that I can tell, no one watching me, no one that will think it suspicious if I get up and walk to the arcade.

I'm getting into the habit of making some pretty poor choices.

Leaving the cafe behind me, I take my time walking the two blocks to the arcade. The building itself is a bit run down, but there are a few kids playing on big, bulky gaming systems. The place could use a new paint job, a decent cleaning, and new games to stay up to date. I'm surprised it's still in business at all given technology today. I meander into the arcade with my hands in my pockets and mark every person in the building. There are several boys, a couple young girls, and an ancient man working the ticket counter. A glance at the ceiling and around the doors tells me there's hardly any surveillance on this place—just the solitary camera at the front door. I also realize something else as I pass the group of boys and the girls trading places on the dinosaur hunting game. Everyone in this building is a werewolf. I can smell it on them, that little something that sets them apart from normal humans.

I feel the manager's eyes on me as I walk to the very back of the arcade and almost walk into a low hanging sign that says *LASER TAG ZONE*. Black curtains section it off into a creepy back corner. Shaking my head at my own stupidity, I silently part the black curtains and take soft footsteps inside, eyes peeled for any sort of danger. If this were a movie, Phoenix would be yelling at me on the screen not to go in here.

Just inside the threshold I pause as the curtain falls back into place behind me to lock me in the darkness. What am I doing? I spin around to the entrance and freeze with my hand about to part the curtain again. Am I not just confirming the suspicions the IMS has about werewolves? I haven't told on a fugitive. I'm about to have a clandestine meeting with said fugitive—one, for all I know, is in league with the monster that killed my parents and cursed me.

I close my eyes and exhale sharply. I'm being so stupid.

I push the curtain aside to leave, but stop when I hear quiet voices behind me that my sharp hearing picks up.

"Do you think he's going to come?" There's no mistaking who it is. Witty.

I don't even catch Genna's reply as I storm into the depths of the laser tag zone. I find my way through the black walls and streaks of florescent lights until I reach the most secluded alcove to find a trio waiting for me. Genna's blonde wig has an odd glow to it under the black lights. A few feet away from her stands Rosalyn with her arms crossed and a scowl on her face, the same as ever. And between them Witty stands looking rather nervous, twisting his hands together and biting his lip.

I come to a jarring halt.

Witty is standing. Wheelchair-bound Witty is *standing*. And standing with two of the most dangerous girls I know.

For once I find myself at a loss for words. I know Phoenix told me that Witty had left because he wanted to be healed of his disability. I didn't think it would actually work. It's a miracle. I'm in shock and there's a twisting feeling of happiness, relief, and deep sorrow in my gut. What's the price of his legs?

"Well, I think this is a first," Rosalyn says with a smirk. "Cat got your tongue, Hawk?"

Ignoring her, I walk forward until I'm directly before Witty. I can't help but find the sight odd—we're at eye level. Actually, I think Witty is an inch taller than me. I never knew. His smell's changed. He's a werewolf for sure.

"Curse it all, Witty," I say at last. "I'd hug you if you hadn't shot me in the back."

"I'm sorry," he says and tries to give me a smile, but his face collapses into a worried frown. "You can punch me if you'd like. That'd be fair."

"Don't tempt me," I growl. "But I don't think it'd be fair. I'd have to do a heck of a lot more damage for it to be *fair*, Witty."

He drops his gaze.

"You're getting to be as high-strung as your sister," Rosalyn comments.

I whip about on her with a growl. "You don't get to talk about Phoenix."

She smiles in her usual pompous way. I take a step forward but find Genna suddenly between us.

"Let's not," she says flatly and gives Rosalyn a reproachful look before settling her attention on me. "You came."

"I shouldn't have." I gesture widely to Witty. "So this is your trustworthy, reliable source? Really? *He shot me in the back.*"

"We've been friends for a long time," Witty says and wrings his hands. "That was the hardest thing I've ever had to do. Helping Dasc escape, I mean, and making you think I had betrayed you and Phoenix."

"You *did* betray us."

Rosalyn laughs as if I told a joke. "Is this going as well as you hoped, Genna?"

"Go stand guard at the entrance," Genna says sharply.

"Yeah, go stand guard," I add with a sarcastic nod.

She looks like she wants to stick my head in an oven but she stalks out at Genna's command. Right—because Genna is Dasc's right-hand. How could I forget?

"Please," Witty says. "Let me explain."

"Genna keeps saying the same thing and yet I haven't heard any explanations yet," I snap. My blood is boiling with the pain under my skin and this situation is in no way helping. Maybe Rosalyn's right. I *am* getting as temperamental as my sister.

"Okay. Yup. Right then." Witty clears his throat and straightens a bit as if he's about to give a presentation to Director Knox. "First things first, we're not working for Dasc. Well, I guess we *are*, but that's not really what we're doing. It's sort of complicated—"

"We're using him," Genna cuts in.

"Yes!" Witty pipes up. "That's what I meant."

"Using him," I say. "How?"

"When I was first discovered by Phoenix and . . . and my dad—" Genna takes a deep breath as if it physically pains her to think of Jefferson, "—I explained that Dasc is the only one who knows where all of the werewolf cells are. I only knew so much. From the progress of the interrogations, it was clear Dasc was never going to give them up to the IMS. He was biding his time until someone broke him out."

"Someone like you," I say flatly. "I guess his plan worked."

"It was the only way to earn his complete trust."

"And did you?"

"Did I what?"

"Earn his complete trust?"

She pauses a moment too long.

"I guess I have my answer," I say and scoff.

Her eyes narrow. "I knew it wouldn't be that easy. Dasc doesn't truly trust anyone. I only needed *enough* trust. Then I needed some help."

Witty raises his hand shyly in such a way it's like he's admitting he just farted or something.

"Why Witty?" I ask and keep talking directly to Genna since Witty isn't the best conversationalist.

"Because Dasc only sees weakness he can exploit. He doesn't see the strength created by weakness."

I hold up a hand. "Backup, Yoda. You've lost me."

She crosses her arms over her chest looking rather superior. And beautiful. Dang it.

"He saw Witty's condition as an opportunity. If you were stuck in a wheelchair your whole life, wouldn't you jump at the opportunity to walk again? In his own roundabout way, Dasc proposed it to him. Help set him free and walk again. He thought it a sort of selfishness he could use to his advantage."

"I don't think that's selfish," I say quietly. Witty bows his head and averts his eyes. I can understand desperately wanting freedom from chains. How can I blame him for wanting that for himself?

"So Witty's played his part," she says and shrugs a shoulder at him.

"I've been the grateful conspirator," Witty says sheepishly. "You know, wanting to help because he fixed my legs."

I cross my arms over my chest. "Helping him how exactly?"

The two of them share a look as if deciding what they can tell me.

"Don't be shy," I say. "You got me all the way here. Might as well let the pixies out of the bag."

"Using my tech skills," Witty says quietly. "I know the frequencies the IMS uses so I've been able to help the werewolves avoid detection. You know, slip under the radar, that sort of thing. And—well . . ."

"*And?*"

He glances to Genna as if looking for help.

She turns her dark eyes to me. "Helping find targets to hit—monsters and IMS alike."

Now that sounds awfully traitorous despite their claims of being on our side.

"You've been helping Dasc attack the IMS?" I say in a deathly calm voice. "You do realize that I work for the IMS, my sister is a Spartan, and my friends are agents?"

"It's not what you think," Witty says weakly.

"Have you gotten any of your friends killed? And I mean more than those who died in the attack on Underground. Because those deaths are on your head too."

His hands shake and Genna takes a step forward as if to protect him from the venom in my voice. I'm not usually like this but I have nasty fits of rage at times. Learning that they are exactly the traitors they've been made out to be is really burning my insides.

"We couldn't go back to Dasc empty-handed or he would know exactly what we were up to the second we walked out of there," Genna says, matching my tone. "And Underground was going to be hit regardless. Echidna's forces were veering in that direction. We just gave them a little more encouragement to act as our distraction."

"People *died*."

"People would have died somewhere else if not there. People will always die. You make necessary sacrifices to win when you're playing for the stakes of the world. Sometimes there are no good choices."

"How very utilitarian of you."

"If I told you that the sacrifice of those few meant saving thousands of others, what choice would you have made?"

I don't respond.

"I do what I have to," she continues. "I won't apologize for it."

"Well, too late. You already apologized to me."

"That was different," she says quietly.

"Why?"

She looks away. "It doesn't matter. What's important is that with Dasc free, he's been in touch with his contacts and preparing his followers for war. And now with Witty's help, we've been able to track him."

"What, you've bugged him or something? Surely you didn't need Witty to be able to do that."

"You can't bug him," she says matter-of-factly. "He'd smell anything foreign. Trust me. It's been tried before."

"Then how?"

Witty finally speaks up again with a gleam in his eyes. "Technology is everywhere, recording everything, watching everyone. If you know where you to look, you can find almost anything or anyone. But it's—well, it's a process. It takes a lot of sifting and we have to be careful that he doesn't know what we're doing. He thinks we're tapping into IMS communications here in Seattle."

"But in reality?"

"We're liberating one of Dasc's cells," Genna says with a touch of pride.

My eyebrows shoot up. "You've found one?"

"This is the second one, actually. It's taken a lot of work—a year's worth—but we're doing it. We're freeing the werewolves from Dasc and also steering them clear of the IMS black hole."

"The Fields," Witty adds.

I swallow and turn away from them to think this over, running my hands through my hair and massaging my scalp in fidgety circles.

"That's why you led me to Jason's file," I say, facing them once again. "So I'd know why you didn't want them at the mercy of the IMS."

Genna gives a single nod. "Free of the IMS. Free of Dasc. That's the deal."

"But then . . . where do they go?"

"Dasc might be a possessive, manipulative psychopath, but he did know how to build a strong community. We've set up a hidden sanctuary—much like your Underground—where the werewolves will be safe and able to make their own choices. They won't be cannon fodder in Dasc's quest for revenge."

"Hmm." I roll my lips, tap my foot, and flex my fingers against the constant ache in them. "Confined to one little sanctuary? Sounds like a prison to me."

"It's temporary because that's only step one."

"Oh, there are even steps involved! Why didn't you say so?"

Witty chuckles uncertainly and Genna smirks.

"The plan actually came about before Phoenix ever put Dasc in the hospital," she says.

I blink. "Err, what?"

"We both know what your sister can do to the werewolf disease, and what she might be capable of in time."

"You're not going to try to kidnap her are you? Because that would end badly for everyone."

For the first time she gives me a wide smile. "We don't need to."

Witty starts counting his fingers and scrunches up his face like he's doing math in his head. "There are over seven billion people in the world. Do you really think that Phoenix is the only one on the planet with abilities to manipulate magic? The odds are generous that there is at *least* a handful if not more that can do the same. So, we've been searching for them."

I look around the bare room. "Geez, you guys really

need to have a chair around for absorbing this kind of information." I start to pace as I take it in. Phoenix is an anomaly, there's no doubt about that, but we've also thought—perhaps selfishly—that she's the only one that can do what she does. But from the way Witty puts it, it makes sense that there would be others in the world, right? Perhaps others that have stronger abilities than Phoenix? Maybe even strong enough to actually cure the werewolf disease.

"Have you had any luck?" I ask breathlessly, a bubble of hope rising in my chest.

Genna's smile only grows. "We have."

"It was pure luck though," Witty says and releases a breath as if the memory still stresses him out. "Genna crossed paths with him by accident while we were snooping into what Dasc's been doing. It took a bit of convincing but he's agreed to help us. But he's—well, he's odd."

"Being over a thousand years old has made him a bit of a loon," Genna adds.

"Wait, what?"

"He's what the majestics refer to as a Magus, and what the majestics will also thoroughly deny exist."

Magus. I know that term. Phoenix told me about the Magi after one of her sessions with Scholar—who in reality is Terra, a majestic in hiding so she would know the truth about the Magi. Way back when the majestics were desperate to get an advantage over Echidna's forces, they had humans drink their magical blood and it turned them into something else entirely. They're supposed to be incredibly powerful, on par with the alphas of the monster races. More powerful than any Blessed. And if Phoenix, who is Blessed, is able to do what she can do, surely a Magus would be able to do so much more.

Witty clears his throat as I continue to pace, thinking.

"A Magus is a person—" he begins.

"I know what a Magus is."

"Terra told Phoenix," Genna says softly.

Angry once again, I glare in her direction. "Yeah, you know that majestic dragon that you used as a distraction so you could make your getaway. She almost died because she came to protect Phoenix. That's on you."

"Add it to the list," she says so quietly I almost don't catch it.

Ignoring my anger to be able to ask what I truly want to hear, I say, "So can he do it? This Magus, can he cure the werewolf disease?"

Genna remains stoic but Witty's head and shoulders droop. He's always telegraphing how he feels. How on earth is he able to fool Dasc if he's really working against him? I feel like Dasc would be able to see Witty's true colors a mile away. But his reaction tells me everything I need to know.

"No," Genna says but I'm expecting it. "But his abilities rival Phoenix's. At the moment he's playing guardian to the werewolves we've rescued. It's a start, and I hope that if we find a few more like him, with their combined power they'll be able to finally free us from this curse."

So, find more of the Magi or other Blessed with powers like Phoenix, string them together and—presto! Werewolf disease cured. I like imagining it. No more compulsions, no more beast hiding inside, no more serum including the pain it brings.

"It sounds great," I say. Witty looks like I just passed

him through the agent trials, his whole body rising as if he's ballooning with happiness. Then I add, "But it also sounds unrealistic. If it really were possible, wouldn't someone have done it by now? Like, I don't know, the IMS? And you never mentioned any of this when you came on board."

"I didn't trust the IMS. It was difficult enough giving them the locations of the compounds I knew about, much less my plan for locating the Magi. And as I said before, the majestics will refuse to acknowledge that the Magi even exist. They came about by means that make them seem more like monsters than anything else. Made by drinking the blood of a majestic dragon? The same way Echidna's alphas were created? They'd never admit that. And from what I gather, they've gone into hiding to keep away from both the IMS and monsters who would try to use them. There's also a rumor that Draco attempted to wipe them out, afraid of what they could do."

"So how exactly do you plan to find them if no one else has been able to for hundreds of years?"

She nods. "We have something that no one else has had before."

I shrug. "A positive attitude?"

"Me. A werewolf on the inside of Dasc's operation, one not devoted to him. One that's looking forward to the day I can kill him."

Well, she certainly sounds convincing enough, but she also did that before letting Dasc out of his cage. Can I trust her? Can I trust Witty? I mean, Witty certainly seems sincere—even if he did shoot me in the back—but he could be hoodwinked by Genna just like the rest of us were. But if they're not telling the truth, if they're in cahoots with Dasc, why come to me? How does that accomplish anything? And then there's that point Genna made earlier. If Dasc was going after me, Phoenix would know about it because of the deal she made.

"How does being inside Dasc's operation help us find these Magi?" I ask.

"Because there's someone Dasc entrusted to find them. A man who goes by the name Erebus. If we can get to him, I can convince him to tell us where the others are. I came so close before when—" She pauses and that crinkle returns in the middle of her brow. "James and I found him in Paris but we watched him die. Yet, somehow, he survived and escaped. I don't know what he is, but I don't think he's a werewolf or human for that matter."

And Dasc trusted this man—this Erebus—to find the Magi for him? It's a bit hard to believe. "Why was Dasc looking for them?"

"To blackmail them into becoming weapons in his arsenal against Echidna."

Things just keep getting more complicated. "But you think this man will help us?"

"To him and Dasc, I'm still the Dark Whisper. I'll persuade him."

"Well . . . that's good, right? Where is he then?"

Witty gives a dramatic sigh. "We found out he was arrested by the IMS six months ago but we can't find where he's being held."

Ah, it all becomes clear. "But I have access to the IMS servers."

"I can't risk hacking in," Witty says. "There's literally magic integrated in the software. The second I try, a shock would go down the computer, freeze me in place, and a Spartan team would swoop in. Why do you think nobody's been able to hack the IMS servers from the outside?"

I realize then what they're truly asking of me. Treason. Use my access to find a prisoner for them.

"You realize what you're asking me to do?"

"Yes," Genna says quietly.

"How do you—how can I make a decision like that?" I gesture widely to Witty. "How did you?"

I don't actually expect him to answer, but then—

"I knew," Witty whispers. "I knew you weren't taking the serum."

I stiffen, eyes going wide.

"There were occasionally flags that would go up on inspections of your serum log, but I caught them," he continues hardly above a whisper. "I—I deleted them or showed them as resolved. You and Phoenix were the only friends I ever had and I saw what the disease and the serum did to you. I knew. I also knew there wasn't anything I could do about it where I was. Until Genna showed me another way. I feel like—like I can actually do something now."

It's difficult to form words. All this time and he knew. All this time he was taken for granted and not given the proper respect he deserved. Rule-abiding Witty—breaking a very serious law to protect us. We should have been there for him more somehow.

I feel raw. My heart beats in a painful rhythm sending blood to every ache where the serum is pitted against the disease in my veins.

"You're a better friend than we deserved," I say at last. "And . . . I'm glad you got your legs back."

Witty wilts with relief and there's a subtle shift in Genna's posture to show that she's relaxed somewhat as well.

"So?" she prompts. "Are you going to tell the IMS where we are?"

I think on that for a moment, really considering what's in my heart and mind before I answer.

"No."

"Are you going to help us?"

"I want to," I say, surprising myself. "Curse it all, for better or worse, I want to."

"But *will* you?" She steps closer and cocks her head to the side so her hair brushes across her shoulder. "No more Jasons. No more Dascs. Freedom."

I know my next words are going to make or break me but that part of me deep down and writhing knows there is only one answer I can give.

"I will."

8

Phoenix

Who knew a wastewater treatment plant could be so dangerous? I duck beneath a metal tool of some sort thrown at my head and slide into a nearby office, slamming and locking the door behind me. I stay low as the workers start pounding on the door. It won't be long before they shatter the glass window in the middle of it. I quickly tug on my special gloves with built in dragon's barriers, ready for combat. Using my brief respite to my advantage, I take a deep breath, close my eyes, and send out tethers of my magic looking for the source of the problem here. I follow the threads that hang off each of the workers and follow it down, down, down until I sense the core of dark twisted magic. There's a monster somewhere below me, there's no doubt about it, and it's got hooks into everyone somehow. Everyone except me.

The glass breaks. I rocket to my feet with my bio-mech

gun at the ready. I shoot the first body that tries to wiggle through the broken glass to unlock the door. The man goes limp and blocks the single opening. As the rest of the workers yank their fellow out of the way, Melody's voice comes through my ear piece.

"We're nearly there," she says. "Status?"

"I'm okay. I've holed up in an office," I say. "Everyone except me is under some monster's control. It got John and Jaeger."

"Some kind of infection? Stingers? Spit?"

"No, I was with John the whole time. It's none of those."

Another man manages to get his hands around the knob to try the lock. A blast from the bio-mech gun has him slumped over.

I stretch out a hand and focus on the next man attempting to breach the office space. The others have spread out and are banging on the walls and a single window overlooking the plant. I latch my magic onto him and will the web to wither and break. For a second he stands up straight, free of the control, takes a deep breath, and then is instantly ensnared once again. Okay, so we'll have to take out the source. There's no point trying to cleanse the infected if they become reinfected in an instant.

I draw in my senses as the men start to hack through the door. I don't feel any of that dark magic even reaching for me, so my own power isn't protecting me. But why isn't the monster going for me too?

Then it hits me as I watch the men barrel into the door until the hinges break and it flies open.

"Charlie, Theo, stay back!" I shout before I'm bull

rushed by the workers. I drop them one at a time but it's a small office and a lot of them. They blunder over each other but then their hands are on me. They clearly aren't trained fighters of any sort but they're like rabid animals and attack me with a single-minded focus. I'm scratched across the face and receive a punch to the ribs before I manage to drop the rest with the bio-mech gun.

"It's a siren," I pant. "All of the infected are men. That's why I'm fine."

The sound I thought was a normal radio playing in the background is actually the song of a siren to ensnare men, control them, and do the siren's bidding. She could even make them kill themselves if she wanted. What on earth is a siren doing here?

I vault out of the office, race past the massive tanks of water, and take a set of metal stairs to the level below. I expect to run into more workers but it's eerily empty. I could have sworn there were more people in this building before. My instincts tell me to stay put so I crouch in the shadow of one of the water tanks, keep my bio-mech gun up, and carefully inspect my surroundings. It's reasonably well-lit but crowded with pipes and areas where it would be easy to hide.

"Alona and I just breached the side entrance," Melody says quietly. "There's no sign of John, Jaeger, or anyone else."

"I'm down one level at the south end," I whisper. "The siren's down here somewhere."

"You've seen it?"

"Not yet." But I can feel it. Its song is like a sneaky breeze wafting through the building, almost white noise in the background but it's there. Not too far ahead now.

Moments later I hear footsteps. Melody and Alona tread softly down the stairs until we form up.

"That way," I say and point through the maze of pipes.

Melody, our temporary leader with John in the wind, motions to Alona. "Scout ahead and circle back."

With a nod, Alona leaps upwards. Partway into her jump, a black cloud puffs around her and she emerges as a raven that swoops through the pipes and disappears. Melody gestures silently to me and we move forward without a word, footsteps near silent on the cement and metal beneath our feet. The haunting song grows louder as we sneak along, checking each hallway we pass to make sure we're clear. I keep my senses on high alert. Melody's void follows along beside me, I keep Alona's earthy vibes on my radar, and feel the powerful mass of twisted magic coming closer with every step we take.

Alona swoops back, gracefully touching down as her human self at a crouch before us.

"She's got the rest of the workers, John, and the specialist surrounding her as human shields. John and Jaeger have their guns out and the rest have tools for weapons. We've got no clean opening."

Great. And there's not a doubt in my mind that the siren won't hesitate to use the men not only to fight us but also kill themselves just to spite us. We're in a bad spot, that's for sure. If only Charlie was here and I could keep him from being affected—he could port us right to the siren so we could stab her with a bronze blade and drop the enchantment. But that would expose me, and I don't even know if it would work. I've never tried something like that before.

"Entrances?" Melody asks in a whisper.

"Two," Alona says. "One straight ahead and another door leading to the outside I think."

"Okay. You have the best shot of getting past the siren's defenses fast to deliver the killing blow. I'd rather take her alive to figure out what's going on but it's too much of a risk. Phoenix and I will provide a distraction while you fly in through the other door and drop in behind her. Our priority is saving those hostages."

Alona and I nod, each pulling out our special daggers that are a blend of bronze, silver, gold, and inlaid with wood—the perfect, versatile weapon to handle a number of monsters. Melody does the same as Alona sweeps away as a raven once again to get into position.

"And our distraction?" I ask after she disappears.

"We'll rush in and knock out as many of the hostages as we can before they can harm us or themselves. She can't use them if they're unconscious. Focus on them so we can give Alona her opening."

"Right."

Falling silent once again, we sneak down the hall of pipes. Not too far in I see a pair of doors with small windows in their frames. There's our entrance. Melody and I keep low and quiet until we're right up against the doors. There we wait for the signal.

"I'm in position," Alona says barely audible through my earpiece.

Melody nods to me and gives a countdown with her fingers. On the count of four, I throw myself against the doors—bursting them off their hinges—and Melody glides inside with her bio-mech gun raised. One pulse after another ripples the air and men drop like flies before I can even take aim. I have maybe two seconds to take in the room as I bring my own weapon to bear.

It's some sort of storage room for equipment. There are several shelves lining the wall directly across from me stuffed with boxes, supplies, and bulky things my eyes simply glaze over. In the very center of the room is the ring of men Alona spied earlier with half of them now on the floor thanks to Melody. In the middle stands the siren clad in hardly anything at all. John stands before her with gun raised and a mean look on his face. At her back is Specialist Jaeger with his gun trained on the other door to my left where Alona is supposed to slip in.

I let a wave of my energy surge off myself to momentarily snap the enchantment over the men to give us a chance to take them safely down, but I can't keep that surge up without giving myself away.

John's gun—not a bio-mech, a human make with bullets meant to kill—aims at Melody. I send a bio-mech pulse in his direction but one of the workers jumps in front to take it for him. Melody fires next but John manages to dodge it, rolling sideways as Jaeger pulls the siren out of harm's way behind himself.

Then it's Melody's turn to dodge and evade as John advances on her. The small cement room resounds with the ear-splitting sound of his gun firing. I focus on knocking down the rest of the workers but am a second too late to stop one from plunging a pair of scissors into the chest of an unconscious comrade and then turning the makeshift weapon on himself. I hit him before he manages to stab himself but he falls lopsided on top of the scissors.

The siren's song stops as she laughs. "Dance, little princess!" she shouts, her eyes on Melody. "You've no skin to sacrifice for them this time!"

Melody and John have gotten into an intense battle of fisticuffs, giving me no clear opening to take John out without accidentally hitting Melody too. Instead, I focus my fire on Jaeger. He rolls and props up the body of a fallen man to use as a shield. He's not able to hide well enough though, and eventually he falls limp to the ground.

With him momentarily out of the way, the siren is vulnerable.

I hardly hear the side door open before Alona streaks through the air and lands directly behind the siren. Victory is within our grasp.

A gun shot rings out and Alona stumbles backwards, a spray of blood erupting from her shoulder. The siren spins around and clutches at Alona's throat.

I don't have a chance to see where the shot came from. I've got an opening. I'm ready to fire at the siren's exposed back when my gun is suddenly wrenched out of my hand. A breath of wind tickles the hair on the back of my neck and a magical presence appears beside me. I have a momentarily glimpse of Charlie's face out of the corner of my eye before he disappears again. Crap. If Charlie's here, then I guess Theo is too and that shot must have come from our marksman. Despite being told to stay back, they've been ensnared somehow.

Having trained and fought against Charlie before, I instinctively sidestep to avoid what I'm sure will be his next blow from behind. I'm almost a second too late to avoid a dagger to my ribs. The next several seconds I'm so focused on not being killed by Charlie that I almost miss what's going on around me. I catch Alona shift back and forth several times, puffs of a smoky haze erupting from her quick transformations, and Melody struggling fiercely with John. I finally spot Theo out of the corner of my eye as he advances on Alona with gun raised. Apart from that, I twist and turn, block and dodge as Charlie performs a dizzying spectacle of teleporting as he tries to either shoot or knife me.

Our second mission in and our biggest threat has become each other.

I don't want to hurt Charlie but I also have to put a stop to him. Behind me the siren gives an earsplitting cry. All of the men momentarily glance in her direction as if sensing the imminent danger to the monster holding their leash. Unfortunately, Alona only managed to slice her arm, not stab her.

In that momentary opening Alona has given me by distracting the men, I manage to rip the gun out of Charlie's hand. But then he's moving again. I feint to my left before swiveling right but he knows how I move. I find him there waiting with a blade. Instinctively, I drive my arm to the side to push the dagger away. While I avoid getting it to my gut, it rips across the sleeve of my tactical gear but the fabric holds and protects me.

Grimacing, and realizing this entire fight is only going to end badly, I make a bold move in the hope that Charlie will suffer memory loss like our rogue werewolf agent did. As he drives the blade at me once again, I don't bother to dodge or block the incoming blow. I focus instead on the magic inside myself and push it out towards him as I extend a hand towards his chest. His dagger halts with its tip touching my abdomen as the bonds around him snap and he comes back to his senses. I keep that surge going, let my magic wrap him in a protective bubble but it takes a lot of focus to keep it in place. I can feel the siren's web-like tethers pushing against my power.

Charlie's sharp green eyes widen as he takes in what's going on around him. Acting almost blindly, I grab the dagger out of his hands, clutch onto the front of his shirt, and forcefully yank him around so he has a clear view of the siren and Theo doing their best to either strangle Alona or riddle her with bullets. She's putting up a valiant effort as she switches back and forth between her forms so they can't get a hold or bead on her.

"Go," I say on an exhale to Charlie.

He knows exactly what I'm asking, and on the same breath, he ports us directly behind the siren. Blade in hand, I wrap my arm around the siren's neck to hold her in place and thrust the dagger into her heart through her back. She lets out a coughing cry and slumps to the floor. I know she's truly dead when I sense her web of magic shrivel up and evaporate into nothing.

A hush falls over the room as the men recover themselves and Melody and Alona realize the siren is dead.

"Everyone okay?" John says a bit breathless.

"Oh *God*, did I shoot you?" Theo says loudly and rushes to Alona as she keeps a grip on her freely bleeding shoulder.

Alona rolls her eyes as he extends shaking hands towards her. "I'm fine. Just a graze. I'm good."

"We're okay," Melody says, sporting a cut lip. "But you might need a couple stitches, John. Sorry about that."

"It was a good hit," he says passively, holding a hand to his bloody forehead.

Charlie sways on his feet next to me and gently tugs back the sleeve of my uniform to see the painful, red welt where he almost got me with his dagger. His cheeks redden as if thoroughly embarrassed.

"You okay?" he mumbles and avoids looking me in the eye.

"We're good," I announce to the others.

As soon as the team has given their assurances of no life threatening injury, Melody immediately gets up to attend to the man who had scissors driven into his chest. She gestures wordlessly to Theo and he hurries over to assist her—neither having magical blood that could contaminate their patient.

Now that the threat has passed, we move back into action. Melody tosses around some of her medical foam and a tight wad of white bandages for us to patch ourselves up with while she and Theo work on the poor unconscious man on the floor. Alona calls in a cleanup team and nearby field agents to assist with a sweep while she holds a wad of gauze to her bicep. Charlie hovers around me and keeps staring at my arm as if it's going to spurt blood. But the suit did its job. I'm going to have a nasty bruise, I'm sure, but I'm fine. Charlie doesn't look so good though. I have to grab his shoulder at one point to keep him from falling as his knees buckle.

"Charlie, what's wrong with you?" I ask sharply. He looks far too unsteady to be okay.

He waves me off and teeters to the side. "I'm fine."

"I think you should sit down."

"No, no."

Ignoring his false assurances, I put pressure on his shoulders and push him to the floor. He's much too pale for my liking. He tries to reassure me yet again as I give him a quick once over and don't find any apparent injury. Then it hits me. He had been teleporting nonstop in his attempt to kill me. He's completely drained from overworking himself like that.

"Just take it easy," I say. "You're worn out from trying to stab me."

He sighs and hangs his head. "I'm so sorry."

"Shut up, Charlie. I'm fine. What's a little attempted murder between friends?"

I smirk but instead of my joke lightening the mood, he puts his forehead in his hands looking utterly defeated.

"Oh, pull it together, man," I grumble and rise to my feet to see how I can help the others.

John's in the middle of wrapping a bandage around his forehead so I help him finish and tuck in the ends.

"Thanks," he says. "Well, we best check the rest of the facility and make sure there aren't any more surprises waiting for us." He nods in Alona's direction. "You'll cover them?"

"I'm good for it."

Once John's patched up, he and I explore the rest of the treatment plant, scour the lower levels, clear the offices, check the sludge tanks, and inspect the effluent where the clean water is released into the waters of the lake and start of the Mississippi River. We pause at the top of the bank overlooking the water and the peaceful evening outside— such a drastic difference to what just happened inside.

"Do you see that?" John says. He gestures to something

on the edge of the water and squints at it. "What does that look like to you?"

"Something . . . kind of gross."

He chuckles and starts walking to the water's edge. "Is that your professional opinion?"

"My unprofessional one, sir."

I follow him to the water and we both kneel to inspect what caught John's eye. At first glance they look like chipped bits of rock covered in a sickly green goop. So, basically the kind of thing I might expect in the sludge tanks, but there's something unnatural about them. I pick up a nearby stick and prod one over. The other side has a nice glossy curve with a gray sheen. I prod some of the others and find the same thing. They're all curved, all cracked, and broken in small scattered fragments close to where the effluent meets the lake.

"These are egg shells," I murmur.

John straightens and peers across the surface of the water. "Well, they certainly didn't come from a chicken."

I poke the green goop with the end of the stick. It has the consistency of a booger. Disgusting. "Something monstrous popped these out. But not a siren. They don't do eggs."

"Not a siren, but something the siren was obviously protecting. It tried to make us leave the facility first so it could keep doing whatever it's been doing here. It only attacked once it was threatened to be exposed by you." His eyebrows draw together and he looks positively grim. "We'll need to take some samples and get them analyzed, find out what exactly this siren was cooking up."

While John grabs an evidence bag from the car, I nudge what shell fragments I can find out of the water with my stick. John comes back and scoops them up, careful not to touch them directly since we don't know if the slime is poisonous or something equally nasty. It's better to be safe than sorry when messing with the leftovers of monsters. We return to the facility and share our discovery. They've managed to stabilize the man that was stabbed and Charlie has a bit more color in his face as he munches on an energy bar. Alona doesn't look fazed by her injury at all.

Some of the men start to wake up and we deal with their confusion as best we can. Before long, the emergency cleanup crew arrives, including a faun assistant that uses its empathetic influence to calm the civilians and dull their memories of the event. After more backup arrives from nearby field offices, we continue our sweep of the city but come up empty.

It's well into the night by the time we leave. We're all subdued and quiet—except Specialist Jaeger who's seething about what happened. I'm not sure if he's more upset about the fact that he was used as a puppet or that it wasn't Dasc behind the encounter. Although, he still seems inclined to blame the werewolves in some capacity.

"They could have been in league together," he says as we board the Osprey to return to Camp Ripley. Another team has come in to take our post in monitoring the city. "There's no way to prove that the werewolf was being controlled by the siren."

No one responds.

In flight, I page through the previous case files on Melody's tablet to verify that all the agents that went rogue were not only werewolves but men. It's a little hard to concentrate when I feel the eyes of Charlie, John, and

Specialist Jaeger on me. I do my best to appear unassuming and completely oblivious to their curiosity. I'm worried they were more observant about the circumstances of taking down the siren than I thought. But my suspicions about the other attacks are proven right—mostly. Nearly all of the previous incidents involved male agents but there was a handful of female agents that also turned on their fellows. I make a quick list of those. If not siren influence, then perhaps Dasc had been at those sites after all.

When we finally land at the base, night is well settled and the buzz of bugs fills the air. Sweat coats the back of my neck and I'd love to sit down to enjoy a refreshing drink but there's still more work to be done. John leads the way to headquarters and we open up a link with the IMS servers to start analyzing the egg shell fragments, anything of import around Bemidji that the siren might have been after, and applying what we now know to the previous attacks.

It gets quiet except for the clicking of keyboards and the barely audible murmurs to each other when we find something of interest. It's far too quiet and I suddenly imagine that if Hawk were here, he would drag in a radio from somewhere and insist on a spontaneous dance party to lighten the mood.

I smile to myself and it doesn't go unnoticed.

"Find something funny?" Charlie grumbles, clearly still irritated about what happened earlier today. His eyes flash to my injured arm so often that you'd think he's worried it's going to suddenly combust.

I shrug. "Just thought of something Hawk would do right now."

"Oh yeah?"

"Yup."

There's a beat of silence. "So, what would he do?"

I shake my head. "Never mind. Only my brother would think it's funny." I pause for a moment and battle that swelling ache in my chest. "I wish he was here, that's all."

He sets aside his tablet and scoots closer in his chair, bending his head until he's half a foot away. "Well, I'm here. If you ever feel the need to say something that you'd tell your brother, you can tell me."

I raise an eyebrow. "Okay. Do you want to have a random dance party?"

He considers me for a long moment, wrinkles forming at the edge of his eyelids, his mouth pursed in puzzlement.

"Right. I guess that would be normal for you two," he says at last.

I laugh under my breath and keep reviewing the map of Bemidji before me.

Theo enters the room a few minutes later—I didn't even realize he left—wearing hot-pad gloves and carrying a steaming pan of something that smells of sugary goodness. He promptly sets it before Alona who sits back in her chair alarmed.

"I'm so sorry!" he says loudly, jolting the rest of us out of our reveries.

"You baked me a cake for grazing me?" Alona says flatly.

He looks truly nervous and clasps his enormous mitts together. "I cook to express myself, you know that. And this cake was made with the tender, loving hands of deepest regret and scattered with the tears from a man most aggrieved—"

"No one wants a salty cake with your man tears."

He throws up his hands. "What more do you want from me!"

"Could you two love birds shut up?" Specialist Jaeger snaps.

Theo laughs. "I didn't know you had a sense of humor."

"What?"

"Love birds? Because she's a raven. I get it."

Specialist Jaeger facepalms, then gathers together his things, and leaves the room.

Despite Theo's claims of crying salty tears into the cake, when each of us women gets a piece for our troubles today, I find it scrumptious. More cake is dispersed and the men get some too. The mood lightens somewhat until I find John's hand on my shoulder.

"Can I talk to you for a second?" he says quietly.

I swallow the last bit of food in my mouth and nod. I follow him out into the hall, through headquarters, and into the midnight gloom. He doesn't say anything as we continue to the rolling hills of the camp where they sometimes test munitions. Nice and far away from everyone else. That's not a good sign.

"How did you know something was wrong?" John finally asks and turns about to face me with his arms crossed. "Back in Bemidji with the siren. You knew something was wrong with Specialist Jaeger before there was any reason to suspect anything out of the ordinary."

My heart thunders in my chest. I knew this would happen eventually. I had been too brazen today, but what other choice did I have? Ignore it like everything was fine and move on? We never would have discovered the siren if I hadn't said something when I sensed that strange magic latched onto Specialist Jaeger. What would Scholar think of me exposing my secret so quickly? So much for protecting my secrets.

"I had a gut feeling," I respond automatically.

He takes a step closer and tremors work their way into my fingers. "*Why?* What tipped you off? There's always something."

I don't have a clue what to say that will satisfy him. He's not some random agent, someone who won't do a double take or let it go. He's a Spartan leader and my commanding officer. I'm cornered.

He sets his feet wider apart and rolls his shoulder, settling into his stance, before he says, "Let me tell you a story. I once came across a man who could sense magic. Sure, vampires and werewolves seem to be able to sniff it out but this was a Blessed. Before him, no one had ever heard of such a thing. He was crazy as a loon, kept insisting he was Merlin from King Arthur's time, but he was powerful in a way I've never seen before or since."

"What happened to him?" I ask. I refrain from immediately questioning him about this man that has *my* ability. I thought I was the only one, but if there's this man then surely there must be others like him as well.

"He came in to be tested to see what he could do. Draco took over from there and he's been doing lab work ever since."

Lab work. Or stuck in a lab under Draco's heel.

"Now here's the point of my story," John continues. "Ever since this 'Merlin' decided to help the IMS, bio-mech guns were invented, probation rings came around, and even the werewolf serum showed up. What that man can do has saved millions of lives. Now think, what shape would the world be in now if he had kept his abilities to himself?"

I know what he's getting at and my face burns.

"I can only imagine that if someone else had abilities like that, more tools could be made to save lives. Would it be right for them to hide it?"

My chest heaves as I fight to control my breathing. "And what if revealing those abilities meant losing everything they had?"

"Some sacrifices are worth it." He leans in so close his warm breath washes over my face smelling of Theo's cake. "I'm disappointed in you, Phoenix."

He walks away leaving me frozen and shaking. Never have a person's words cut me open so thoroughly that even I could see the coward hiding beneath.

9

Hawk

I'm not sure how I manage to make it back to my apartment without walking straight into lampposts or buildings. Did all that really just happen? Witty standing. Rosalyn acting as lookout. Genna convincing me to join her cause. Me agreeing to help.

I know the weight of secrets. They get heavier and heavier over time, especially when you don't have anyone to share them with. Right now I feel like I weigh a thousand tons but I'll have to keep up the appearance of a feather light load if I'm going to make it through work each day without suspicion. I'm playing a dangerous game, but I've been playing this game since I was a child. I know how to keep my secrets.

That cheers me up slightly and I walk a little straighter, hoist my chin as if I've got my entire life in hand. Come on, world. Bring it on! But, you know, not too much. A few agents pass me on their way to their own apartments but no one gives me a second glance. Good. First stage complete. I make it to my apartment without arousing suspicion. Yup, I'm definitely a pro at this already.

Once safely in my own private corner of the world, I strip off my socks and toss them to the side, find an open bag of beef jerky I forgot about peeking out under the couch, and settle in to mull things over as I chew a tough strip.

Genna gave me the details of the man I'm supposed to be looking for. While searching subtly for clues on his whereabouts, she hopes I can also keep my ears open for any word of agents scouting near the other werewolf compound she located. Now *she* is a person who really seems to have a handle on her life. So determined and confident. Unyielding. Pretty—

My phone rings and I flinch, nearly choking on the piece of jerky. When I check who it is, my sister's name glares at me as if she already knows what I've done. Oh, man. Should I just let it go to voicemail? Or can I be convincing enough that she won't know anything's going on?

Relax, Hawk. This is just a telephone call, not a face to face. Of course I can pull this off. Plus, she might get more paranoid if I *don't* pick up. Or she could be in trouble herself. I can't leave her hanging like that.

Shoving the rest of the jerky in my mouth and trying to chomp it to pieces as quickly as I can, I answer the phone, lean back on the couch, and let myself sink in. The physical relaxation will help me not sound tense on the phone. It's the little things in life.

"Sup?" I say around the huge mouthful.

"I'm sorry, I must have gotten the wrong number," she says with the tell-tale whimsy of a sarcastic joke. "I'm trying to reach my brother but I seem to have called a troll eating a garbage can."

"You're just jealous of my delicious jerky," I say and manage to accidentally spit out part of it.

"Oh, so jealous. How about you finish so you can talk like a normal person? I'll wait."

"Ar' right."

It takes a while to finish chewing. Phoenix hums an old song Celina taught us while she waits. My jaw aches by the time I'm done.

"Ta-da!" I announce.

"Geez, Hawk, did you put a whole bag of the stuff in your mouth?"

"How else am I supposed to test my limits?"

I smirk and can picture her rolling her eyes on the other end of the phone wherever she is.

"So, is this our daily checkup?" I ask. "Everything good?"

There's a long pause on the other end before she says, "Yeah. You?"

"Please wait for a pregnant pause before receiving my answer." I count to ten in my head and hear her sigh. "Yup, I'm good."

"Ha ha, you're so funny."

"Just making sure you know that *I* noticed that pause. Are you sure everything's okay?"

Something must be on her mind because she takes another long pause before answering again.

"Do you ever wonder if we've made the right choices? You and me. Our secrets. What we've done. All of it."

Pixies, she *does* know, doesn't she? *How* could she possibly know? Did she sneak to Seattle without telling me?

I bolt upright and glance to the window as if I'm going to see her face pressed against the glass.

"Why do you say that?" I ask, all pretense of humor gone.

"No reason. I just . . . I don't know."

"You know how much I love cryptic answers, Phoenix, but even that one's a bit too much for me."

"Well, we sort of had a run in with a siren today."

I make a fantastic shocked face even though there's no one around to see it. "Wait, a *siren*? Where?"

"Bemidji, in a wastewater facility of all places."

"Eww."

"I know. It smelled."

"Are you okay?"

"I got nicked, but nothing serious."

Well, if she says it's nothing serious, I'm sure she's fine.

"Did the siren scratch you?" I ask, prodding for more information. A siren. In Minnesota. What on earth?

"Charlie got me actually. The stupid thing put the guys on my team under its spell along with all the plant workers."

"*All* the workers? Aren't there any female employees?"

She chuckles. "Well, yeah—up until about a month ago at least before the siren made the boss fire them so it had a better chance of not being discovered."

"I bet those women were thrilled."

"Oh, yeah. The cleanup team discovered they were preparing lawsuits against the facility for being sexist."

We both laugh at the irony of it. But eventually our laughter fades and that deep thought remains between us.

"So?" I prompt when Phoenix doesn't continue.

"So what?"

"Why did that make you decide to reconsider your life choices?"

There's some rustling over the line, faint footsteps, and a heavy sigh before Phoenix answers.

"I could have done more," she says quietly. "I *should* have done more. When you have the power to do something, don't you have a responsibility to despite any consequences to yourself? When did we decide to let fear dictate who we are?"

Her words strike a delicate cord and I can see that fear inside myself. It's shaped our choices for better or worse—fear of the consequences for what we've both done, fear of being forever separated, fear of being ripped away from our dreams.

But haven't those fears been realized already? We're permanently separated for the first time in our lives. We're both trapped by our secrets. My dream to be a field agent, a Spartan, has been ripped away. Because of fear. Because of worry.

Genna's words ring in my head.

Aaron is the most selfless person I've ever known. Certainly more than you or Phoenix.

Have we been so selfishly caught up in ourselves and failed to notice the rest of the world crumbling around us when we've had the power all along to stop it? Phoenix is a burgeoning magical cure-all. I have the keys to the kingdom to set the werewolves free from Dasc and the IMS. But fear has always stopped us. Do we have the strength to press forward and face the consequences? Am I willing to do the impossible? Am I willing to let Phoenix go?

I swallow back my eddy of dark swirling thoughts,

remember the person I'm supposed to be, and say as casually as I can, "This conversation got heavy real fast."

"Yeah. Yeah, it did." No joking, no deflective sarcasm. I guess we're both giving this a lot of serious thought.

"Well," I say and clear my throat. "Now that we've gotten the light-hearted stuff out of the way, it's time to talk the real dark stuff. Have you survived the social interactions with your squad mates?"

Phoenix snorts. "Oh, it's been misery. Having to *talk* to people. It's the worst."

"Preach."

"But seriously though. We have one pain in the butt that I'd like to kick off the planet for everyone's sake." She lets out a throaty growl of irritation. "We've been assigned to work with one Specialist Laurence Jaeger. Name ring a bell?"

I go stone cold and my stomach drops out of me. The beast slumbering inside raises its hackles at the name. The man who questioned Jason and helped to push him over the edge, sending him into a spiral that led to Jason's suicide. A cold, heartless bastard.

"Charlie's uncle?" I ask quietly, attempting to sound curious.

"Yeah, and he's every bit the jerk that Charlie made him out to be."

"You don't say." I feel myself become more distant as if I'm an observer watching myself talk on the phone. I close my eyes and can picture Jason curled up in his cell, alone and at the end of his rope. I know that feeling. And this Specialist Jaeger—this *monster*—sped things along. In his interview with Jason I could read the hate between the lines, the blinded view on werewolves. My hands start to shake and the beast inside gives a vicious roar. I have a sudden urge to rip something apart with my hands, to sink in my teeth, to shred—

"Hawk?"

As if cold water has been dumped over my head, I inhale sharply and hold the phone away from me for a second to catch my breath. Focus. Calm down. I'm fine. I've got a lid on it. I bring the phone back to my ear.

"Yeah, sorry," I say with a grimace. "My mind was wandering for a minute."

"You okay?"

Always worried the second anything seems off. Anger rears up almost faster than I can wrangle it. I'm not some dog to be leashed. But this is Phoenix. She does what she does because she cares. I know that.

"I'm fine. You were saying?"

"I gotta run. We're still digging into this siren and trying to figure out what she was doing. I'll talk to you later, okay?"

"Okay."

"I love you, dog breath."

"I love you too, Fifi. Bye."

"Bye."

The line clicks and I quickly set the phone down before I hurl it. I grab the nearest pillow, thrust my face into it, and scream into the padding that attempts to suffocate me as I let out this wild burst of rage. Pain shudders through my body and I know that this is the effect of the serum eating away at me. But I don't know if it would have happened without that trigger, without mention of Specialist Jaeger leading me to Jason yet again.

It takes me a long time to finally stop screaming, put the pillow aside, and catch my breath. I lie full out on the couch and stare up at the ceiling with an arm draped across my forehead.

"The best we can do is honor their memory," I say to myself, the only present company I have. "So, what are you going to do, Hawk? Scream out life's frustration into a pillow? Or are you going to do something about it?" I close my eyes. "What are you afraid of?"

Eventually I go to sleep but it's a fitful night full of tossing and turning with the decisions looming before me. It isn't until the morning as I'm in the middle of brushing my teeth that I make a connection that I should have made last night. Specialist Jaeger is a werewolf hunter. If that's so, why has Phoenix and her team been assigned with him? They couldn't possibly be hunting werewolves, could they? No. Phoenix would have told me. She wouldn't go along with it. They must have crossed paths or needed his expertise on something else. Yeah, that must be it.

Despite reassuring myself that it can't be true, the thought continues to lurk in the back of my mind.

Well, I have the weekend to really roll things around and consider my options for how to proceed next. I can't just walk into work on a Saturday and pretend I have important things to do in order to look up Genna's mystery man. No one except security will be there so I won't have an excuse until Monday to be in. The best way to avoid detection isn't by sneaking around but by blending in. It makes you less obvious that way.

So, I decide to go for a run. Exercising helps to clear my head. I change into my running gear and am in the middle of locking my apartment door when someone walks up behind me.

"Hawk."

My heart lurches in my chest. It's Spartan Knox.

I give him a cordial smile and tuck my key into my pocket.

"Sir."

Well, he doesn't look stern or angry so he hasn't found out I met with Genna and her co-conspirators.

"I wanted to check up on you yesterday but didn't see you at the diner," he says.

"Oh, I needed to get out for a bit. Stretch my legs. It—it had been a rough day. But I'm okay. I appreciate your concern."

Knox nods and gestures one-handedly to my getup. "Mind if I join you?"

Maintaining close proximity to Spartan Knox is not what I had in mind today. He's ultra-sharp. I'm going to have to be at the top of my game. "Uh, sure. I could use some company, I suppose."

"Let's go."

Not having much of a choice, I follow him out of the apartment complex and we jog down the block to warm up. It's a beautiful morning. The clouds have parted for sunshine and the air is crisp. There's the smell of the bay lingering as always but I'm getting used to it. I let Knox take the lead on our run. Once we really get going, he sets a fast pace but that's what we Spartans do. We're always pushing ourselves, keeping ourselves sharp.

"Sand run?" Knox says between even breaths.

I make a whatever gesture with my hands and shoulders. "That's one way to wake up."

He smiles and we head for the nearest beach. We race each other and dodge around pedestrians enjoying the nice morning sunshine. All the while, the only thought in my mind is that I've already gone behind this man—my hero, my mentor—and spoken with multiple traitors. Come Monday, I'll be going a step further and using the IMS servers to help them. Like a broken record, I ask myself if I'm doing the right thing here.

Knox finally leads us off the beach, back into the city, and we slow to a walk to cool down for the last half-mile.

As we catch our breath and glisten with sweat, I decide I need to know more before I do something I can't take back.

Steeling myself, I say, "Can I ask you something?"

Knox nods as he brushes sweat out of his professional man beard. "Shoot."

"What do you know about Specialist Laurence Jaeger?"

He cocks an eyebrow at me. "Why do you want to know?"

"Phoenix mentioned him when I talked to her last. I'm just curious. Do you know him?"

"Yeah, I know him. He's a werewolf specialist among other things. I've butted heads with him a few times."

I would have liked to have seen that. "Yeah? How come?"

"Disagreed about how to handle a couple of cases."

I wait for more details but Knox isn't very forthcoming.

"Is that all?" I say to prompt the conversation along.

"Spartans don't gossip, Hawk," he says and gives me a very critical eye.

"It'd be gossip if you were telling me rumors. I'm just trying to get a feel for this guy's character. Professionally."

"Hmm." He doesn't say anything else for a long time until we reach the apartment complex. Instead of entering, Knox bobs his head to the side in a gesture for me to follow him. "Come on."

We walk past the apartments and keep going until we reach a quiet little park shadowed by enormous willows. Knox leads me to a nearby bench and we take a seat.

"You ever hear of the Kentucky uprising that happened a few years back?" Knox asks in a conspiratorial tone, one arm slung across the back of the bench and his eyes frequently scanning the area for eavesdroppers.

"No. Should I have?"

"It was kept very quiet and nothing was put out on the feeds about it. The only people that really know about it are those that were involved."

"That sounds ominous. Let me guess, you and Specialist Jaeger were there?"

He nods. "We were both called in to assist. A man by the name of Harvey Downs had been bitten in the months prior. He was given the serum and went through all the usual protocol. Something happened with him—not sure if he had issues before he was turned or not—but he lost it. He started claiming the serum was poison and the IMS was trying to kill werewolves. He managed to gather quite the following in the area. This Harvey turned into some kind of cult leader. Things got bad. People were getting turned or hurt, they held a couple violent protests, and eventually I was called in when they took an IMS facility hostage."

My mouth goes dry. Harvey Downs claimed the serum

was poison? Could it be he had the same kind of reaction I do to the serum? That drove him crazy . . .

"Things went from bad to worse," Knox says and sighs, sagging against the bench as if the memory still manages to defeat him. "Harvey started threatening to kill hostages unless the IMS told the truth about the serum. The man was clearly deranged. I wanted to negotiate and rehabilitate those people, but not everyone else did."

"And Specialist Jaeger?" I ask, even though it's pretty obvious his opinion must have been polar opposite considering Knox's tight-lipped expression.

"Argued to breach the facility and take them out using any means necessary. He managed to convince the director in charge of the crisis. So we breached."

"What happened?"

"Specialist Jaeger blew in too soon so the cultists had time to react before we were able to control the situation."

The blood drains out of my face and pools in my feet. "They killed the hostages?"

"No. Killed themselves."

A jolt goes through me. My imagination falls into a black void as I think of Jason bleeding to death in his cell and these werewolf "cultists" in drab robes with angry faces shooting themselves. I shudder and drop my gaze to my hands.

Knox sighs. "They said it was better than being controlled by the IMS."

My entire body wilts on the seat and I bring my head low so I can run my hands through my hair, elbows planted on my thighs to keep myself upright.

"Why tell me this?" I whisper.

"You wanted to know what kind of man he was," he says simply, then angles himself closer to me with a stern brow. "And I know you've been having difficulty adjusting to our current situation."

I let out a harsh, humorless laugh. "And this is supposed to help me?"

"Those people needed treatment, but they were also a threat. *We* are a threat, Hawk—what we are. This precaution of taking us off the front lines is the right thing to do. Things will get better eventually, but until we're no longer an immediate threat, it's better if we sit out this fight."

I can hear it in his voice. He truly believes that. He believes that we're animals to be caged at the slightest hint of provocation. We're dangerous. We're monsters. It's a battle to keep my face reflective, to make it seem as if I'm considering his words for the wisdom he thinks they are.

And maybe they are the words that I need, but not in the way he thinks.

My mentor, the greatest werewolf I know, has agreed to accept his cage and not acknowledge the truth of the serum. He'd rather be the monster and has even put up the bars of his own prison. We aren't werewolves by choice. This life has been forced upon us, but I'm not willing to accept it. I'm not willing to sit on my hands and let the truth remain silent. Because we are all suffering, some more than others. Knox doesn't know the pain and the horror inflicted by the serum. It sears my veins even now and I clench my fists against it, fight to keep myself together as Phoenix's pendant grows warm against my skin trying to keep me together. Her magic is the kind we need—a warm embrace that soothes away the nightmare.

"Hawk?"

I nod as if I accept the reality that he has—that we are to submit to our suffering by the rules of those who can't even begin to understand us.

Knox pats me on the shoulder and we walk back to the apartment complex together. As we go, my spine straightens and I see the path ahead of me that I need to follow. We part ways and I enter the emptiness of my apartment alone.

There are so many others out there that are helpless against the werewolf disease and the threat of the IMS and Dasc alike. But I am not. There's a way I can free them, free us all. Genna has a plan and I have a part to play in it. I see that now. No one is going to come save us. We have to save ourselves.

And come Monday, I know exactly what I'm going to do.

10

Phoenix

The morning dawns bright and humid as a typical Minnesota summer day. As with everything else, we wake up as a team and immediately split off to the facilities before we can be summoned away. I walk with Alona and Melody into the bathroom where other women are getting ready for the day. After a quick shower, I dry off and am in the middle of combing my hair in front of a mirror when I find Alona at my side.

"John gave you a colorful speech?" she asks quietly.

I almost drop the comb in my hand. "Excuse me?"

"I thought Scholar told you to keep your secrets secret."

I startle and face her head on. She's completely mellow with a bit of a scowl as usual. She continues to braid her long hair without even looking at me as if we're discussing what's for breakfast this morning.

"So it *was* you," I whisper. "The raven at the bus stop that took me to her?"

"Took you long enough."

I roll my eyes. "I figured it out the first day—well, I guess technically the second day—that I met you. I just wasn't *sure*."

"Uh-huh."

"You know, you seem awfully crabby all the time," I grumble.

"It's called dry humor."

"Uh-huh."

She finishes her braid, loops it up so it rests in a tight bun at the base of her neck, and spins on her toes to face me. "I'm not crabby. I just have a natural disposition to not like people. People are idiots."

"I'm not an idiot."

She shrugs and glides away. It would be nice if Scholar's contact could be a little more friendly. I grumble a few choice words under my breath and keep working on my hair when Melody comes over to take Alona's place.

"Making friends?" she says with a smirk.

"Oh, yeah."

She laughs. "You'll get used to Alona eventually."

"Aren't you supposed to say she'll warm up to me eventually?"

Melody fervently shakes her head before whipping her hair up. "Alona doesn't warm up to anyone. She just becomes gradually less annoyed with you. Usually. A bit like Charlie, actually."

"Wonderful," I grumble.

I wrap my wet hair into a bun and find I'm unable to contain my curiosity anymore.

"Can I ask you something, Melody?"

"Of course."

I'm not sure how to phrase it in a soft way so I decide to go blunt. "That siren, it called you 'princess.' Theo is always calling you 'your majesty.' Are you . . . royalty?" Her expression falls so I quickly add, "I'm sorry. I don't mean to pry. You don't have to say anything—"

"No, no. It's okay. Really." She gives me a worn smile. "The subject was bound to come up sooner or later, and we're a team. You ought to know." Melody tugs at a loose strand of her hair as if giving herself a moment to collect her thoughts before she says, "My full title is Princess Melody of the Northern Seas. Although, technically I'm not a princess anymore since I lost my skin."

Her skin? Wait a second—princess of the northern seas, as in around Scotland and Ireland? Combine that with her British accent and the way the selkies in Duluth treated her—

"You're a selkie?"

"Born one at least, but without my skin I'm stuck as this. A hollow."

I remember how protective the selkies were of their skins back in Duluth. It's an integral part of them and is the essence of their magic.

"But—selkies are Scottish." It's the first thing I can think to say. "Your accent—"

"Is a ruse," she says with a sigh. "It was just . . . easier for me. Pretending to be someone I wasn't, I mean. I've always been good at accents."

"Can I ask what happened?"

Melody finishes putting her hair into an orderly bun before facing me. "Short version, a monster got its hands on my skin and then it was a decision between saving a friend's life and saving my own skin."

"You saved your friend."

"Yes."

What kind of awful choice is that? Lose a loved one or a crucial part of yourself.

"Do you regret it?" I ask quietly.

"No. I became a Spartan knowing that one day I'd have to make sacrifices. It . . . hurt but I'd do it again if I had to because some sacrifices are worth making."

I swallow and turn away, busying myself with tucking a few loose strands into place. She's given me more to think about than she knows. She must sense something, though, because she claps a hand on my back.

"And if *you* ever need to talk," she says, "I'm here."

I give her a wan smile. "I appreciate that."

Ready for the day, I start walking out with Melody when Alona wings back into the bathroom with our black suits over her shoulder.

"Suit up," she says. "We've got bad news."

"Yeah?" I take my suit from her outstretched hands.

"Lab got back on those egg shell fragments. Hydra."

Things can't get much worse than that. Hydra are level five monsters with lots of heads, lots of acidic spit, high speed healing, and incredibly tough hides.

"Oh, bloody hell," Melody says under her breath and snags her suit.

The three of us rush back into the bathroom, shrug out of our clothes, and slip into our special Spartan suits. We check each other's buckles to make sure they're on correctly and then jog to our bunks to snatch up our helmets and my magical gloves. The guys come out from the other bathroom and John meets us at the door to the outside.

"We're going to start sweeps down the river and nearby lakes for signs of other eggs or—heaven forbid—adult hydra. From the amount of shell fragments, our experts think there was more than one egg at that facility. And if we only found shells—"

"Then here there be baby monsters," Theo quips as he adjusts his belt. He makes a motion like a t-rex at Alona who doesn't react in the slightest.

As usual, Specialist Jaeger has something to say on the matter. "Our mission is Dasc and the werewolves."

"Level five monsters on American soil trump everything else," John says flatly. "Nearby teams are being called in to assist. We'll be coordinating and working closely with Tango. Since there haven't been any sightings in the area, we'll be checking the water ways as that's their most likely hiding spot. I don't need to remind all of you that those waters lead to the Twin Cities and Underground. If there are any loose hydra in the area, we need to stop them before they hit a populated area."

Specialist Jaeger just shakes his head and walks away muttering something about contacting headquarters.

"Leave him," John says darkly and waves the rest of us on. Feeling a bit of relief at leaving the specialist behind, we hustle to the Osprey in our matte, black suits. It's a quick ride up and out with the rotors changing from helicopter to airplane position. As we head up to Bemidji once more, John raps his knuckles on the hull and the sound outside becomes muted so we can talk freely.

"Patching us in now," Alona says from an intercom overhead.

A moment later, we join the channel along with the other Spartan teams responding to the area.

"Sierra is en route," John says.

"Tango five minutes out from the headwaters," a female answers.

"Whiskey reporting in. ETA twenty minutes."

"Foxtrot on your heels, Whiskey."

"This is Tango, passing lead to Sierra."

John hangs onto cargo straps overhead as he stands and uses the radio on the side of the hull. "We have evidence of a level five monster in the Bemidji area. There's a strong possibility we have more than one hydra out there. A single one of those can wipe out an entire city. We'll do an expanding search from the wastewater facility concentrating on the waterways. Tango will secure our initial starting point. Eyes and ears open people. Molon labe."

The other leaders echo back "molon labe" and the radio falls silent once again.

Hydra. In Minnesota. I can't believe this is happening. And I thought the lamia were bad.

"Anyone else think this is crazy?" Theo says.

Charlie already has his nose in *Pride and Prejudice* but raises his hand without taking his eyes off of it. Melody, John, and I raise our hands in unison as well.

"I mean," Theo continues, "Why here? Why now? And *hydra*?"

"We'll leave that to the analysts for now," John says. "For the time being, let's just focus on killing the things."

"Amen to that."

The rest of the ride is carried out in silence except for Charlie muttering something about a character being a jerk in his book. Despite how much he insists he doesn't like it, he sure seems to be wrapped up in it.

Before long, we arrive at Bemidji. Instead of making for the airport like before, we set down right in front of the wastewater facility. Tango has already secured it and we'll be using it as our base of operations. We disembark, leaving the air sprites behind to guard the aircraft. I look to the road where confused and curious civilians watch us but are redirected by a line of IMS agents—members of the cleanup crew—in FBI uniforms moving them along. We're going to be the talk of the town but no one's going to know the real reason why we're here.

Inside the building, we find Tango setup in the office where I had locked myself in the last time I was here fighting a mob of siren-controlled workers. Since the office is too small to accommodate us all, only John enters while the rest of us linger just beyond the door.

I get a quick glimpse inside to take stock of the re-purposed office space. They've got a map of the area spread out on the desk with overlaying grid lines. A woman, who I suspect is Tango's leader, stands with hands braced on the tabletop. Like John, she too has a prominent scar on her face but it's a horrible burn that trails from her jaw and disappears into the collar of her "SWAT" uniform. At her side is a tall, willowy man I recognize as Spartan Yetka, one of my instructors during Spartan training who's back on rotation it seems. The other is Amanda Fry with her hands clasped behind her back and a fire sprite in the form of a hawk perched on her shoulder. I guess her pyrokinetic abilities nabbed herself a friend.

The rest of Tango stands outside with us and we nod to each other or pass quiet greetings as our team leaders discuss strategy. We're a fairly young crowd. There aren't many old warriors amongst the Spartans. Most either die young or . . . well, that's it really. Even our instructors, like Spartan Yetka, are simply rotating between teaching and active duty. Spartans don't retire. I've discovered it's a fact of life that a Spartan will stay on the battlefield until the very end. Melody has been the rare exception of a Spartan taking time off, if you can even call it that. The world needs us now more than ever. We can't afford to give anything less of ourselves.

"You catch the chatter out of France?" a woman from Tango asks us. She's got a tattoo of a gryphon on the side of her neck that I try to discreetly inspect without being weird.

"Not yet," Theo says and points at the woman's neck. "Nice tat!"

She looks a little stunned and I catch Charlie rolling his lips out of the corner of my eye as he tries not to laugh.

"What's happening in France?" Alona asks.

"Word is they've been scrambling their *Spartiate* for something going down in country, but their divisions are refusing to share what's going on."

"Sounds suspicious, but I thought we're not supposed to gossip," Charlie says flatly.

I nudge him sharply in the ribs at the same time Melody does on his other side. He glares at us both in turn.

"Sounds like France covering up something they aren't supposed to be doing. That's not gossip. That's called analyzing intel." One of the woman's teammates behind her laughs.

Thankfully, John comes out just then before Charlie can port the stranger into the middle of the lake or something.

"Let's get a move on, people," he says. "We've got our grid so let's search it."

He gestures with two fingers to us and we follow him out into the bright morning sunshine. It's a cloudless day and already humid and warm. In our black Spartan outfits, we're going to be melting by the end of the day, but that's the job.

From sunrise to sunset, we and the other teams scour the edge of the waterways and surrounding forests, grid block by grid block. Under the blazing sun, I start to wish we could be searching directly in the lakes and rivers but a pack of water sprites is already on that job. I keep my senses alert and use what Scholar taught me in order to detect magic in the area. If there's a hydra out there—egg, hatched baby, or grown-up—I'll be able to detect it. For everyone else, it's a search by sight and experience. We draw attention but our FBI liaisons clear a path for us through snooping civilians and curious children. Everyone knows something is going on but our liaisons have setup the ruse of hunting down a dangerous criminal. They even put a plug in with local reporters to cover up what we're doing.

If only they knew we were hunting down monsters with the ability to spit acid, regenerate from almost any attack, and snap a car in half with their teeth.

By day's end none of the teams have had any luck. Our

grid expands and we continue the hunt. None of us really get any sort of break. It's go, go, go the whole day and by evening, I really start to feel it. Team Sierra stops back in our Osprey for a quick meal of protein bars and water before we're in a van moving to a new start point for our search further south along the river. As we drive, I close my eyes and push out my sensory feelers, focusing past the interior of the vehicle and grasping at the surrounding area as we pass. There are specks here and there of magic that we sweep by but nothing exceptional.

The van rumbles down a straightaway when something catches my attention. Almost out of my range, like a wisp of smoke on the edge of the horizon, I sense something foul. Twisted. Seething.

Theo claps a hand on my shoulder and I jump.

"Taking a nap?" he says with a smile.

I blink and the magical fishing line I've stretched out comes whipping back in. It takes a lot of concentration to reach out so far. I can't sense that presence any more but I can't get it out of my head either. I've never sensed something like that before. The closest thing I can compare it to was when a baby leviathan swam upstream to assault Underground. Could it be the target of our search?

We eventually slow to park on the side of the road and I immediately rise to exit. The very last rays of sunlight pierce through the trees bordering the road and a rogue breeze brushes across my sweaty skin. It seems so peaceful but I know what sort of darkness can hide behind pretty lies.

"Okay team," John says as he disembarks. "We've got water sprites combing the lakes and rivers to the east. We're going to head south through here before cutting west."

I look to the east where I had sensed that presence. I *know* that's the way we ought to be going, but how do I explain myself? The rest of the team moves to the trees.

John's words from the night before ring in my ears. He knows there's more to me than I've let on. He knows I have powers that could help them, help everyone. Scholar said I need to protect my secrets but . . . at what cost? At the risk of innocent lives endangered by the threat I know is east and not in the direction we're about to go? I've been waging this battle with myself since I discovered what I can do.

Am I right to hide my abilities?

Selfish. Coward. That's what John implied of me and even said directly. I'm a disappointment because I won't make the necessary sacrifice.

The others start to walk south but I march up to John.

"Are you sure we shouldn't head east?" I say in an undertone.

He gives me a searching look. "Is there something you know, Phoenix?"

"I think we both know my senses are a bit more attuned than others. I'm asking you to trust me. Please."

A long moment passes between us as he realizes what I'm saying and doing. I'm taking the risk to do what needs to be done.

Without breaking eye contact, he says to the others, "Wrong way, everyone. We're heading east."

"You said south then west," Charlie says with a confused look.

"Did I?" John gives me a significant look and turns around to head into the trees. I follow after into the dimming shadows. We head south through the trees before we reach a wide field of tall grass that reaches up to my elbows.

Our team pauses briefly and I hear Theo whisper, "Don't go into the tall grass!"

Charlie squints at him. "What?"

"Man, have you never seen *Jurassic Park II*? There's gonna be raptors out there!"

"Raptors?" Alona scoffs. "Really, Theo?"

"We're hunting down a hydra and you laugh at the possibility of raptors?"

"If anything, there's more likely to be kappas trying to drown us in the marshy areas."

"Gee, thanks, Alona."

"No problem."

John clears his throat. "We're going to walk staggered formation for a while. Phoenix, why don't you take lead for a change?"

He says it very casually as if he's giving the new girl a chance to learn the ropes, but in reality he's giving me lead because I'm the only one who knows exactly where to go. He swings an arm forward motioning for me to lead the way. I take a deep breath and start the trek across the rolling hills and swampy areas. Alona shifts and circles our group overhead while I lead us on.

The light continues to dim and eventually we click on our flashlights. John walks a short ways behind me with a thermal imager in his hands to help spot any waiting surprises in the growing dark. The others march along in silence with the radio occasionally squawking with the other teams reporting in. We keep on moving at a slow pace to avoid treacherous footing and I keep our pace deliberately casual so I can try to focus on stretching out my feelers again for that source of twisted magic I sensed earlier. After twenty minutes of walking, I sense it again like smoke on the wind. No one says a word as I shift our trajectory towards it. We head back into a wooded area and before long we come to train tracks running through the forest. Whatever I've been sensing, it's close. Very close.

I pause on the bank of the tracks and look up and down the rails. It's quiet. Actually, it's a little too quiet. There's no sound of flies buzzing, crickets chirping, or birds calling to each other. Everyone single one of us stands motionless listening to our very deadened surroundings. John raises a hand to get our attention, turns the radio on mute, and motions for us to go silent. Our flashlights click off in unison and I tug on my special pair of goggles, switching them to night vision mode. John motions wordlessly to me and I lead the way down the embankment as soft as a shadow with my bio-mech gun raised.

We hardly make a sound as we step carefully between trees and brush, and come to a small stream choked with green algae. The water runs directly beneath the train tracks through a large culvert that a person can easily stand in.

There. Directly before me like a poisonous cloud of bitter energy, I locate the source. An enormous egg sits against the wall of the culvert covered in green slime. I approach it cautiously with John as the others keep an eye on the forest behind us. The top of the egg almost comes up to my waist and I would be hard pressed to be able to wrap my arms around the thing. Beneath the slime is gray marbled eggshell and within . . . a baby hydra yet to hatch.

John motions to me and points to something on the

floor. I look down and spot massive paw prints in the muck made by some kind of beast. If the last place we discovered hydra evidence was guarded by a siren, it looks like this one is being guarded by a monster as well. These tracks look feline, as if a tiger or a lion took a stroll through here.

We bend closer to inspect the egg and I'm glad to find no cracks or splits in the shell. Once we're sure we're not going to have a baby hydra spitting at us, we clear the rest of the area. There are more paw prints in the moist soil along the sides of the murky stream but no signs of the creature that left them. Alona continues to circle overhead but returns without spotting anything else out of the ordinary.

With the perimeter established, John clicks on his flashlight to better inspect the egg as he calls in what we've found.

"Tango is inbound," I hear over my earpiece. "We'll bring the Osprey in and load it straight into the air. There's no way we're taking care of it down there."

Despite how much all of us would like to. The situation is complicated to say the least. Hydra eggs are notorious for several reasons. For one thing, they can lie dormant for decades, centuries even. Second, the shells are basically indestructible. Meaning, you have to wait for the hydra to hatch before you can even attempt to kill it. Now mix those things together and you have an extremely deadly time bomb that could decide to go off whenever it feels like it. We obviously can't leave the egg here but it's in a tricky area. If we can at least transport it out, we can get it to an area we can control. The problem is getting it there before the thing bursts out.

We guard the creepy egg until the shadow of the Osprey

falls over us, its approach silent with its own pair of air sprites keeping the sound of its engine and rotors contained. The ramp lowers and the inside of the bay is illuminated by the fire sprite still perched on Amanda's shoulder. She and her team lower a line with a net attached to the end since there isn't enough room for them to land. While John and Melody unhook the net and start to drag it down to the culvert, Theo keeps his sights on the trees, Alona circles overhead, and Charlie and I inspect the problem that is the egg.

"Port it?" I whisper.

Charlie makes a face as he leans close to the egg, hands braced on his knees. "I don't know what that would do—if I could even bring it with me."

"You don't think you can?"

He shakes his head. "I've never tried porting something like this before. And that twinge of pain might wake it up."

"Okay. Better not."

"Agreed."

John and Melody stalk into the culvert with the net between them and lay it beside the egg. At John's word, I very delicately place my hands upon the egg—grimacing at the slime beneath my gloves—and ease it onto its side into the net. It's certainly heavy and for a normal person it'd be like trying to budge a boulder. Thankfully for us, my strength is coming in handy. Even so, it's difficult to maneuver it without jostling it too much. We all move softly with our breath held at each bump and jarring motion. Eventually we lay it out in the net then bring up the sides as Melody and John guide the Osprey closer so we can latch the hook onto the netting.

The moment it starts to rise into the air, I blow out a

breath. The team above hauls it up and carefully pulls it into the belly of the aircraft. Well, that was nerve-wracking. Not that it's over, of course. It still has to make it to a safe landing site where it can be secured and dealt with.

We wait anxiously until we hear the Tango team leader say over the channel, "Package is secure. We're heading to the landing site now. Be ready."

John looks to me and I give a single nod. We're good. That's it. We can—

I snap my head to the sky as I feel another dark presence closing in fast. Alona gives a sharp caw in the air above us in confirmation.

I hit the radio button as fast as I can. "Tango, you have an incoming bogey!"

Our team looks up as a shadow swoops across the sky—leathery wings, four thick legs, a long segmented tail, and two heads, one lion and one goat. A chimera, and it's heading straight for the Osprey. The thing comes alongside the aircraft just as it starts to pivot and bathes the hull with a torrent of fire from its two mouths.

"Theo." It's all John says before Theo immediately whips his sniper rifle off his back, drops to the ground, and gets a bead on the chimera.

"Alona, try to draw it towards us," John commands over the radio.

Her raven form, a mere speck in the sky, darts for the flying monster that circles the Osprey blasting it with brilliant orange flames. Scorch marks adorn the hull but it doesn't seem to be doing much damage otherwise. The Osprey circles back around to head towards us and lead the chimera right into Theo's fire. At least, I think that's what the plan is supposed to be. One second the aircraft is flying steady and the next it veers dangerously to the side and almost skims the treetops before heading back up at an odd angle.

John keeps a finger pressed to the radio in his ear. "Tango, talk to me."

"The damn thing is hatching!" their team leader shouts back. "It got our pilot in the back. Amanda, light that thing up!"

The blood drains out of my face as I watch the horror unfold above me, unable to do anything about it. The chimera is moving too fast and too close to the Osprey for Theo to get a good shot. More than once Alona almost gets caught in the monster's flames only to dart away before returning to taunt it some more. It lets out the roar of a lion and high-pitched shriek of a goat. Freaking chimeras.

"I can get up there," Charlie says as if to himself. "If they can lower the ramp, I can help."

John immediately passes along the message to Tango but I think they're a little preoccupied at the moment. The Osprey continues to jerk around in figure eights and tight circles with the chimera bombarding it. At one point I think I see light peeking through the hull of the aircraft and the flicker of flames from within.

"It's burning through the hull," Melody says breathlessly beside me. "Hydra spit."

Acidic hydra spit. Pixies.

The chimera takes a wide turn when the Osprey nearly runs into it and Theo lets off a shot. It gives an ear-splitting scream but continues its relentless attack.

"Open the door, open the door, open the door," Charlie

chants beside me, eyes fixated on the aft of the Osprey. He's already got his dagger out in his hand with the tip saturated in dark blood. The only way to kill a hydra is by stabbing it through the heart with a blade dipped in magical blood. But first you have to get past their jaws, acid, and thick hide.

"You aren't going up there alone," I say and clamp a hand on Charlie's shoulder.

He doesn't protest, merely nods.

Then the ramp starts to lower.

"Get ready," John warns us. "You get that thing out of there. Understood?"

"Understood," Charlie and I say in unison.

The Osprey turns about but we can't actually see into the aircraft at the angle it's spinning. Charlie curses under his breath.

"Do you trust me?" he asks.

Without hesitation I respond, "Yes."

Then we vanish. Not into the Osprey. Nope. Into the middle of the air near the aircraft with nothing beneath us but a very long drop. I suck in a sharp breath but Charlie's eyes are steel, locked onto the Osprey where we now have a much better angle to see inside. But then we're falling.

And suddenly we're in the midst of the battle raging in the belly of the aircraft. Metal hisses around us as flecks of acid eat through everything they touch. Amanda and her fire sprite have turned the inside into a tornado of fire but it isn't stopping the acid or the monster flinging it around. The broken bits of shell roll back and forth as the aircraft moves madly through the air. The other Spartans do their best to keep their footing, avoid the acid, and attempt to stab the monstrosity before them.

It's a slimy thing of molted white and gray scales, sharp claws, a whipping tail, and three long necks supporting three very angry heads. The baby hydra's eyes—all three pairs—glow with a greenish, venomous light as they swivel back and forth while it projects acid and snaps at the blades thrust towards it. It's surprisingly fast and agile, its thick trunk of a body jerking out of the way of the Spartans' weapons and gripping the floor with its deadly little claws. It hisses every time Amanda and her sprite touch it with fire but the burns heal alarmingly fast.

Charlie lets me go as he alone ports to the side of the hydra and drives his blade towards the monster's heart. He's fast. But so is an enraged baby hydra.

One head swivels around and launches a glob of acid spit directly at his face. Charlie vanishes to the beast's other side and the acid hits the metal hull. The other Spartans rally at Charlie's distraction and swarm towards the hydra with metal shields and blades in hand. The hydra heads swivel this way and that firing spit in every direction. I duck and stagger out of the way, acid hissing past me in some very close calls.

The Osprey lurches downwards to the left as the chimera slams into it from the side. Everyone, Spartans and baby hydra alike, lose their footing and stumble or roll to one side of the aircraft. I think the only reason we haven't crashed yet is because the air sprites must be doing everything in their power to keep us aloft. They start to level us out but it's already too late.

The hydra rolled right on top of Charlie and all three heads focus on him, vicious mouths lined with glowing acid.

So, as usual, when someone I care about is in deep trouble, I do something really stupid.

I launch myself forward as the Osprey levels out, wrap my arms around those three heads, and throw the hydra with all my might away from Charlie. The hydra's claws hook onto me, dragging me along as we go tumbling away.

Right out the open bay ramp.

"PHOENIX!"

Charlie's shout rings in my ears before there's nothing but the wind whipping past me, the roar of fire, and the thrum of the Osprey's engines.

Mid-fall, the hydra heads turn their nasty little eyes towards me and I know I have a split second to react before I find myself covered in acid. I shove the monster off me and the dragon's barriers in my gloves activate as I lift up my hands to shield myself. Half a breath later, sizzling acid hits the barrier and I can feel it chewing through. Oh, *pixies*.

Not that I have any time to worry about it. Two more seconds and I'm going to be impaled on a spruce tree.

I don't think. I react. All my focus goes into the gloves Scholar gave me and the barriers immediately expand, growing larger and larger until I'm encased in a bubble of shimmering magic.

Tree branches rise up to meet my face.

Then I vanish.

Charlie's arms wrap around me one second and the next I fall two feet into shallow water. The barrier around me bursts like a popped balloon and I suck down a breath at the cold water soaking me through. Charlie does the same beside me and I realize he managed to port us into the stream beneath the train tracks. He doesn't say anything as he keeps an arm around my waist and ports us once again out of the cold water and woods to the train tracks.

My eyes turn upwards and I see Alona dart into the body of the Osprey as the aircraft veers dangerously close to the trees. The chimera is distracted as it looks for the fallen baby hydra and moves far enough away so the rest of our team can open fire. John and Melody send up a wave of bio-mech pulses to herd the thing right into Theo's sights. Three powerful shots later and the chimera falls with a heavy thud to the ground below.

A moment passes and the Osprey rightens and moves off as Alona says, "I've got control. Setting her down nearby."

Now for the baby hydra.

I can feel its wretched essence as that of the chimera drifts away into nothingness. Panting, I wave the others over and we converge on where the hydra fell. It spits and hisses as it snaps its legs—bent at an odd angle—back into shape. Before it can make a move to escape, we surround the thing. I take Charlie's hand. We vanish and reappear directly behind it. Focusing on my gloves once again, I will the barrier to expand but this time to encase the heads of the baby hydra. It spits and spits but the acid stays within the sphere I've created. Anger courses through me, white hot and blazing.

It tried to kill Charlie. It almost killed everyone up in that aircraft. The acid burns against the shield smothering it but the barrier holds. Now free to deliver the killing blow, Charlie drives his blade home and there's a sizzling pop as the hydra's heart bursts. The light goes out of its many eyes and the heads fall limp inside the barrier bubble.

My concentration wavers as I realize what I've just done and the bubble vanishes, the acid and heads hitting the ground. Greenish smoke rises and fills my nostrils with a ghastly smell.

The world grows still and I realize each and every one of my teammates is staring at me.

In order to save myself and Charlie, I just manipulated dragon's barriers. In front of all of them. Despite the fact that the battle is over, my breathing quickens. For so long I've been hiding this secret and in one fell swoop, it's over. They know. My magic isn't just strength. It is so much more.

Charlie's eyes pierce through me, calculating, studying. In a deathly calm voice, he asks, "Do you mind explaining what exactly you just did?"

11

Hawk

For the first time since I moved to Seattle, I'm excited to go into work. Who cares if it's because I could get arrested for what I'm about to do next? At least it's *exciting*. May I go out in a ball of fire rather than in a dusty, stuffy office. And this is a mission. I've trained for missions. I've been dying to go on a mission. But *nooooooo*. Of course I got kicked before I could go on any mission. Murphy's Law just loves to laugh at me. Stupid jerk Murphy.

But this—despite the circumstances of, you know, treason—has made me come alive again. Sure, the serum is still eating away at me and causes a constant ache, but at least there's some purpose in this. The paperwork I do here does not count as productive or held in high aspiration for life goals in any fashion.

Riding the elevator up to our floor, there's some excited chatter and I realize it's because Dylan has brought a big box of donuts today.

How exciting. At least if I get caught, I can grab a donut before I'm arrested.

Oh, but there are *cream-filled* ones. Wow! It's like Christmas or something.

Maybe being arrested wouldn't be so bad. At least I wouldn't be here anymore.

As soon as the elevator dings and the doors open, I escape the confection-adoring public and hurry to my cubicle—but not too fast. I don't want to draw attention. When I round the stacks to my desk—surprise, surprise—Doug is already here.

"So, how early exactly do you come into work?" I ask as I sling my jacket onto the back of my chair. When Doug doesn't respond, as usual, I start carrying on the conversation by myself but using a very deep and nuanced voice to convey Doug's side of the conversation. *"The papers aren't going to correct themselves!"* I step to the side to portray myself. "Doug, the papers don't care if they're typo free or not. You're stripping them of their individuality too early in the morning." I step to the other side with my head scrunched into my shoulders and voice changed. *"But I love the feel of carpal tunnel in the morning! Don't you?"* I step back into my own role. "And I love eating fried chicken dipped in chocolate. Doesn't mean it's good for me."

I mime playing drums and say, "Ba-dum, tsss!" before spreading my arms wide with a smile. Doug blinks slowly and returns to making scratch marks on a document. I glower at him.

"The centaurs called. They want their sense of humor back," I grumble and take a seat.

One thing I've discovered about Doug is that the more

outgoing I tend to get, the less he cares to pay attention. Meaning, he's not even going to look my way for the next fifteen minutes which is exactly what I want. While he's occupied with typos, I log into Jefferson's account. In the search function, I type "Erebus." The search comes back with a single record and my heart beats a little faster as I click it.

And am promptly denied access.

This account does not have the proper clearance to access this record.

Well, crap. I keep up my bored poker face as I think this over. The fact that a record was found at least proves there *is* a record of some kind. There's a trail in the system that leads to him. I just have to be able to get to it—which means I need higher level credentials. *That* is going to be a problem. Like Witty said, we can't hack our way in. We have to be clever. More accurately, *I* have to be clever. I quickly log out of Jefferson's account and into my own before Doug decides to look up again. Not that he can see my screen but . . . still.

I type random words into the document processor as I form a new plan. Who would have high enough clearance to access the record for Erebus? I doubt most of the people here have anything higher than my own, let alone Jefferson's, but there are two possibilities. Milton and Knox. The latter I would rather avoid at any cost because not only is he my mentor but a Spartan commander. Milton on the other hand . . . wringing credentials out of him could actually be a pleasure.

Speak of the devil—

"Hawk, good morning." Milton shuffles into our little space with a cup of coffee in hand. "Doug, good morning."

"Good morning," Doug replies. It's the only time he ever speaks. I roll my eyes.

"And how are we today? Ready to make the paper world a better place?" he says and swings his arm with gusto, almost spilling his coffee.

How can *anyone* be so enthusiastic about this job?

"Today is swell," I say with a falsely cheery tone.

"Good, because I've got about twenty papers I need you to clean up by the end of the day. I've e-mailed them to you. Chop chop."

He turns around and shuffles out the way he came. The second his back is turned, I mime giving him a good kick to the butt and turn to Doug with a wink. Doug promptly returns to paperwork. Pretending to do actual work, I open Milton's e-mail and find the list of documents to review along with links to the server where I'll find them. I print off the first and walk to the copier where I stand a bit longer than necessary to survey my surroundings.

Milton's office is at the far end of the floor. He has his own little enclosed space with tinted glass walls while the rest of us sit in our stuffy cubicles. He's currently making the rounds with the employees as if he actually cares about them but we all know he only cares about the bottom line. I stand with my hot-from-the-press papers and watch out of the corner of my eye as he goes into his office and sits at his desk. How am I going to get his credentials? Milton is very by the book when it comes to security and safety and blah, blah, blah. There's no way he's going to just tell me what his login information is, but I can't think of a way to spy it either. His computer monitor faces the window, he actually covers his hands when he types in his password, and he'd see me a mile away. In fact, his head comes up to pin me at the printer. Instead of ducking in an obvious move that I was watching him, I give him a thumbs up with a wink while holding up the paper to show I got his e-mail. He gives me a thumbs up in return. What an idiot.

Despite how much I would enjoy choking it out of him—I have a very clear mental image of strangling him with his mouse cord—that would obviously draw too much attention. This needs to happen under the radar, so to speak. The less anyone else knows the better. Besides the fact that I really don't want to be arrested, it'd be safer for everyone involved including Genna and Witty. So, now the question becomes, what do I do?

Heck, I don't even know if Milton has the proper clearance to access the file I need. I can't exactly go around asking about it either. It'd be a little suspicious saying, oh by the way, who can access high security level files? I'm asking for a friend. Then again, in the right environment with the right variables, some people will spill anything if given the chance. I lean sideways against the printer as I calculate my objective against the assets at hand. Alcohol is always a tongue loosener, but I doubt even that tactic would open Milton up. No, it needs to be someone who knows a lot of gossip, is a keeper of secrets as it were, and feels compelled to share such juicy information when plied.

Ah. Of course. Vicky.

From what I've gathered during water cooler talk and

eavesdropping, Vicky has been here longer than anyone and is relied on heavily by Milton. She's his go to person and has her paws in everything. If anyone could tell me Milton's clearance apart from Milton himself, I'd say it's her. It's a good place to start at any rate.

Objective number one: confirm Milton has the clearance I need.

Plan of attack: persuade Vicky to give me the information on Milton.

Obstacles: well, Vicky's kind of a stuck-up jerk with the laugh of a hyena and I think I made things awkward when I brought her dinner the other day as my excuse to come up here. Oh, geez. This is going to be just super.

Well, I guess here goes nothing.

I go back to my desk but keep my eyes and ears open. Needless to say, I don't get a lot of paperwork done—so, nothing unusual there. As the lunch hour draws near, I make multiple trips out to the copier for random things I've printed just to see where Vicky is. She'll be heading out for her lunch soon and that'll be my golden opportunity. When she starts glancing at the clock I know it's about time. I hurry to the bathroom and make some quick adjustments—finger-comb my hair, pop a breath mint, and straighten my outfit. One last check in the mirror—oh yeah, I've got this—and I walk calmly to the elevator just as Vicky gets there.

She spots me and ducks her head. Oh, boy.

"Hi, Vicky." When she glances up I give her my tried and true, award-winning smile. Her cheeks go red.

"Oh, hi."

She's pretty but always holds herself stiffly and makes

faces at people sometimes so she's off-putting. She makes a little grimace even now. Yikes. The elevator doors open and we both step inside.

"Which floor?" I ask politely and stand next to the buttons so she has to tell me and can't ignore me to press one herself.

"First floor."

I hit the button. "Right. Lunch time."

"Yup."

As we start to move down, I stick my hands in my pockets, lean against the doors, and cross one foot over the other.

"Look, I wanted to apologize about the other day," I start off. She keeps her lips rolled in and gives me a doe-eyed stare. "When I brought you food, I mean. I hope I wasn't too forward—and I was a little rude at the time. I didn't mean to make things awkward."

"No, it was a sweet gesture," she says quietly. "Thank you."

I turn up the smile. "You're welcome."

The silence settles a little and she shifts on her feet before she says. "They were really good eggs."

"Good. I'm glad. They were from a local cafe I like to visit. The Montrells. You heard of it?"

"It sort of rings a bell."

"Well, if you're free tonight I could introduce you to their amazing pies."

Her cheeks turn a darker shade of red. "I—I really have work I ought to do . . ."

I lean in an inch but she doesn't shrink back. "You're such a hard worker I'm amazed the rest of us even have work to do. You've earned a break. One night. I'll buy. You won't regret it. A woman like you deserves to be treated now and again."

She finally unrolls her lips and gives me a shy smile. Bingo.

"Just one night," she says.

"Whatever the lady wants."

She narrows her eyes slightly. "Are you flirting with me, Hawk?"

"No, no, of course not." I step away from the doors as the elevator slows to a stop and give her a sideways look. "But if I was, is it working?"

Vicky laughs—like a baby hyena. "I'll meet you outside the doors here at seven?"

"Sounds like a plan."

She steps off and when I don't follow, she turns back around confused. "Weren't you getting off?"

"No. Just needed to stretch my legs a little." I wink and the doors close.

The second I'm alone, I do a victory jab into the air. Ha! They really should have made me a specialist—of smooth talking. I laugh to myself and am still laughing by the time the doors open again at the office floor. A group of people are waiting to leave for lunch and give me odd looks. I do a double point with a wink and a click before walking off with a bounce in my step. Now, if Vicky gossips with her friends, they'll be able to tell her how excited I was after she accepted my date proposal.

Oh, wow. A date. How old is Vicky again? Is this weird? How did I not think of that earlier? Well, too late to care about that now. The plan is in motion, and if all goes accordingly, Vicky is going to tell me exactly what I want to hear tonight.

After another slow day of work, I do my usual routine with the gym but skip the cafe in order to prepare myself for the evening. I put on my sharpest outfit along with a new leather jacket—my old one turned into a pile of ash when the cabin in Moose Lake blew up. It's a shame, really. That other one was my good luck charm. This new one that Phoenix got me for Christmas is nearly identical though. I do one last check in the mirror, test my smile at my reflection, and head back to the office.

Vicky's waiting for me outside already. Dang. I wanted to beat her here but I guess she was more enthusiastic about this than I thought. She's dressed herself up and shed her usual gray suit attire for a flattering red dress. Geez. Maybe I played my part too well. I'm actually starting to feel a bit guilty about this.

"Hey, Vicky," I say and jog a few steps to reach her. "You look great."

"You too. You clean up nice for a wolf."

And that guilt instantly disappears. It's a true test of my skill to keep my smile from completely faltering. It wavers ever so slightly but I duck my head to the side to cast it more as embarrassment, as if she's caught me. When I meet her eyes again she doesn't seem fazed in the least. I let it slide . . . for now. The comment sparks something inside me as if there's a sudden itch I need to scratch or it's going to drive me mad.

Happy thoughts, Hawk. Make that smile genuine. Eggs

and bacon and ham at the diner. Mmmmm. Yup. Those are happy thoughts.

"Shall we?" I ask and gesture politely towards the sidewalk.

She nods and we walk step in step into the city. We swap small talk on the way there—how are you enjoying Seattle? How's work been? Have you visited the Space Needle yet? Taken a boat ride out in the harbor? Any plans for the weekend? Vicky's very good at filling any dead air—or taking any air there is—to talk and talk and talk. I let her. This is exactly what I want. Now that she's away from work, she's even chattier. In fact, she's in the middle of gossiping about her new neighbors when we finally reach the diner.

I hold the door open for her.

"What a gentleman!" she says full of surprise. Why is it surprising? Probably better if I don't linger over that one as the itch inside grows a little stronger.

"And where would the lady like to sit?" I ask instead.

"Oh, uh . . ."

"I would recommend the booth right over there." I point it out for her, leaning in a little closer than necessary. "Has a great view."

Her cheeks go bright red again. "Sure."

This is almost too easy.

We take our seats across from each other and moments later Daisy appears with a waist apron and pad of paper. She studies me briefly as if reassessing what kind of man I am to have now been seen with two different women in this cafe as well as flirting with her. I suppose I should have brought Vicky somewhere else but this place is a known entity. It's nice to have a little comfort when diving into a sticky situation.

"What can I get for you?" Daisy asks.

I order my usual and Vicky takes her sweet time making a deal about what to get. The longer Daisy remains at our table side, the more irritable she seems to become. She at last heads back to the kitchens, brings out our drinks, and then it's just me and Vicky again.

"So . . ." she says and spins the straw of her drink round and round in her glass. "This is nice. It's a different change of pace for me."

"Well, you can't be working all the time."

She shrugs. "You could probably stand to work a little more."

My eyebrows shoot up. "Oh, ho ho, what's this now? You don't approve of my work ethic?"

She laughs and the sound could make a baby cry.

"There is no work ethic with you," she teases.

"What can I say? I'm just not made for office life. I get it's important and there are people that really excel at it." I make sure she picks up the compliment. I may hate my work but it's clear Vicky doesn't. I wouldn't be making a good impression if I just started complaining about work and degrading her own position. "I just don't think I'm built that way. I miss being out in the field. I feel that's where I can do the most good."

She bobs her head to the side. It's clear that's not her dream job.

"There are some great stories I could tell you," I say and position myself to start talking about what I really want to. "My sister and I were involved in—oh, wait. Sorry."

"What is it?"

I do my best at an embarrassed smile. "I can't tell you that one. I don't think you have the right clearance."

"You're such a tease," she says and gives me a smile that turns my gut a bit.

I lay the bait. "It's true though. In fact . . . I don't think I can tell anyone that story at the office. Except maybe Spartan Knox. I don't think I could even tell Milton."

"That's true."

Come on. Say something more. Stick up for Milton who you seem to like so much. But she doesn't. Dang. I guess that one was too easy.

"Well, I have a story for *you*," she says.

"Oh, by all means." I gesture for her to continue and prop my chin on top of my interlaced fingers. Our food arrives just then—delivered by a somewhat stiff Daisy—but Vicky is gobbling up the attention I'm giving her.

"I probably shouldn't say anything myself," she says in a low conspiratorial tone over our plates of ham and pancakes.

"You can't leave me hanging now," I say in a perfect mimic of her tone.

She glances around the diner as if everyone is listening in to our conversation. "I heard something's been going on in France. They've restricted access to other IMS authorities and even booted some emissary officials out of the country."

My face draws into a frown. "How come?"

"No one's sure, but from what my source tells me, their Spartans have been posted on high alert and recalled from outlying missions."

What's going on over there? Let's just add this to the list shall we? But I certainly haven't heard anything about this.

If France is keeping a tight lid on this and the rest of the IMS is trying to hush it up to keep the situation under control, whoever Vicky got this information from might have the clearance I need. Maybe we're steering in the right direction after all.

"Who's this source of yours?" I ask blatantly, but she's given me a good cover for being curious.

She shrugs dramatically and cuts her pancakes into fourths. "A reliable one."

"Hmm." I cut into my ham with lips pursed. "You aren't just pulling my leg, are you?"

"Of course not," she says sharply.

"Okay, does this source of yours know anything else?"

"Probably, but he only told me about France because it might affect our work."

That has to be Milton. He's the only person apart from Vicky that actually cares about what we do in that office building. It's not concrete evidence—not by a long shot, really—but it's about as close as I'm going to get without tripping any wires. I'm relatively pleased with my progress. Vicky spilled more than I thought she would to be honest.

Then she keeps talking.

"I mean, our work has already been affected by the whole—" She throws one hand out to gesture at me. "—werewolf problem."

A nerve snaps laced with the bitterness built up in me by the serum. I'm generally good at keeping a lid on it or acting like it doesn't exist but I've discovered that the right trigger sends that pixie shooting out of the bag like a firework. I slam my knife and fork so hard on the table that the whole thing rocks and the silverware jumps up an inch before falling noisily back down.

"If you're so disgusted by us, why did you agree to come here, you blasted hypocrite?" I snap.

Vicky stares.

It's an effort to rein in my snarling grimace so I duck my head and run a hand down my face to smooth my features into complacency. When I look back up, Vicky is leaning as far away from me as she can in the booth.

"Sorry," I say as lightly as I can. "It's . . . I'm sorry, that was rude of me."

She tucks her hands into her lap and averts her eyes. "I thought you were cute," she says quietly. "I guess appearances can be deceiving."

And she promptly gets up and walks out of the diner. I sit frozen in my seat and close my eyes. Well played, Hawk. Real smooth. I open my eyes to find Daisy standing nearby staring at me along with other patrons. I run a hand through my hair, throw some cash on the table, and make a hasty exit.

My feet carry me swiftly away from the diner and down the sidewalk while I clench and unclench my fists. I feel a growl working its way up my throat and claws trying to poke out through my fingernails. The beast inside me is restless and trying to break free. The stupid serum isn't helping one bit. In fact, it almost feels like it's making everything worse. Phoenix's pendant burns hot against my sternum in response. It's almost like my sister's hand on my shoulder telling me to cool it.

Thinking of my sister hits a different sort of trigger and I want to howl at the twilight skies, but instead I end up heaving a shaky breath and fight back tears. I miss my family like a deepening ache in my chest that grows and grows the more I think about it. I stumble around the corner of a business into an alleyway and brace my hands against the wall as I work myself out.

This isn't me. This isn't remotely like me. As I think through the despair and rage waring in my head, I do my best to focus on the pendant hanging around my neck. Eventually the oddly sharp emotions ebb away and I can think clearly again. I remain there with both hands planted against the brick wall and my head hanging low between my arms as I sort out what just happened. A shadow of fear looms over me as I consider myself—and make the comparison to Jason. Phoenix only saw a little of his condition but I was much more privy to Jason's slow sink into insanity brought on by the serum. He'd have sporadic fits of rage, of weeping, of lifeless depression that only got worse over time.

Am I heading down that path already?

No, Hawk. Pull it together, man. You're overthinking this. You just got upset and you have a lot of pent up stress. Anyone would go crazy being stuck in that office all day and then dealing with prejudices from everyone. That's it.

My self-assurances help and I return to the sidewalk to head deeper into the city. I loop back over the route I've already walked to make sure I'm not being followed before making for the video arcade. The manager stares at me when I enter and walk to a big, boxy arcade game in the middle of the building. A sign above it proclaims itself SUPER KART SMASH. I pause for a moment as I recall

Witty's secret code before entering a quarter into the game. Okay . . . red button three times, blue once, white three, blue twice, joystick tapped up twice and . . .

Message away displays briefly on the screen before vanishing.

And now I wait. I stay at that game for a little bit pretending to play but really just crashing the kart over and over again until I wander aimlessly around plugging quarters into random games to pass the time. The clock on the wall ticks out ten minutes, fifteen minutes, twenty minutes until the manager creeps over and hands me a ticket.

"Try the laser tag zone. I think you'll find it very fun," he says in a monotone then shuffles away again.

I guess that's my cue. Where did they get that bag of bones anyway?

Through the black curtains at the back, I find Witty waiting for me alone.

"Just you?" I ask.

He nods and fidgets with a set of car keys in his hands. "It's safer if it's just one of us at a time. Plus Rosalyn is busy gathering information and Genna—well, she's reporting to Dasc right now."

My heart thunders in my chest. "Oh. I see."

"It's okay," Witty says but he doesn't sound or look convincing that it's not a big deal. He's twitchier than usual. "She has to keep updating him or he might decide to come here. He might decide to do that anyway . . ."

Witty stares off with wide eyes as if imagining the terror that would bring. I can't say I blame him. I want Dasc to remain as far away from me as possible. When he controlled me that one night in Moose Lake and almost made me attack Phoenix—I shudder and push the thought from my mind.

"So," Witty prompts. "Why'd you send the message? Did you find something already?"

"No, unfortunately. I hit a bit of a roadblock and I could use some help getting around it." I shove my hands into my pockets and roll back my shoulders. "I think I know someone's clearance I can use but getting it is the problem."

"Well, we can't hack in," he says and he narrows his eyes at something invisible in the distance, eyes going back and forth as if reading his thoughts on a piece of paper. "Maybe if we . . . well, no—but maybe . . . I guess that could work . . ."

"Earth to Witty," I say. "What are we talking about?"

"Oh, sorry. Follow me." He waves me deeper into the maze of black curtains and spray painted walls until we reach a little cubby crammed full of computer equipment.

I inspect the four monitors, venting overhead, wires draped in meticulous fashion, and a series of multiple keyboards. "I didn't realize you brought your whole apartment with you when you left," I comment.

"Perk of the job," he says off-hand then gasps and goes wide-eyed. "I mean—it's not a perk. Or a job. It's equipment for spying. Not that I'm spying on you. I mean—"

"You can relax. Just tell me what you're doing."

Witty clears his throat and takes a seat before his setup. "I was just thinking—if you can't hack in or steal the login information, maybe you can access a computer where someone is already logged in."

"And how, exactly, am I supposed to do that without

them noticing? Personnel always log off when they leave their computer."

"Normally, yes, *unless* they are diverted elsewhere temporarily and *think* that they've logged off." He starts typing rapidly. "I think I can put together some code that won't tamper with the IMS system at all but the computer itself."

"Okay . . . I think I follow. Sort of."

"Let me work something out. Go ahead and grab a seat. This will be a little bit."

I pull over a stool I hadn't noticed before and sit beside Witty as he brings up complicated lines of code and starts making modifications that I can't even begin to understand. As he works, I bounce my toes on the ground and spin slowly back and forth on the swivel top of the stool.

"She was worried about you, you know," Witty says quietly without pausing his work. "Genna, I mean."

I don't know what to make of that precisely. "I'm flattered."

"No, really." He stops to look at me fully. "After she heard about the mandatory probation rings and serum, I've never seen her so angry. She was beside herself, wanted to pull you out immediately."

I guess I really am flattered then, and yet at the same time feel like I'm being babied. She doesn't think I can handle myself.

"So why didn't she?" I ask. "If she was so concerned about my well-being."

"Because she knows the lives of the many outweigh the lives of the few . . . or the one. Her words. Said she knows that personally."

Witty turns back to his computers and I'm left to ponder that in brooding silence. If what Genna says is true about returning to Dasc in order to save the rest of the werewolves, then she's sacrificing her own happiness—leaving behind her father and returning to the man that enslaved her and killed her mother—to free the rest. I lean back and cross my arms. She had called me selfish before. Phoenix and I have been hiding ourselves for a long time. Now, in light of what she's going through, I guess I can see her point. We have been selfish.

"And just a few more tweaks . . ." Witty says under his breath as he types furiously away.

"Until what?" a loud, unfamiliar voice booms behind us.

The next second I'm out of my chair with fists up ready for a fight. Though expecting an attacker, the man I face makes me pause and blink in surprise. He's an old geezer with gray hair and a beard so long it trails past his belt. His squinty eyes are framed with wrinkles and although a bit bowed, he plants his hands on his hips as if about to scold me. Then my eyes settle on the robe he's wearing—as in "hello from the medieval ages" robe of dark blue.

"Well," he says loudly and throws up his hands. "Until what, Wallowitz?"

I note the British accent. What the heck? Who is this guy?

"Oh, I—yes, sir." Witty clears his throat and straightens his shirt. I lower my fists only slightly. "Just putting together some code to help out Hawk here." He gestures to me as an afterthought with both hands and a slight bend in the knees. "I—I didn't realize you were coming. I thought Genna asked you to stay at the compound."

"Bah!" the old man says and waves a hand at us before inspecting the computer screens. "I like to know what's going on."

"Witty," I say out of the corner of my mouth. "Who is this guy?"

The stranger turns about and looks down his long nose at me. "*I*, young lad, am Merlin." He spins on the spot so his robe swishes around him and he raises his hands when he comes about to face me again. Blue and white sparks fly up in twisting symmetrical patterns to frame him and set the dark space alight. The old man—Merlin—looks rather pleased with himself at his spectacular introduction.

"Merlin the magnificent."

12

Phoenix

In the first few minutes after my abilities are revealed, I consider running. But I don't. It'd be useless anyway. Charlie's here for one and could teleport after me. I could try to stop him but I don't want to do that. He's my friend. He deserves an explanation after everything we've been through together.

The team is quiet as we focus first on checking on the other team, assessing the damage, and making sure both the hydra and chimera are dead before calling in the cleanup crews. My attention is split between what's going on around me and what on earth I'm going to tell the others.

I can only imagine what Scholar would say if she was around. I blew it big time. I was careless but what else was I supposed to do? Let Charlie take acid to the face? Just fall and impale myself on a tree? Besides, John already knows I'm unique. He just didn't know *how* unique. Considering what we've been facing, it'd take a miracle for me to get through each day without using my special abilities.

The last of the light wanes and night falls around us as the cleanup crew finally arrives. We guard them as they load up the dead bodies of the monsters into the Osprey then make sure to get rid of any other supernatural evidence in the area. It's well past midnight by the time we trek back to our van left on the side of the road. The drive to the airfield is tense to say the least but no one asks me anything until we make it to the safety of our own aircraft and Alona closes the ramp so we're in complete isolation. I can't help but feel trapped. My palms turn sweaty. Maybe I should have run after all.

Then it's just me and my team. Alona leans against the entrance to the cockpit, Theo and Melody take seats, but John and Charlie remain standing, Charlie with his arms crossed and John with a hand gripped on a line above his head. My eyes automatically flick to the switch on the hull to lower the ramp behind me. When I look back, Charlie's eyes have narrowed as if daring me to try it with him there.

"So, Red," Theo says loudly to break the silence. "That was unexpected. You're not actually a dragon, are you?"

I roll my lips and shake my head.

"Dang. That would've been really cool."

No one laughs.

"I thought we agreed no secrets," Charlie says coldly. "At the very start, that's what we promised. Everything out on the table, including all of our abilities. What was that back there, Phoenix? And why hide it?"

Behind the questions I hear the hurt. I lied to him. He trusted me but I didn't trust him enough to share this secret.

"You don't understand," I say quietly.

"You're damn right I don't," he growls. "So, please. Enlighten us."

Where do I even start? What do I reveal? I catch Alona's eye but she doesn't give me any indication what to do despite being Scholar's confidant and knowing more than any of the others. Although, this morning she told me to protect my secrets.

But secrets could have gotten Charlie killed today—could have gotten me killed too.

"You can trust us," John says gently.

Trust. That's the problem, isn't it? How many times has my trust been broken? First Dasc masqueraded as my teacher, then Genna was my friend, and Hawk told me everything was under control. How many times have I trusted someone only for that trust to be used against me? My cheeks grow hot and I stare at the metal flooring with my arms crossed. It was never supposed to come to this.

"*Can* I trust you?" I mutter.

Charlie is suddenly before me and waits until I look up before he says, "I asked if you trusted me earlier tonight and you said yes. Or was that a lie?"

I glare at him but he holds my angry gaze.

"*Fine*," I snap.

"Fine." Then he takes a step to the side so I'm open to explain to all of them. I don't fail to notice him keeping by my side, though, and also subtly shift closer to the ramp switch at the same time.

"I've never told anyone," I say at last. "Well, just about."

"Hawk knows," Charlie says for me.

I nod. "And Jefferson figured it out—my old mentor," I say for the benefit of the others, in case they don't remember him from when they rescued us in Moose Lake. And then there's also Scholar, but that's not my secret to tell.

I find my eyes starting to water even though I don't know why. I don't cry. I rarely cry. But there's something intensely personal about revealing what comes next.

"It started when I was four years old. My parents had just been murdered by a werewolf..."

For the next half hour, maybe more, I tell them about Hawk and me running away as kids, my power coming into its own, discovering the reality of what I was after returning to Moose Lake and meeting Jefferson, the warnings given to me about revealing my capabilities, receiving training from "a source I'm not going to talk about," realizing my abilities affected more than werewolves, learning how to detect magic, and still discovering new ways to control my own magic and those around me.

When my tale comes to an end, there's a long moment of silence and my eyes once again go for that ramp switch. I wait for them to be aghast at what I've said, to tell me off for not revealing what I could do earlier, to arrest me even.

But none of them do.

Their silence bores into me so I say, "I know I should probably go to the IMS and let them take my blood, try to make a cure for the werewolves or whatever, but I can't. Not yet. I can't go until I know for certain that I can cure the werewolves—that I can cure my brother."

Melody's the first to speak. "You probably won't reach the pinnacle of your powers for another couple of years or so. Life experience and self-awareness do more to boost magical abilities than sitting isolated somewhere."

The others nod and a spark of hope flares in my chest.

"Well, I guess that settles it," Theo says and claps a hand to his knee. "There's no point setting the authorities on you until you can really juice up."

Alona marches over to him and slaps him upside the head.

"*Really?*" Theo exclaims and massages his scalp.

That spark of hope expands into a kindling fire. Are they *supporting* me on this? They aren't going to turn me over to Draco?

"Melody and Theo are right," John says, soft-spoken as always. "But it *is* your plan to hand yourself over once you get to that point, isn't it?"

I swallow. It's never been put in so little words to me before and so bluntly. But that is the trade off, isn't it? Spend the next few years living my life before . . .

"Yes," I say quietly. "For my brother, I will."

"Then I'm inclined to let your performance tonight remain a secret for now."

I loose a breath and turn to Charlie who still hasn't said a word.

"And you?" I ask.

Those green eyes rake my face over and over again as if trying to peel away the layers to see the magic and intentions underneath.

"Why are you so afraid?" he asks.

"I told you—"

"You said you were warned, but warned about what exactly? If you can't make a cure yet, then why are you so afraid of anyone finding out? I can understand Dasc not wanting a cure but we're talking about hiding it from the IMS."

His gaze is steel and I realize he isn't going to let this go. What more can I say?

"Not all of my secrets are mine to share," I say.

"That's not good enough."

"*Charlie.*" It's Alona, her voice cutting across him. "You realize what she can do puts her in danger, right? Do you think dragons would like the idea of someone being able to manipulate their magic? Threaten their power? The fewer people that know, the less danger she's in."

"She's a *Spartan*," he argues, gesturing widely to me. "She's in about as much danger as you can get on a daily basis."

His continuing argument is really dampening my spirits. For a brief moment I thought everyone on the team was onboard with protecting my secret and understanding my reasons. But not Charlie. Not the one person I thought would out of everyone. My eyes remain downcast as the sting goes deep. I trust him but apparently he doesn't reciprocate the feeling.

"Are you going to report this to the IMS?" I ask without looking at him.

His brooding silence unnerves me but eventually he says, "Not at the moment."

Well, that's *something*, I guess.

"Regardless of what your opinion is," John says, "we protect our own. If Phoenix could be targeted for this, then I'm going to respect her wishes and keep this low-key for the time being."

John nods to me. With his vocal support, the others nod as well. They'll have my back.

"Thank you," I say, unable to express my gratitude enough.

"But now that we know about this, we aren't going to ignore it either," he continues. "What you can do will benefit us in finding and killing these hydra. I have a feeling this is only the beginning."

"You can count on me."

"Good. Now then—"

The radio in the cockpit comes alive. "Sierra, come in. This is Camp Ripley tower, over."

Alona slides up front and gets on the horn. "We hear you, over."

"Sierra, you have orders from Director Knox to report back to base to wait on standby. Teams Romeo and X-ray will be coming in to replace you and Tango, ETA ten minutes."

"Roger that, tower. Sierra is oscar mike in ten." Alona slips back into the bay.

"Back to the base, huh?" Theo says. "Thought we'd be out here snooping for more hydra."

Melody pats him on the back when he looks disappointed. "We'll be in the thick of it again soon enough. Those were some great shots you took, by the way."

"I appreciate that, your majesty."

For the next ten minutes we wait. Charlie keeps his eyes

on me as if I might still run. Before long we hear from the replacement teams that they've made it. John passes the lead and Alona takes us up. I sit in my usual spot and my eyelids grow heavy. I'm exhausted. But my team supports me. They're going to keep my secret.

And then there's Charlie who's still making up his mind.

It's in the early morning hours by the time we land again. An officer greets us and confirms we're on standby until new orders come in so we stow our gear, prep the equipment for our next takeoff, then immediately head for the barracks to catch some shut eye. I remain in my gear but undo some of the straps to make sleep a little more comfortable. When my head hits the pillow, I doze off immediately.

It would have been wonderful to get some actual sleep but I guess that's not for me to decide. I sense movement nearby and when I open my eyes, I find Charlie snatching up my hand. We vanish a moment later, then again and again until we're well away from the barracks and on the outskirts of the camp. Adrenaline has my heart pumping fast and I'm fully awake again in no time.

Once we stop moving through space and time, I shove Charlie off of me.

"You said you'd never do that without asking first," I growl. "Why on earth did you bring me out here?"

He comes in close—like, *really* close. Almost touching noses close. I freeze.

"I need to know the whole truth," he whispers as if the very shadows could be listening. But who knows? Maybe they are.

"Charlie, I already told you that I'm not going to give up secrets that aren't mine."

He grips my arm, not painfully but enough to frighten me. "Who is it you don't trust in the IMS?"

"Does it matter?"

"It matters. I *need* to know."

I study him as he studies me, his eyes catching the flood lights shining from the doors of the mess hall. Something feels off about this.

"Is there something you aren't telling me?" I ask.

"That would be so touché, wouldn't it?"

My eyebrows knit together. "Look, I've told you everything I can. If I say more, I could be putting someone else in danger."

His hand doesn't leave my arm. "I was there the night those vampires attacked, remember? We let that dragon go. Melody and the selkies wanted us to. Is that who you're protecting?" I blink. He put that together? "And why? Who in the IMS wants that dragon? I looked through the records ages ago. There are no search warrants outstanding for any dragons in the area. If there's nothing official, but you still think the IMS is a danger, then there has to be something underhanded, am I right?"

Too much. He's worked out far too much.

"Charlie . . ."

"And on another note, if you're so sure there's something shady going on in the IMS, why stick around? Why join the Spartans?"

"Look, the less you know the better, okay? I'm trying to protect you."

"And maybe I'm trying to protect you!" he says sharply. He glances behind us as if someone might have overheard and then drags me deeper into the darkness. "Just give me a name. You don't have to tell me why. I'm only asking for a name."

I can hardly make out his face anymore in the shadows of the gun range.

Just a name. I can do that.

"Draco," I whisper.

He exhales sharply and lets loose a choice swear.

His fingers fall away from my arm and he begins to pace back and forth.

"I know," I say. "Head of the IMS? Majestic class dragon? Not who I would want labeled as a shady character either."

"No, that's not—*crap*."

"Charlie?"

He stops and grabs me by the shoulders. "Do you remember that day during the trials when we were here? And I went off with Draco for a bit?"

My heartbeat quickens. I don't like where this is heading. "Yes..."

He exhales sharply a second time. "Phoenix, I didn't know."

"What are you saying?"

"Draco asked me if I'd noticed anything unusual about you. I said you're strong and that's it. And then he told me... he told me to keep an eye on you. He said that you might be caught up in something unwittingly, and if you ever did something out of the ordinary, that I should report it."

I shrug out from his hands and take a step back. "Tell me you didn't."

Charlie. *Charlie* is Draco's undercover source? I had been worried that clever dragon might be following me somehow in order to track Scholar through me. But this...

205

"He's the founder of the IMS. I had no reason not to trust him. And if you were in something deep—"

"So you've been spying on me?"

"Not exactly."

I take another step away to distance myself from him. "That is *exactly* what you just said! I thought you were my friend, Charlie. After all the crap we've gone through—"

"I was trying to protect you!" he shouts, no longer caring about the sentries and guards roaming the grounds.

"Wait a second." I hold up a finger as it clicks into place. "That's why we were assigned to the same Spartan team, wasn't it? Draco pulled strings so you could keep tabs on me."

"Phoenix—"

"*Why couldn't you just ask me?*" I shout. "Flaming hydra crap, Charlie! Don't you think I've had enough friends stab me in the back?"

"Don't you think I wanted to ask you?" He throws up his hands and we're right in each other's faces. "I had orders not to! You of all people should understand *perfectly*."

It's a punch to the gut. Of course he has to mention *that* painful memory—when I was ordered to shadow Genna and it nearly ruined my relationship with Jefferson forever. And in my surge of anger of it being brought up, I slap him across the face. For a second I forget how strong I am, how angry I am, and gasp as Charlie stumbles so much that he has to brace a hand on the ground to keep from falling over. Both hands cover my mouth as I watch him stagger upright.

"Charlie," I murmur. "I'm sorry, I—"

He holds a hand to the side of his face with a grimace. "Whatever you think of me up there on your high horse," he says through gritted teeth, "I'll have you know that I never told Draco anything. And if I would have known that he posed a danger to you in the slightest, I would have told him to go to hell."

For a moment the world goes still and the last vestiges of anger bleed out of me. My face grows hot as I really consider what he's saying. He would have defied the orders of a majestic class dragon to protect me. By-the-books Charlie. For *me*. And I just viciously accused him of betraying me when he'd done nothing of the sort. My mouth awkwardly hangs open like a fish as I try to think of something to say but come up empty.

The darkness swallows him up as he vanishes. I swivel and hunt for him guided by that beacon of magic within him.

"Wait!" I run after him even as he teleports again. "Come back! Charlie—you—MOVIES ARE BETTER THAN BOOKS!"

Charlie whips about and appears directly in front of me so close that I jerk backwards and almost fall over.

"That's it!" he shouts. "That's the final straw—"

"Calm down, I only said that to get you to come back." I grab his arm before he can vanish on me again. "I'm sorry. I—I'm just sorry, okay?"

"For which part?" he grumbles. "Slapping me or accusing me of selling you out?"

"Both." I gently pull his hand away from the side of his face. There's a red handprint across his cheek. "So so sorry. Come on. Let's get you some ice for that."

"That's it?"

"You need some pain meds?"

"No, I mean—you're not angry anymore? Just like that?"

I only need to mull it over for a couple seconds before I nod. "I guess that . . . I trust you. And if you say you didn't tell Draco anything and were trying to protect me, then I believe you."

His face softens. I offer an apologetic smile, wishing I could offer something more substantial. I point towards the mess hall and he ports us to the door. The lights are on but there's only a couple of guards hanging around at this hour. I gesture to Charlie's face and they don't stop us as I lead the way into the kitchens. There's a freezer stuffed with an assortment of ice bags due to the number of injuries that crop up from the intense physical training around here. I grab a big blue one and pass it over. Charlie leans against a metal table behind him and lets out a relieved sigh as he presses the compress to his face.

I bit my lip and grimace at his pain. "I didn't mean to hit you so hard."

"Uh-huh. Berserker." His lips twitch upwards.

My grimace changes into a smirk. "Unicorn."

I shut the freezer and lean against it opposite him. It's quiet except for the hum of the refrigerators, the soft footsteps of the guards in the hall beyond, and our near silent breaths.

And if I would have known that he posed a danger to you in the slightest, I would have told him to go to hell.

I watch Charlie as he closes his eyes and shifts the compress against his cheek. I can still picture him tied up to that chair when the lamia held us hostage, how pale and death-like he became after having his blood drained. How even then he still managed to teleport me past a dragon's barrier to save my brother. How he kept me company at the hospital in Moose Lake when I felt so alone. How he stayed by my side even when everyone else was angry at me after discovering my secret orders to keep an eye on Genna.

"Draco's not the dragon we think he is," I say quietly. Charlie cracks open an eye. "He's done things in the past that almost no one knows about, but my . . . *friend* told me. He has a vendetta against Dasc and my friend for her unwitting role. As for me . . ." I sigh and cross my arms over my chest. "I've been a useful pawn to him as a way to find my friend. And if he found out what I'm capable of, that'd be it. I'd be shipped to a lab and would never see Hawk or my friends again. Bio-mech guns, the serum, and all that other 'dragon tech'—they come from people like me. People who disappear."

He lowers the compress and sets it down before bracing both hands on the tabletop behind him. "But you've stayed with the IMS."

"Even if the head is crooked, that doesn't mean the rest of the body is corrupt."

"How poetic," he mumbles.

"You saw what we did today. We took out a hydra and chimera. That's good work, Charlie. *We* do good work. I work for the people of the IMS, not Draco himself."

He nods slowly but keeps his eyes on me. "You're scared."

"Terrified," I whisper.

"But you'll turn yourself over anyway once you think you're powerful enough."

"Yes."

"And if you're never powerful enough?" he asks softly.

I stare at the worn tiles between our feet. "No matter what. Once I plateau, if there's even a chance..."

A chance that Hawk can finally be free of the monster that binds him, of the old hatreds that condemn him, of the prejudices that mar him... for that, I'd be willing.

"Does Hawk know that's your plan?"

I shrug. "Sort of. We both know that I'll try to be the cure, but how exactly that happens... not really, no."

I've tried not to linger on such thoughts to be honest. In the vague plans I've imagined for myself, I give a sample of my blood and a cure covers the world. But the cold, harsh reality is that I'll be contained somewhere, a supply too valuable to lose. Safe and secure but not free. That's what the rest of my life is leading up to. A black void. Just like where the werewolves go, never to be heard from again. It hurts then as the thought of it sinks its claws into my heart. No more movie nights with Hawk, no more pestering Charlie, no more flying in to save the day from rampaging monsters. Just needles and tubes and doctors and emptiness.

I swipe the back of my hand across my cheek, angry at the stray tears that fall to show my vulnerability.

I don't want to be alone.

"You are a rare individual, Phoenix Mason."

"Not really."

He rolls his eyes. "Could you just shut up and take the compliment?"

"Could you just shut up and give me a hug instead?"

He gives an exaggerated sigh and steps forward. I push off the freezer to meet him halfway and we wrap our arms around each other in a warm embrace. I tuck my face into his shoulder and squeeze my eyes shut.

"Thank you," I murmur into the fabric of his tactical gear.

His breath tickles the top of my head as he says, "It's a good thing, you know."

"What is?"

"That you made it to the mystical rainbow island of besties. Or this would never happen."

I snort and his body shakes with silent laughter. What a good thing indeed.

"I am curious though," he says. "If you can sense magic, what do you sense from me?"

I consider that for a moment as I feel his heartbeat pulse under his skin. "Bright, prestigious light."

"Prestigious, huh? Can light even be prestigious?"

"Oh, it's prestigious all right."

Footsteps storm into the kitchen and we hastily pull apart. Theo stands framed in the doorway, his mouth slowly turning into a ridiculous smile.

"What were youuuuuuu doing?"

Then John appears over his shoulder. "I hope you guys at least got a couple minutes of sleep because we've been called out."

"Where?" Charlie and I say in unison.

"Duluth. They tracked those eggs back to a bulk freighter called the *Tregurtha*."

"T-the *Tregurtha*?" Charlie sputters.

"Yeah. Why?"

"That's the biggest freighter on the Great Lakes. It's over a thousand feet long. If they managed to smuggle eggs over on that thing—"

Then we could be hunting for a *lot* more eggs.

13

Hawk

When Genna told me about a Magus helping them out, I guess I imagined a dark and brooding hero that could shoot lasers out of his eyes or something. Nothing could have prepared me for Merlin. Although he may look like a version of Merlin from the old Arthurian legends, he acts nothing like it.

"Do you have any gum?" he asks Witty and holds out a hand.

"Oh, I . . . no. No, I don't. Sorry."

"I do love gum, especially that peach mango stuff." Merlin eyes me up next. "What about you? Any gum?"

"Fresh out."

He snaps his fingers in disappointment. With a wave of his hand, the stool I had been using slides over to him and he takes a seat. I expect him to give some rapturous speech next or something. Instead, I watch as he pulls an iPod from inside his robes and starts scrolling through his music as if we're not even there.

"Er . . ." I glance to Witty but he just shrugs. "It's a pleasure to meet you."

"I should hope so indeed," Merlin says without looking up. "Did you know I missed the wedding of Prince William and Kate Middleton? A real shame. I hadn't missed a wedding of the royal family for four hundred years and then there goes my streak just like that." He snaps his fingers once again for emphasis. "Did you see it live?"

"No." I'm typically better at coming up with responses but this guy is throwing me for a loop. I clear my throat. "Unfortunately, I was otherwise detained." By sleep, I believe.

Merlin makes a sort of harrumph sound and nods. "As was I."

"Oh?"

He gives me a sharp look. "Of course I was."

Witty raises a hand to get our attention as if in class. "We haven't told him much about you yet, Merlin. Just that you're a Magus."

"And that you might be able to help cure the werewolves," I add.

"Hmm." The old man tucks away his iPod and gets to his feet. "That I might. The Y-S serum comes from me after all. And if this sister of yours is as powerful as I've been told, then perhaps together, and with a few of the others, we can be rid of the disease once and for all."

I blink and take a step back. "The serum . . . it comes from you?"

"Yes, so I imagine there will be a shortage of supply for

the werewolves rather soon since my absence from the IMS has been lengthening."

That's really not what I'm concerned about. It's more the fact that this man before me is the cause of the poison battling the other poison in my veins—the source of what's driving me mad. I consider him for a very long moment as he digs out his iPod again to shuffle through his music. I know that the powers of Blessed develop in correlation with their personality. Amanda Fry who's a bit of a hothead gained the ability to control fire. One of the girls during the trials could repel bugs because she hated them so much. Charlie can teleport—though I don't know what his deal is. And then there's Phoenix with the ability to—well, I can't put a definite cap on what she can do because her powers seem to keep growing. But she's strong and for some reason can tame werewolves and stop lamia. I guess she's always felt the need to protect me and that's where her powers stem from.

So what is it about this Merlin character that led to the serum and his other magical tricks? What's his motivation? And why do I react so adversely to it?

"So. Merlin." I begin and cross my arms over my chest. "You're over a thousand years old?"

"Yes, although I've rather lost count at this stage."

"Then are you the Merlin from the stories over in—"

Witty gestures frantically at me to stop talking. When Merlin glances up, Witty pretends to be rubbing his neck instead. While normally I would respect not talking about a topic that is clearly not intended to be talked about, I need to know who this Merlin person really is.

"You were saying?" Merlin says with a bit of a bite to his words.

"I can't help noticing your accent and name. If you're that old, are you the Merlin from the Arthurian legend?"

As soon as I say it, objects in the room start to float and move on their own as Merlin's eyes glow with literal sparks shooting out of his irises. Witty gives a squeak of fright as his computer setup begins to shake and hover as well until everything in the room is spinning around us. A chill crawls down my spine. Merlin raises his hands on either side and the objects pick up in their frantic dance around the room. Cables from the computer whip past and one catches me in the leg.

Witty scuttles over to me and grasps my arm. "Why did you do that?"

"I, uh . . ." Well, I'm starting to think it was a bad idea. I wanted to rile Merlin up a bit and get the truth out of him. I didn't think he'd start levitating everything in the room like some mad magician.

In fact, *I* start to levitate and Witty along with me. My feet leave the floor and I feel pressure form against my chest as if an invisible hand is clutching me.

A sharp, clear voice comes from the other side of the room. "Merlin! Starlight shines!"

Genna steps forward through the floating chairs and cords and computer monitors with a hand outstretched towards Merlin. The old man turns aggressively on her then freezes.

"Through darkened night comes moon divine," she continues.

Although her words seem like gibberish to me, it must mean something to Merlin because I gravitate back down until my feet touch the floor. The circling objects slow and settle into their previous positions until the room is as normal as it had been before. Genna strides forward completely unfazed and stands toe to toe with Merlin.

"What happened?" she asks.

His eyes dart to me and narrow. "He brought up some old wounds."

"He mentioned *back then*, didn't he?"

"This young fool certainly did."

"Merlin."

"What?"

She plants her hands on her waist like a parent addressing a naughty child and yet her words aren't demeaning. She ignores us as if he's the only person in the room.

"The past hurts," she says simply. "I thought you said you were okay, though."

He ducks his head. A mighty Magus cowed before Genna. "I am."

"Why did you leave the compound?"

"You know I don't like to stay in confined spaces for long."

She nods, being ever so patient with him. "I know. Neither do I. I thought you might have run to a concert or something but when I didn't find you, I came here."

Merlin perks up and his dower expression immediately changes into that of unabashed curiosity. "A concert? Is there one going on right now?"

"Some heavy metal festival."

"Maybe I should go check it out," he mutters to himself and turns away as if he's going to walk off right then and there.

"I thought you already decided you didn't like heavy metal."

He lifts his chin. "Art is subjective by the day."

"Uh-huh. Look, you shouldn't be away from the compound for long."

Witty and I continue to stand off to the side as we witness their interaction. It's an interesting relationship to be sure. Genna almost seems like a caretaker for this extremely powerful man who's also incredibly old. I feel the roles should be reversed and the old, wised wizard should be teaching the young woman. And I also pick up how he isn't dismissing her either. There's camaraderie here to be sure.

"I wanted to know what was going on," Merlin says and gestures to me in particular. "You keep telling me things but I like to see the world for myself, not secondhand through other people's eyes. You understand."

"I do."

"And?"

She cocks her head to the side, considering him. "Well, I'd say we should take a field trip to the compound but Hawk's tagged. They can track where he goes."

Merlin waddles over to me and picks up my hand with the probation ring. He wiggles his fingers over the metal, mutters something under this breath, and then gives Genna a big toothy grin.

"There! Now we can go."

She frowns. "What did you do?"

"I've befuddled the magic. It'll think it's still here while the lad is elsewhere. The magic has been . . . how shall I say it? Frozen, I suppose. A few hours of a stand-still reading should not be detectable. Now, shall we?" He sweeps his arm to the exit.

"Wait a second." A stroke of inspiration takes me. "If you can befuddle it, can you make it think I'm taking the serum even if I'm not?"

Merlin strokes his beard. "Lad, there's a difference between translocation adjustment, temporal looping, and bio-magical magnetism. I fear the matter is too complex to sufficiently fool."

"Sorry, what? I didn't get any of that."

"It can't be done."

My heart sinks. "Are you sure?"

"Very. Perhaps an adequate study encompassing three years would yield results, but not spur of the moment calculations."

I guess it was too much to hope for. But I least I have this other escape. "I'm good to leave without them knowing, though?"

He claps a wrinkly hand on my shoulder with surprising strength. "*Of course.* You can shift even and they wouldn't be the wiser. Like I said, the magic is frozen. I know what I'm doing. I'm Merlin! The magnificent."

Genna shakes her head. "If he says so, then I believe him. He keeps surprising me with the things he can do."

"That's because I'm magnificent," Merlin says.

"Well, what do you say, Hawk?" The three of them look to me.

I nod vigorously, excitement building in my bones. "Let's go. I want to know exactly what I'm helping with. And I wouldn't mind bailing on this city for a while."

Merlin's the first to hurry out of the dark laser tag zone. Genna and I follow next as Witty quickly checks his computer equipment for any damage. When we reach the main area of the arcade, I don't see Merlin anywhere. I pause for a moment when a teenager grabs me sharply by the arm out of nowhere.

"Boo!" he says loudly in my face.

His short black hair sticks up in all directions above his extremely animated face that's currently set to taunt me. He's dressed oddly with a red scarf and rawhide jacket that looks overly large on his gangly body.

"*Merlin*," Genna says sharply and pulls the teenager's hand off my arm.

Wait . . . Merlin?

The boy giggles and scampers away to the door.

My face must show my confusion because Genna says, "It's how he remains undetected. Don't ask me how he does it but he can change his appearance from young to old whenever he feels like. And also enjoys scaring people like that whenever he gets the chance."

"I wasn't scared."

She raises an eyebrow and moves for the door.

"Well, I wasn't," I call after her and jog to keep up.

Genna and Witty wait at the doors as Merlin strides carefree outside. Witty watches surveillance on a tablet that I realize is of the street outside and surrounding area. After a minute of watching the feeds, he nods.

"All clear," he announces.

"Let's go," Genna says. We walk calmly outside and around the corner to a car waiting for us. Merlin's already behind the wheel with a big smile on his face. He waves at us to hurry up and revs the engine.

I open the front passenger door but young Merlin immediately starts shooing me out.

"No, no, no!" he says angrily. "Genna sits there, then you sit on that side, and Wallowitz sits on that side."

"Okay..."

Genna slides up to me and says quietly in my ear, "He has a bit of OCD. Some things have to be a certain way. Just go with it."

She slips into the front passenger seat and I sit where I'm directed to behind her. Witty takes the spot behind Merlin. I grab my seat belt to latch it but find myself frozen and unable to move my body.

"What the—"

"Me first," Merlin says and clicks his belt. Then Genna does hers. They both look to me and I can finally move in order to latch my belt. I can't say I enjoy being robbed of movement. It's pretty freaky actually. Witty waits patiently for me before doing his last. "If you would dear," Merlin says to Genna. "Track one."

She hits a button on the dashboard and when the first note plays, Merlin pulls out in sync with the music. I sit in shocked silence as I realize what the music is.

I point hesitantly to the radio. "Is this..."

"*Spice Up Your Life*," Witty says with a solemn nod. "Spice Girls."

"Number eight please," Merlin requests and Genna

turns up the volume as directed until we have "Spice Up Your Life" blaring in our ears. I watch with horrified curiosity as Merlin sings along at the top of his lungs. He knows every word. Well, I guess I wasn't expecting this. The great and powerful Merlin is a major Spice Girls fan. He continues to sing loudly and slightly off key as we move through Seattle, transitioning to "Never Give Up on the Good Times"—as Witty informs me—and proceeding through the rest of the Spice Girls' hits. It's a sharp contrast to the context I find myself in. Upbeat, pop music as I ride with a bunch of fugitives on our way to a hidden werewolf compound.

Merlin drives almost erratically through the city, taking unnecessary turns and back tracking now and then. I keep looking this way and that out the windows trying to figure out if he's avoiding someone or what.

"The cameras," Witty informs me as we perform almost a zig-zag pattern at one point. "I figured out where they are so we can come and go undetected. Well, unless there's an agent that sees us." He glances out the window to check but appears satisfied and gives me a shy smile. "I created a program that tells me exactly where we can and can't go."

I just stare at him. "You were seriously underutilized in the IMS."

His eyes widen and I look away.

Some ugly truths are starting to become glaringly obvious to me. Phoenix and I have generally held the IMS on a pedestal as if they're a righteous agency defending mankind. But if that were true, why have I been in fear of them since I was a small child? And yet still wanted so desperately to become an agent and earn their admiration?

Then here's Witty, a boy who did everything asked of him and more for the agency, and his plethora of skills were severely discarded. He ran surveillance in the penitent cells and before that catalogued weapons in the armory. Now here he is having successfully outmaneuvered the whole of the IMS and Dasc himself for a year. Legs or no legs, he could have done this as easily from a wheelchair. More and more I'm glad that Witty found some bit of freedom, even at the cost of this mess. Maybe fighting the system is better than being crushed beneath it after all.

"Hawk?"

I snap my head up at Genna's voice. "Yeah?"

"I asked if you've heard anything about the area I wanted you to keep an eye on."

I clear my throat. "No, nothing yet. I don't know if I will even if there is news, to be honest. I doubt they'll let us werewolves know if they discover one of Dasc's camps nearby."

"Hmm."

"Reconsidering my usefulness?" I ask off-hand.

She turns around in her seat to face me. "Never."

"You're that confident in my abilities?"

"It's never been about how useful you are," she says and turns back around. "Only who you are."

I look to Witty but he shrugs.

We drive for what feels like hours. As we go, I carefully mark where we are and how we've gotten there. We move out of Seattle and the Olympic National Park looms before us. Merlin pulls over to the side of the road, and the three of them turn in their seats to look at me.

"Please tell me this isn't the part where you rob me and leave me on the side of the road," I say.

"I don't need to rob anyone," Merlin says casually. "I'm filthy rich."

Witty stares at him. "I thought you said all of your money is held in an account you can't access anymore."

"Even so, there's a lot of money in there. I'm filthy rich."

Genna ignores them and pulls out what looks suspiciously like a black hood. "It is, however, the moment that I'm going to ask you to put this on."

"Really? I thought you trusted me."

"I trust you, but I also know you have a rather tried and true vulnerability. If someone gave you the choice between saving your sister and keeping this location a secret, which one would you choose?"

The air grows heavy inside the car.

"And you?" I ask. "You still have Jefferson out there. They could do the same to you if they caught you."

"I'm willing to end my own life in order to protect this place," she says so matter-of-factly it makes me fear for her, because I believe her. She would do it. Genna extends the hood to me. "I don't want to place that burden on you too if I can help it."

I take the hood but don't immediately put it on. Every other encounter I've had with Genna, I've had each of my senses available to me. This is a true test. Do I trust Genna? After everything that she's done, *can* I trust her? At least enough to put on this hood? Perhaps. Genna's had ample opportunities to do away with me if she wanted.

But if she ended up handing me over to Dasc?

No. She wouldn't. Dasc would want his life debt intact with Phoenix. I'm sure it's of great value to him to have a Spartan—my sister—in debt to him. What that means for the future, I'd rather not think about.

I take a deep breath. "I better not end up in Chechnya with my liver cut out."

And tug the hood over my head.

"Why would we take you to Chechnya for that?" Genna asks. "We could do that right now."

"That's not funny."

She laughs anyway and the car is in motion once again. I'm sensitive to every jarring movement of the vehicle, every turn and straight stretch as I try to figure out where exactly I am and where we're heading. We keep driving long enough to make me nervous and only be able to retain a vague idea of where we are. After traveling at a slow pace for some time and heading up an incline, we finally stop.

"Stay put," Genna says.

Doors open and shut three times as the others get out and I'm left alone in the car. My fingers itch to pull off the hood and see where they've taken me. I'm extremely curious—and I've also got a pit in my stomach that keeps telling me I'm a big idiot for ever agreeing to this.

The door directly beside me opens and I smell pine needles. A warm hand grasps mine and leads me gently out of the vehicle.

"This way," Genna says.

I get out with her guidance but don't move any further. "You know, I could very well trip on something and break my ankle and pride."

"Well, we don't want that," she says and I can almost hear the smile in her voice. "Trust me."

"Can I?"

She's silent a moment before saying, "You can."

"Did James trust you right before you killed him?"

The thought's been simmering in the back of my mind like a fire I can't put out despite dousing it with reassurances and excuses. I need a straight answer to be rid of this itch of curiosity. It's almost getting as bad as the itch I feel between my shoulder blades and the tense muscles down my back urging me to shift into the beast.

"If I tell you what happened, will you trust me then?" Genna asks quietly.

"It's certainly a start."

"I think we already got past the start when you didn't tell the IMS where I was."

"That was . . . me giving you a chance."

"Oh?"

"To prove us wrong about you," I say and squeeze her hand. "Well, not all of us."

"Hmm." She readjusts her grip so one hand holds my far elbow while her other guides my right hand. "How about I make you a deal? Let me walk you in blind and I'll tell you the story on the way there. It's not far."

"Fair enough."

"Then I'll warn you that it's mostly uphill from here. Be sure to lift your toes so you don't trip."

She begins to walk me forward and I think I hear the other two moving on ahead of us. Leaves rustle, bugs hum and buzz nearby, and the air lies heavy with the smell of a hundred different plants. We're definitely in woods somewhere. As instructed, I make sure to take higher steps than normal to meet the uneven incline.

"James and I discovered information leading to Erebus a couple years ago," she begins as we begin the climb to wherever it is we're going. "We had been devising plans to escape for years but couldn't leave the others behind. And we knew we would never truly be free unless we could be cured or kill Dasc. It was around that time that my guardian—Susan—discovered some enlightening information from the shapeshifters. Watch your step here."

We move more carefully up a steep rise until the ground levels out again. I keep silent, determined to absorb her story rather than interfere with it.

"I knew about the Magi already, but Susan found out one was behind the serum. Dasc had kept that from us, told us the serum was a way to control us. He never mentioned there was someone out there powerful enough to counteract the disease to help us. Susan . . . she died delivering that information to me."

Genna's pace slackens and we walk rather slowly towards our secret destination.

"Dasc had told me just earlier the same day that he had a man seeking out the Magi in hiding. He was interested in using their abilities against Echidna to serve his vendetta. But I saw the other possibility—uniting the Magi to bring about a cure. Then as luck would have it, Dasc summoned us to meet him in France where this man, this Erebus, was last known to be." She looses a sigh. "Things got complicated. The French IMS captured James and me and we made a deal to take down Dasc together. I hoped to capture Erebus in the same move."

"It was a trap," she says quietly. "One of Echidna's lamia had infiltrated the IMS and posed as an agent. Everything went wrong. In the end, Erebus was killed—or so I thought—and James . . . he was poisoned with wolfsbane. It's a slow, painful death for someone like us." She's silent for a moment and we stop walking altogether as she lingers over such a terrible memory. Before she says anything more, I think I already know where this story is heading.

"Dasc survived and found us," she says hardly above a whisper. I've rarely heard her sound so fragile. Genna's made of stern stuff. It takes a lot to make her appear even remotely vulnerable. "He saw through our deceit and we instantly became expendable traitors. That's when—" She takes a deep breath and her hand tightens around mine. "James sacrificed himself. He took responsibility for everything and set the stage to paint in me a loyal light. He said I had only been tagging along to uncover his plans to overthrow Dasc. I knew what James was doing. There would be no point in both of us dying. One of us had to escape to fight another day. We both knew what it was going to cost us. So I played my part."

Her hand shakes and I hold onto her a little more tightly.

"You have no idea how hard it is to lie to Dasc when he's compelling you to tell the truth. James and I couldn't lie but we could twist the truth to our own interpretation. James told a convincing story but there was one last test to make Dasc truly believe. He made me kill James."

My thoughts are subdued, weighed down by such heavy revelations. To be forced to kill your best friend—possibly only friend. I got a taste of such control myself when Dasc's compulsions tried to make me attack my own sister. It was impossible to resist the urges he fed into my brain. At least, impossible until Phoenix showed up and I felt her own strength protecting me. If Phoenix didn't have her unique abilities, that situation would have ended much differently. I shudder to think of it.

"I will never forget," she whispers. "And I will never forgive."

I lick my dry lips. "We'll make Dasc pay for everything he's done."

"I didn't mean Dasc."

She tugs on my hand and we start moving again as I wonder how Genna has ever been able to smile at all with that sort of guilt eating away at her. My own troubles feel like petty, insignificant trifles compared to what she's been through. Killing Duke wrecked me. I don't think I could have survived what she's endured.

"We're almost there," she says.

The sound and shape of the air changes as we leave the woods. The ground smooths out and I guess we're in a manmade tunnel of some sort. Footsteps echo from the four of us as we head down, down, down to wherever they've brought me. A gate creaks open ahead of us and Merlin mutters about it needing oil. Genna leads me on and the gate closes behind us. Another five minutes pass by my estimate until we at last come to a halt.

The first thing I see when the mask is lifted is Genna standing before me in the darkness. My eyes adjust to the low light from a single bulb overhead to take in the wide chamber we've come to. My nose twitches at the dank smell of mildew, perspiration, and dried blood. There's a steady drip of water somewhere and dull, muffled voices further in past a barred door on the other side of this cement antechamber. Merlin and Witty stand past Genna waiting for me to get my bearings.

From out of the shadows in every direction appear hooded figures that walk with an odd gait, hands curved into claws at their sides. I spin about where I stand to find we're surrounded by them, whoever—or whatever—they are.

That really pessimistic and occasionally logical side of my brain yells TRAP.

"Ahhhhh . . ." one of the figures says with a hiss to his voice. "Fresh meat."

I pinpoint which one spoke a second before he draws back his black hood to reveal his deathly pale skin, bloodshot eyes, and wicked fangs when he smiles. The others do the same with identical tell-tale features.

Vampires.

14

Phoenix

The *Tregurtha*, a massive bulk freighter, hasn't responded to our hails or those of the coast guard since we reached the area twenty minutes ago. With the ramp lowered, I stand with a hand on the line above my head waiting. The ship seems to stretch on forever, its dark red hull mostly above the water. It must be running light without much by way of cargo. What sunlight manages to pierce the thick clouds glimmers off the white paint of the bridge. Wind buffets the Osprey and freighter and turns the surface of Lake Superior into a roiling pitch.

Charlie and Melody stand beside me wearing their slim masks and goggles same as me. We already have our lines secured for the moment we get the word to rappel onto the deck. I don't know what we're going to find down there but chances are good we're in for a fight. We've been hovering for a while with Alona skimming us through the lower portion of the clouds to keep us out of sight and for the air sprites to collect a mass of clouds around us for when we decide to descend.

And as we wait, I stretch out my feelers for signs of magic on that ship. I expect to brush against spots of bitter darkness but there's nothing. Finding nothing is actually worse than finding monsters in this case.

John comes up beside me and gives us the signal that we're going down. When he turns to me, I form a zero with my fingers and nod in confirmation. Theo joins us and secures his own line before we start our descent out of the clouds and to the deck waiting below.

The coast guard is standing by for the time being. They have orders to steer clear until we can secure the vessel. Then we'll bring them on so they can take the freighter to a safe harbor. Once we're in position over the stern, Theo rappels to the tower above the bridge with his sniper rifle to cover us. The rest of us rappel to the deck below and unlatch our lines. Alona moves off with the Osprey like a ghost as the air sprites spin a web of mist around it and keep its engines near silent. We quickly take stock of our surroundings, of the unnatural quiet apart from the slap of the choppy waves against the hull and the fact that there's not a sign of life on board. I'm not sure what I had been expecting, but I'd rather see men running at us under the control of a siren than this foreboding emptiness.

Two other Spartan teams, Romeo and Lima, come aboard behind us as we secure the landing site for them. Not a word is spoken as we split our designated ways to search the vessel. John leads point into the bridge that—like the rest of the ship—is eerily quiet. We walk with our bio-mech rifles drawn and turn sharply around the equipment in the room. There's no one here.

But then I see it at the same time as the others. Blood. Lots of it. It's splattered across the floor and smeared towards the other side as if something—or someone—had been dragged through it. Melody bends down and runs a finger across a large splotch. She lifts her glove to show us it's dry. Whatever happened here, it wasn't recent.

"Bridge is clear," John says quietly into the radio. "But we have a lot of blood here."

We keep moving and I dread what we're going to find. The smear leads down a flight of stairs to the passenger stateroom hallway, then past the empty captain's quarters and small galley. Down and around we go, clearing to the deck without a sign of anyone except for the blood here, there, and everywhere. When we reach the stairs that descend into the belly of the freighter, I pause as I see a sign taunting us. Someone left an arrow pointing down the stairwell painted with blood.

Melody swears under her breath. Charlie's eyes gleam with anger and I almost crush the bio-mech rifle in my hands.

John signals to us and we continue down the narrow steps, back and forth along some seventy steps until we reach the tunnel swathed in darkness beneath the cargo holds. We turn on our night vision goggles before continuing on. A massive conveyor belt runs along our right with a series of gates closed above it used to drain out the cargo bays.

Blood smears and droplets lead the way along the ever

so long tunnel that runs the entire length of the ship. It's cool and moisture slick. We must be below the surface of the lake.

"Engine room is clear," Romeo reports in.

"Top deck is clear," Lima says.

"We've cleared the state rooms and are in the conveyor tunnel," John says. "Whoever did this left us a sign to come this way."

"Romeo is coming to assist."

The radio falls silent once again and we move steadily but slowly through the tunnel. We pass door after open door that marks the separation between the different cargo holds. We come to one where an enormous guillotine, as it were, has been locked down into place over the conveyor belt and the waterproof door is shut before us in the tunnel. There's another message waiting for us on the door.

Please enter. Again, in someone's blood.

My own blood boils. There are monsters and then there are *monsters*.

We move into position around the door, Charlie and I covering John as he opens the door, and Melody breaches in first. She gives a sharp intake of breath and I find out why a second later when we enter behind her.

Bones litter the floor. Wait, not littered. Arranged. Arranged into lines and piles of odd shapes. I step carefully around them when I see more writing on the wall.

You should have killed me sooner. - ε

"Phoenix," Charlie breathes.

I look to him but he's not looking at me. He's walked further into the tunnel and is staring at the piles of bones. I move to his side and see what he sees. My heart stops.

He didn't say my name to get my attention. He said my name because that's what the bones spell out on the floor. *Phoenix.* The taunting, the blood on the walls, the dead crew that have been reduced to piles of bones—it's all for me. I can't breathe as I numbly sink down and realize there are patches of fabric lined in a neat row before the bones.

Smith. McNab. Spencer. And so on. The crew's tags.

I rise and stumble over to the door hatch, heaving and hardly able to see. Charlie's there a second later with a hand on my back. I lean over and brace myself on my knees before ripping off my mask and emptying my stomach.

"We've found the crew," John says over the radio. "They're dead. Whoever took the ship left a message for one of our team. They knew we would be coming."

This can't be happening.

"Phoenix?" Melody comes up beside me.

"Epsilon," I choke out and gesture weakly to the signature "ε" at the bottom of the taunting message. "It's Epsilon. I had two chances to kill her and blew it. Now she—this is my—"

"Don't you dare say this is your fault," she says sharply. "That lamia would have done this anyway but she put your name there because she wants to break you. It'd be a bloody shame if you let her."

Maybe that's true. Maybe Epsilon would have massacred them anyway, but it still doesn't change the fact that I didn't stop her at Scholar's house or in Underground during the siege.

Team Romeo arrives and Charlie gently grabs me by the shoulders to move me away from the death message. I spit out the bile left in my mouth. My face is on fire and sweat gathers on my brow. I feel dizzy and lightheaded.

"Hey, *breathe*," Charlie says and keeps a grip on my shoulders.

I gesture to the blood and bones behind me. "Charlie, I can't—"

"Steel goes through fire and becomes stronger for it, okay? Don't be broken by this. Turn into the weapon that ends her."

"I can't believe you can be so metaphorical at a time like this."

"Read enough books and it becomes engrained. At least listen to what I'm saying, okay? Don't break. Get angry."

I curl my hands into fists. "I *am* angry."

"Well, you don't look like it."

My stomach roils in response and I shrug his hands off my shoulders.

"Phoenix. Charlie."

We turn around as John calls us back over and points to a spot amongst the bones. I swallow before bending low to see what it is. Cracked, grayish shards are scattered amongst the remains of the crew.

"Eggshells," he says.

Another taunt. We came here looking for the source of the hydra eggs but we're already too late. And considering the size of this freighter, there's no telling how many hydra have been smuggled inland.

I remain in a daze as Lima reports in that they've cleared the rest of the ship and are escorting the coast guard to the bridge so they can bring the ship in to port. The lights come on after ten minutes, the engines come to life, and we start the slow procession towards Duluth. Melody, John, and members of Romeo start cataloging everything, taking pictures, and noting every detail.

"I've got Director Knox on the horn," Alona says over the radio. "He wants our team in Underground to debrief him directly. Especially Phoenix."

Of course. Now that I've been made a target by our enemy, I'm sure the council and director are going to want to chat with me. The other teams will remain with the ship to bring in the cleanup crews and go over every inch of this massive freighter for any other clues left behind. Every monitor, computer, and electronic device will be checked to see where exactly this ship's been in order to find leads on our missing hydra.

But as for me and the rest of Sierra, we return to the deck and hook onto the lines Alona drops from the Osprey and we winch up into the hold. As soon as the ramp closes, the rotors tilt and we make haste for the Twin Cities.

Any sound within the aircraft is drowned out by the engines as the air sprites do what they can to give us the fastest speed possible. That's fine by me. I don't want to talk and I don't want to hear what the others have to say. And as that deafening silence consumes me, the rage under my skin boils hotter with each passing minute. I hadn't been strong enough or quick enough to stop Epsilon before. I'd been weak. I'd been slow. With the image of those bones and blood etched into my mind, I vow that I'll never be either again. The next time I see Epsilon, I'm going to rip off her head.

With murder on the brain, I walk with resolution when we

land at the Minneapolis airport and make for the transport waiting for us. We pile in—crammed a bit tightly carrying our gear—and our driver hastens us through the messy traffic. No one says anything to me, but Theo and Melody have a whispered conversation in the back of the van and I sense Charlie's eyes on me. It's a solemn time as we finally reach the power park and hidden entrance to Underground.

We take the lifts down, down, down into the depths and eventually enter the cement halls of the hidden city. I don't have a thought to spare about how odd it feels to be back here with my team and in my tactical gear. In my mind it's been an age since I was here last, even though it's hardly been two weeks since my graduation. Murmurs follow us as we march straight through the center of Merchant Square, the colonnade, and into headquarters.

"The council is gathering," the receptionist informs us. "It'll be about ten minutes. You're welcome to wait here or in the council chambers."

"I'm going to call my folks," Theo announces. "I'll meet you in the chambers."

He makes for the communications room but we all follow him.

"Calling friends in Scotland," Melody says.

"Checking on my sister," John says.

"Letting my grandma know I'm alive," Alona says.

"I need to talk to my brother," I mumble.

Charlie shrugs. "I'm providing moral support."

Theo gives a dramatic sniffle and says hoarsely, "You're too precious for this world, Cranky."

"You know, the only one that's been making me cranky is you."

Theo beams. "Then my work here is done."

The rest of us shake our heads and enter the communications room. As usual, it's in a flurry. We move out of the way of a couple of runners that sprint from the room with papers in hand. I watch the chaos briefly before heading to the row of wall-mounted phones. The others do the same and Charlie leans against the wall, hands in his pockets, as I dial the number for Hawk's cell phone.

It rings and goes to voicemail. "You've reached the one and only Hawk Mason. Leave a message."

I sigh and brace a hand against the wall, hanging my head. "Hawk, it's me. I just wanted to check in. I—" What do I say? I don't really want to leave today's events in a message. "Today wasn't a good day. Just . . . keep an eye out for yourself, okay? I love you. Call me."

I hang up and go to lean against the wall beside Charlie, his shoulder rubbing mine.

"Why didn't you tell him?" Charlie asks quietly.

I stare unfocused at the computers and operators around me. "He's got enough on his plate. I don't need to add to it." The scene of bones and blood from the ship floats before my eyes. "I can't get it out of my head," I whisper. "But maybe I should have told him. If Epsilon is taunting me, she knows the best way to get to me is through my brother."

"Hawk's smart and a Spartan," Charlie says. "I'm sure he'll be fine even if Epsilon's stupid enough to do something like that."

"She's not stupid. She's ruthless. And because of me, she's—"

"Don't do that," he says sharply.

I blink and bring him into focus beside me. He looks angry.

"Do what?"

"Blame yourself. You heard Melody on the ship. This is *not* your fault."

"Easy for you to say," I grumble. "It wasn't your name spelled out in bones."

He smacks me upside the head.

"Hey!" I step away from him and massage my scalp.

"Just trying to jar your senses."

Heat rises in my face and my free hand curls into a fist. "You jerk."

He steps forward even closer than before and angles his face towards mine. I freeze.

"Do you remember our talk before heading to the *Tregurtha*?" he murmurs.

I'm not likely to forget it any time soon. He said he'd tell Draco to go to hell if he knew the dragon was a danger to me. He called me a rare individual. I remember the hug reclusive, anti-social Charlie gave me.

His expression is cold. "Don't make the mistake of thinking you're the only person upset about this."

I swallow and he looks away.

The others are wrapping up their conversations. John assures his sister he'll come by when he can, Melody talks in what sounds like fast Gaelic, Alona converses softly in what I've learned is Ojibwe, and Theo sounds like he's arguing with someone about how to make something called chocolate religieuse.

"And I didn't hit you *that* hard," Charlie whispers. "You've hit me harder."

The handprint from last night has turned into more of a reddish patch across his cheek tinged with green and purple on the edges. I bite my lip and vow to never mention it again.

There's a series of clicks as the rest of our team hangs up their phones and we walk together through headquarters. I look to the arch in the center that pulses with energy. I don't even need to be actively looking for it to notice it. It's a glaring beacon that washes Underground with waves of its power, saturating the entire city. We eventually move past it and to the other side of headquarters, then down the ramp to the council chambers. Charlie and I share a look. The last time either of us was here, we were intruding on a closed meeting and ended up in the penitent cells for it. At least we're invited this time.

The two guards at the bottom open the towering doors for us. John spearheads the way into the room and we fall in line behind him. Most of the council sits or stands around the circular table in the middle of the room while two look on from video monitors on the opposite end. Director Knox stands before them in his usual crisp suit. John goes straight to him and they shake hands. Then the director insists on shaking hands with the whole team and I come last.

"Spartan," he says and gives me a solemn nod.

"Sir."

He turns back to the table and we stand in rigid formation beside him to face the rest of the council. Then the nasty dragged out process begins. I've been in this position before. After the assault on Underground, I was questioned thoroughly about my part during it and was made even to question myself. Of course, it's always easier to judge the actions of someone when you weren't there yourself. This time is no different. The council wants to know everything about the hydra mishap in Bemidji, the battle with the siren, and what we discovered aboard the *Tregurtha*.

"And the message was intended for you?" the centaur councilor asks. "Why?"

I roll my shoulders. "Probably because I ticked off Epsilon one too many times."

"I see your attitude hasn't changed," he says coolly.

"You asked a question," John says, not rising from his usual soft-spoken self. "And she gave you the answer. Monsters aren't particularly motivated in more refined terms, councilor."

The centaur's hooves clack on the stone floor and he flicks his tail in agitation.

"And if you're done questioning my team about their actions during combat, I'd like to discuss what we're going to do next."

I want to cheer for John for being so calm and collected yet unexpectedly sassy in the face of the council trying to tear apart our report and methods. I puff out my chest a little and I'm not the only one. The rest of the team does the same and we make an impressive bunch—if I do say so myself—coated in a layer of hard-earned grime in our tactical gear. Mind, I would like to go shower somewhere.

Before the councilor can make another remark, Director Knox knocks a fist on the table.

"What are we going to do indeed," he says and steers the meeting towards proactive measures and what the techs have found.

"According to the ship's tracking logs and in coordination with the teams in Duluth, we've located a number of shipments that went out from the *Tregurtha* not only in Duluth but across ports along the Great Lakes. We've got planes, trains, and automobiles, people. Hundreds of them. The hydra egg Sierra found in Bemidji is only the beginning. We've already begun passing along the word. Now that the other divisions are on the lookout, we've uncovered an alarming number of suspicious deliveries. There's now the possibility of a hydra attack in nearly every state of the U.S. and in other countries as well."

Oh, pixies. It's starting. The great war Dasc had been teasing for months. Echidna is spreading her troops across the ground.

"As of this moment, we're reassigning all Spartan teams to this hydra threat. We'll adjust the load of unrelated code blacks to veteran field agents." Director Knox plants his hands on the table. "There are no two ways about it. We're spread thin and the odds at this point are stacked against us."

He looks more tired than I've ever seen him. "Sierra, I suggest you get what rest you can. I fear you won't be getting much of it in the near future."

We salute in unison, which the director returns, and then file out of the chambers. The councilors murmur farewells and blessings. When we exit, we find a faun waiting to take us to accommodations that have been prepared for our brief stay. We follow her cloven hooves into the living quarters of the city and to the bastille-styled apartment complex. When she leads us to a familiar door, Charlie and I pause, glancing to each other, before we enter what had once been Witty's apartment before he defected.

Gone are the rows of computer equipment and hanging wires, along with his little shrine to the majestics, comic book collection, thick black rugs, collection of video games and movies, and enormous television. It feels oddly bare despite being fully furnished with new couches, a smaller TV, six beds to accommodate the entire team, and plush golden rugs. It's been converted into a Spartan way station. I guess that just goes to show how active we've been lately.

"If you need anything," the faun says, "Underground will be more than happy to assist our dutiful Spartans. Have a good day."

She bows herself out of the room as if we're royalty and closes the door behind us. Theo immediately goes to the closest bed, drops his bag at the foot of it, and then flops onto the mattress. The rest of us spread out claiming our own beds, before pulling straws for who gets to use the bathroom first. Charlie gets the first privilege and the rest of us lounge about, pulling off the outer layer of our dirtied gear, taking a snooze while we wait, or eating from the plate of pastries left for us on a table.

I take a seat on the couch as I eat a doughnut and turn on the television to see what's on the feeds. Melody and John join me, both propping their feet up on the coffee table. The feeds aren't really any comfort. France is still on lockdown and word is going around about the dispersal of hydra eggs. The anchor asks all agents to be on the lookout.

"This is too depressing," Theo grouses behind us. "We're going to have enough crap to deal with after this pit stop. If we're going to relax, we need to *relax*."

John silently passes over the remote and Theo quickly changes it to a cooking competition show featured in Britain.

Charlie comes out of the bathroom squeaky clean— looking handsome as usual—and trades places with Melody who's up next.

One by one we take our turn getting clean, then lounge about the apartment. Theo and Alona leave at one point only to return an hour later carrying a meal Theo made himself. We sit around the table like a big family to eat through the most delicious bowl of pasta I've ever had in my life. For dessert, Theo sets what he calls chocolate religieuse in front of me.

"It's my grand-mère's recipe," he says and pats me on the back. "Best served on bad days."

"Why's that?"

"Well . . . because *chocolate*."

Alona chortles. "The answer to life itself."

"Yes," Theo says and nods vigorously.

"Thank you," I say and look in wonder at the confection perfection he made.

"And I can also give you a hug, unless those are only reserved for Charlie."

He ducks the roll Charlie hurls at his face.

The chocolate *is* delicious but when I finally go to sleep, it can't keep the nightmares at bay. I dream I'm on the *Tregurtha* as Epsilon sneaks aboard and captures the crew members, but they have the faces of my team, of my friends, of Jefferson, and Hawk. Then she sinks her teeth into them and starts to rip them apart while I'm trapped and helpless. As she digs those shark teeth of hers into Hawk's neck and blood flows down his chest, I wake with a sharp gasp and nearly launch myself out of bed.

Cold sweat covers me, the sheets are tangled around my legs, and my hands shake. Every breath is sharp and when I run a hand over my face, I find tears there. My breathing eventually slows as I focus on the room and try to push those horrible images away. Then I realize I don't hear the steady breaths of people sleeping. Everyone's awake. I wonder if I had cried out in my sleep and woken them. Frustrated with myself, I slip out of bed and move silently out of the apartment. I keep walking. It feels good to have the air move against my face. I hug my arms to myself and try to see the walls around me instead of the bloodshed in my mind.

My bare feet carry me to the arena and I walk through the tunnel between the stands to the middle of the stadium. The fire sprites burn low at this hour and give only a faint orange glow. When I stop to watch their glittering embers, a rogue wind sweeps over me and twists my hair up off my sweaty neck. I look around and spot two air sprites like puffs of clouds swirling in a spiral around me. The torrent of air drops and one of the sprites glides down to spin in figure eights around my legs while the other gently wafts to me. I hold out my hands and it settles in my palms like a snow-touched wind. Two bright lights glimmer at me out of its shapeless form.

It pools into my hands and makes a sound like a cat purring. I actually manage to smile.

"So who are you?" I whisper.

With its ability to manipulate air and sound, the one cradled in my hands unmistakably says *Flitter*.

The other one racing figure-eights on the ground makes a slew of loud farting noises and my smile grows.

"Fart and Flitter. Hello. I see you managed to sneak away from the Osprey."

The one in my hands trills and gusts up into the shape of a bird. Its wings spread wide and a funnel of air swirls around me, cooling the heat off my skin. The effect it has on me is immediate and my muscles unwind. This amazing little creature, that still manages to purr and trill despite seeing what the Spartans face every day, softens the jagged edges that have been forming around my heart.

There may be horrors in this world, but there is also light. And it is worth protecting.

"Thank you," I whisper to Flitter as it swoops up high with Fart and they tease the fire sprites with gusts of wind.

Moments later, the rest of my team comes wandering into the stadium in their pajamas. They don't crowd around me or give me a pity speech, but meander about as if they all randomly decided to explore at the same time.

Theo walks to the turf in the middle of the track and rips up a clump of grass.

He gives me a big smile. "Watch this."

He throws the chunks into the air and the air sprites zoom down to catch it before it falls. They carry it along currents of wind and eventually dump it right on top of a fire sprite. The flames hiss and smoke rises from the brazier. Fart and Flitter dart to hide behind Theo and me as the fire sprite rises up and peers over the edge of its nest. A few sparks fly from its eyes before it settles back down.

For maybe fifteen minutes, we move aimlessly through the stadium, watching the air sprites play and Alona shifts to fly among them. They do some acrobatic moves and we watch in fascination. No one says much of anything.

Although Epsilon's taunt has set me apart, I'm not alone.

One by one, we leave the stadium and return to the apartment. Fart and Flitter follow in my footsteps before floating away to play with others of their kind along the ceiling. At last I return to my bed and sleep through what remains of the night, ready for a red dawn to rise.

15

Hawk

So. Vampires.

What the heck?

"Easy, Claude," Genna warns the vampire standing nearest. "This isn't the delivery."

Delivery? And again, what the heck? I thought I was being taken to a werewolf compound, not some vampires' hidey hole. I stand at the ready and on my guard, hyper aware of everyone in the room and every movement they make.

"So who is he?" Claude the vampire asks.

"An associate. We're showing him the compound."

The vampires give me nasty looks.

Claude bares his fangs. "I thought you said the less people who know about this place, the better. Why are you bringing someone else in if he isn't staying?"

"Are you questioning me?" Genna asks with lethal calm. At her tone, the other vampires ease up a step. Geez, what kind of reputation does she have around here?

"Of course not, Dark Whisper." Claude actually bows to her. "Whatever you desire."

"Claude."

"Yes?"

"You can drop the act. You're hardly intimidating."

His feral smile turns into a goofy, crooked one. "We have a reputation to uphold."

"Uh-huh." Her expression softens. I blink and keep glancing between the two. "The delivery should come in tomorrow. Can you hold out until then?"

Claude and the other blood-suckers look to each other in confirmation, nodding their heads a little sadly.

"We'll make do," Claude says. He gestures widely to the door at the other end of the antechamber. "Shall we?"

Genna spearheads the way forward and I hesitate before following. Merlin and Witty fall into step behind us and the vampires bring up the rear. To say the situation is confusing is an understatement. I don't have a clue what's going on.

"So, I have a million questions," I say.

"I'm sure you do."

"Delivery?"

"Blood for them." She jerks her head in the direction of the vampires tailing us. When my shocked expression gives me away, she adds, "From a blood donation rig, don't worry."

"Vampires? Really?" I ask quietly while attempting to keep a keen eye on them behind us.

"This area is historically their territory. It's the last place Dasc would think to look for us."

"But I thought Dasc sent you to Seattle in the first place," I say as we walk down another sloping tunnel to where the muffled voices I heard earlier become more defined, along with the clink of metal and movement of feet.

"As an undercover mission to keep an eye on the IMS, not work with the vampires."

I'm still having trouble wrapping my head around any of this. My frustration is driving my temper up a steep incline and I run a hand through my hair, clutching at the strands. The serum and Merlin's presence aren't really helping things in the "don't go crazy" department. I let out an aggravated growl and fight that temptation to shift into a beast with claws.

Genna lays a hand on my arm but looks to the others. "Go on. We'll meet you up ahead."

Merlin and Witty give me sideways looks as they walk past, the vampires sort of slinking behind.

I swallow and pace away from Genna. Her act to shelter me as if I'm a badly behaved child having a tantrum doesn't help my current mood.

As soon as the others are far enough away, I spin about on her. "I don't need to be babied."

"Good. I just figured you didn't want an audience."

"Audience to what?"

"You going mad."

Her words are like a slap to the face and push my anger over the edge.

"Excuse me?" I snarl.

She doesn't back down or look even remotely defensive. "The quick to anger bit really isn't you, Hawk."

"How would you know?"

"I might not have known you for very long, but I saw

enough. I'm a pretty good judge of character and I had you pegged the moment I met you."

My lip starts to curl and I want to strangle her. I want to break free of this shell and into the monster raging inside. Two seconds. That's all it takes to slip into this mode. A hair trigger. That's what I'm living with day in and day out without Phoenix here. The pendant against my chest burns.

Genna grabs me by the upper arm to keep me still. "Your jokes, your persistent positive attitude, your love for your family—that's the real you. You're a man of compassion and action with a quick tongue. That's who you are. This right here—this is the demon on your back."

I let out a loud huff and look anywhere but at her. "You spent years without the serum. How did you manage it? Is there a way to control it without the serum?"

"Yes."

My eyes snap to her. "How?"

"By knowing your demons," she says simply. "And being meaner than them."

I throw up my hands. "What does *that* mean?"

"It means that sometimes if you want to tame the beast, you have to become the beast. You've been fighting this for so long, I don't think you know another way."

"You mean give in."

"I didn't say that."

"Well, you're not making a lot of sense regardless."

She's so good at making no expression of emotion at all that I feel the need to sigh on her behalf—and I do. A big, over the top dramatic sigh that earns me a small smile from Genna.

"For now," she says, "whenever you feel your wolf half coming through, focus on who your pack is. It helps."

"I don't have a pack."

"Yes, you do. The sooner you figure that out, the better off you'll be."

She leaves it at that and keeps moving along the tunnel. I'm so confused that I forget to be angry—like flipping a switch. I scratch my head and jog to catch up.

"Can't you just tell me the secret?" I ask.

"There's a difference between telling someone and them actually getting it," she says.

"You think I won't understand?"

"That's not the problem." She gives me a sideways look. "I know you'll understand the words if I say them but that won't make a difference. You have to experience them. Look, I'll explain it later. We're here."

Indeed the others have stopped outside a large metal door with rusted bolts and a big handle. Well, it certainly looks like the door to a creepy monster lair. I really don't know what I'll encounter on the other side. There are only two types of werewolves that I know. Those on the serum and Dasc's playthings. The wolves behind this door are a new, untested category—werewolves without the serum and also free of Dasc. Will they have more in common with me? Or with the werewolf alpha?

Only one way to find out.

The vampires lead the way in, three of them having to work together to open the heavy door. When I step into the light of fluorescents, I expect dingy walls, the smell of mildew, and rat droppings in the corners. And this place . . .

well, it certainly meets all my expectations. It's not very clean or nice smelling. It's a dirty hideout for monsters.

But what I don't expect are the small children running past laughing and playing a game of tag. I don't expect to find several of the adults tidying up their lair, sweeping up the rat turds, and scrubbing the floors. I don't expect colorful curtains sectioning off different hallways that branch off from the entrance chamber. And yet there they are. Children laughing, adults trying to make this dingy place a little more like a home, and bright colors in defiance of the grim shadows that fall over every werewolf. We're all cursed but these people—they look happy enough. I don't see anyone foaming at the mouth anyway. If I didn't know this was a werewolf compound, I wouldn't be able to tell.

The vampires split off and pass through a pair of bright green curtains to the left while Merlin holds open the red curtains directly ahead of us to let us through. Witty joins him on the other side so they make a pair of welcoming guards. Genna and I enter another tunnel that leads to what I assume is the central chamber of this place. It's huge. A short flight of stairs leads down to the main floor that's filled with mismatched tables and chairs in varying states of degradation but draped with patterned cloths to hide their ugliness. The sweet smell of bread mixed with the tang of something spicy fills the air. Children and adults in shabby clothes sit and talk or carry their empty plates to basins at the back where they pitch in cleaning up the dishes. Looks like we just missed supper time.

Everywhere I look there's a sense of . . . belonging. My shields begin to lower, the ones that hide the true pain I always feel deep inside. The aches begin to ebb away and I stare at a group of children playing musical chairs.

"What is this place?" I whisper, my words nearly lost in the din of conversation and children's laughter.

"A right mess," Merlin grumbles and stomps down the steps.

Genna smiles at the grumpy wizard but says to me, "This is sanctuary. This, Hawk, is what a werewolf community should be."

I've no argument there.

Below us, Merlin raises his hands as if he's about to conduct an orchestra and begins swirling his hands and twiddling this fingers. Tables, chairs, and people alike start gliding around like some sort of puzzle game. There are a few startled gasps and shrieks of delight from the young ones as they magically float into position at Merlin's behest. When at last he drops his hands and dusts them off, I realize what he's done. The tables and chairs are in exact orderly rows, everything is squared and centered, and there's a very clear symmetry to how he arranged the room including the people in it.

"That's better," Merlin says and walks calmly away through another tunnel with his hands clasped behind his back. As he goes, his young appearance shifts back into that of an old man—robe, beard, and all. That's a neat trick.

"Would you like a tour?" Genna asks.

"I'd love one."

She leads me down the stairs and another tunnel to a series of conjoined, dome-shaped chambers that act as the living area. We walk slowly with Witty trailing behind, and Genna explains the hows and whats to me.

"This place was actually built by the vampires ages ago during the gold rush, I think," she says. "It stayed off the IMS radar for years. When one of the entrances was discovered, they actually made a pact with the agent to keep this place safe. Claude and his coven don't kill humans. In fact, they offered to help nearby agents against other monsters in exchange for sanctuary here. They live off blood donations."

We pause outside a play room of sorts where kids read books and create buildings out of blocks.

"I just . . . I can't wrap my head around that to be honest," I say. "I've never heard of vampires acting like that. Not ever."

"Claude and his family used to be vampire hunters," Genna says softly and her eyes become unfocused as she stares into the play room. "They were turned out of spite. So, they spitefully killed the vampires that changed them and have been living their lives peacefully like this ever since. Not all monsters are monsters. We know that better than anyone."

"Touché."

We walk step in step through more tunnels with rusted pipes and low ceilings illuminated by single bare bulbs. The place certainly looks old and could use some repairs, but it's hidden and has room enough to spare which is the most important thing. They're self-sustainable, I'm told, as we visit a sweltering greenhouse the length of my office floor. Apparently the room had been converted—it used to house cells where the vampires stored their meals. I'm not sure how to feel about that. A part of me wants to make a crack about going vegetarian—the other part of me wants to throw up. Further past the greenhouse there's a generator powered by an underground river.

"Witty got it working, actually," Genna points out. "It kicked out several years ago according to the vampires but we have electricity now thanks to him."

"Just helping out," Witty says and shrugs his shoulders with a sheepish smile. "We needed to power our surveillance equipment."

"Speaking of which," Genna says and we turn into the next room that has clearly been claimed by Witty. Cables run in orderly groups to a large computer setup with six monitors each displaying different footage from what I assume is the surrounding area.

"Well, you've certainly been busy, haven't you?" I say and inspect the different feeds before me. They're mostly forest locations but one looks over a road.

"There's one last place I want to show you." Genna takes my hand and tugs me out of the room. I let myself be led down yet another hallway and staircase to a short tunnel guarded by two young men and a girl. They're playing a card game on the floor while the girl keeps glancing up at a monitor on the wall next to them. It's more surveillance video but this time it's of someplace inside the compound where there are a lot of wolves running about.

The three quickly abandon their game and scramble to their feet when they see Genna.

"Ma'am," they say in unison.

Wow. They sound like they could be soldiers under her command but they certainly don't look like it. Dressed in jeans and dirty t-shirts, they look like a group of teenagers hanging out after school.

"How's it going?" Genna asks and strides up to the three.

"All's well," the girl answers. "No incidents."

"Good." Genna nods and moves over to the monitor to watch the action. "We're going in for a little bit. We need to stretch our legs."

"Yes, ma'am." The taller of the two men stands beside Genna to check the screen as well. "The door's clear. Go ahead."

Genna motions to me and opens a very thick, solid steel door. Witty and I join her in a very small room with yet another heavy steel door. Genna shuts us in and we hear the lock click on the other side. Trapped. A small panel opens in the door we just walked through and the girl peeks in at us.

"Just a second." She looks over her shoulder to her companions before bobbing her head. "Okay, you're clear."

Genna opens the next door, ushers us quickly through, and shuts it again. When I turn about to survey the room, I realize this is what the monitor is looking over. It's an enormous room that stretches on and on like someone decided an underground football field was an excellent idea. There's even fake grass covering the floor that I toe with my shoe. And everywhere, running wild and free, are wolves. They play, howl, yip, and race each other.

I can feel that itch on the back of my neck, that urge to change shape and run out to join them.

"This room is completely sealed off," Genna explains, having to raise her voice a bit to be heard. "Someone is always watching the door. Everyone in the compound can shift whenever they like as long as they do it here. We're free to be us."

"In a locked room," I say.

"That door unlocks the second someone wants out and can shift back to their human self. If they can't, then they stay here until they can. This isn't how the IMS operates," she says a bit stiffly. "And this isn't how Dasc operates."

That's something I've always wondered actually but Genna's never talked about, even in our long chats. "How exactly did Dasc operate?"

Genna steps away so her back is to me and she rolls her shoulders. "Whenever we shifted, he locked us in cages until we could figure out how to shift back under our own willpower."

No wonder she's never talked about it. My anger at my own circumstances seems a bit pitiful now. At least no one's ever locked me in a cage. I can't even imagine how that would help you figure out how to control your wolf half.

"How long?" I ask quietly, the noise from the wolves nearly drowning out my words.

She doesn't turn to face me when she answers. "I wasn't in the cage the whole time but . . . seven months."

"I'm sorry."

"Don't apologize. I hate apologies."

How could I so foolishly forget?

"Come on," she says and hunkers into a crouch.

I watch as her form changes and reforms into that of a black wolf. Once fully shifted, she turns to me, her dark eyes rimmed with gold. Most of the world sees that particular coloration as a mark of danger—the sign a werewolf is not under the control of the serum to keep their senses in their human mind. But the world fails to see the beauty in it, the golden flecks that catch the light. In fact, the beauty's been lost on me until this moment. It's not necessarily that it's

Genna's irises that are gold-rimmed, but the fact that she can show her eyes proudly here without threat of discrimination or fear. In fact, the golden-yellow shows more prominently than I've ever seen them as if in this place she can let her true colors shine.

Genna is a wolf and in that she shows no shame.

She waits patiently as Witty shifts to my left. I watch him curiously to see what his appearance will be. While Genna is a shadow, Witty is a gray ghost with long limbs.

I let loose a breath that releases the tension in my shoulders and I let the itch take me. Pain blossoms down my back and I hunch over with my palms planted flat on the ground. My senses warp as everything human about me changes. I keep my breathing even as practiced many a time but my fingers still dig into the ground at that pain as I become something else entirely. This part has never been easy.

But then it's over. Paws replace hands, muzzle replaces nose and mouth, twitching ears stand tall and alert, and the familiar sensation of my tail settles on me. A thin whine escapes through my teeth as I feel the serum fighting me and what's in my mind. Phoenix's pendant radiates as usual like a peacekeeper and makes the pain less but doesn't make it go away completely.

The other side of me awakens—a side that runs on instinct and smells and noise. The scents of a hundred different wolves bombard me, of fake grass, of stale air, of blood and saliva. Yet oddly enough, one of the things that still feels the most disorienting is a lower disposition to the ground.

Genna yips at me and races out to join others in what looks to be a game of tag. Witty's tongue rolls out of his mouth and he looks the most lively I've ever seen him—despite being what he is. He runs away with a very awkward gait but happily nonetheless.

And then I'm running too. I don't know how long I stay in that man-made—or rather vampire-made—field letting loose. Even back in Moose Lake with our community "werewolf games," I never felt the freedom I do now to bark as loud as I want, to not look over my shoulder, to not test the air for scents of strangers nearby. In fact, I run so hard and for so long that I run myself ragged. It's not until Genna shoulders me towards the door that I finally stop and realize that most of the others have left already.

Reluctantly, I trudge alongside Genna and Witty to the door and plop down on the floor beside it panting hard. I don't shift back immediately. The pleasure of stretching my legs to their fullest is a hard feeling to give up. Right now I'm a lazy wolf. I don't want to turn back into Hawk the completely bored and frustrated office assistant.

Witty takes no time at all shifting back. He doesn't seem to struggle in the least with the transformation and something like jealousy stirs in my chest. It's always been a struggle for me if I'm being honest with myself. I really have to remember my fingers and toes and which way my joints go. It's difficult recalling being human once I've been overtaken by the wolf, but if I think hard enough on it, my body follows suit.

Genna, as expected, shifts seamlessly and stands within seconds to plant her hands on her waist.

"You can't hang around all night," she says sternly. "We need to get you back."

I swipe a weary paw at her and huff. It earns me a smile.

Nearly everyone else has exited the field and only a few stragglers remain. I want to stay—boy, do I ever—but Genna's right. Someone could go looking for me and discover I'm not where my probation ring says I am. I need to go back. I need to return to my ever so terrible day job in order to find the key to making the world more like this. Freedom. Who'd have thought I'd find it in a cement bunker?

So I picture my fingers and toes and joints as usual. My body reacts and the fur starts to disappear on my body. But then something unusual happens. I can't make the picture clear in my head. Arms and forelegs get confused and I sort of freeze up stuck between the two halves of myself, unable to decide on either. The beast growls at me to stay. Sharp pain spikes all over as if I'm being stabbed by a hundred knives and my thoughts turn into a jumble.

Up. Down. Teeth. Fangs.

Wrong. Wrong.

I'm wrong. This world is wrong. Tear it! Rip it!

"Hawk!"

My muscles lock and start to twitch sporadically as I try to piece myself back together. The world loses focus and I have no control as I start to convulse. My shoulder bashes repeatedly against cement until hands hold me up to keep from harming myself.

"Hawk, listen to me."

Genna.

Claws. Paws. Hands. Fingernails. Wrong. *Wrong*.

"Focus on my voice."

I can't focus. I can't fix myself. Not again.

Not again.

Not again.

"You're human. You're a boy who cracks jokes and makes friends with everyone you meet."

Am I? But I'm a wolf. I'm somewhere in between. Fur. Hair. Wrong—

"You are Spartan Hawk Mason. If there's anyone that can pull themselves back together, it's you. You are Phoenix's twin. You are a warrior. You are my friend."

Yes, that's . . . that sounds like me. Doesn't it?

"Red hair. Long limbs."

Yeah, that's me.

"Green eyes. A bit of freckles."

The pain becomes focused and I stop convulsing so much as my legs lengthen out and my joints line up the way they're supposed to.

"You're clever and caring. You also think far too highly of your own sense of humor but sometimes you're right about it anyway."

Heh, yeah. That's me.

The fur disappears and I can wiggle my fingers. My face pulls in, everything becomes so much less sharp on my ears, and my panting turns into deep breaths. My head swims but I blink and blink until the ceiling comes into focus—then the faces hovering above me as I lay on my back. I tilt my head to find Genna bracing my head in her lap. Witty releases his grip on my arms while a stranger lets go of my ankles. How much had I been thrashing?

I close my eyes, feel the heat roll off my body and the sweat gather on my skin. Shame runs its fingers over my burning face and I want to hide or slip out of my skin.

"Not again," I whisper.

The others don't say anything but give me time to rest

and catch my breath. Twenty minutes later, after I've walked embarrassed past the field guards and curious onlookers that whisper until Genna's gaze finds them, I sit at a table alone in their great hall. It's late into the night and the others have gone to bed. I've been subconsciously rubbing at my scar just below my ribs that continues to haunt me. I can hardly remember the night I was bitten except for the pain and the confusion. Through it all Phoenix stayed by my side even when the adults tried to keep her away when I turned. They kept me secluded in a glass cage and she sat there pressed up against the other side through the night. It's funny. I'd forgotten about that until just now. The memory of it's been buried beneath the terror of the serum.

Phoenix had always been there. And now—when I need her the most—she's not.

A chair scrapes across the floor and Genna takes a seat across from me. She doesn't say anything for a long time and simply sits there with her hands clasped together on top of the table.

"You said 'not again.' When did this happen before?" she asks quietly.

I clench my jaw and don't look her in the eye. It's a secret I've kept for so long, I thought it'd stay buried forever. I never thought it'd come back.

"When I was five," I say, my voice small. "Nearly a year after I was first turned."

"Does Phoenix know?"

I exhale slowly through my nose. "No."

She nods and doesn't question me on my decision. Maybe I *should* have told Phoenix, but I didn't know how.

"What happened?"

What indeed? I swallow and shake my head. "I'm not sure. It's only happened when I've been taking the serum." I wet my lips and keep my eyes on a motley chair draped with a green sheet to hide the ugliness beneath. "When I was first bitten, I felt so lost and confused. I was just a little kid. I had Phoenix to help me—more than I realized at the time—but still, I . . . I didn't know who I was. Was I still the boy my parents loved? Or was I something completely different? The serum hurt me and things just got worse. It got to the point that I—"

I pause and knead my hands together. I've never told anyone this before. It's difficult bringing it up even now.

"I started having seizures after I took my injections," I continue on hoarsely. "I was real good at hiding it. I'd be sure to hide myself away in the bathroom or somewhere and wait it out until it was over before going out. Phoenix already looked at me like I was some leper. I didn't want her to think any less of me. And no one else reacted to it the same way I did. I was a freak among the freaks. I tried telling one of the nurses about the pain once, but she didn't believe me. She thought I was whining about needles or something. I sure wasn't going to tell her about the seizures then. But I should have told someone. Instead, I stopped taking the serum and told myself I could handle it. To my surprise, I actually did. At least I thought I could—until I found out it was because of Phoenix, not because I'm stronger than I thought."

"You *are* stronger than you think," Genna offers.

"No, I'm not," I say sharply, the memory of the seizure downstairs vivid and fresh in my mind. "I'm weaker. Have you heard of any werewolf having seizures because of the serum?" She shakes her head. "I didn't think so."

"It doesn't make you any less than what you are."

"And what exactly am I?" I finally meet her eyes with a furious glare. "Please, *enlighten* me, because I don't have a clue myself."

"You're the person who took that pain and turned it into something useful. Don't do yourself a disservice by back peddling now." She leans forward on her elbows. "Hawk, your own suffering drove you to be more compassionate to those around you—like me. Like Witty. Like all the werewolves in Moose Lake. It didn't make you weak. It made you a better human being."

"Am I?" I ask quietly.

"Are you what?"

"Human?"

Her stern expression softens. "I don't have all the answers, Hawk. I don't know if Phoenix with the Magi can wipe the slate clean and make us who we were before. I don't know if what we are can be fixed. All I know is that being a monster isn't an excuse to become a monster."

"That's very new agey of you."

She smirks and shakes her head. "What I mean is—who cares if you have claws? Claws, fangs, fur, it doesn't matter. If you don't want to be a monster, then don't be a monster. It's not pretty. It's not easy. It's a struggle every step of the way. But when have things worth having ever been easy to get?"

I give a single laugh. "Changing the werewolf image one wolf at a time."

"That would be ideal."

"If I decided I wanted to become a superhero, do you think that would work?"

"You can be whatever you want to be," Genna says.

"That would be ideal," I parrot and we both smile. "What about you? Who do you want to be, Genna?"

She leans back in her seat and her dark eyes glimmer. There's nothing malicious looking about her but she does hold herself a certain way that belies the fact she knows she's a force to be reckoned with. I don't doubt that for a second.

"I want to be the dagger in Dasc's back he never sees coming."

16

Phoenix

Despite the air conditioning inside the van, sweat trickles down my neck beneath the layers of my Spartan tactical gear. Plus, it's not running full blast because Theo keeps complaining he's too cold. Alona will roll her eyes and crank up the A/C to spite him for a minute before turning it back down. John just shakes his head and Melody offers him the emergency tarp to keep warm.

I've been popping bullets in and out of the magazine of my mother's gun for the last half-hour. It's the one piece of gear I have that isn't standard issue. When I find Charlie giving me an all too knowing look, I pop the magazine into place, pull back on the slide, then tuck it into my shoulder holster. The pearl handle gleams in contrast to the matte black of my gear but I find it fitting that I carry it with me as if I'm continuing my mother's legacy—even if she *was* a Constantine.

"There she is," John says from the front passenger seat.

I look out the side window at the looming structure before us. The Sartell Paper Mill is a giant complex of buildings along the bank of the Mississippi River. I see it in blips between the trees alongside the road. We don't go to the parking lot on the other side of those trees. We'll be walking in from a safe distance away to not draw attention. Dusk is settling in and the sun is sinking beneath the horizon as we come to a stop near the north end of the complex behind a row of oak trees. When Alona parks the van, we sling on windbreakers to disguise the gear we're wearing until we can get inside the paper mill itself.

We hop onto the street and move casually in the direction of the river as if we're out for an evening stroll and want to take in the sights. That's when I get a good look at the mill. John tells me it's been a cornerstone of the city for a hundred years but took a recent turn. I can see where part of the roof's caved in, blackened and charred. There was a horrible explosion and fire in May of this year and the mill's been shut down ever since. The place may be locked up but that hasn't stopped the local monster population from utilizing it. In fact, it appears to be a prime location to hide a hydra egg.

Unfortunately, our team's on our own with no backup to speak of. The more information the techs and investigators uncover, the worse the situation gets. Now the Spartans are spread from here to Texas and we don't have the man power to check every suspect location with two or more teams. No, our job now is to scout and subdue, and only call in backup if we have to.

John motions to us in his silly looking windbreaker that has an orca stitched over the chest. "We'll cut across to the river and head south in two teams through the complex. Alona, Melody, and I will take the west entrance. Phoenix, Charlie, and Theo will take the east."

We nod and continue on quietly but on full alert as we approach the backend of the paper mill. A thunderous engine catches my attention growing ever closer. I pause and turn around as it approaches.

"I know that engine," I say.

"You *know* that car engine? That one specifically?" Charlie scoffs.

"Like thunder in the mountains."

I take a step to the left so I can see it. The last of the light reflects off the shiny finish of the green 442 as it pulls to a stop behind our van and parks. The door opens a moment later and Jefferson steps out burly as ever. After everything I've seen lately, it feels like a miracle to cross paths with him again. He spots me and hastens over to join my team that's also stopped to observe.

"Jefferson!" I move forward to intercept him and give him a generous hug.

He claps me one-armed on the back. "Hey, kid."

We pull apart and I beam at him. "What on earth are you doing here?"

"I was about to ask you the same thing. I heard a rumor that all Spartans are on hydra duty."

"We are."

His squinty eyes get even smaller. "Well, I'm here about werewolves."

I turn partway to the buildings behind me. "At the mill?"

"I take it you think there's a hydra in there?"

"That's the word on the street."

Charlie comes round and extends his hand which Jefferson gives a hearty shake.

"Good to see you," Jefferson says gruffly.

"Likewise."

John comes over next and they exchange the same courtesy. "Barnes."

"Kessler."

"What have you heard?" John asks and gestures for us to move behind a row of trees and shrubs right along the river's edge.

Once more out of sight from both the houses and mill, Jefferson says, "Came across some wild ones in St. Cloud. I managed to tag them and tracked them here. From what I can tell, a lot of werewolves in the area have been using this place as shelter since the place closed. They come in from all over so I thought I might be able to get a lead on Dasc or my daughter."

"No luck so far?" I ask quietly and he shakes his head.

"You think there's a hydra here though?" he asks in return.

He and Melody exchange a nod of greeting before she answers for us. "Techs tracked a supply truck that took cargo from the *Tregurtha*. One of its stops was here."

He looks to the mill over my shoulder and I do the same.

"Are we close enough?" John asks quietly.

I nod.

"Close enough to what?" Jefferson says.

"Let her do her thing," Theo says as if it's obvious.

I close my eyes and let my feelers do the work. They stretch out past the bright lights of Alona and Charlie beside me to the mill. It's almost like pulling on the ends of a rubber band. My reach can only go so far but it's enough. I suck in a sharp breath as I open my eyes and that band snaps back into me.

"There's definitely a hydra, along with three less powerful monsters that could be werewolves."

John nods and motions for the team to move ahead as if this is now a very normal part of our routine.

Jefferson yanks on my arm. "What are you doing?"

My heart twangs at the note of panic in his voice. "It's okay. They know. I told them."

"What were you thinking?" he growls. "Do you know what kind of danger you've put yourself in?"

John puts a hand between us. "Phoenix is one of us. And no one's hauling her away until she decides to go."

His squinty eyes narrow on my team leader. "Did you tell Merlin the same thing?"

I blink. "Wait, you know about Merlin?"

"How do *you* know about Merlin?" Jefferson says, eyes darting between us. His hand squeezes tighter around my bicep.

"John told me about him. But how do *you*—"

There's a sharp pop in the direction of the mill that's unmistakably a gun shot.

"Conversation for another time," John says and we burst into a sprint to catch up with the rest of our team converging on the buildings. Jefferson stays on our heels but John barks at him, "You're not coming with. You're a civilian now."

"Like hell I'm not going in there."

For the first time, John truly looks angry. "Then at least stay back and out of our way."

There are two more pops before we reach the first door. I rush forward, give it an almighty kick that blasts it off its frame, and take point with my bio-mech weapon that looks like a slim shotgun that I had hiding under my windbreaker. The others follow into the large and dark interior of the warehouse portion of the mill. I push out my power and sense where those spots of bitter magic dwell inside the building. The largest and most profane—the hydra—is further in near the river's edge but the other two—wait, two? There had been three other things in here before. But then the second sputters out as well until there's just the one.

Someone else is here killing them.

I hustle forward with my sights aimed before me as I take a door on the left, clear through another large open room, and enter the area where the roof is partially collapsed. Two furry bodies lie on the floor in expanding pools of blood just inside the door. And beyond—

A man in dark clothes from head to toe faces off against a werewolf. The latter leaps with jaws open wide for the man's throat. I shoot a bio-mech pulse but too late. Three gunshots ring through the empty room and the werewolf falls to the floor, rolling over itself until it lays still.

"Drop the gun! Hands where I can see them!" I shout and the rest of my team surges in to surround our mystery shooter.

Melody checks on the wolves on the floor. She doesn't need to say a word for me to know they're dead. The last spot of bitter magic vanishes as the third werewolf dies at the man's feet.

The man carefully sets his gun on the floor then raises his empty hands up to either side.

"Hands behind your head," John says. When the man does so, John moves forward to kick the gun out of reach. "On your knees."

"This is really unnecessary," the man says as he does as he's told. That voice is unmistakable.

John snatches the balaclava off the man's head to reveal none other than Specialist Laurence Jaeger.

"Can I get up now?" he asks unfazed. He just murdered three werewolves but sounds as if this is a minor inconvenience for him.

"I'm debating," John says coldly. "Melody?"

"They're dead," she answers.

"What the hell were you doing?" I hiss.

Specialist Jaeger's eyes turn lazily to me. "My job. I'm authorized to use deadly force if it's used against me. These three were on the serum but attacked me anyway."

"How could you even know that?" Charlie asks and shakes his head.

His uncle's attention falls on him next and you can feel the temperature in the room drop.

"You should know firsthand the answer to that," he says.

What is *that* supposed to mean? No one says anything but the specialist rises to his feet and dusts himself off. Then I hear hurried footsteps as Jefferson enters the room. He pauses beside me to take in the scene, the three dead werewolves on the floor, our guns still aimed at the specialist in the middle of our formation.

"Who let you in?" Specialist Jaeger drawls at him.

Jefferson's eyes widen and he snarls, "*You.*" Then immediately makes a beeline for him.

I smell trouble a mile away and grab his arm to wrench him to a halt. "Woah, woah, woah. Don't do something you'll regret."

"I wouldn't regret this," he growls.

Yeah, I probably wouldn't either but I've got more backing from the IMS than he does right now if he takes a shot at the specialist. "I take it you two have met before."

He tries to wrest his arm out of my grip so I let him go. "We've crossed paths."

"He's been interfering with my investigation," the specialist says and takes a step towards him.

Jefferson does the same until they're closer than I'd like—nearly within strangling distance. I inch towards to Jefferson although my eyes linger over the bodies of the werewolves.

"You've been making a mess," Jefferson says and curls his hands into fists. "These people deserve help but you'd rather feed them a bullet."

Nearby I sense that other bitter presence still biding its time. We're getting sidetracked here. There's a freaking hydra in the complex we need to take care of.

John knows the same and tries to step in. "Gentlemen—"

"Isn't that what you're looking for?" Specialist Jaeger says, ignoring him completely and moving even closer to his opponent. "To put a bullet or twenty into Dasc?"

"I'm doing whatever it takes to end this."

"Even if that means putting your dog of a daughter down?"

I don't even bother holding Jefferson back as he connects a punch with the specialist's jaw. There's a resounding crack as bone meets bone and the specialist's head snaps back.

Jefferson goes for a round of blows but John steps in like a slippery shadow. He moves so fast I almost don't follow but one second he's there and the next he twists Jefferson around and pushes him away.

Our team shifts to stand between the two in the opening John makes. Specialist Jaeger straightens as he holds a hand to his jaw. Jefferson only has eyes for him and breathes like a bull ready to charge.

"Both of you back down," John commands. "We have a hydra here to deal with."

Instead of listening like he should, the specialist moves around us and produces a pair of handcuffs. "Jefferson Barnes, I'm placing you under arrest for assaulting an IMS agent."

My jaw actually drops. "*What?*"

He puts a hand on Jefferson's wrist and when Jefferson moves to pull away, the specialist quickly slaps one end of the cuffs on. "You don't want to add additional charges to the list, do you?"

"You son of a—"

"Under Title 51, section 7—"

"You can't be serious!" I hiss.

John's hand snags my arm to hold me back when I make to rush the specialist. "We have a hydra to deal with. After that thing's dead, then we can worry about this. You got that?"

Steam could roll off my face in my anger as Jefferson is placed into handcuffs and the specialist starts to march him out of the building.

"I'll catch up with you later," he says directly to me before moving out the door.

"Come on," John says and tugs on my arm again. "Which way, Phoenix? I need you to focus. We each depend on each other and if you can't get your head—"

"It's this way," I snap and swing about to head deeper into the complex.

My fingers curl around my bio-mech rifle and I breathe through my teeth. I'm *furious* and so frustrated I couldn't punch Jaeger myself. And Jefferson—*flaming hydra crap*! I want to go after them but I can't. That cloud of corrupted magic lies ahead and we can't leave until it's taken care of.

So as angry as I am, I do my best to move quietly even though I'm pretty sure that thing already knows we're here. We move out of the warehouse portion of the mill and into the wood room. It's mostly empty but there's still a layer of sawdust and wood chips. Through the stagnant debris I see footsteps and trails of something big having slithered through the dust.

I can feel it. Directly before us down a stairwell it waits for its prey—meaning us—to walk past its hidey hole so it can attack us from behind. There's no guardian to speak of protecting it. I gesture to my team to indicate where it is. While Alona flies up to get a better view, John and I move forward as the distraction. Theo sets up at a cross angle. Charlie and Melody wait with their blood tipped swords out, ready to deliver a killing blow. We need to move precisely in order to kill this thing without giving it time to pin us down.

And I'm angry. That can do a lot for a person. I draw in every little bit of my power except for a sliver stretched out to the hydra like a string so I'll know the moment it moves. John and I walk cautiously forward around the front of the stairway and continue on. My magical tether lets me know when the hydra starts to creep up on us from behind. Its presence doesn't feel much bigger than the one in Bemidji. Perhaps it only hatched recently and hasn't had time to grow.

The second I sense it coiling up to strike, Alona lets out a caw to signal the others. I whip about as the hydra lashes out three acid dripping maws. Using the power I've reined in, I thrust out a hand to manipulate the barrier in my glove. I force it to expand using myself as its power source and trap all three heads within a shimmering bubble the size of an exercise ball. Six eyes leer at me only three feet away behind that barrier. Six eyes that taunt and rage and gleam. It's a hideous sight and one that would make a normal person cower or flee in terror. *This* is a monster.

But it's not the only monster here.

The expanse of that barrier quickly shrinks as I curl the fingers in my hand. I think of the bones and blood on the *Tregurtha* as I will that barrier to crush their skulls. The hydra tries to fight it. Each head lets out a wretched shriek and acid spatters the inside of the barrier but to no avail. And some part of me takes pleasure in the first crack that sounds as their bones begin to break.

Before I can go any further, Charlie appears on the beast's back—it's no more the size of a pony—and thrusts his sword through its scaly hide. There's a sizzling pop as the hydra's heart explodes in its chest. A shiver runs down its body before it lies still. I release the barrier bubble and the heads hit the ground with a squelchy thud as acid and black blood alike seep out. Its bitter essence shrinks and shrinks until it's gone.

A young level five monster and I rendered its greatest ability inert as if it were nothing.

Then I become aware Melody is staring at me. And Charlie. And the rest of the team.

Maybe they realized how powerful I can be.

Maybe I just realized it too.

"It's dead," I say flatly. "Can we go now?"

I turn to leave, not even waiting for an answer, and am struck so hard by a dizzy spell that I would have fallen flat on my face if not for Charlie porting to catch me. I sag in his arms and breathe heavily as the toll of that manipulation hits me hard.

"*Pixies*, that came out of nowhere," I pant.

"You could say that," Charlie mutters.

John comes up beside us as Charlie helps me take a seat on the floor. "What was that?"

"I wasn't sure I could actually pull that off," I mutter.

"No, I mean the fact that you drained yourself so thoroughly that if Charlie hadn't killed the thing, it could have easily killed you."

My cheeks burn. "But—"

"When we do anything, we do it as a team. I don't want to see you doing something so reckless again. You were just supposed to throw up a shield between us to distract it. I understand you have abilities that frankly could make a monster crap their pants but I want you to use them wisely."

I nod and take the offered protein bar Charlie passes me.

"Is there anything else in the building?"

"Nothing magical."

"Good. Alona, Theo, you're with me. We'll clear the rest of the building any way. Melody call in the cleanup crew. Charlie, keep an eye on her." He points to me as if I need a babysitter to make sure I don't go running off to crush more skulls.

But I did that, didn't I? I literally began crushing the skulls of that hydra. And I had *enjoyed* it. I look over my shoulder to the bloody mess I made as Melody calls in the cleanup crew. The jaws are slightly crooked and three pairs of eyes stare blankly into space. On the *Tregurtha*, when I saw the blood and bones, I threw up. Now with this other bloody scene before me, I don't feel an ounce of pity. In fact, part of me wishes I had done more.

As usual, Charlie watches me carefully as he stands and I finish the protein bar.

"What?" I snap.

"Nothing." He looks away and rolls his shoulders. "I just remember a girl that couldn't fire a gun properly after shooting her first monster."

I get to my feet and shove the empty wrapper at him. "Well, maybe if that girl had been a little tougher, we wouldn't be in this position right now."

He doesn't say anything when I stalk away to inspect the corpse of the hydra. What's the point of this thing? Why here? And why Bemidji? Of all the places to let a hydra loose, those seem like pretty useless targets. This isn't an IMS installation. I note a pile of bones down the stairwell where it's made some kind of nest. It clearly hasn't bothered to go anywhere else. The only thing special about this place are the werewolves using it as a way station. Could that be the link? Was there something about Bemidji connecting it to the werewolves such that Echidna's forces would target the area?

A headache forms in my temples trying to sift through the random pieces of information in my head. I just want to get out of here and find Specialist Jaeger so I can give him a piece of mind, maybe squeeze a bubble around *him* until he decides to let Jefferson off the hook.

We wait longer than I'd like for the cleanup team to arrive. Theo, Alona, and John come back after scouting the rest of the facility. There's no one and nothing else here. When at last the IMS crews come to clean up the crime scenes and dispose of the bodies, I'm in a rush to leave. None of my teammates bring up what I did back there. I wonder if some part of them is now afraid of me. Maybe I shouldn't have gone overboard like that.

It's well into the night when we exit the paper mill and return to the van. We drive back to the nearby airport and walk to the Osprey to await new orders. I check my cell phone once we reach the aircraft and find a text from Specialist Jaeger with a room number for the hotel next to the airport. Good. Then I'll go harass him. Since the rest of the team will probably stop me if I tell them where I'm going, I say I'm grabbing some snacks for the road while they fuel up and do final pre-flight checks.

I change into my civies up in the cockpit before walking across the tarmac, nabbing a taxi outside the terminal, and riding to the hotel on the other side of the highway. I don't bother to stop at the front desk and bypass it while the clerk is busy checking in a family of seven. The maroon carpet hushes my footsteps as I march down the hall until I find room 107 and bang on the door. It swings inwards a moment later.

"I'm glad you came," Specialist Jaeger says. He's changed out of his vigilante outfit for something bland and gray.

I push past him into the room. "I don't think you should be."

There's a single bed inside with an array of weapons spread across it and a duffle bag open with clothes spilling partway out. Jefferson's not here.

I spin about and cross my arms over my chest. "Where is he?"

"Waiting in my car before I drop him off with the local IMS authorities for processing," he says and moves around me to fold shirts and stuff them into his bag.

"I want you to release him."

"Of course you do. And under what legal reason, I wonder?" He says all this without looking up from bundling a pair of pants and shoving them haphazardly in with the rest of his things.

I bite the inside of my cheek. "You incited him to act. You shouldn't have taunted him about his daughter."

He laughs quietly but the sound builds until it fills the whole room. My fingers itch to strangle him so I squeeze my biceps instead to resist the urge.

"You know, you have an awfully strange fondness for werewolves despite everything that's happened to you. Dasc murdering your parents, turning your brother, then putting you through the wringer in those useless interrogations—not to mention an entire town of werewolves trying to kill you at one point, and then Jefferson's own daughter throwing all of your effort back in your face."

I breathe heavily through my nose but controlling my

temper has never really been my strong suit. "And you have a fondness for outright killing them."

He pauses, turns sideways to face me, and angles his head to the side. "Do you know why I was tracking those particular werewolves?"

"You're looking for Dasc."

"Yes and no. I came across them on my search but realized they didn't have any information to offer me. What I did find out, however, was that they had recently gone on a hunt in the city." A muscle feathers in his jaw and that handsome face holds cold malice. "They came across a young woman walking home after a long day waitressing. I found her mangled body ripped to shreds along the river."

The bloody scene aboard the *Tregurtha* flashes before my eyes. My pulse quickens.

"They went off the serum," I say quietly.

"No, actually. They didn't." He rolls up another shirt and chucks it into his bag. "I checked. They've been taking the regular doses, but the magic in their blood turned them into something horrific. When I confronted them in the mill, they attacked me. Can you really be angry at me for defending myself and killing them?"

I don't say anything but inside . . . no. No, I can't be angry at him for that.

"That's my job, Mason. I don't take pleasure in finding the victims and watching the murderers walk away because they claim a disease made them do it. They've played the victim card so many times that the system has lost sight of who the real victims are. So forgive me if I seem callous, or rude, or even cruel. I don't care to waste time trying to sway people from a viewpoint that, by my definition, is woefully ignorant."

He continues to pack and I just stand there, heat radiating off my skin as I contemplate his words. I've seen the good and the bad side of werewolves—like Hawk and then Dasc. I still believe it boils down to an individual's choices but . . . what if having the werewolf disease made one inclined to go the more violent route? There have been times Hawk has scared me with violent spurts. Then again, I've scared myself by what I've done.

"I thought you of all people would understand," he continues and zips up his duffle. My face is starting to hurt from holding a frown for so long. "I've read all about Dasc and your interrogations, not to mention what he did to your parents. And then there's Charlie."

"Charlie?"

"Yes, my darling nephew you seem so fond of." He pulls out a military style carry bag and begins loading it with the pieces of weaponry off the bed.

"What about Charlie?"

He pauses with a gun and magazine in either hand to appraise me. "He never told you, did he?"

My anger spikes again. "Tell me what?"

"How his parents died."

Cold seeps into my veins. This is something I should be hearing from Charlie when he's ready, not his jerk of an uncle. But will he ever tell me? I made the connection a long time ago that his sordid past with werewolves had something to do with his parents. I still don't know the what, where, when, or why though. And curse it all, I'm too curious for my own good.

I'm in the middle of debating telling him to shove it or explain when he continues on without my prompting.

"I think he was . . . maybe six? Just a kid when everything went to hell." He shoves the magazine into the gun and tucks it into his bag before moving on to another. "Charlie's father was my brother. We were pretty close but he went and married that psycho wife of his. I don't know what he saw in her."

Specialist Jaeger doesn't look at me as he tells his story. It's as if he's rehearsing it to himself as he checks each of his many guns, daggers, and ammunition supplies. I don't move. I'm frozen to the spot as I listen.

"They fought all the time. Didn't have a great marriage. Ended up getting a divorce when Charlie was little. My brother came to live with me for a while. Charlie got shipped back and forth between them. Things got nasty. That witch of an ex-wife tried to steal Charlie away when he was six and ran off into the Rockies. My brother and I went and hunted her down with the police. Found Charlie by himself at a hotel. Kid didn't have a clue what was going on."

I can picture it in my head. Little Charlie with big green eyes sitting alone in a hotel room, quiet and probably trying to read a book while even that young.

"We couldn't find his mom. Charlie said she got hurt—wouldn't tell us how—and thought she went to a hospital. Turns out she was bitten by a werewolf when off trying to use an ATM in town."

A shiver travels down my spine. Oh, Charlie.

"I thought she was a loon before but the werewolf disease made her so much worse." He zips up the main pouch with extra force. "We all stayed the night at the hotel. My brother and Charlie were in one room. I was in the one next door. I heard a scream in the middle of the night. Ran to their room and found a wolf had ripped out my brother's throat while he slept. It was her. Charlie woke up in time to see his father murdered."

My stomach churns and hands shake. After my parents died and I grew up in Underground, for years I wished I could remember more. I could only vaguely recall the night they were murdered. I so desperately wanted memories but now that I know the truth, I wish I could forget. Does Charlie remember that horrible night? Does he remember seeing his father torn into by a wolf? His own mother?

"Of course, the wolf fled out a window and I had a hard time explaining what I had seen to the police. Then an agent showed up with the FBI." He gives a small shake of his head. What he's really saying is that an IMS agent arrived. "She believed my story and said Charlie was in danger. So, she set up a trap for the wolf using Charlie as bait. I didn't understand what was going on at the time but I wanted to help, even got myself a gun. And sure enough, when Charlie was asleep, his mother came back for him. Human that time."

He finishes loading up his bag but leaves a single magazine out on the bed. He takes a seat next to it, crosses his arms over his chest, and finally looks me straight in the eye.

"She must have spotted me and the agent. Went wolf mode in an instant. Charlie saw his mom turn into the thing that killed his dad. She went for me. The agent missed the shot. Charlie hopped out of bed to protect his mother but too late. I gunned her down—emptied a whole clip into her."

Fire works its way up my throat and it becomes terribly difficult to breathe. And suddenly I imagine myself in that dark room, little Charlie rushing for his wolfish mother that looks exactly like Dasc's form, and I empty the entire clip from my gun into her chest. I close my eyes and an unbidden tear slips down my face.

"Charlie's never forgiven me for it. I've tried to look after him but he's always had too much of his mother in him."

He sighs and gets to his feet.

"Why?" I manage to squeeze out and open my eyes. "Why send me your room number? Why tell me this?"

The specialist picks up the magazine and walks over until we're only a foot apart. "Because I've read the reports, Spartan. I know you have a personal score to settle with Dasc but have been conflicted because of the situation with your brother. But I also know you once put a full clip into that *schweinhund's* chest, and I have a feeling you're eager to do the same again."

He holds out the magazine to me. It's full of red .45 bullets—wolfsbane.

"It's an extra-long magazine, just in case," he says and pushes it into my empty hands. "I figure a Constantine ought to be prepared for the worst, don't you think?"

The weight presses into my palms and I stare at it. Without even checking, I know it'll fit my mother's gun— the same gun that had its own set of wolfsbane bullets when I first found it. My mother's legacy. A werewolf hunter. A Constantine. That blood runs through my veins. Blood that currently runs cold.

Specialist Jaeger picks up his bags and slings the duffle over his shoulder. "Take it or leave it. It's your call."

Then he walks out of the room and I'm left holding a magazine of werewolf-killing bullets in my hands. I ought to pitch it or turn it over to the proper authorities so they know he has illegal ammunition. These things are meant to kill people like my brother. I can't keep these. I'm trying to work towards a cure, not kill them off before there's a chance I can save them.

But then I think of little Charlie seeing both of his parents being killed. I think of my own parents. And I think of that smug smile of Dasc's face—the father of the werewolf disease—as he escaped Underground with Jefferson's daughter.

Ten minutes later I leave the hotel with a heavy weight in my pocket.

17

Hawk

Going back to work is like being in an alternate reality. The world I'd much rather experience is the one tucked away in the woods where werewolves can be themselves without prejudiced eyes on their backs. Despite my . . . lapse, I truly enjoyed being able to run free with others like me. But maybe someday we won't have to hide anymore. Phoenix will play a key role, I know it, and so will I. Together we can put an end to the curse of the werewolves. If there were two people I'd bet on that could pull it all off, it'd be Phoenix and Genna. I don't know of anyone else so keen on curing the disease.

So I walk as normally as I might into work with the usual crowd of employees. I say good morning to Spartan Knox, throw my usual jokes at Doug that bounce right off him, and make the typical water cooler small talk. The second Vicky sees me, she turns heel and disappears somewhere amongst the cubicles. Despite my casual attitude, I'm hyper aware of the mechanical trigger hidden in my back pocket, a gift from Witty. In order for this to work, I'm going to have to set the scene and play my part perfectly. There's no room for doubt or error, but I'm motivated to see this through now more than ever. At this point I'd do anything for a cure after what happened last night.

The first thing I do when I get to my desk is check the IMS feeds, especially the local ones for any indication that agents might be on to the secret base outside Seattle. Then I check for any reports of Dasc's compound that Genna's preparing to free. Once I'm satisfied the IMS isn't aware of either, I finally pay attention to the urgent message at the top of my screen. When I see Team Sierra mentioned in the first line, everything else is pushed to the side of my mind. They uncovered what they believe to be a massive infiltration of hydra eggs in the United States and possibly Canada as well. All agents are advised to be on the lookout and that veteran agents will respond to code blacks for the time being while the Spartans track down the hydra.

A flurry of whispers and chatter swells in the office as one by one the rest of the employees see the message or tell their co-workers about it. Hydra. Lots of hydra. I knew Phoenix and her team had found an egg that hatched, but this . . . I have to let Genna know, just in case. There's no telling if any of those hydra eggs have made their way to Seattle. I do know the sort of chaos this is going to create though—tying up our elite forces, causing panic, and giving the IMS tunnel vision to deal with this threat. I get it. I do. But I know how clever Dasc has been and how clever Echidna must be. Is there more to this plan than just releasing hydra?

Later. I'll get a message to Genna later today. For now, I have a mission to accomplish.

And it starts with a bit of dramatic acting. Pressing the trigger in my pocket, my monitor goes dark.

"Dang it!" I say loudly and slap my hands on my desk.

Doug peeks at me around his monitor. I ignore him for once and stare very focused like at my computer and pound at the keyboard for a bit before picking up the phone and dialing the in-house technicians.

"Tech support," a dull voice answers.

"Hi, my monitor died on me. I have no idea what happened."

"Have you tried turning it off and then on again?"

"Yup."

"Is the power light on?" he asks and sounds so lifeless that I wouldn't be surprised if he's a zombie.

"Yup. There's a green light."

A long, nasally sigh comes through the line. "Are all the cables plugged in?"

"Oh, the cables are supposed to be plugged *in*? How foolish of me. I've been using them to make friendship bracelets."

"*Sir—*"

"Yes, the cables are plugged in."

There's a long pause before he says, "We could try—"

"You know what? I've got it to work again. Tried an old trick my friend taught me."

"What?"

"Thanks, pal." I promptly hang up on him and release Witty's trigger. My screen flares back to life as if nothing had happened.

While the conversation in itself to tech support was useless, having Doug listening in was not. I've guessed on more than one occasion that Doug is here for the sole purpose of keeping an eye on me—Milton's whipping boy. Well, now if anyone questions me during the next phase of my plan, I'll have little weasel Doug to back me up.

I make sure to wait exactly a half hour before getting up and searching for the devil's advocate himself. I find Milton in the break room. He's got his morning schedule in hand as he fills his mug with coffee.

"Oh, good," I say with great exaggeration of relief. "I'm glad I caught you." Even though I know this is where Milton is every morning at exactly this time. People fail to realize just how observant I can be. I'm going to use it to my advantage.

"Hawk. Good morning," he says a bit stiffly. "If you could give me a minute, that'd be great."

"Of course. Meeting in your office in say . . . fifteen minutes?"

His little piggy eyes tear away from his schedule and narrow at me. "Meeting? For what?"

"I have a proposal I'd like to discuss with you. I wanted to make sure I had your approval before I did anything."

He straightens a bit at that. He *loves* being the boss around here and having people suck up to him.

"Fifteen minutes then."

"Great." I give him an eager smile but nothing too ostentatious. Everyone knows I don't like it here. I can't overplay my part by smiling too much. Heaven forbid if they think I'm actually happy. They'd be suspicious straight away. But as I step out of the break room and walk back to my desk, it *is* a little difficult to keep from smiling. I'm finding a devious amount of happiness in doing something behind Milton's back. Dang, this feels good.

As long as everything goes to plan, I'm really going to enjoy this.

I return to my desk to wait out the fifteen minutes while aimlessly paging through papers without really looking at any of them. With three minutes left to go, I return to the break room to get what I like to call my "contingency plan." Grabbing one of the white mugs from the cabinet, I pour myself a hot cup of coffee and then walk to Milton's office. Glass walls separate him from the rest of the floor on the east end. He has his back to the windows so all he ever does is stare through those glass walls keeping an eye on everybody, making sure we're doing what we're supposed to. I recall similar glass panels at Werevine Pharmaceutical—back when I was actually doing something.

Milton looks up when I approach and waves me in. I close the glass door behind me and take a seat in one of the chairs on the opposite side of his desk. I make sure I have Witty's trigger in my hand tucked between my hand and coffee mug.

"Thanks for seeing me," I begin.

He straightens a few papers until everything is square on his desk, aligning his pen ever so neatly, before he clasps his hands in his lap.

"What did you want to talk about?" he asks.

"Well, you read the news on the feeds this morning, didn't you?"

"Of course."

"So you know about the hydra threat."

"Yes. Please get to the point soon."

One of these days, I'm going to put super glue on his chapstick, I swear.

I clear my throat. "Okay, here it is. We have a lot of computing power here. I thought if we pooled our resources, we could really help out in a big way." I squeeze my palm against the trigger but it only looks as if I'm clutching my coffee cup a bit more tightly. "The Spartans need eyes on everything. If we could just shift our focus away from typo checking—"

"They already have analysts working day and night on the problem."

"But if there are hydra here—"

"*Hawk*." He temples his fingers together and gives me a knowing stare across his desk. "I understand you don't appreciate the intricacies of the work we do here, but it is important."

My brow draws into a deep frown. "Then is it possible for me to transfer somewhere where I can actually be useful?"

He sighs and gives a sideways glance to his computer. It's obvious he's ready for this conversation to be over. To be honest, so am I. He does a double take at his computer and jiggles the mouse a little. When he doesn't get the response he wants, he pecks at the keyboard and mutters under his breath. I keep my palm pressed tight to the trigger.

"What?" I ask and make it sound as if I'm irritated at being interrupted mid-conversation.

He pounds more aggressively on the keyboard. "It just turned off or something."

"The monitor went black?" I ask.

"Yeah."

"I just had that this morning."

Milton picks up his phone and starts to dial. "I'm calling tech support."

"No, no, no," I say and stand. "You don't want to do that. They wasted my time and almost screwed up my computer earlier. Let me help. I can fix it."

He eyes me with suspicion. Yeah, I get it—*me* trying to help *him*. Who wouldn't be suspicious?

I wave my free hand at him. "They'll just give you the usual run around anyway. Turn it off and on again. Is there power? Blah, blah, blah."

"Well, what did you do to fix it?" He doesn't move from his chair.

Stupid, stubborn Milton. I need him to leave.

"It has to do with the BIOS and a snap charge and a disconnect with the . . . motherboard." I spew out words Witty gave me incase this happened. It's good to simply confuse your enemy with technical terms, he told me. To his credit, he's right. Milton blinks and then grudgingly moves out of the way so I can sit down. As expected, he then hovers behind me to watch my every move. Time to initiate my contingency plan.

I scooch forward in his swivel chair really fast with my coffee in hand and splash it wildly so it gets all over Milton's pants.

"Oh, shoot!" I exclaim.

He makes a loud, unintelligible growl and flicks the hot coffee off his hands.

"Here, let me." I grab a handful of tissue off his desk and act like I'm going to pat the coffee off his pants. He immediately backs away and puts his hands up.

"I've got it," he says sharply. "Just get my computer working."

"Of course. I'm so sorry." He marches out and I yell after him. "I heard grape juices helps take out coffee stains!"

He keeps on marching and I laugh quietly to myself as I release the trigger and his monitor instantly comes back to life as if nothing had happened. Good old Witty. That's a neat trick. I immediately set the coffee aside and open up the search function with Milton's account still logged in. Perfect.

Erebus.

I hit enter.

This account does not have the proper clearance to access this record.

I blink. Then glower. I move to knock the coffee cup clean off the desk in a fit of rage but catch myself an inch away from shattering ceramic. It didn't work.

A shadow fills up the doorway. "What are you doing, Hawk?"

I whip my head up to find Spartan Knox watching me with the same kind of look my drill instructor gave me whenever he thought I was hiding something.

"Milton had a computer glitch," I say.

"But what are you doing?"

I look him straight in the eye and fight the urge to swallow. "I was meeting with him when he had the same issue I did earlier. Tech support would take their time getting up here so I figured I'd help."

His unflinching gaze doesn't lose its hard edge. He knows I wouldn't help Milton out of the kindness of my heart. I've made my distaste for him too obvious. If Milton really did have a computer problem, I would have enjoyed watching him squirm with a red face as he waited for tech support to come and fix the problem.

I lean over the desk and lower my voice. "I figure the faster it's fixed, the faster we can get back to our meeting. I swear he's just trying to blow me off."

The words work. Knox nods in a knowing sort of way but doesn't move on.

"So? Did you fix it?" he asks.

I turn back to the computer, randomly click the mouse a few times and announce, "All done."

"Good."

He hangs around until I vacate Milton's seat and return to the other side of the desk. Only then does he walk away. As he heads to his cubicle, I watch his back through the glass panes of the office. Milton may have been a bust but I know someone who would have the credentials to get what I need. The Spartan commander—even if he is temporarily grounded—would have access. I'm sure of it. Only, a Spartan stands in the way of getting said access. A Spartan and a friend. This just got a lot more complicated.

Milton finally returns with his pants wet and a scowl on his face. He goes straight for his computer and gives a sigh of relief when he sees everything is up and running again. Then his beady eyes land on me.

"What are you still doing here?"

I shrug. "Waiting for us to finish our meeting."

"Meeting's over. You already know my opinion on the matter."

"But—"

"You have reports to go over. I suggest you get to them."

He ignores me and types angrily on his keyboard. I shove out of the chair and return to my desk in a huff as one would expect me to after leaving Milton's office. When I sit down, I stare blankly at my computer screen and twirl a pen between my fingers thinking over my next move. I'm also aware of Doug staring at me from around his cubicle.

"Take a picture. It'll last longer," I say dully.

The road from here is bumpy and one I was hoping not to take. Spartan Knox is a very intelligent man. Getting the slip around him isn't going to be as easy as spilling some coffee in his lap and hoping he leaves his computer unattended. With greater security access comes greater responsibility. He'll be very careful about leaving his account open. But what other choice do I have? What other option is available to me? I'll have to be clever. *Very* clever. Maybe Witty can give me some other gadget to help too. I don't know what but *something*. Being a traitor is tough work.

As soon as I have the thought, it tastes sour in my mouth. I've been loyal to the IMS my entire life. I've fought for them. I've bled for them. I became a Spartan for crying out loud. But what I'm doing . . . it is traitorous, isn't it? But traitor to whom, I wonder? The IMS betrayed the werewolves with their forced serum injections, secret Fields facility, and probation rings for those of us that have been loyal from the beginning.

But this is an internal debate for another time, not here in the middle of the work place. I sigh and open up the first document I'm supposed to be reviewing.

The rest of the day I spend split between pretending to work and taking as many water breaks as I can without suspicion in order to pass by Knox's desk. He's always there and the few times he isn't, he's logged out. People talk to him and he gives them his attention with a hand still on the mouse or stands not more than a couple feet away from his computer. As I suspected, he guards his clearance carefully. This isn't going to be an easy task. I feel a bit slimy every time I think about how I'm going to sneak around my friend's defenses to get what I need.

After work I do my usual routine. Apartment, gym, diner. Daisy doesn't stop to chat and it hurts a little. It was nice having a normal conversation with a normal person who thought of me as normal. So, as soon as I'm done with my food I make for the arcade. The manager makes a cranky face when I arrive and enter the code to let Witty know I'm here. While I wait for someone to show up, I make the rounds on the video games. I get fairly good at them but I'm sure I'm nowhere near as good as Witty.

I'm in the middle of shooting zombies when someone tries to sneak up behind me.

"Oh, how the mighty have fallen." Rosalyn comes around my side sporting a smirk. She's hiding beneath a bright red wig with short curls. "From saving Underground to shooting pixelated zombies."

My heart sinks a little. "Rosalyn. I didn't think you'd be the one to show up."

She picks at something under one of her fingernails. Right. Because that's her thing. Making sure people know she doesn't care.

"Genna's busy sucking up to Dasc and Witty's helping her."

"So, you're stuck babysitting the compound?"

She glowers at me. "Someone has to keep those idiots alive."

"You have such high regard for your comrades, don't you?"

"Just because we're all werewolves doesn't mean we're family or even friends. That's like saying all humans are chums."

I bob my head. "That's true, but you did help rescue them."

She rolls her eyes. "Is there a reason I'm here?"

"I wanted to pass along some intel. A bunch of hydra eggs have shown up in country. Have you heard anything about it? You guys ought to be careful."

"We know," she says simply. "We don't know much, but we know they're around."

"Oh." Guess my intel isn't as useful as I thought it was going to be. I guess I should be relieved that they're already aware of the situation. "Well, since you're here . . . I want to go back to the compound."

"No."

"Why not?"

Without even looking, she raps her knuckles against my hand with the probation ring. "Because you're tagged. Can't risk it."

"Well, where's Merlin? He could—"

"It's too risky for him to come here too often."

She crosses her arms over her chest and pins me with those icy blue eyes of hers. She's really quite pretty despite the fact that she looks like she wants to kill everyone she meets. While Genna's made of stern stuff, Rosalyn's made of sharp thorns and I don't think she cares who she hurts with that prickly personality of hers.

"You know," I say to break the tension, "You pull off the cold-blooded killer look very well."

"Good."

"If you didn't slightly resemble your brother, I wouldn't think you two were related."

Her chin lowers so she's no longer looking down at me but rather through her eyebrows. If I thought she looked intimidating before, it doesn't compare to the psychopathic stare she gives me now.

"Don't ever talk about my brother," she says quietly.

"Why not?"

Instead of giving me an answer—or moving to gut me which she looks liable to do—she turns about and makes for the door.

"Why does Genna trust you?" I call out to her. She pauses. "Of all the people in the world to trust, why choose you? You made your love of Dasc plain enough before."

She whips about and a flash of steel leaves her hand. My training gives me the speed and judgment to dodge it. Whatever it is smashes into an arcade over my shoulder in a loud crash of glass and sparking electronics.

"Oh, good," she says lightly as if her mail arrived on time and the world is sunny. "Glad to see you're not out of practice."

My heart beats in my ears. I don't chance a glance at what she threw but I'll bet it was a dagger.

"Was that a warm-up?" I say and press a hand to my heart. "Why, Rosalyn, I could have sworn I touched a nerve."

"You're just as annoying as your sister," she snaps.

"Thank you. We pride ourselves on our belligerence."

Her eyes narrow to slits. "That's clever. You should turn your act into a show. You can call it 'how to make everyone want to stab you.'"

"Actually, I wanted to go with Ginger Snap but I'm afraid people would show up expecting cookies and be terribly disappointed."

She blinks. "What?"

"Gingersnaps."

"I don't get it."

"They're cookies."

"What's that?"

I cock my head with a smirk. "You're messing with me, aren't you?"

She smiles. "I think I'll turn it into an act. I'll call it 'snapping a ginger in half.'"

"That doesn't really roll off the tongue, though, does it?"

"Do you ever stop talking?"

"You never answered my question."

Rosalyn rolls her eyes. "Having to explain how trustworthy you are makes you *not* look trustworthy. There's no point trying to spell it out for you. I guess it comes down to, do you trust Genna to trust me?"

That's a fair point. Genna's smart and clever. If Rosalyn was actually working for Dasc as some double-double-agent, Genna would know . . . wouldn't she? And I trust Genna. I think. Still—trustworthy or not, Rosalyn is a hard person to like.

"Well, since we've established you aren't going to the compound and there's no reason for me to be here, I'm leaving." Rosalyn makes for the door but it swings open a second before she reaches it.

Merlin as his younger iteration pauses and looks down at Rosalyn. "You left."

She grabs his arm and hauls him inside off the sidewalk. "What are you doing here?"

"You left," he repeats.

"For such a brilliant wizard you do some really dumb things."

"It makes me nervous when I'm left alone," Merlin says, unfazed.

Before Rosalyn can sneak him away, I step in between them. "Well, since you're here, Merlin—"

I hold out my hand with the probation ring and Rosalyn rolls her eyes.

"He wants to visit the compound again," she explains when Merlin gives me a puzzled look. "We don't have time for this."

"You had time enough to come out to meet me," I argue. "Bringing me to the compound is just going back the way you came."

"Who says I was at the compound?" Rosalyn says but then waves her hand. "Fine. Whatever. Merlin, do your thing."

The young wizard smiles, wiggles his fingers over the probation ring, and mutters something.

"You're so overdramatic," Rosalyn sneers. "Let's go before I change my mind."

Feeling the burden of the day lifting from my shoulders, I follow the two outside and take the same route as I had with Genna, Witty, and Merlin before. After we leave the city, Rosalyn happily throws a hood over my head and we travel some more before exiting the car. Rosalyn is a lot less worried about me falling on my face than Genna was. I stumble a few times without my sight and Rosalyn not being much of a guide. When we reach the gates, the vampire guards greet us and we're allowed inside. As soon as we're there, Rosalyn splits off, grumbling about finding peace and quiet away from whiners.

"Don't mind her," Merlin says with an old man's voice and when I look back at him he's got his long white beard and wrinkles again. "She's had a difficult life."

"So I've heard. And you?"

"What about me?"

"I'm a naturally curious person and I don't know a thing about you."

He gives me a sad smile and pats my shoulder. "Perhaps another time I'll tell you. You should join the others in the level below. That's why you came, isn't it?"

Before I can say anything, he walks away hunched and bowed.

It's true. My mind has been on the indoor field when not preoccupied with getting into secure accounts at work. There's no point hanging about then. I make straight for the stairwell that leads to the false field. I pass the stationed guards who question me briefly before letting me pass once the way inside is clear. I step through the thick double doors and give a big sigh that loosens the muscles in my back. The pain of the serum doesn't feel so bad right now, not when I get to experience this kind of freedom. There are already plenty of others running around and playing games. My kind of people.

I hesitate before attempting to shift. The last time things

went about as bad as they could go. The tension returns to my muscles.

The door creaks open and clangs shut behind me.

"Stage fright?" It's Rosalyn again.

I do my best to ignore her and roll my head around my shoulders. "I'm fine."

"Living in fear isn't really living at all. I should know."

She shrugs past me, rolls her shoulders, and shifts into her silver wolf form with a mask of black. Such an odd coloration. At least it's easy to mark her out in a crowd of wolves. It always seems wise to keep a tab on Rosalyn if she's in the vicinity. She tilts her head and her tongue hangs out as if she's laughing at me. I give her my best vicious smile until she moves away.

Without an audience, I take a deep breath and will myself to change. The pain comes at me as usual but there isn't a loss of identity in the mix like last time. I keep my head, the pendant grows warm against my chest, and I become Hawk the wolf. Well, that's a relief. With all four paws firmly on the ground, I move at a trot then a full on sprint around the field. Wind in my face, senses alert, scents in the air. No shame. No hiding. Freedom.

I run and run and run and eventually Rosalyn starts to shadow me. I slow to a walk, panting from exertion. Rosalyn bobs her head at me, flicks her tail, and then moves off to join the others in what looks to be a game of freeze tag. It's pretty hilarious watching the werewolves pretend to be statues while their teammates rush around trying to unfreeze them. When I don't follow immediately, Rosalyn barks at me and motions with a forepaw.

For the next hour—or at least I think it's an hour—I

play like a young pup with the others. I feed off their energy and join in the fun. Despite freeze tag seeming like a childish game for a bunch of werewolves to be playing, there's a sense of combat to it and no one minds if they look silly. The whole time it's go, go, go—leap, dodge, tag, slide, roll. I'm pretty good but the others are better. I'm not used to the feeling, actually, so I'm determined to become better. I watch Rosalyn closely whenever I can—she's clearly a master of her wolf form. It's unclear who finally calls the game, but we leave en masse for the double exit doors. The majority of the group hangs back and one or two move forward at a time to shift, exit, and shut the doors again before the next few go up. Safety protocol.

Rosalyn and I are the last to leave. She changes back to herself in a hurry but it takes me a little longer. At last, I rise sweaty on two feet, a smile on my face. No freakish seizures today. That's a relief. It would have been extra embarrassing in front of Rosalyn. She waves at the camera and the door opens for us.

"You were good out there," she says as we exit together.

I blink. "Was that . . . was that a *compliment*?"

"Don't get used to it."

"Of course not. I'll take it for the singular treasure that it is."

"You're weird."

I shrug. "You were pretty amazing out there."

She cracks her knuckles. "Years of practice. Still not good enough."

"That's nonsense."

"No, it's not." She walks a little faster so I speed up to match her pace. I don't say anything and she gives me a long sideways look as if sensing I'm not going to leave until she spills. She huffs. "Sure, I'm good. I know that. But I've never been the *best*. It makes a difference where I'm from."

"Meaning . . . Dasc's encampment."

She nods. "Growing up there was always a competition. Who could be the fastest? Who could be the strongest? Who could be the most loyal?" She huffs again. "I'd try *so* hard but I was always second best. Do you know what it's like always being in someone else's shadow? It's like you—you're—"

"You're not even you're own person sometimes," I say quietly. "Everything you are is defined by someone else—knowing you can never be them. Yeah. I know."

As much as I hate to admit it.

Rosalyn slows to a normal walk.

"I guess you do, don't you," she says. "I think it was even more frustrating knowing that the other person didn't want it as much as I did. I wanted to be the best more than anything, to be named Whisper and be recognized as the better woman."

"And now?"

"And now . . ." She grimaces. "Well, I still want to be better. I always will. I'm too competitive." I nod in agreement. "I mean, I could turn Genna over to Dasc right now and take up her place as the Dark Whisper. I'd be recognized as the best but I still wouldn't be *better* than her."

"That's not the most comforting thing you've said . . ."

She keeps on talking, gesturing animatedly with her hands. "She always beat me in the war games and on missions and gaining Dasc's favor—"

"Seriously, this conversation is not taking a good turn—"

"But turning her in to Dasc would be a cheat. And as satisfying as that might be just to win—"

"You're making me really nervous—"

"It wouldn't be the fulfillment I'm looking for."

She at last comes to a stop and slaps her hands to her sides with a great sigh.

"So, where does that leave you?" I ask, almost dreading the answer.

"Attempting to outdo her at her own game."

"Meaning?"

"She wants to cure everyone and free us from Dasc. Well, I'll beat her to it. I'll prove that I'm better."

"Uh . . . that's the spirit?"

She plants her hands on her waist and narrows her eyes at nothing in particular in the distance. "I'm motivated. I can do it."

"I've no doubt."

"And I owe her," she says grudgingly. "She got me back to my brother and kept him safe." For the first time in . . . well, *ever*, she looks sad. "It was good seeing him again if only for a little while. No matter what happened, I was always the best in his eyes. I knew it."

And at last I think I finally understand why Genna trusts Rosalyn. She may have her own twisted way of thinking but she'll be loyal in this endeavor.

"I'm glad you told me that," I say.

She shoots me a sharp look. "Don't get all emotional on me now."

I wipe at fake tears and sniffle. "I'm sorry. It was just so beautiful."

"Geez." She rolls her eyes and stalks away. "I don't have

a clue what Genna sees in you. Come on. We need to get you back before someone realizes you're gone and you screw everything up."

I shake my head and follow after. Same old Rosalyn, but at least now I understand a little better what drives her. I go out the way I came and Merlin meets up with us. Meaning, once we reach the entrance Rosalyn has the pleasure of throwing a bag over my head before leading me clumsily out. We at last come to a car and after a few minutes of driving, Rosalyn rips the bag off my head with a smirk. I run a hand through my static-wild hair.

"I think you pulled a few hairs out," I say.

"Baby."

"I wasn't *complaining*. It was merely an observation."

She just smiles and we continue to Seattle in silence. We zig zag through the streets until we reach the arcade. The car comes to a stop behind the building and Rosalyn motions for me to stay put as she pulls out a cell phone from the glove compartment. She hits a speed dial number.

"Reese, are we clear?" she asks. "Perfect." She spins towards me. "Okay, loser. Get out."

"You give me all sorts of warm and fuzzy feelings, Rosalyn."

She rolls her eyes. Merlin, however, gives me a big smile and waves enthusiastically.

"You should be fine now, lad. I'll see you again tomorrow, yes?"

My chest feels lighter at the thought of being able to escape to that safe haven once more. I beam at him in reply.

Rosalyn shoots Merlin a nasty look. "What?"

"Yes, I think I'd rather like a daily excursion. It's settled then."

"You are *not* sneaking out here every day—"

"Until tomorrow then, Hawk!"

"MERLIN!"

I slip out of the car and Merlin guns it through the rear lot seconds later. Laughing to myself and feeling lighter than I have in ages, I enter through the back of the arcade with thoughts of tomorrow's adventure at the compound already filling my mind.

18

Phoenix

The clip of wolfsbane bullets in my bag feels like a bomb waiting to go off. I'm aware of its presence at all times like someone staring at the back of my head. Between the bullets, lingering over what I learned about Charlie's past, and Jefferson's pending charges, it's hard for me to keep my focus despite needing a clear head more than ever.

We're hunting hydra after all.

The IMS analysts have been working around the clock to find us leads. The IMS has never been in such a flurry before. Of course, that means the information they spit out gets sent to us to investigate.

By the time I got back to the Osprey from meeting with Specialist Jaeger, we had already received three new locations to check. After thirty-six straight hours awake and on the move, flying from Edina to Hibbing and now Duluth, we're starting to feel the strain. Two of the locations were a bust but it was obvious *something* had been there recently. An

IMS cleanup crew has been moving along in our wake trying to pull clues from the sites while making sure anything magical is secured or disposed of.

Our third suspect location ends up bringing us right back to the northern end of Duluth.

"Wish they could have figured this one out when we were here before," Theo grouses.

His eyes are heavy-lidded and his words are starting to slur with a lack of sleep. He's the second most energetic one of the bunch, though. Melody actually manages to beat him on that count. Her perpetual optimism somehow gives her more energy than the rest of us. While Alona brings us in, we switch between sitting and dozing or stretching to try to wake up. It's not like we haven't done stints like this before. Being able to function on no sleep for a long period of time was part of Spartan training. It's not fun by any means and no one looks forward to it, but at least we can face times like this knowing we've persevered through it before.

As we pass through the darkness near the midnight hour, I do my best not to stare at Charlie—although it's pretty easy to keep my eyes glued to him without being noticed when he's dozing and the others can't be too bothered to care. I'm pretty sure Theo's been staring at the same spot on the wall for the last half hour so my doing it isn't too suspicious. So, I watch Charlie slumber as I fight my drooping eyelids. He looks so peaceful. His chin rests almost touching his collarbone, hands folded neatly in his lap, and *Pride and Prejudice* tucked into the crook of his arm so it doesn't fall while he's out of it. That, or maybe Melody put it there when I wasn't looking.

I can't imagine what he's been through. I mean, partly I

can. We both lost our parents at a young age, but my situation wasn't nearly as tangled as his. An evil man killed my parents. It makes it easy to hate Dasc without any reserves. But Charlie . . . someone he loved killed the other person he loved, and then that person was killed by the man who ended up raising him. What a twisted mess. No wonder Charlie was so bitter and snappish when I first met him. Granted, he's still kind of bitter and snappish but his hard edges have softened somewhat, at least towards me. I don't know how I managed that, actually. Or if it had anything to do with me at all. What I do know, is that beneath the pain and anger is a man who puts every bit of his heart into the things he cares about. There are no half measures when it comes to his friends.

The Osprey gives a bit of a shake as it encounters some turbulence and Charlie jolts awake. When our eyes connect for a brief moment, I simply nod in acknowledgment and then gaze unfocused on the hull across from me.

I wonder what Charlie would think if I told him I have a magazine of wolfsbane bullets in my bag tucked beneath my seat.

Then again, maybe I already know what he would think.

"Wake up, everyone," Alona says over the speaker. "We're a minute out."

Charlie rubs at his eyes, grabs hold of the harness above his head, and gets to his feet. "I can't believe they think there's a hydra here. First Enger Tower has vampires, now this."

"What's special about this place?" Theo asks.

"It's Glensheen Mansion," Charlie says. When Theo and

I give him blank stares, he rolls his eyes. "It's a famous, historical site and museum in Duluth. Geez, guys."

Theo slaps his hands on his knees and turns furiously wide-eyed to me. "*Is nothing sacred anymore?!*"

Melody rather unceremoniously snorts a laugh and I spot John hiding a smile.

The sound in the bay warps as the air sprites make our approach near silent. Time to get to work. We don our special masks, stand, and take hold of the netting over our heads to keep ourselves steady as Alona loops over our destination. A copy of what she sees on thermal is relayed to us on a monitor. According to that source, there's no one and nothing in or around the impressive estate. When they say mansion, they mean mansion.

But I know that thermal can be very deceiving.

At a nod to John, he hits the controls to lower the bay door. The wind doesn't even hit us despite the fact that on any other aircraft it would. The air sprites have formed a soundless bubble around us. We won't feel the wind until we escape their magical sphere. I step forward to the edge of the open bay and keep one hand on the netting above me while the other I hold out palm first before me. For whatever reason, it helps me focus. I close my eyes and stretch out my tethers of magic. I sense something almost immediately and let my hand stray in its direction so when I open my eyes I know the exact direction and my comrades do as well. There's something monstrous lurking in the boathouse positioned on the edge of Lake Superior. Two things, actually.

I hold up two fingers to my team and point at the

boathouse below. John nods in acknowledgment and hits another control to alert Alona to hold the Osprey steady. The aircraft gently eases into a hover as we hook up our lines. One by one, we rappel out of the aircraft, past the protective bubble, and instantly get slammed by the sound and force of wind below. Once we're on the ground, kneeling on cool grass with our bio-mech guns pointed outwards, Alona swoops down in her raven form as the air sprites keep the Osprey in position in the air. She scouts ahead as a bird while the rest of us walk in a staggered line to the boathouse. Our formations have become much more cohesive within a short amount of time.

Once within forty feet of the boathouse, John has us split into pairs—Alona transforms to join Theo—in order to surround the boathouse.

"It's in the water inside," Alona says softly over our headsets. "Couldn't see too well, but I'd say it's a pony-size hydra with a basilisk protecting it curled up near the door. That door's the only way in. I had to peek through the mesh of the sealed sea door but there's no way we're getting in through there."

A basilisk? *Pixies*. A memory crosses my mind of facing one during my agent trials—a giant snake with a crown-shaped crest on its head. Its gaze is deadly so avoiding its eyes is essential. I had thrown a weasel at it back then. But since we're out of weasels at the moment...

The silence presses against my ears as John takes a moment to think and devise a plan. I fight the pull of my eyelids. We have to be ever so careful here. We're all tired and one slip up could end up getting any one of us hurt or worse.

"Charlie, Alona—scout the mansion and bring back a mirror that a single person can carry. Not too small though."

A rustle of wings signals the two taking off into the darkness. We wait in silence with our eyes and ears on the boathouse for any sign of movement while those two search the mansion behind us. Several minutes pass before they return. Alona drops out of the sky smoothly and shifts on the ground a second before Charlie appears beside her carrying a large mirror with an ornate frame that's about half his size.

John gives them a nod. "Perfect."

When he finally explains the plan, it's clear that precision is still expected of us despite our sleep-deprived state. We're Spartans. We always have to be at our best. But the plan also involves trust in each other. Trust has been difficult for me lately but I have to take a leap here. That's the only way this is going to work.

At John's signal, we converge on the boathouse. John and I move as a pair to the door. Senses on high alert, I feel the basilisk just on the other side of the door. John holds the mirror out before him facing the door. The others bunch up behind us, Charlie keeping a hand on Melody's arm as Alona the raven perches on his shoulder. Theo keeps low with his bio-mech gun trained on the area at our feet.

I count off on my fingers before pushing the door in wide. A startled, angry hiss responds to our intrusion. Keeping my eyes closed, I duck down so the mirror is in clear view and activate the barriers in my gloves. A bio-mech pulse rushes past my legs as Theo fires at the body of the basilisk waiting for us. With the mirror and the pulse, the thing is distracted and thrown off balance. Keeping my eyes closed nonetheless, I sense exactly where it is, plant my feet, and put the full strength of my magic into my fist. I swing in hard. Bones break beneath my blow and the basilisk is sent crashing into a wall.

"Go!" Theo says.

I open my eyes and take a second to spot where the basilisk has landed and my footing to reach it before racing forward into the darkness and grime of the disused boathouse. I don't give a second thought to the hydra rising out of the water in the middle of the room with Charlie, Melody, and Alona corralling it.

The basilisk flails its huge trunk of a body and tries to bring its head about. Whipping out my retractable sword, I snap the segments into a single blade, close my eyes, and lunge towards its head. A shock passes through the sword in my hand as it goes clear through the basilisk's skull and hits the stone floor beneath it. With it pinned, I throw my body weight on top of it—its rough scales scrapping against my battle gear—and hold its head in place facing the wall.

"Clear!" I shout to the others.

With the basilisk unable to set its piercing gaze on anyone, the rest of the team is able to move much more freely. I open my eyes and watch as Alona distracts one hydra head while Melody blinds another with a quick cut of her blade across its face, and Theo shoots the final head. Before it can heal from any of their attacks, Charlie teleports with a loud splash into the water directly over the hydra's back and plunges his blood-tipped sword through its hide. I fear the retractable blade might break from the force it takes to pierce that thick skin but thankfully it does its job. The hydra lets loose a hiss from each head before it falls limp partway in the water, two of its heads thunking heavily on the dirty floor.

In the meanwhile, I keep the basilisk pinned despite it thrashing madly. John comes about with the mirror and places it to the side of the giant snake's head.

"Ready," he says. "You got it?"

"Sure thing," I grind out as I wrestle the stupid basilisk. Freaking snakes.

Charlie suddenly appears directly beside me and flicks water on me. "I've got you."

He sets his weight with mine to keep the basilisk pinned. Behind us, there's a sharp clang as Melody and Alona stab swords through the end of the basilisk's tail to keep it in place. It'd be great if we could just chop this thing's head off but that wouldn't kill it. There'd just be a very angry head snapping around until its body grew back.

"Eyes shut everyone," John says and nods to me.

I find the basilisk's eye—that now firmly shut with the mirror directly before it. Grimacing, I peel back its eyelid and force it to look at itself while I keep my own eyes averted. The basilisk gives a shuddering gasp and then wheezes out its last breath, at last lying still. Charlie and I wait a few moments before carefully easing off it. When it doesn't move, I feel to make sure both of its eyes are shut before giving the all clear. Even a dead basilisk can kill if you aren't careful.

John comes around from the mirror and gives both me and Charlie a solid clap on the shoulder. I take a second to catch my breath and take in the room. I imagine this boathouse must have been nice in its prime but right now it's ... not something I care to look at for long. Especially not with two dead monsters in it.

"Ugh, it *smells* in here," Theo says and holds the edge of his sleeve over his mask.

"It gets better the longer you're on the job," Melody assures him.

"Seriously?"

"No," John says. "You just go nose-dead eventually."

Theo's expression falls flat. "Great."

Once we've double checked that both monsters are dead, Alona flies to the Osprey to call in the cleanup crew. Charlie ports into the mansion to return the mirror to its proper place. John and I split off to scout to make sure there's nothing else in the surrounding area while Theo and Melody guard the boathouse. My feet are dragging and I'm dead tired by the time Duluth field agents come to take our place to wait for a cleanup crew to arrive. Finally given our leave, we load into the Osprey and head south to wait at Camp Ripley until we receive our next orders.

I'm pretty sure most of us doze off on the flight but we're not the only ones tired. Alona's been awake just as long if not longer than the rest of us flying the Osprey. The air sprites can keep the aircraft in a hover but they can't fly it on their own to give Alona a break. So, to help her stay awake—and startling the rest of us in the process—John starts singing at the top of his lungs while standing behind Alona's pilot seat.

"Oh, what a beautiful MORNING! Oh, what a beautiful daaaaay!"

I jerk awake out of a semi-coma and accidentally hit Charlie beside me in the process. Theo groans but Melody laughs.

"What *is* that?" Theo says and wiggles a finger in his ear.

John continues to boom his song and doesn't answer until he's finished. "It's from *Oklahoma!* Gotta love the classics." Then starts up an encore performance. In fact, he repeats it over and over again until he starts going hoarse and we finally land. As soon as the engines wind down and we make to depart, John reverts to his usual soft-spoken self.

"Thanks, boss," Alona says.

"Happy to help," John says and pats her on the back. "Okay, everyone. Get some sleep before we're called out again."

There's a collaborative "hooray" but it's very lackluster with weak fist pumps in the air. Leaving most of our gear in the Osprey, we trudge to the barracks, take a short pit stop in the restrooms, then fall into our bunks. I'm asleep within seconds.

It also feels like I'm woken back up within seconds.

The two-tone alarm goes off loud and clear but I'm still sluggish to rise. I don't have a clue what time it is or how long I managed to sleep but there certainly hasn't been enough down time. The six of us blink blearily at each other before getting out of our bunks.

"Wake up," John says and slaps me pretty hard on the back. It jolts me to my senses a bit and I straighten, stretching both hands towards the ceiling. John slaps everyone hard on the back to get them up and moving.

We file out of the barracks and get a move on to the Osprey. No one bothered changing out of their gear so we don't have to worry about that at least. Fart and Flitter trill at us when we enter through the bay door, then they resume their positions on the rotors. We filter into our own positions, John and Alona heading up to the cockpit to get our orders. I notice the cycle starting to form—getting orders nonstop, us rushing to save the day, returning to base only to get little to no sleep before we're summoned again. This time it's to Brainerd to back up Spartan Team Tango. When we show up, they've cornered a hydra at a small lake with bones scattered along the shore and a group of grindylows protecting it. Amanda Fry and her fire sprite are irritated at their lack of effectiveness with both monsters using the lake for cover.

But we're tired and just want to sleep so we decide to end things quickly. Charlie ports me directly on top of the hydra hiding at the bottom of the lake and I spear it through the back. The grindylows try to flee with their big, scary charge dead but the other Spartans make quick work of them.

"Well, I'm feeling a bit more awake now," Charlie says as he shakes water out of his hair.

I laugh—a bit delirious—and his shoulders quake with suppressed laughter himself. Leaving Tango to wait for the cleanup crew, we return to our Osprey. The air sprites dry us out with some very forceful gusts that I have to squeeze my eyes shut against. With both Charlie's and my hair a windblown mess, we head back to base once again. When we touch down, we make the long walk to the barracks and —with a prayer up to the heavens that we can get a few uninterrupted hours—almost instantly fall asleep.

The next couple weeks pass in a blur of sleep deprivation

and bloody battles between ever larger hydra and their companions. We settle into a rhythm amongst ourselves, and day by day, accepting the continuous solidarity becomes easier. I'm not exactly anti-social, but I've never spent so much time constantly with people other than my brother. I get to see them at their worst—angry, crabby, freshly woken in the morning—and at their best—constantly supporting each other despite the extremely dangerous and tense situation we're in. It wears on each of us and I'm sure I have the same bags under my eyes as the rest. I wouldn't really know. I haven't stopped to look in a mirror in ages.

Charlie's the first to really crack. After a particularly rough bout with a teenage hydra and its siren friend, we return to the Osprey where Charlie trips over Theo's bag strap sticking out from under his seat. He manages to catch himself just barely, but the string of curse words and absolute fury that exits his mouth leaves us sort of shell shocked. He kicks Theo's bag then ports it out the bay ramp. I stand motionless with my mouth slightly agape watching him rage. I don't think I've ever seen him so unhinged before. I don't say anything, partly because I don't know what to say and I also don't want that anger directed towards me. After his temper tantrum, John has him walk it off outside and I catch sight of him pacing past the ramp now and again still looking furious. Theo retrieves his bag and shoots nasty glances at Charlie whenever he walks past outside.

John stands in the middle of the bay massaging his forehead.

I take a seat near the open ramp watching Charlie pace out of the corner of my eye. Moments later Melody joins me to do the same.

"It was bound to happen at some point," she says. "We're all wound up."

"I've never seen him flip out like that," I say quietly.

"I have. It usually happens around this time on his birthday."

My head snaps about. "It's his birthday?"

She nods. "He's never had a good one, or so he's told me. Now he gets upset whenever it comes round, very on edge."

"Yeah, you could say that."

He paces past the ramp again with his hands planted on his waist and a scowl on his face.

Something pulls at me deep inside my chest. I know exactly how Charlie feels. It's hard to celebrate my own birthday when it's also the anniversary of my parents' murder.

"We best cheer him up, don't you agree?" Melody says and gives me a winning smile.

"I don't know what to say to him. I never know what to say."

"Then don't say anything." She winks and turns to John. "Will we be getting a break soon?"

He crosses his arms over his chest. "The break's right now. Not sure how long it's going to be. If you plan on doing something, better do it now while you can."

"Excellent." She grabs my hand and pulls me sharply to my feet. "Put off your weapons and let's go."

I narrow my eyes but start removing my weapon holsters as she quickly undoes hers. "Where are we going?"

"Shhh! Follow me."

She grabs my hand and tugs me down the ramp. Charlie stops when he sees us and looks like he's readying himself for defensive mode, but we jog right past and keep on going. Melody is positively giddy as our feet beat across the tarmac. We've stopped at the Mankato Regional Airport for the time being after killing a hydra hiding in the river and its siren buddy. Despite being tired as usual, I hurry along with Melody to the airport terminal where we flash our badges to get past security and get ourselves a taxi into the city. Our driver looks at us with a mix of curiosity and caution—we're in our tactical gear minus the weapons. Melody manages to ease the man's fear when she asks with a bubbly voice and smile that he take us to the nearest shopping center.

After getting dropped off at a Walmart—and getting alarmed looks from other shoppers—Melody's quick to find the book aisle.

"We should hurry," she says. "We probably don't have much time to pick out presents for him."

I worry my lower lip and scan the selection before us. The task makes me feel extremely nervous. I never know what to get people—except Hawk. Get the wrong thing and it makes the occasion seem insignificant or off-hand but then it's impossible to find the *right* thing. Then you don't want it to be too expensive or too cheap, or too small or too big—

Melody laughs and claps a hand on my shoulder. "You look like you'd rather be facing a hydra."

"I think I would," I grumble.

"Come on! Don't over think it. There aren't any expectations you need to worry about. Charlie's not used to getting gifts." She wanders to a selection of sci-fi stories and pulls one off the shelf to read the back cover. "Think he'd like one about artificial intelligence?"

Shoving my hands in my pockets, I blow out a breath. "I don't think there's any book he says no to. Except maybe *Pride and Prejudice*." I give her a sideways look.

Melody makes a face. "He's still reading it though. He hasn't called it quits."

"Why are you so determined that he read it?" I ask and pluck out a thick thriller to read the description.

"Diversity is good for him, and I really want him to appreciate the genius that is Jane Austen." She sets the artificial intelligence novel back on the shelf and skims her hands over a row of books. She adds under her breath, "Hope it might open his eyes a bit."

"Whatever that means."

Melody gasps and stops in front of a glass case. "Ooohh! Let's get this!"

Ten minutes later, we walk out of the store carrying a new ebook reader and case of cupcakes fresh from the bakery. The world seems oddly ordinary as we walk under a sunny sky beside ordinary people doing ordinary shopping. We end up sitting on one of the cart racks and setup the ebook reader together. We just about collapse into a fit of giggles creating an account for Charlie, making his password "I luv pretty kitties," and loading a couple of Jane Austen's other works on it. I'm snorting into my hand and feeling the most at ease I've felt in ages. I haven't really had close female friends. Ashley was the only one—I don't count Celina since she's more of a surrogate mother—but that blew up in my face. But with Melody it's like having an older sister.

Eventually we return to the airport, wrap the ebook reader in the plastic shopping bag, and return to the

Osprey. We find Charlie sitting at the bottom of the ramp talking with Theo. They seem to have worked things out and are on friendly terms again—at least that's what I assume since they're discussing weapons politely with each other. John hovers in the background like a parent supervising. Alona swoops off the top of the aircraft in her raven form when we arrive and immediately starts asking about what we brought back.

We shush her and walk directly to Charlie. Together we hold out our presents and his eyes grow wide.

"What's this?" he asks.

"Happy Birthday, Charlie!" we say in unison.

The expression of shock doesn't leave his face and it takes Theo shaking his shoulder for him to take the offered presents. He's quiet as he unwraps the ebook reader and cupcakes. Crinkles form at the corners of his eyes and it looks like he's fighting back some strong emotion behind his rigid jaw and tightly clamped lips. Melody and Theo fill in the silence, Melody explaining his account, and Theo telling us about the ingredients in the cupcakes. The treats are soon broken into and shared amongst everyone as we sit at the bottom of the open ramp enjoying each other's company and the sunshine. Charlie remains speechless but there's warmth radiating off him in the looks he gives us.

It's then I realize that Melody's not the only sister I have and Hawk isn't the only brother. Theo, John, Melody, Alona, and Charlie have become like family to me. We're a team but also more than that. I trust these people. I trust them with my life every day and they do the same for me.

We're in the middle of recommending books for Charlie to add to his collection when we hear the radio chirp from the cockpit. There's a simultaneous group pause before Alona ducks in to receive the incoming transmission.

"Looks like break time's over," John says and dusts off his hands.

"Well, you know what they say." Theo stands and stretches his arms up high. "The family that slays together, stays together."

I laugh and we file into the bay as Alona starts up the engines. Looks like we have another mission. Settling into my spot for the flight, I spot Charlie lovingly tuck his new ebook reader into his bag and give it a good pat. I smile and turn away only to have John catch my eye. He gives me a single nod of approval with a lingering smile of his own.

A sensation of warmth blossoms in my chest and it becomes clearer than ever that this is where I belong.

19

Hawk

My eyes never stray too far from the clock on the wall above my desk.

T-minus five minutes until freedom—not only from work but everything.

Almost every night for the past several weeks I've been picked up at the arcade and brought to the secret werewolf compound for the evening. It's an escape from the maddening reality of my day job but also something so much more. For the first time I truly feel like I belong somewhere. Sure, I always had Phoenix but we were the odd ones out. Werewolves just don't fit into normal society. But at the compound, there's no one giving me sideways looks or moving away out of fear when I walk past.

T-minus three minutes to freedom.

I strum my fingers on my keyboard impatiently. Doug keeps giving me the evil eye from his desk and dramatically flips papers over when he's done reviewing them to let me know he's irritated with me. Like I care.

The second the clock hits the end of the hour, I launch out of my chair and rush for the elevator. I'm the first one out of the building.

"Why the rush?" Spartan Knox calls at my back.

"Gotta beat my high score!" I shout over my shoulder and wave.

He thinks at the arcade. Good for him. But what I really mean is capture the flag at the compound.

I follow my new routine. I skip the gym entirely, along with the diner, ditch my stuff at the apartment, swap for loose clothing, and hurry to the arcade. I'm not the only one excited for the end of the day. Merlin is already waiting for me in his teenager guise playing Pacman. He huffs when he sees me and keeps playing.

"You could give me a little more time to have fun," he says. "It gets stuffy in that place."

"I can understand that." It's not what I think of the compound at all, but I get it. Just thinking of the office leaves a bad taste in my mouth. "If we get going, I can teach you a few moves."

He immediately abandons the game. "Let's go."

I smirk as Merlin waves a hand over the probation ring on my finger and hustles to the front door. Genna appears out of nowhere in front of him and grabs his arm. She's in her blonde wig again and sunglasses.

"Merlin, you know the drill," she says.

He lets out a noisy huff again. Genna gives us both a smile and looks to Reese the manager. He checks the surveillance camera behind his counter and nods. Genna still does a sweep of the street outside before we leave and jam in the car to Spice Girls.

"Anything new?" Genna asks over her shoulder.

Merlin has me positioned in the middle of the backseat this time to keep our seating arrangement an even triangle.

"Nothing today. Just more news about hydra everywhere." And reports from Phoenix's team taking care of business like pros. Phoenix and I haven't chatted in a while. She's been too busy. That makes these daily excursions even more important to me.

"Hmm."

"Do *you* know anything new?"

"Just speculation on my part."

"Speculate away. I'm all ears."

She hesitates as Spice Girls blares through the car. In fact, she doesn't say anything until the song ends and a quieter one begins.

"Don't you find it curious how the hydra got in?" she says at last over the softer song so we don't have to be yelling to be heard. "They weren't slipped in one at a time like most monsters manage to cross borders. They came in on a massive ship, and by all accounts, brimming with hydra eggs. There's no way something of that magnitude could have slipped in without being noticed by the IMS or otherwise. Meaning the IMS has either grown extremely sloppy . . . or they were let in."

"You think someone from the IMS let a brood of hydra in? No offense, but that sounds kind of ridiculous."

"It wouldn't be a single someone," she continues. "Something of that magnitude would involve a lot of people. They could be with the IMS or . . ."

"Or?"

"I don't know. It's not like every single inspector could have been replaced by shapeshifters. That'd be too many people, and from what I know, there are safeguards against it. The IMS would notice. Like I said, I'm just speculating. Then there's something else."

I run a hand through my hair. "There's more?"

"From what you've told us and what we've learned on our own, it doesn't make strategic sense to place the hydra in the locations where they've been discovered. What is there to be gained from hydra in an abandoned mill? Or an old boathouse no one uses anymore? There aren't any hard targets in those areas to make the hydra actually useful. Why ship in so many and throw them around if they aren't going to do anything significant?"

"They've got the Spartans up to their eyeballs in it. Code blacks are being delegated elsewhere, making a mess of things," I say. "That's significant."

"Yes, that is," she murmurs and falls silent.

Perhaps I should be giving this more thought like Genna instead of letting my mind be consumed by daydreams of where we're currently heading. Eventually I take the dark bag from Genna and pull it over my own head. We don't say much as we go through the usual routine of guiding me blindfolded up rocky slopes and into the vampires' secret hideout. Genna tugs the hood off my head and Claude the vampire—today's lookout—gives me a brief nod of acknowledgment. The vampires haven't exactly warmed up to me but they don't really warm up to anyone. They mostly avoid the werewolves and only talk with Genna or Rosalyn. You know, I think Rosalyn might be the only one they actually like. They fist bump when I come in with her. It seems significant in its own way.

We pass the guardroom and enter the main compound. As usual, several small children are running amok playing tag and drawing with chalk on the floors. A few adults meander in the area keeping an eye on them to make sure they don't try to rush into the guardroom or—heaven forbid—outside.

Before Genna and I can make for the "playground" another level down, Merlin grabs my arm and starts dragging me towards the common room.

"You have some new moves for me?" he asks barely containing his excitement. "I've been working on my *sprinkler* and *fishing rod.*"

It's hard not to laugh. "We really need to up your game, Merlin. Think you can handle something a little more advanced?"

"Of course!"

Genna rests a hand on my back and I can feel the warmth through my shirt. "I'll be in the greenhouse if you need me."

She walks away and I gaze after her while Merlin drags me along.

After one night when Merlin asked me about current dance styles and discovered I'm a "professional," he's been insistent on having me teach him some moves. I don't think I've ever seen anyone so overjoyed to dance, even if it's ridiculous moves like the sprinkler. His excitement is infectious and when I teach him, several others tend to join in. It's no different today. When I introduce him to the highly respected "robot," several children and a few adults come over to join us doing our best robot moves to the sound of a small CD player.

I eventually take a break from the dance party as my stomach gives a particularly loud grumble. I'm always so excited to get here that I forgo eating. Then again, I also feel bad eating here when it's difficult getting supplies to this place. A lot of things have to be discreetly smuggled in every day just to be able to feed everyone. That's why their massive greenhouse is so important here.

Rosalyn appears at my side without making a sound and holds out a cinnamon roll in a plastic wrapper. "Here, you idiot."

"Where'd you come from?" I ask and take the roll. "And this?"

"I was picking up supplies. Snagged a few of those for Merlin while I was out."

"But you're giving me one?"

She crosses her arms over her chest and stares straight ahead. "Just keep making Merlin happy. We need him."

Then she abruptly walks away. I don't try to hide my smile as I rip into the cinnamon roll and watch Merlin and the others from a distance as they keep dancing. The atmosphere is happy and upbeat. It's a nice change of pace, and knowing I get to come here each day makes getting through work easier.

The sound of fast footsteps catches my attention and I turn as a young boy dashes into the room out of breath.

"Merlin!" he shouts. "We need you!"

The dance party abruptly stops. Merlin rushes after the boy out of the room and the rest of us follow on their heels. We run through the hallways towards the sound of snarling.

Merlin skids on the cement in a pair of flip flops, slams into the door of a side room, and comes to a halt. His eyes go to whatever is happening inside the room and the rest of us bunch up behind him. I watch in astonishment as Merlin slaps his hands together and a wave passes through the air like an expanding bubble from him. The snarls beyond the doorway fade into silence as Merlin maintains his stance, hands pressed tightly together, hair fanning out as if he's trapped in a whirlwind, and eyes aglow.

"So dramatic," Rosalyn grumbles and pushes past him into the room.

In the opening she creates, the others and I crowd around behind Merlin's shoulder to see what's caused the fuss. Two wolves stand shaking in the bunk room beyond. A thin white one is clearly facing off against a dark gray that's got its tail tucked between its legs. Rosalyn goes to stand between the pair and stare down the one with its tail tucked, head bowed, and acting ashamed.

Looks like we just had an incident with a werewolf going off the rails. It's happened once before when I was here and it startled me to be sure. I know that Merlin's here to help the werewolves but it hadn't been clear to me until that moment. He's the source of the werewolf serum so even though Genna said the werewolves would be free of the serum under his influence, I honestly couldn't tell the difference. I figured it would be the exact same. I didn't understand, but now I do. It's moments like these that show the truth of it.

Both werewolves in the room calm down and shift into humans as Merlin maintains his stance and uses his power to compel the werewolves into their right minds. But it's not a constant cloud. It's directed to those that need it when they need it—like medicine for a flare-up. That's the true difference having Merlin here instead of keeping werewolves under constant injections. It's an emergency response only, not a compulsory thing.

Merlin eventually lets off his surge of power and his arms dangle at his sides. There's almost a collective sigh of relief with the situation settled. Rosalyn starts telling off the one guy whose name I can't remember. He doesn't look much older than me though. There's a very strong ping of empathy for the guy struggling with this part of himself. It's the same struggle I'm still going through.

"Walk it off," Rosalyn says loudly and gives him a hearty slap on the back. "Go on. And you idiots, too." She turns and points at those of us lingering in the doorway with a scowl. "Go burn off that stupid in the playground."

She makes a shooing motion and shoves the other two out of the room.

"You have such a gentle hand," I comment and several sniggers follow.

Instead of shooing us, she starts kicking about our legs to get us moving. We scatter and with the excuse of being herded by Rosalyn, I escape to the "playground" which is where I've wanted to go since I came here. Some of the others that I've gotten to know—and who sniggered after my comment to Rosalyn—start chatting with me along the way. They're a lively bunch and it's such a nice change of pace. I fill them in on what's going on outside since they're pretty cut off in here. They want to know celebrity gossip and any new movies they can request to have brought in. Apparently Witty is working on setting up an entertainment center.

Along the hallway, we pass the open doors to the greenhouse. I pause and look inside. Genna's working on replanting something with a subdued smile on her face.

Max nudges me in the back. "Well, go on."

They're all smiling at me and winking.

I roll my eyes. "Really?"

"Play it cool. Don't blow it."

"You're a bunch of jerks."

Multiple hands start shoving me into the doorway to the point I just about trip. Genna looks up and the others vanish leaving laughter in their wake. My face grows warm and I clear my throat, run a hand through my hair, and put a crooked smile on my face.

"Hey." I walk casually to her and take a gander at what she's doing.

"Sounds like you're having fun," she says offhand while keeping her eyes on the leafy thing she's folding soil in around.

"Yeah, I am. I can't thank you guys enough for letting me come here."

"It's been good. For everyone."

"Oh?"

"You've become quite the morale booster."

I blink. "Really?" That's unexpected.

She straightens and dusts her hands off. "You have an infectious energy."

"Well, I guess that's better than an infectious disease."

Her laughter warms my chest.

"Anything I can help with?" I offer.

"Sure." She waves me over and directs me to repot a bunch of plants.

Rolling up my sleeves, I say, "Okay, you can't blame me if they die since you're putting their lives in my hands." I make a dramatic grimace as I pull up a plant and transfer it to another pot.

"But they're such capable hands."

I almost drop the plant and catch her smirking out of the corner of my eye. Taking better care of my charge, I carefully replant the thing that I don't even know the name of and mimic Genna's movements to cover it up, gently press the soil in, and give it a little water. We go down a row of plants doing this. By the end I've got dirt compacted under my nails. Genna's hands look even filthier. She stands and stares at her hands for a moment before slowly trailing one dirty finger down her nose with a vacant expression.

She catches me watching, but I'm too curious to play shy.

"What was that?" I ask and brush my hands off on my pants.

Her expression changes to something... haunted, is the best way I can describe it. She slowly rubs her thumb and forefinger together to get rid of the soil on her skin.

"It's something my mother used to do when I was little," she says quietly. "After I was taken by Dasc, I used it as a sign of defiance between James and myself. It was our secret code to say that we weren't the toy soldiers Dasc wanted us to be. In a way it kept me sane, reminded me who I was."

Sometimes it's easy to forget what Genna's been through. Sometimes it's impossible.

"That must have been hard."

"It was."

As usual, she's not one to shy away from the cold, hard facts or the reality of her situation. She hasn't been made fragile by her trials and isn't a fan of pity. I don't think anyone can call her damaged either. Maybe someone else of lessor fortitude would have broken under the pain she endured in the past, but not her. It's one of the many things I admire about her.

One of her many traits I wish I had.

"We might as well head down," she says. "I'm sure you didn't come here to garden."

"Oh, nonsense. I was looking forward to replanting . . . uh—"

"Spinach."

"Spinach all day. Wait, spinach? Really?"

"Yes."

I do a double take of the plants. "Well, anyway. The company wasn't too bad either."

"That's good."

We walk out together and descend a level to the playground where most of the compound residents have already congregated. By the time we join in, they've already started a massive game of capture the flag. Rosalyn is running around and barking like a crazy animal. She's not the only one though. Everyone's rowdy and barking and rolling on the ground. No judging. No holding back. I've talked with several of them that were willing to tell me their stories. It was heartening to talk to other people like me and know I'm not the only who struggles controlling my other half and dealing with the prejudice that comes with being what I am. Not only that, but simply accepting what I am.

I run free for hours with the others. Genna and I join the team against Rosalyn. There's no end to our close battles. I've gotten better with each successive day and have only had one other seizure since being back on the serum. Somehow it was actually tolerable. I was here and despite being embarrassed by it, the others didn't find my situation something to be embarrassed about in the least. Genna, Rosalyn, Max, and a few others sat around a table with me and took my mind off things by debating over the best kind of meat for half an hour.

But the time comes when I have to leave and return to the world I'd rather never go back to. One by one we leave the field. The others head to their bunks but my path takes me to the exit. Merlin appears as usual to escort me out but we're joined by Rosalyn this time.

"Where's Genna?" I ask.

"Helping some brats go down for bed. I need fresh air." She huffs and looks ready to strangle someone.

"Little kids not your idea of fun?"

She rolls her eyes and mutters, "My idea of going insane."

With one last look of longing back at the compound, I turn around and follow them out. Another evening come and gone. I sigh and before I can ask for the bag to toss over my head, Rosalyn savagely throws it on me.

"You enjoy doing that far too much."

Her evil little laugh is her response.

Twenty minutes later, we pull into the rear lot of the arcade next to a dumpster. I chuck the bag back at Rosalyn. I aim for her face but she skillfully catches it. Without missing a beat, she pulls out her cell phone and calls the front desk manager to make sure it's safe for me to go.

"Reese, are we clear?" she asks. "What? Oh, sh—" She grabs me by the collar unexpectedly and shoves me towards the car door. "Knox is in there looking for you. He's in the back right now. Go in through the bathroom window, go!"

My heart pounds in my ears as I hurtle out of the car and to the building. There are several windows but Rosalyn points to the one on the far right. I sprint for it as Merlin and Rosalyn hustle out of the car to help.

"He's heading for the bathroom," Rosalyn says with the phone still pressed to her ear. "Reese, can you stall him? Damn it."

The window's locked from the inside. I try to jiggle it loose but it won't move. From the way Rosalyn is muttering curses under her mouth, I'd say I have seconds to get into the bathroom and pretend I've been there the whole time. Merlin practically shoves me aside to wiggle his fingers over the window mechanism. The lock pops open. I slide the window up. Rosalyn hoists me up and I slip through the small opening to land lightly on my toes at a crouch. Just as the door to the bathroom opens, the window behind me shuts, and I angle myself towards the sink as if just about to wash my hands.

Knox appears and takes up most of the doorway with his tall frame. I glance up as if startled but it's not much of an act. I *am* startled. My heart is racing and I have to focus on keeping my breathing even after rushing in here. I have a feeling my face is flushed, though, from the heat rising off my cheeks.

"Knox?" I say curiously. "What are you doing here?"

He doesn't say anything for a moment as he takes in the scene, watches me, and scans the small, dingy bathroom. Relax, Hawk. You were here the whole time. You've been playing away the day's stresses in the arcade and stopped for a bathroom break. That's all. He can't know any different because my probation ring should show that I've been here the whole time.

"I've been looking for you," Knox finally says. "I know you always come here."

"Yeah, it helps relieve stress," I say and turn on the sink to start washing my hands. "Why were you looking for me?"

Knox steps in and shuts the door—trapping me inside with him.

"Word reached me through the grapevine. I heard what you told Milton, about helping on the hydra hunt or wanting a transfer."

"That was a while ago."

"Yes, but you've been off ever since we came here. Are you okay, son?"

I almost want to laugh but that wouldn't be the appropriate reaction. No, Knox is looking for me to open up to him honestly, confess my desire to escape, have a talk man to man. I guess I should give him what he expects if I'm to deflect suspicion and not have him search around the building to find two fugitives lurking out back. I turn off the sink and dry my hands while looking pensive.

"I want to do more, you know that," I say at last. "And when I know I have a good idea but it's just shot down, it's frustrating. We're men of action. We're Spartans. Milton doesn't understand that."

"We are Spartans, and as Spartans we follow orders. We've been ordered here, Hawk. This is our mission."

"Correcting typos?"

He steps away from the door and closer to me. "Being exemplary werewolves and human beings in the face of everything that's going on. We have to show the community that not all werewolves are monsters to be feared."

No, of course not. We're monsters to be cowed. We're supposed to be obedient dogs to the sheep who cower before us—sheep that lead the legendary community. Sheep that want their warriors to be sheep too.

"I suppose." I chuck the paper towel into the trashcan. "You came all the way out here to check on me?"

"Spartans never go it alone," he says simply.

Right. And those with suspicions follow up on their leads. I'm on his radar now, I can tell. That warm, bright spot in my chest sinks into a cold abyss as I realize what that means. With his eyes on me, it'll be too dangerous to escape to the compound again.

As of this moment, I am alone.

20

Phoenix

I don't remember the last time I slept in an actual bed. We've been chasing down hydra leads for the last couple months with hardly any breaks between battles. Team Sierra has gotten quite the reputation lately. We've become one of the most efficient Spartan teams in clearing out the hydra threat. Officially, John likes to account our success to integral teamwork. I mean, that is true, but in reality, it's more a combination of my abilities, Charlie's abilities, and our awesome teamwork. No other team has a teleporter or someone with the ability to sense magic and manipulate it to their will. We've purged hydra from Duluth to International Falls to Fargo and beyond.

But being so successful also puts us in high demand. Despite how many hydra and protective monsters we put down, there always seem to be three more to take the place of every one we kill. We're always moving, always on the go, running and gunning.

I wake up stiff from my sleep on the floor of the Osprey's bay. Melody's body warms my back and Charlie's foot rests against my calf. We're crammed together on the metal floor with a mat of rubber for our mattress. A shirt and pair of jeans are rolled together beneath my head for a pillow and the emergency tarp is spread over all of us as a communal blanket. Only Alona sleeps off by herself. I can see the edge of her black feathers as she curls up in her raven form on one of the seats beside us, a wing draped over her head. Even the air sprites are resting inside on the opposite row of seats, the only sign of them the subtle movement of the straps next to them as they let out silent gusts of air while they sleep. It takes a lot to wear them out and you know a sprite is truly drained when they nap.

We're woken up by the usual sound—a voice over the radio calling us to action.

"Sierra, this is Minneapolis Division. Come in, over."

Alona rustles her feathers and the rest of us groggily sit up where we lay.

"Sierra, this is Minneapolis Division," the voice says more urgently. "We have a situation in downtown Minneapolis. Come in, over."

John gets to his feet first and follows Alona who flies into the cockpit. The rest of us rub the sleep from our eyes and listen to the conversation. A code black was just called in from an agent checking Werevine Pharmaceutical. That gets my attention fast.

"Didn't you set that place on fire once?" Charlie says, one side of his hair smushed and the rest sticking up giving him a very lopsided appearance.

I give a big yawn before saying, "There was a spider. I had to make sure I got it."

The others laugh softly. We get to our feet and work as a team to fold up the tarp.

"I was expecting something more along the lines of 'their drapes were hideous' or something," Theo says.

We tuck the tarp under the left seats and belt it down.

"You got chilly," Charlie quips.

"You couldn't find a light switch to see," Melody offers.

I roll my eyes. "How sarcastic do you guys think I am?"

"Very," the three say in unison.

The ramp lowers just enough so the air sprites can dart outside to the rotors as the engines start up. John stretches his arms to the ceiling when he walks back to us.

"Werevine Pharmaceutical has a hostage situation," he says.

Oh boy.

"Hydra?" Melody asks.

He shakes his head. "For once, no. Werewolves."

Crap.

"Under their own volition?" Theo asks. "Or the alpha? Or a siren?"

"Won't know until we get there."

"Super," Charlie mutters and casts a sideways glance at me as if remembering the first time he encountered a siren and became its puppet.

John yawns and sets off a daisy chain from the rest of us.

"Wake up, everybody!" he says loudly and segues into a rambunctious version of "Oh, What a Beautiful Morning" from the musical *Oklahoma!* which we discovered he's quite a fan of. After that first time serenading Alona to keep her awake, he now does it every morning to get us moving. He's sung it enough that the rest of us join in to add to the clamor as we straighten our uniforms, cinch our straps, and click the buckles on our tactical gear. Through this experience I've discovered Charlie and Theo both have beautiful singing voices. I'm still off key but it's the spirit that counts, right?

"We'll be at Werevine in fifteen minutes," Alona says over the speakers.

"So, what do we know?" Charlie asks.

"An agent went to check up on the company after they'd been silent this morning," John says. "They have a button someone is supposed to press every half hour as part of safety protocol. I guess having a couple of shapeshifters under their nose freaked them out."

I duck my head but catch the others grinning.

"Any way," he continues. "She got there and saw the hostage situation. She called in the code black but then went dark. We don't know the condition of her or any of the other hostages. It's a work day so I can expect there's going to be a lot of people trapped in there that need our help."

"Backup?" Melody asks but we already know what John's going to say.

"Nope. There's a team of field agents that have surrounded the building discreetly to make sure the werewolves don't make a run for it, but otherwise we're it."

A skyscraper full of people—potentially all of them being used as hostages—and we're it? Great.

"They make any demands?" Melody asks.

"Flea medication?" Theo mutters. I give him a sharp look and he pointedly looks away whistling.

John holds onto a strap over his head as the Osprey picks up speed.

"They want the truth," he says. "About the serum."

"The truth?" I ask. Which one? There's so many to choose from.

"They want to know why people go missing when they react badly to it."

Their eyes press in on me so I focus on the bio-mech rifle in my hands. If only I could cure the werewolf disease, we wouldn't be in this position. Those werewolves—people like Jason—disappear because they can't handle the serum but the IMS can't allow them to live without it either. They're a danger to themselves and the people around them.

We're trying to fight a war on too many fronts. As if Echidna's lethal monsters weren't enough, we have to deal with the werewolves now too.

"I'm surprised they took us away from cleaning up hydra dung," Theo says offhand.

John gives a short bob of his head. "I know, but they wanted a team that could get in and out without things getting messy. Division headquarters doesn't want this getting out, especially with the werewolf lock down they've established on our agents."

Another secret. Another lie. To keep the werewolves in line. We're playing a dangerous game here and one I'm afraid we're going to lose.

The minutes tick by fast and soon the Osprey slows to a hover as our plan goes into action. The ramp drops and the air sprites keep us steady as Alona flies out to circle Werevine Pharmaceutical to make sure the way is clear for us. If they get any indication that we're coming, they could do something rash and rash is a very bad thing when hostages are involved.

One minute. Two minutes. Three minutes until Alona sweeps back into the Osprey and the ramp closes behind her. In a poof of curling and shimmery black smoke, Alona shifts into her human self and shakes out her arms.

"The roof is clear for overhead infiltration," she reports. "We'll go in high through the cloud cover and drop straight down or they might see us coming."

John nods. "It's show time, people."

The team assembles in the bay and we hook onto our lines as Alona pilots us into position. My stomach feels odd as we go straight up, forward, and then slowly maneuver back down directly over the roof of Werevine. The ramp opens and I walk to the edge to drop my line. At John's signal, I begin my rappel through the open air with nothing but clouds above me and emptiness around me. I'd love to take in the sights from this angle but I'm a little busy. My feet touch the roof top and I get into a defensive position by the door as the rest of my team follows me down. After Melody, John, Charlie, and Theo get their feet under them, the Osprey rises vertically into the clouds. We stay put until Alona radios that the air sprites are keeping our ride in place and she's going to circle back around in raven form to scout through the windows for us.

"I've got eyes on the floors below you," she says. "Take the stairs on the southeast corner of the building two levels and it'll take you right to a group of them holed up in a cubicle area."

We breach the door as quietly as one might and descend the stairs on soft soles to minimize the sound of our passage. There's an eerie sense of déjà vu when we pass the executive floor. It's been redecorated since the last time I was here—probably due to, you know, the fire. We continue down the stairwell and pause behind the door to the next level. At John's signal, Alona flies past the windows cawing loudly to draw the attention of the kidnappers as we breach. There's a volley of bio-mech pulses, each precisely aimed, and the group of werewolves toting guns and knives fall but we move in fast to catch the dropping bodies and ease them gently to the floor to minimize the sound.

Alona lands on the parking ramp to shift and gives us another update to guide us. We do this level by level and efficiently take out the kidnappers before they know what's going on. That is until we reach the floor where the majority of the hostages are being held. It's made up of cubicles and the werewolves have taken to hiding in them, each holding onto a hostage to shield themselves. We crack open the door to the floor and Charlie ports me and him to the other side of the office. Together we quickly crouch out of sight beside a copier machine before lobbing out a series of smoke grenades at the same time John, Melody, and Theo do from the other side.

Chaos stirs as the smoke swallows up the room. The werewolves shout to each other. Hostages cry, scream, and some even make a run for it. I move as a ghost through the smoke with Charlie at my back, our masks and goggles on to protect against the haze. Led by my senses, I move to each werewolf from behind as Charlie sneaks on the other side and ports the hostages out of harm's way. With fast strikes and a torrent of bio-mech pulses, I neutralize the werewolves on the floor as John and the others do the same on the other side until we meet in the middle. The smoky haze slowly clears as the ventilation draws it out.

"Floor is clear," Alona says from her perch outside. "But you've got five making a run for it on the level below you. Take the stairs to the west!"

Charlie takes my hand and we vanish to the other end of the floor facing the stairs. We burst through the doors then boom, boom, boom—landing, landing, door in quick successive teleportations. I thrust open the door so Charlie has a clear view to port to the exit and block it. Between me and him a pack of five people running with guns stutter to a halt.

"Weapons down or we fire!" Charlie shouts and I close in on them from behind. "You're surrounded!"

They stop and glance uneasily between myself and Charlie. Pounding footsteps sound in the stairwell we just came from and moments later the rest of our team comes to box them in. A woman who stands closest to Charlie nods to the others and they slowly put their guns on the floor and raise their hands up to shoulder height.

"Take five steps towards me," Charlie commands.

They do and walk away from the guns on the floor. Theo and Melody sweep in to make sure they can't go for them.

"On your knees."

They do and the woman in front gives a bone chilling laugh. "Only for you, darling."

"Hands behind your head. All of you."

They comply and the woman's attention remains glued to Charlie. The rest of us move in to zip-tie their hands. I reach the woman and finally get a good look at her face. She seems vaguely familiar somehow but I don't recall ever meeting such a werewolf. She has the same bitter magical essence as the others but there's something . . . off. She's extraordinarily pale and her black hair doesn't look natural, as if it's been dyed. I think of her laugh . . . I swear I've heard it before . . .

"I know you," I breathe.

Despite the dyed hair and the contacts she must have in her eyes, I can see it—the ghostly lamia I encountered at the castle in Scotland. The very same that was later killed by Draco in Underground. How on earth is she still alive? And she must have werewolf blood in her system. That's why I couldn't distinguish her until now.

I whip about my bio-mech gun and send a pulse into her chest before she can move. It knocks her back but she's not out. She laughs and flicks something free with her tongue along her teeth and bites down.

"Lamia!" I shout and whip out my collapsible sword.

The others are quick to action as the lamia gives a sing-song whistle and takes my sword in her outstretched arm. I cleave through flesh and she lets out a cry of pain but she can take it. She'll survive anything unless I cut her head off.

A bio-mech pulse hits me in the back and I slump forward at the same time Melody hits the floor across from me. I don't go unconscious as my own magic protects me but I'm sluggish to rise. John and Theo advance on me with their guns raised. Oh, pixies. This stupid lamia must have taken a sip of siren blood and put them under her control.

She laughs as another bio-mech pulse hits me in the back and I almost fall forward on my face. The werewolves with their hands zip-tied quickly scuttle out of the way and those that get their feet back under them make a break for it.

Charlie appears out of thin air in front of me and gives the lamia a hand up.

"Oh, you're *handsome*," she purrs. "I could just gobble you up."

Yeah, she probably could—literally. That really gets my blood boiling.

It takes a great amount of will power to not let my power explode out of me in all directions. As Scholar taught me, I pull it in and then stretch out single tethers to each of my male counterparts. There's no holding back or hiding like the last time I encountered the power of a siren. I look up as Charlie realizes what's happened and his sword flashes into his hand. A second later he slashes for the lamia's head but she grabs his wrist mid swing with a snarl. Her eyes go to me.

"You're ruining my fun."

Can she tell I'm the one doing it? Setting them free from her chains?

She sings a few notes as Charlie winces from the hold on his arm. I feel that web reaching out to my teammates but she can't get through, not with me protecting them and simultaneously putting pressure on the force keeping her alive. I'd rip it clean out of her right now but I'm having a bit of a struggle after having been shot by bio-mech pulses and keeping up constant protection for the guys. I don't dare drop that protection even for an instant.

"Fine," she says and throws Charlie into me.

Theo and John unload once Charlie is out of the way and she staggers from the shots but doesn't go down. Instead she pulls out a vial from her jacket and downs it in one go. Theo continues to fire as John advances with his own blade out. Charlie and I untangle ourselves a second before a piercing scream rips through our skulls. I clamp a hand to the side of my head as it tears through me. My cries of pain mingle with the others as the lamia uses the power of a leviathan scream against us. I drop to my knees again and do my best to fight it but it's so, so powerful and jarring.

"Ah, that's better," the lamia says and rolls her shoulders. Charlie falls backwards beside me and Theo and John are in no better shape.

I can do this. I have to do this. Warmth radiates off me and despite what John told me about not pushing my power too far, I think now's as good a time as any to throw that advice out the window. Like I did back in Underground, I'll have to rip that power right out of her body.

"I hoped that would do the trick!" the lamia says cheerfully, kicks away my sword and takes my chin in her hand to tilt my eyes to hers. She gives me a shark's smile.

I fight against the building pressure in my head, against that horrible hideous scream—and feel another presence closing in fast.

"I just want you to know," the lamia continues, "that I take great pleasure in being the one to defeat you after you and your little dragon friend killed my twin sister." So she's not the same lamia Draco and I fought in Underground. The one before me is an identical twin. I didn't even know monsters could have twin siblings. "I will be glorified for this moment, a feat not even Epsilon could achieve. Your comrades will forever curse the name Iota. I am the glorious, the terrible, the undefeated—"

I latch onto the magic in her blood, close my fists as if I

have its essence in my grip, and pull. Her body locks up and she makes an odd choking sound.

"You talk too much," I snarl.

A small blur hurtles into the room. Black smoke explodes in the air, Alona plummets out of it, and in an effortless, fluid motion slices her blade through Iota the Chatty's neck. Dark blood splatters across my face. The lamia doesn't even have time to register a look of surprise before her head falls free of her body.

Alona, panting hard, gives the corpse of the lamia a disgusted look. "Caw caw, sucker."

"Alona!" I exclaim. "Perfect timing!"

She gives me a rare smile. "I figured you could use some help."

"Yeah, you could say that." I wipe the edge of my sleeve across my face. Yuck.

"You've got a little blood coming from your eyes, you know. And nose. And ears."

I nod weakly. "Yup. I bet I do."

She gives me a hand up and I stagger on wobbly knees. Ugh, I freaking hate going through that. Once I'm on my feet, she moves to Charlie, then Theo and John, to help them stand. They take some time to reorient themselves as I kneel next to Melody.

"The other werewolves," John says and holds a hand to his forehead. "They got away."

"No, they didn't," Alona says and preens. "While you guys were getting your butts kicked, someone had to cover the exits."

Theo groans, staggers over, and gives her a hug. She freezes up and makes an exasperated face before lightly patting him on the back. I take a seat next to Melody and keep a finger pressed to the pulse on the inside of her wrist as if its steady beat can calm my own. I'm glad she's okay, only unconscious.

John bends down to inspect the body of the lamia. "Iota. That's Greek alphabet."

"Then there's Epsilon," Charlie says.

"And Zeta. She's dead," I add. "But there will always be thirteen."

"What?" John asks. "Where did you hear that?"

"My mystery friend."

"Ah." He stands and patches in to division headquarters for a cleanup crew to meet us at the building.

After backup is confirmed to be en route, John has us "walk off" the side effects of the leviathan scream by hauling the unconscious werewolves to the first level while Theo escorts the hostages to the second floor to account for everyone. Charlie and I ride the elevator up and down, picking up groups of werewolves throughout the building, and gather them in a long glass-paneled hallway. Each of us keeps itching at the drying blood in our ears, noses, and corners of our eyes.

It takes the cleanup crew forever to arrive. When they show up they complain about Minneapolis traffic but considering what we've been dealing with for the last two months, we don't have much patience for their issues.

At last we get a call from Director Knox himself. Alona patches him through to the team's headsets so we can all hear.

"Excellent work as always, Sierra," he says. "You've been topside for nearly two months straight, is that about right?"

"Yes, sir," John says over the radio.

Charlie and I are off by ourselves leaning against the glass walls of the hallway watching the cleanup crew identify each of the werewolves we captured.

"Every team's been making sacrifices and feeling the strain," the director continues. "Unfortunately, I can't allow much of a respite for any of our Spartans considering the current situation."

"And we wouldn't ask for it, director."

"I respect your tenacity but we both know that a worn soldier can easily become a dead soldier. I'm authorizing a week's leave for Sierra, effective immediately. Get some R&R, recharge, and return to the fight fresh. We need you."

A week long break. I sag a little where I stand.

"Get your team checked out in Underground's medical unit first," the director continues. "I want each of you cleared after dealing with that leviathan scream."

Melody comes on the line, finally having come to. "We're in tip top shape, sir, and I'll dust them off."

"As long as you do. Good work, everyone. Come back in one piece."

I find a grin on my face and I look sideways to Charlie. He has the same weary, dopy smile. I hold out my fist and he bumps it with his own.

"Everyone meet on the top level of the parking ramp," John says. "We're done here."

Charlie and I walk past the IMS agents in FBI jackets and take a side exit nearest the parking garage. My feet drag and I take a deep breath of the evening air. The others file out behind us and soon we walk as a group to the top of the parking structure where the Osprey is waiting for us. I'm too tired to talk and I think the others feel the same from their own bleary-eyed expressions. We've had a long go of it without much of a break whatsoever.

Once we're back in the Osprey, John takes a seat and says, "So, where to, team?"

"I've got some friends visiting in New York," Melody says.

"I need to check in with my family," Alona says.

"Same," John says. "My sister and nephew are over in Montana at the cabin."

"I want to go see my brother in Seattle," I pitch in.

Charlie twists his hands together over and over again as he stares at the floor.

I nudge him with my shoulder. "I could use some company."

His eyes sparkle when they meet mine and he nods slowly. "I hear they have some cool libraries and bookstores."

"I do owe you a trip, don't I?"

"Well!" Theo says loudly and claps his hands together. I think he's the only one with a bottle of energy still. "Before we wander our separate ways, there's a stop we absolutely have to make. No arguments. It's our professional duty."

I frown. "And where is that?"

He gives me a big, dazzling smile. "To grand-mère's house we go!"

21

Hawk

I can feel the early symptoms about a minute before the seizure starts. A headache quickly comes upon me, I feel . . . odd—it's the best way I can describe it—and I've got a tingling in my hands. I get up and make a quick beeline for the old records room where they store rows and rows of boxes. Hardly anyone ever goes back there. Mere seconds after I make it inside and close the door behind me, I slip away. The things surrounding me turn into ghosts on a slide and I forget everything.

When I come to, I'm on my back. I'm dizzy and it takes me a while to realize where I am and what I'm doing on the cold, hard floor. My shoulder and hip ache from my fall and I taste blood in my mouth. I readjust to lie easily on my back and take deep breaths. Man, I feel exhausted—like bone weary. I close my eyes and listen to the ticking of a nearby clock on the wall. I inspect my mouth with my tongue and realize I must have bitten my cheek hard during my lapse.

Eventually my head clears and I ever so slowly sit up and lean against the nearest row of file boxes. I perform a check over myself. Arms are okay, legs are okay, I didn't wet myself, thank the stars for that. Things went better this time.

I've had four other incidents since being barred from Genna's super-secret hideout. They came out of the blue, twice at my apartment, once when I was out for dinner, and the other at work. That time I made the mistake of trying to hide in a bathroom stall only to come to with a black eye, a sprained ankle, and a witness who saw me staggering out a bit ragged. I had to say I fell off the toilet. Yeah, never living that one down.

To say it's frustrating is putting it lightly. It's infuriating. For one, these episodes aren't even being triggered by trying to shift. In fact, I haven't been able to shift since that night at the compound with Rosalyn. It's been too risky for me to go to the arcade to make contact, much less visit the compound, with Knox keeping a closer eye on me. So, I've been stuck in the monotonous hell of work without true company, without my friends, and without the support of my sister. I haven't heard from Phoenix often. She's been too busy fighting hydra nonstop. If I had the choice, I'd rather be facing hydra than sneaking away to hidden alcoves to lose myself in a seizure. I've rarely felt so helpless before.

I keep thinking I should tell someone or go to a doctor, but what could I possibly say? I can't go to a normal doctor, pretend everything's normal about me, and get anti-seizure medication. I have to go a licensed werewolf doc and if I do that, they'll realize I'm reacting to the serum and I'll be shipped away to the same graveyard Jason was. No, my best chance is to keep this secret and help find Erebus so we can find the Magi.

Granted, there's been next to no movement on that front. In my head I've started referring to Knox as Fort Knox. I've had no luck devising a way to get access to his account without being caught. I have one job to do and I'm getting stonewalled at every turn. But one way or another, I have to end this.

I remain in the records room over long and I know it, but I'm so, so tired. I rest my head against the file boxes behind me and close my eyes. Just a moment of rest. That's what I need.

The door to the records room creaks open. Crap. I hastily scoot so I'm leaning against a shelf out of sight and hope whoever it is doesn't walk this way. The door shuts again but whoever has entered remains without turning on the lights.

"Okay, what did you hear?" someone asks in a whisper. I probably wouldn't be able to make out their words if it wasn't for my keen wolfish hearing.

Another voice answers, "I told you my friend is a Spartan on Team Yankee, right?"

"Yeah."

"Well, he passes word along when he gets the chance. His team just got in the area. They found one of those werewolf cult compounds."

My stomach gives a jolt.

"Where do you think they found them? In the city?"

"No, I think it's near the Canadian border."

"So, what are they going to do?"

"What do you think?"

"Ohhh..."

"It's about time, if you ask me." The one makes a sound of disgust. "Wish they'd do something about the werewolves they threw in here. It's only a matter of time before one of them snaps and wolfs out on us."

"So... when are they moving in on that place?"

"I'm not sure. But, hey—don't tell anyone I told you, okay? I'm not technically supposed to know."

Footsteps pass outside the door and the two fall silent for a moment.

"Let's go before Milton finds us," one of them says.

Their feet shuffle across the floor, the door opens, and then there's a sharp intake of breath.

"Spartan Knox, s-sir," one of them stutters.

"What are you two doing?" Knox's deep baritone echoes from the doorway. I remain hidden behind the shelf, my body trembling from a mix of exhaustion and anger.

"We were just—just—"

"If I catch you passing information on Spartan movements again, Brian, I'm not going to give you a second chance," Spartan Knox growls. "I'll have you arrested."

"Y-yes, sir."

"Get back to work."

I hear the two make a hasty exit before the door closes again. I remain where I am for twenty seconds to make sure Knox isn't hanging around before rising to my feet.

Spartans are on the move against the werewolf compound. Whether the one with the vampires or the one Genna's trying to free, I'm not sure. Either way, I have to warn them. There's no time to lose. It might already be too late. I exit the records room and walk casually to the elevator.

The way's clear and no one pays me any mind. Knox thankfully isn't in sight. Milton's secluded in his office with the door closed and focused intently on his computer. Before anyone notices me, I slip away as a gaunt and tired shadow.

I escape into the elevator and brace a hand on the railing, sagging somewhat, as it moves much too slowly to the first floor. When it dings and the door opens, I keep a casual pace to the doors but stop just before the corner and edge around to see if the guards are there. They are, but they're hunched over their computer together. I walk calmly past and am given only a cursory glance. They're probably more concerned about people coming in than going out. Once I hit the street and am out of sight of the entrance, it's difficult to not start running. I pick up my pace for sure but I'm quickly out of breath. That seizure really took it out of me. Weaving through traffic and pedestrians, I make for the arcade as fast as I can. I do what I can to make sure I'm not being followed but I feel out of whack. There's still a chance I'm being followed or monitored via my probation ring but I have to chance it. Genna needs to know.

At last I make it to the arcade out of breath, stumble to the Super Kart Smash machine, and brace my hands on either side of the console. Geez. Stupid seizures. No time to pity myself, though. I input the series of actions and get the notification that the message has been sent. There's no telling how fast someone will be able to get here, though. By the time Rosalyn, Merlin, or Genna shows up, it could already be too late. I leave the game console in search of the manager, Reese, who's not at the front counter. Rosalyn's called him before so he must be able to call her. If I could just get a message to them a bit quicker—

I sense movement behind me and circle behind one of the game consoles to come around on whoever is following me. Medium build, blonde hair, t-shirt button down. I freeze.

Doug—boring, dull Doug—spins around on me with a bio-mech gun drawn.

My first instinct is to knock the gun out of his hand. I could do it easily, but that would also be too suspicious. Sure, he's already come here armed after following me somehow undetected but does he actually have any evidence? Can he prove anything that I can't maneuver out of? I don't know if the charade is up or not.

"Doug, what on earth are you doing?" I ask angrily and hold my hands up at my sides. "Put the gun down, you idiot."

"I saw what you did."

I think those are the most words he's ever spoken to me before.

"Saw *what?*"

He jerks his head in the direction of the Super Kart console. "You sent a message."

I shake my head. "Doug, it's not what you think."

"You leave as soon as there's word Spartans are going after your werewolf buddies."

My eyes narrow. How does *he* know about the Spartan attack?

"Yeah, I heard about the attack," I say and continue with my irritated tone as if I'm the victim in this. "I got angry. I'm sick of work, Doug. I came here to cool off before I started smashing computers in. I should be out there helping them! Not sitting in a cubicle!"

He smiles. It's a very creepy look. "That's a nice try. Turn around."

"What?"

"I'm placing you under arrest."

"For what?" I shout in his face.

This is bad. This is very bad. I have options at this moment but none of them are good. I could disarm Doug, take him out, and then . . . and then I'd have to run. Option two, let Doug arrest me and try to make up a story the authorities will believe. Chances are slim on that one what with all the anti-werewolf crap going on. And . . . well, those are the only two options I really have right now, don't I? There's no way I'm going to turn over Genna's werewolf compound to the IMS in exchange for some kind of deal.

So attack and flee, or don't fight, take my chances, and probably wind up going to the Fields anyway.

Before either Doug or I can make a move, a figure slides up behind Doug and whacks him hard on the back of the head. He crumples to the ground and the bio-mech gun rolls away from his hand. Rosalyn snarls at me behind the wisps of a black wig, the stock of her gun still upraised in her hand as if she's going to knock me out too.

"What did you do?" she hisses.

"What did *you* do?" I snap and throw a hand out to Doug. "I might have been able to explain myself out of this but how do I do that now?"

"It's not my fault he followed you here! You've put everything at risk—"

"Shut up for a second, will you?"

"I just saved your hide—"

"*The compound is going to be attacked!*" I shout over her. She blinks and lowers the gun. "What? When?"

"Soon. Now, probably. I overheard that a group of

Spartans is moving in on a werewolf compound near the Canadian border."

She swears under her breath and glares at Doug as if she'd like to put a bullet in his head out of anger. I grab her gun hand before she can do anything stupid. She yanks out of my grip and immediately pulls out a cell phone to place a call.

"Genna, it's Roz. The Spartans are moving in on the western Watch Guard right now. You have to get your butt in gear." She listens to Genna's reply and her face changes from irritation to alarm. "What do you mean there's a hydra there?"

"*What?*"

She throws a hand up in my face and keeps on listening. "Then get them out of there before they decide to drop splinter bombs on that place! I've got the vampire cave covered, you just *get them out of there.*"

Rosalyn hangs up and shoves the phone into her pocket.

"How can I help?" I ask.

"*You* are not helping with this. You still have another mission to finish."

"Do you really think I can go back after what *you* did?" I gesture to unconscious Doug.

"I've got that covered." She gives me a vicious smile and my gut twists unpleasantly. "Don't move."

"I really don't like the sound of—"

In a blur, she clocks me with the butt of the gun and the world tilts before darkness consumes me.

I'm not sure how long I'm out of it. Long enough to be moved, tied to a chair, and have my head pound with pain. I wince and feel sticky blood crinkle on the skin of my forehead. Dang it, Rosalyn. I blink and bring the room into focus. The black walls of the laser tag area surround me, a single bulb hangs overhead, and directly across from me is Doug tied to his own chair. Footsteps circle around from behind and Rosalyn appears. She paces in front of me and when her back is to Doug—he's beginning to stir awake—she winks at me and presses a finger to her lips. I don't acknowledge that she's sent me any signal as Doug's eyelids flutter and his gaze falls on me.

I understand what her play is. At least, I think I do. She's cast me in the light of a victim, tying me up just like Doug. Both she and I are going to have to give quite the performance, though, to persuade Doug. There's just one downfall here. Her exit strategy. If she "interrogates" us and then simply leaves, that's too suspicious. Someone in Rosalyn's position would continue to use us as hostages or kill us. Otherwise, the only way this ends with me being received back into the open arms of the IMS is if agents come to rescue us. Meaning Rosalyn will be captured or killed. If that's her play, then she's made a very dangerous gamble and her life could be the cost.

Will she actually go through with it? Or does she have something else up her sleeve?

"Wakey, wakey, little birds," she croons and continues to circle the pair of us with a gun held loosely at her side. "Song birds need to sing."

Well, she's certainly playing up the picture the IMS has painted of her—crazy and deadly. She eventually comes to a stop directly before me and crouches so she's looking up, the gun pointed at my chest.

"It was stupid for you to come back here," she says. "You do realize that making a habit of where you go makes it very easy for people to find you. I just had to wait here until you showed up again."

"What do you want—"

She jumps to her feet and slugs me across the left side of my face. My head snaps to the side and pain reverberates through my skull. I can taste blood in my mouth again and work my jaw slowly.

"Don't interrupt me when I'm talking," she says and spins around to Doug. "And who are you, ugly? You picked a bad time to come here."

I expect Doug to not say anything as usual but he asks, "Where's Dasc?"

She cocks her head to the side. "You think I'm going to tell you something like that? You're even stupider than you look."

He smiles. Rosalyn punches him.

"You won't be smirking when I'm done with you," she snarls.

Yet when he raises his face, he smiles once more. "Are you sure about that?"

What's he up to? What does he know? I don't think he's the kind of person to put up bravado in the face of danger just because he can. He's not Phoenix, not by a long shot. No, I think he has something up his sleeve that's making him confident. I stare at Rosalyn. She needs to leave. Something's not right. But she doesn't leave. She starts asking us questions about the IMS facility we work at and what we do there. When we both tell her it's about correcting reports, she claims not to believe us, and we both get pummeled some more. It's a weak guise but at this point it's the only one we have.

And Doug keeps on smiling.

We discover why a few minutes later. Rosalyn stiffens and swivels towards the entrance at the same time I hear faint footsteps beyond the room. There's a subtle click and a grenade is tossed at our feet. Bright lights and an explosion of sound fills the room. A flash grenade. My ears ring and the bright light ghosts in my vision. Shouting starts, smoke fills the room, and somehow my chair gets tipped over in the ensuing chaos as IMS agents breach the room. I can't see what happens next, only that there are suddenly several men surrounding me and cutting away my bonds. I fall out of the chair once I'm free and someone helps me stand.

But where's Rosalyn? Did she make it out? Or do they have her?

"Mason, look at me."

Dazed, I turn my head to find Knox next to me in full tactical gear.

"Knox?"

"Are you okay, son?"

I nod weakly and sag against his grip on my elbow. After the seizure and Rosalyn's charade, I'm completely spent. Knox helps me out of the room and I spot others assisting Doug who's still smiling. He must have been able to alert the IMS somehow. There's no sign of Rosalyn but that doesn't mean she's home free, not by a long shot. Agents are spilling out from every corner of the arcade. I guess I'm never coming back here again. I can only hope they don't find anything here pointing to a connection with Genna and her allies. But Doug saw me send a message out on the Super Kart game. How do I explain that away? Out of the corner of my eye I see Doug talking with a couple of agents and they glance towards that specific game. Maybe I should have run when I had the chance.

No, calm down, Hawk. You can explain this away. Doug doesn't know what he saw. You sent a message on a game. Claim it was part of the game, a way to get to a secret level. If no one knows the combination to get to it, then how can they prove me wrong otherwise? Unless they want me to show them what I did as proof . . . then I'm screwed. My only hope is convincing them with my words alone.

"You have some explaining to do," Knox says sternly as he leads me to the front of the arcade. He pushes me into a chair near the door and stands over me like a guard. He props his foot up on the next chair over and leans in with an elbow resting on his upraised knee. I feel crowded, intimidated. He snaps his fingers and an agent with a medic patch on his arm hurries over. Knox gestures silently to my face and the medic gets to work, pulls out gauze, alcohol swabs, and an ice pack.

I wince as the alcohol burns in the lesion on my forehead. "Sir, I—"

"Why did you come here?" Knox says. "Why weren't you at work?"

Well, if I'm going to lie, I better do it consistently and with a half-truth.

"I heard about the Spartans in Seattle and why they're here," I say. "I was . . . upset, I guess."

"Why?"

"I should be out there doing something, not sitting in a stupid office cubicle checking grammar." I throw a hand out towards the window and the medic flinches before continuing to wipe blood off my face with gloved hands. "It really worked me up and I . . . I know I shouldn't have left the building but I was ticked off, sir. So I came here."

"Why here?"

"I told you before—stress relief."

"You bolted out of work for stress relief."

Using the back of my hand, I push the medic's attentions away from me so I have a clear line of sight to Fort Knox.

"You know exactly the kind of crap I've been dealing with," I say angrily. "Is it really so farfetched that I felt like escaping from the seventh circle of typo hell to get a breath of fresh air?"

"Air's not so fresh in here."

He's not going to lighten up on me, is he? "It reminds me of home and I need that right now. In Underground, my sister and I would go to the arcade and the movies all the time. This place—it brings a little of that back, you know? I'm suffocating in that office, Knox. You know that."

He nods and the medic edges forward to finish putting ointment and a bandage on my forehead. Knox eventually rises and crosses his arms over his chest. His steady, piercing gaze never leaves me so I stare back.

"After this incident, we can't let you run around free anymore," he says. "Not if you're being targeted."

Of course not. Why not steal yet another freedom out from under me? Let's just bring the bars of my cage closer together. Obviously there's nothing wrong with that. The itch on the back of my neck returns in full force and wills me to wolf out. Then the serum fights it and Phoenix's pendant grows warm. My head pounds so I lower my face into my hands. I need to get out of here. I hope I've been convincing enough so they think me a disgruntled employee, not a treasonous werewolf.

"Come on," Knox says. "Let's get you back so you can make a full report."

"Fine."

"And there may be disciplinary actions against you, you realize."

"I know."

He lends me a hand and pulls me to my feet. While Knox walks me out, the rest of the agents spread out and keep combing over the arcade. I spot the manager being interrogated. My feet are on thin ice. If they find one crack in my story, I could find myself plunging down into the depths.

When we return to the office building, there's a flurry of activity and whispers as the rumor spreads about what just happened. Doug is escorted into an empty office while Knox takes me into Milton's office. They have me take a seat in an uncomfortable chair and explain everything to the pair of them. Milton looks huffy as usual and Knox is quiet except to ask the sporadic question. A recorder on the desk makes a record of my entire statement. At the end of it, Knox thanks me and then orders me to remain where I am as he and Milton go off to discuss things.

Alone in that big office surrounded by the silence that presses in on my ears, I consider the choices I've made that have led me to this point. A couple years ago, I never would have gone against the IMS, never would have dealt with fugitives behind their back, never would have kept any of this from Phoenix. But as I sit here wondering if I'm about to be arrested or not, I realize I don't regret what I've done.

Genna once said I was selfish and she was right. All my life I've been fighting for my own sake but I've finally put myself forward to fight for others like me. What I've done, I've done to help the werewolves under the thumb of both the IMS and Dasc. I can only hope that my warning about the attack on the compound came in time. Did Genna manage to get the werewolves out? Is she okay? Was she caught? What about the hydra Rosalyn mentioned? And what about Rosalyn for that matter?

Knox eventually returns silent as the grave and takes a seat on the edge of the desk in front of me. He folds his hands in his lap and has that air of stern disappointment about him. We stay that way for a while in the silence—disappointed mentor and troublesome protégé.

"So, how long is it acceptable for a brooding silence to go on?" I eventually ask. I'm in hot water. I know it. He knows it. But how hot I'm about to find out and I'm testing the waters.

He gives me a sharp look but he doesn't appear outraged. That could just be a part of his personality or I'm not in *too* much trouble. But then he doesn't say anything for a while, long enough to make me nervous.

"Hawk, why did Rosalyn Graham go after you?" Knox asks quietly.

So he hasn't made up his mind yet about my excuses and explanation. Knox is a smart man and not easily fooled. I don't think I've fooled him one bit, actually. Maybe he's only waiting to see what I'll do. That's a horrible thought.

"I don't have an answer for you," I say.

"She could have easily gone after any of the other employees here, myself included."

"She'd have to be an idiot to go after you, sir."

Knox isn't easily sidetracked by humor either. "But she waited and waited and went for you."

I swallow and look down at my hands. It's a show of reluctance and possible embarrassment. I need him to think that my next words come from shame.

"Maybe she thought I'd be easy to crack," I say quietly. "They tricked me once before, her and Genna. They played me and my sister for fools. They probably think we're still fools."

I convince myself that I really am embarrassed and summon up the intensity of that feeling from memories of when I truly was. The trick works and I can feel my cheeks grow hot—maybe even have a little color in them for show. I'm a good liar and an excellent actor when I want to be.

The trick works as far as I can tell. Knox sighs, gets to his feet, and pats me on the shoulder.

"Whatever the reason, you're not safe," he says. "We need to be prepared in case Rosalyn Graham or even Genevieve Barnes shows up and tries to do something like that again. Stick to your apartment and work, no other detours. I'm going to be doubling up the watch around here. Do you understand?"

Meaning I can't even attempt to get a message to Rosalyn or Genna or Witty. I'm going to be cut off from the only friends I have, the only lifeline from the seizures and the agony of this place. Even if I manage to complete my mission and find the location of Erebus, I'll be trapped.

There's only one way I'll be leaving this place on my terms.

"I understand."

22

Phoenix

I'm not sure what to expect when we land the Osprey in Theo's backyard. When the ramp lowers, I step out into a meadow blooming with tiny purple floors. The flat expanse of grass extends far to either side, to a lake on my left and a forest on my right. Directly before us sits a colonial style house with red shutters and warm light spills out of the many windows. A string of Christmas lights outlines the back porch and what looks like an event tent as if someone just held a wedding or dance. The scent of lilacs lies heavy in the air, birds sing, and the lake glimmers with the last rays of the sun.

"It's beautiful," I say to no one in particular.

Theo claps me on the back. "Be sure to tell my grand-mère that. She'll love it. Come on!"

He gives us a wide smile and sets off for the house with his bag slung over his shoulder. Laughter and distant talking floats to us from the open windows. It sounds like there's a lot of people here.

"Is that for us?" John asks and points to the tent.

"Oh, man!" Theo exclaims and slaps a palm to his forehead. "I forgot it's Matthew's birthday today!"

"Are you sure it's okay we're here?" Melody asks.

He waves her off. "Oh, yeah. I called ahead. We're good." He walks backwards and cups his hands around his mouth. "Fart! Flitter! You can come too!"

There's a shrill sound behind us followed by a powerful gust of wind as the two air sprites dart ahead of us. Theo's shout also managed to grab the attention of those inside because the back door opens and three people step out onto the porch.

"Theo?" a girl calls. "That you?"

"As handsome as ever!" he shouts and rushes ahead.

By the time we reach the porch, Theo has picked up the young girl and twirled her around in the air before setting her back down. She has a large amount of curly hair that bounces about her shoulders. Beside her stands an elderly woman with white hair and a shawl wrapped around her arms. Theo hugs her next and moves on to a third woman who looks like she could be his mother—they have the same smile.

"Have you been eating well enough?" the old woman asks and gives him a shrewd look. "You look like you should eat more."

"Is that an offer of food?" Theo says with a grin.

"I doubt my grandson will be able to kill many hydra if he's a toothpick. A vampire's fang would go right through you."

He laughs and guides her over to the rest of us waiting on the bottom steps of the porch. Melody walks up first and they share kisses on either cheek. John is next and gives Theo's grand-mère a warm handshake. Alona goes straight for the hug which surprises me.

"Oh, my dear girl," the old woman croons. "Still keeping my boy on his toes, I hope?"

"Of course."

Charlie and I take a step forward awkwardly when Theo motions to us.

"Grand-mère, I'd like you to meet the newest members of our team. This is Charlie Jaeger and Phoenix Mason."

"*Bonjour*," she says and takes both our hands. Her palms are calloused and the fingers that I thought would be fragile hold my hand in a firm grip. Theo had told me before his family is a generational group of vampire hunters. I can see the steel in the old woman's eyes but also kindness.

After passing on our own greetings, Theo strikes up a very fast conversation in French with his grandmother that ends with him promising us food inside. We drop our packs at the back door and enter single file into the rustic looking interior. It's open and spacious, which is very good because there are a *lot* of Benoits currently here. We walk directly into the living room where Theo begins introducing everyone while his grandmother moves into a kitchen on our right.

"This is Maria," he says and puts his hands on the shoulders of the small girl he first ran to when we got here. "Then that's Isabella, Thomas, Adalyn, Fayette, Fernand, Leo—"

The list goes on and on. Each time he says a name, that person gives us a friendly wave, bob of the head, or a short hello. I don't think I'll be able to remember their names but I also don't want to be rude. I give it a good try of matching names to faces. Theo gives us a little more background by pointing to people and saying how he's related to them—sister, sister, brother, aunt, first cousin, father, another brother, third cousin twice-removed, some hermit his grandmother must have let into the house—

"I'm his *brother*," Dorian clarifies with a huff.

"So he claims," Theo says out of the corner of his mouth to us, and then keeps on going with the introductions.

I feel awkward standing there and attempting to bob my head at each person to acknowledge them. I'm also tired and sore and hungry. But the faces looking back at me don't seem to mind that we look haggard, smell rather foul, and have interrupted their family gathering. No, the faces looking at me are friendly, others curious, others happy to see us. It's a nice change of pace, that's for sure.

A bell clangs from the kitchen garnering everyone's attention. Theo's grand-mère comes out carrying a steaming dish of something wonderful smelling in her hands.

"You can eat out in the pavilion," she announces. "Or in the kitchen. I'm afraid there's not an abundance of room inside."

"Nonsense." It's Theo's father—I think. "We can make room for our Spartans, can't we?"

He looks to the others and there's an immediate flurry of everyone getting up, moving out, and rounding up the children to get them out of the way so we can reach the adjoining dining room. Melody tries to tell them to stay, that we can move, but they only give her kind smiles or pat her on the shoulder. Most either go out to the pavilion themselves or vacate to the upstairs area. Children's feet thunder across the floor above us along with the sounds of joyful laughter. There's warmth here that I haven't truly felt during two months of fighting monsters. Away from the danger, blood, and death, there is light, life, and love.

We're escorted into the dining room by the last stragglers who also help bring in food from the kitchen. Melody is still trying to politely refuse their hospitality until grand-mère tells her she can either accept the food or be force-fed it. Theo almost falls off his chair laughing. We sit around the large, solid oak table that's cluttered with torn wrapping paper clearly left over from the birthday party before our arrival. Theo's father, several sisters, and brothers are quick to clear room for the food and bring in clean dishes too. They're mostly loud and boisterous but I don't think I've encountered a more generous family in my life. Theo's mother even anticipates our needs before we realize we need them.

"There's a bathroom upstairs to the right." She points a slender finger to stairs around the corner. "I'll pull out some fresh towels and you can get cleaned up if you want. We'll clear two of the guest rooms. I think Uncle Fernand and his family are about to head out so you can take their place. I'll start on washing the sheets for you."

Theo gives her a tight hug and she closes her eyes with a happy smile. She's a lovely woman with elegant curls, a warm presence, and a rather sharp sense of style if I do say so myself.

"Thanks, Mama."

"I'm just glad you're all in one piece," she says. "Now eat up. I'm sure you're hungry. Don't worry about a thing. I'll take care of the rest."

She hustles out of the room to make arrangements for us.

"You better be careful," Charlie says to Melody. "I think she's giving you a run for your money on 'most accommodating person of the year.'"

He gives her a lazy smile and she suddenly looks mischievous, eyes slightly narrowed, as if she took it as a challenge to out nice Mrs. Benoit.

Then the food is uncovered and we're encouraged to eat as much as we want. The room falls silent except for the clink of silverware and somewhat obnoxious chewing. Everything is delicious. I don't know what most of it is but Theo helpfully names them for me when I say as much—ratatouille, bouillabaisse, and for dessert a strawberry meringue galette. After I've gorged myself, I lean back in my chair ready to fall asleep on the spot. The others look the same. I think Charlie may already be napping as John, Melody, and Alona sip at glasses of wine.

"I don't think I've ever eaten that well in my life," I say. "Thank you."

Theo's grand-mère comes over to pat me on the shoulder. "*De rien.*"

I've learned enough from Theo to know that pretty much means "you're welcome." She bids us adieu and heads up to her room to sleep. The team remains around the table staring absently into space and without much inclination to move anywhere at the moment. Several other Benoits come in to lean against the walls or take the remaining open seats.

One of Theo's brothers—Dorian, I think—takes a seat next to our sharpshooter.

"You hear anything out of France?" Dorian asks.

Theo shakes his head. "No. You?"

"Officially, no."

"Unofficially?"

Dorian takes a long sip of wine before answering. "I contacted one of my old friends in country. Sounds like something went about as wrong as it could over there. Rumor is they lost control of one of their installations. They don't want the other governments and divisions knowing about it until they can fix it."

"Why not?" I ask.

"National pride. Honor." Dorian shrugs. "The French don't want anyone to think they can't handle their own messes—or that they make them in the first place."

It sounds a bit thick-headed to me—but then again, if I was in their position, maybe I'd be compelled to do the same. Silence falls over the table as we consider Dorian's bit of news.

It's during this resting period that little Maria comes over to tug at Theo's arm.

"Theo," Maria says in a small voice. "Have you been fighting monsters?"

He bends low in his chair to her eye level. "I sure have."

"Was it scary?"

"No, *ma chérie*, because I have my friends to protect me." He gestures widely to us.

Melody nods. "And he protects us too."

"Tell me a story, Theo," the little girl pleads and tugs on his arm some more.

"Maria." Theo's mother returns carrying a basket of clean linens. "Our guests are tired."

"It's okay, Mama," Theo says. "I'm not so tired yet."

It's true—he has the most energy out of the team. So, as the rest of us start nodding off where we sit, Theo launches into a story of our exploits. More of his relatives crowd into the room or linger past the doorways to listen. Theo paints us in a very dramatic light and turns our daily assaults into more of an action film than a horror movie—despite how horrific things actually have been. His audience is completely captivated and makes the appropriate gasps, ohs and awes at all the right places. They're an animated bunch and I can definitely tell they're related to Theo.

When Melody's head slips off her propped up arm and thuds loudly against the table top, story time is brought to a swift end. The family disperses and Theo's mother guides us to the rooms she's laid out for us. She makes a point to split up the team by gender so Melody, Alona, and I take one room while the boys take the other. There are only two beds so Melody and I each take one while Alona shifts into a raven form to sleep nestled in the big bay window overlooking the lake. Not wanting to dirty the linens of such a pleasant hostess, we change out of our Spartan gear, take fast showers, and don the silky pajamas Theo's sister brings us. When my head touches the pillow, I only have a second to register the sweet smell of lilacs on the sheets before I fall asleep.

Despite the hospitality, the warmth of the Benoit family, and the wonderful bed, my nightmares still seek me out in the night. This time Iota joins Epsilon in trapping my team in a locked room where they harness the ability of a hydra. I watch helplessly as the skin melts off my teammates' faces and hands.

I'm not sure if I scream or not when I wake up. It takes me some time to even out my breathing as I clutch a hand to my heart. Alona's dark eyes glitter from her corner as she watches me before tucking her head back under her wing. Melody's also awake and extends a hand towards me. I grasp it momentarily and give her a nod to let her know I'm okay. It's only partially true but there's not much I can do about it.

My skin feels hot and sweaty and my throat is dry. Some cool night air and a glass of water might help. I slip out from under the sheets and tiptoe downstairs to the back door leading to the porch. I pause with my hand on the handle when I realize there's someone else nearby.

Theo flicks on the light in the kitchen. He gestures me over and pulls two glasses from the cabinet.

"Can I pour you a drink?" he asks and mimes washing out one of the glasses with an elbow on the countertop as if he's a bartender.

I settle on a stool on the other side of the countertop. "Give me the good stuff."

"For a charming lady like you, of course." He winks and moves to the fridge. I nearly laugh out loud when he comes back with a jug of milk. "Best top shelf stuff I've got."

"Will it take the edge off?"

He scoffs. "Why would you want to be dull?" He fills my glass halfway and slides it over before filling his own and raising his glass for a toast. "Clear minds, sharp knives."

I clink my glass of milk against his and take a swig. It helps with my dry throat.

"Where's that saying from?"

"Old family motto." He rests both forearms on the counter and spins his glass between his hands. "If you don't have a clear head and a sharp blade, it's a little difficult to kill vampires."

"I'll bet."

"Speaking of clear minds," he says and tilts his head to study me. "Why are you up? Something on your mind?"

I purse my lips and swirl the milk in my glass round and round. "Nightmare. Why are *you* up?"

"Just making sure Cranky was all right."

"Charlie?"

He nods towards the back door. "He never went to sleep. Tried to, I think, then came down and went outside."

My brow draws into a frown and I look to the door.

"I'm not sure if he wanted company or not, so I let him be," Theo continues.

"Maybe I should talk to him," I murmur.

"Well, if anyone's going to get him out of his funk, it's you."

I swivel around. "What?"

"Nothing. Go on, then. Bring our teleporter back before he vanishes on us. He needs sleep too."

He returns the jug to the fridge then heads upstairs. I finish my glass and inch out the back door, careful of the squeaky hinges. I can hardly see a thing out here so I follow my senses instead and find his bright spot of magic in the distance near the lake. Using that as my guide, I walk barefoot through the grass, pass the tent pavilion, and to the shore of the lake. In the faint light from the crescent moon, I can make out Charlie's silhouette at the end of the dock.

He swings his arm and I hear a stone skip across the water with a soft plunk-plunk-plunk.

The boards of the dock are rough against my bare feet as I walk out to meet him. He stops mid throw with another rock and gives me a sideways look.

"I don't need a babysitter," he grouses. Wow, I guess he's really in a mood.

"I don't know what you're talking about," I say airily and lift my chin. "I, too, came to skip stones in the middle of the night. This meeting is sheer coincidence."

He snorts—a highly undignified sound for him—and throws a rock so hard it doesn't skip but makes a big splash. I look around and find there's a pile of rocks next to him on the dock. *Pixies*, how long has he been out here? I pick one up with a smooth surface and hurl it towards the water. It makes an even bigger splash than Charlie's last.

"What was *that?*" he says.

"So, maybe I've never skipped stones before—"

"You've never skipped a stone *ever?*"

I stick my tongue out at him like a reasonable adult. "It's not that I haven't tried. I've just never achieved the proper aerodynamics or physics to make a solid object skim a liquid."

He starts laughing quietly and shakes his head. "It's all in the wrist. Here, let me show you."

He picks up another rock, angles it, flicks his wrist, and it skips four times. Gathering my wits with a deep frown, I pick up another rock, try to mimic what he did, and shoot up a geyser of water as the rock plummets into the lake. His laughter belts out of him this time and I punch him lightly in the shoulder.

"And now you know why I prefer skipping rocks at night," I say. "So no one can see."

"Well, no one's perfect at everything."

"Except you," I grumble.

It's too dark to read his expression but I know he's staring at me. I fight the blush in my cheeks and pick up another rock.

"Watch me," Charlie whispers.

I do. He gets into a stance and waits for me to mimic it. Body angled, knees slightly bent, arm stretched back. He makes a slow motion several times of how to throw the stone. I watch intently until he lets it fly. Five skips. I roll my shoulders, pull my arm back, and let the stone roll off my forefinger. Two skips.

"Yes!" I shriek and jump with my arms in the air before I remember there are people sleeping inside the house. I clamp my hands over my mouth.

I turn to Charlie and we burst out laughing.

"I knew you could do it," he says and skips another stone across the lake. "So, what brings you out to skip rocks in the middle of the night?"

"Nightmare." I grab another stone myself and visualize how I'm going to throw it. "Watched the team get acid dripped by Iota and Epsilon."

"Gruesome," he says.

"Yeah." A shiver runs down my spine as I think of it again but it has less bite with Charlie here beside me. "What about you?"

He's quiet for a long time and flips a rock over and over in his hand. He eventually throws it but it sinks immediately.

"Watching Theo's family . . . I don't know. It just stirs up a lot of stuff."

I still haven't told him I know what happened to his parents. I don't bring it up now either, but I can understand how seeing another family so happy and loving might dredge up some truly horrible memories—and longing.

"Do you want to talk about it?" I ask. I won't push him if he's not willing to spill his inner turmoil and secrets. Part of me hopes he will, though. Charlie is a mystery worth unraveling.

He rolls a stone between his hands but doesn't say anything.

"I also enjoy comfortable silence," I say nearly as a whisper.

"Heh, I guess that's become our thing, hasn't it?"

"Just knowing someone is there for you can be enough." I turn more towards him and he towards me. "And I know you'll always have my back. I just hope you know that it goes both ways."

"I know."

I bend down and pick up another stone ready to have a bout of silence skipping stones until we decide we can both go to sleep. The stone skips two times. Charlie doesn't throw his but watches me.

"I've always been jealous of what you and Hawk have," he says so softly it's almost hard to catch his words over the gentle lapping of the water. "And some part of me hurts looking in on the happiness of the Benoits. You already know my uncle is a right prick, but my parents . . . my parents weren't good people either. Even before—before things went real bad, they always fought. I'd be caught in the middle like a bargaining chip and it only got worse when they divorced. Mom had some mental health issues. Dad was always too busy with work. And I was there being shuttled between the two until . . ." He clears his throat and looks out over the water dappled in pale moonlight.

His voice cracks when he says, "I loved them both but I'll be damned if they ever felt the same way about me."

I reach down to take his hand feeling like it's the right move to make, but he jerks away from me.

"I don't want pity," he snaps.

"Charlie, cut it out," I growl. I snatch up his hand and shake it by his face. "This isn't pity, you idiot. It's sympathy."

"Look it up in a dictionary, Phoenix. *It's the same thing.*" He pulls free of my grip.

I throw up my hands. "Fine. Whatever. Turn it into something negative like you always do, but you want to know why I sympathize, Charlie?"

"Why?"

"Because we're family. Me, Hawk, Melody, Theo, John, Alona—we're your family. And family looks after one another. We care—heck, we even *sympathize*—because that's what you do when you love someone. Every single one of us would die for you, Charlie. So, when I hear that your family treated you like crap and you're in pain, of course I want to hold your hand. I want you to know that you aren't alone because *you're not*. So, dang it all, you better get used to people giving you hugs and sending you presents on your birthday and beating the snot out of anyone that hurts you because we're here for you. *I* am here for you. And I just want to freaking hold your hand. I don't care if blood is thicker or whatever."

"It's not," he says quietly. "Everyone quotes that wrong."

I blink, momentarily derailed. "What?"

He takes a step closer until there's maybe a foot between us. "The actual quote is 'the blood of the covenant is thicker than the water of the womb.'" He sighs and takes my hand, our callouses rough against each other's palms. "It means that the bonds we make by choice are more important than the ones by birth."

"Oh. Well, then—yeah. That's what I've been trying to say."

He nods and stares at our conjoined hands as if musing over its implications.

"So, inviting me to come along to visit Hawk wasn't out of pity?" he asks.

I let out a groan. "*No.* I actually do enjoy your company despite your attempts at being cranky. I know there's a ball of fluff and rainbows under that masquerade of sass."

"Uh-huh. Fluff and rainbows."

"I think we should hug this out, Unicorn."

"Berserker," he grumbles but doesn't object when I pull him into a tight hug. In fact, he doesn't go stiff or try to pull away. He sort of melts and holds onto me tight, chin tucked down into my shoulder.

"Thank you, for being you," he murmurs.

I close my eyes and allow the warmth swelling in my chest to overtake me. I have a feeling I'll be able to sleep now. "That's what family's for."

23

Hawk

If I thought I felt alone before, it doesn't compare to the isolation I find myself in now. I'm cut off. I can't contact Genna and company and I doubt they'll be able to get a message to me either. There's been no word of the werewolf compound so I have no idea what happened. There's also been nothing about Rosalyn which I can only assume is good news and that she somehow managed to escape.

I've heard nothing from Phoenix in over a week but I know exactly where she was last. The feeds have blown up over an incident at Werevine Pharmaceutical. I knew something had happened the second I walked into work and saw every head in the vicinity turn in my direction. I thought it was about what happened yesterday with Rosalyn but then I noticed every werewolf in the building getting the stink eye. Once I opened the feeds it all made sense.

A splinter group of werewolves once again openly attacked an establishment. News on werewolves had been quiet for a while as everyone focused on the hydra threat but it's been pushed to the forefront of everyone's minds again. Well, isn't that just peachy.

Reading through the article, Team Sierra is given the glowing respect and admiration they deserve being one of the most efficient teams battling the hydra. Phoenix is out there saving the day and I'm stuck here getting glares from my co-workers and wondering if I'm going to be arrested at any moment. I can't help the tinge of bitterness. It's not Phoenix's fault, I know that, but it's not fair. I feel like a five-year-old thinking it.

I finish the article when Doug finally shows up.

"Morning, sunshine," I say and temple my fingers together. "I thought we'd get here at the same time since you've been shadowing me. I'm shocked you're late, really. Got distracted kicking puppies and drowning kittens on your way in?"

Doug doesn't respond as usual but I'm angry and determined to make him respond. It's a terrible idea but I'm so *angry* all of a sudden. He's the reason I'm in this mess. A shock of pain goes down my back as different parts of magic battle each other and throw me off kilter. One part werewolf battles one part poisonous serum driving me mad. The pendant warms only slightly as if worn out from the constant war raging inside me.

"So you have nothing to say until you're accusing someone of sedition?" I snap and sit forward on the edge of my chair, both hands tightly griping the armrests.

For a moment he looks like he's not going to answer or even acknowledge my presence—then he gives me a sinister smile and winks.

I snap.

My hands grab the closest thing in the vicinity, which happens to be Doug's ceramic mug, and I throw it against the wall where it shatters in an explosive crash. I bare my teeth and snarl, hardly registering the exclamations from others nearby that heard the noise. Doug doesn't even flinch.

"What's going on in here?" Milton squeezes past the shelves into our little corner. He's red in the face and his piggy eyes jump from me, to Doug, to the broken pieces of the coffee mug.

It takes an extraordinary amount of willpower to rein myself back in. I flex my hands a few times and exhale slowly. Doug doesn't say anything as usual, not even to pin me as the one who flipped out and broke his cup.

"There was a spider," I grumble. "I hate spiders."

"Spiders!" Milton throws up his hands dramatically and waddles over to the wall where there's now a sizable dent. "Spiders!"

"Bill me," I say and plop back into my seat. I can't bring myself to care about him or anyone else. My world's shrunk in on itself. It's the only thing I can think about.

Milton looks like his head's about to explode—his face turns bright red, his cheeks puff out, and he draws himself up to his full height which isn't very tall. He stammers a few times, then huffs angrily, and storms away. In his wake, curious onlookers slink back to their desks.

Feeling small and hopeless, I scooch to my computer and stare at the blank screen considering my options. There aren't many. If I stay here, I'll go mad. There's no question about if but a matter of when. I'm already not the same person I was when I came here. Each day I feel a little less, like pieces are breaking off each time I take that serum injection and suffer through the pain that's always there, even when I pretend that it's not. I don't remember what it's like to not be in pain constantly. It's gotten harder to laugh. For a while I could ignore the changes and hope for better but with this last lifeline severed, everything's come crashing inwards on top of me within the last day. If there's a light at the end of the tunnel, I don't see it. Well, maybe it's there but I'm pretty sure it's my life going up in flames.

The clock ticks out the seconds, then minutes, then hour I sit there staring at nothing and contemplating what I'm supposed to do now. On any normal day before coming to Seattle, I'd go to my sister to help me through a rough day—or she'd simply know without me having to say a thing and hound me into feeling better. She's stubborn and extremely annoying at times, but it's also what I need. Genna had become that for me here, as well as Rosalyn, Witty, and Merlin. But now . . . the clock ticks out the empty seconds.

Eventually I get up in search of food which usually has the pleasant side effect of cheering me up. However, when I hear Milton's voice in the break room, I decide hunting for donuts isn't such a grand idea at the moment. Then I hear what he's talking about.

"I knew this would happen," he says in a hushed tone yet still clearly loud enough to be heard by anyone in the vicinity. "Werewolves are trouble. I've always told them that. Then of course the agency piles them on me as soon as they finally decide to deal with the problem. Deal with it. Huh!"

My jaw locks and I stand rigid outside the door, my eyes burning holes into the carpet in front of me.

"I'd bet good money that Hawk was involved somehow with that attack at Werevine," Milton continues. "Most people don't know about this, but he and his sister had their first assignment there as junior agents and almost blew the whole place up. Director Knox tried to hush it all up, of course. I've heard rumors that he has a soft spot for those two. My guess? Hawk set that place on fire on purpose. They're one of the biggest distributors of the serum, you know, and no werewolf is quite right in the head."

"*Milton.*" It's Vicky's voice. The very same Vicky that agreed to go on a date with me despite me being a werewolf. "Someone could hear you."

"So? They already know what the rest of us think of them. I'm just saying it out loud."

So by that logic I could strangle him and it wouldn't be a big deal because he already knows everyone hates him. My fingers twitch thinking about it. It'd be so easy. He's not a soldier. He's nothing special. That itch at the back of my neck grows so strong that a shudder ripples through me and I feel the tips of canines with my tongue. If I wolfed out right here, so what? What would it matter? I'm already on lockdown. I could rip my way through here and—

No. I brace a hand on the wall and hang my head, breathing through my teeth. I can't lose control. There's still the mission. After I get what I need, then I can leave in whatever fashion I want. It's a liberating feeling until the thought of Phoenix hits me in the gut like a giant's fist. I'd be leaving her too. No, I have to make this work. Things are going to get better. I have to believe that. I can't blow everything on a whim.

Pull it together, Hawk. You've got this. Hang on a while longer. Find Erebus. Get the information to Genna. Make the cure. Right.

I finally push off from the wall just as Milton and Vicky exit the break room. They both startle to a halt when they find me directly outside. What they see in my face must terrify the both of them because Vicky immediately slips away and Milton goes purple in the face, stutters something about getting paperwork done, and makes a quick exit. My eyes remain trained on his back until he slams the door to his office.

When I turn away, the other werewolves in the office quickly avert their eyes, but I know they were paying attention. To my shame, not one holds defiance in their eyes. They bow their heads and return to correcting typos like obedient dogs. A scathing thought runs through my mind. Maybe they don't deserve the effort I'm putting into this mission not only for myself but their sakes as well. They aren't even willing to fight for their dignity. When did we become so broken?

My feet drag on the carpet as I return to my desk and plop into my chair. The isolation because of my secrets makes this even harder. I don't have Phoenix to confide in. I don't have Genna or even Rosalyn to talk to. There's no way I can express any of my rage to Knox without setting off alarm bells. The only way truly out of this is to complete the task before me.

Deciding to take another stab at Fort Knox, I rise from

my chair once again despite sitting down a second ago and walk past Knox's cubicle as I pretend to get a print job off the copier. He's there as usual guarding his computer like a hawk. Ha. Like a hawk. Hawk and hawk. Wow, I'm really losing it, aren't I? But as always, there's no opening I can see to exploit. The second he rises to get another cup of coffee, he logs off. He's that on top of security that he actually logs off to get a cup of coffee. How am I supposed to get around a man like that?

I detour into the break room, snag a donut as Knox gets his coffee, and then shuffle back to my desk. Doug's not there. That's a first, and after discovering his interest in what I've been up to, it makes me nervous. Where is he? I rip into the donut—really savoring the feeling of my teeth ripping into something—and decide I can't worry about Doug right now. He's not my focus anyway.

I can't believe that the task before me is impossible. There's always a way. If only I was a serial killer and kidnapper like Dasc. Then this would probably be a breeze.

The weight of the thought hits me. It twists my stomach and the donut turns to tasteless mush in my mouth. So far I've been trying to think of ways to do this within the realm of my own comfort zone and morality. I can justify sneaking a peek at information under Knox's profile because it will benefit the greater good. I can do that. But there are . . . other ways to get what I want. There are things I could do if I was truly desperate. I feel sick even thinking about it.

But how desperate am I?

If . . . if there were no boundaries, I could think of a few different options. I could always get what I need from Knox directly. I know he goes to the gym every day after work. He also takes runs out to the beach. It'd be a matter of timing to make a move. But no. Even if I was truly that desperate, attempting to . . . persuade it out of Knox would be useless. He's a Spartan commander. He wouldn't break and I don't think I could do it anyway.

But maybe I'm coming at this the wrong way. Knox's ability to do his job is a major hindrance but I could use it to my advantage in the right situation. That's the key. I know this office and I know the people that work here. I know that Vicky brings in cupcakes on Fridays for the office meeting. I know that Karen, the cubicle mate next to Knox, always takes one. I also happen to know that Karen is deathly allergic to peanut butter. And if Karen was to say . . . have an allergic reaction right next to Knox and her Epi-pen was nowhere to be found, he would jump in to save her life. And when everyone was distracted, I could slip onto Knox's computer.

I push the donut aside, hang my head, and put my face in my hands. It's an awful thing to think about and I can't believe it even came to mind. Karen is a nice person. She's quiet and keeps to herself but she always says good morning to me even when I'm grouchy to everyone, including her. Doing something like that . . . I could end up killing her. *Pixies*, what kind of monster am I turning into for even thinking about doing that? I can't. There has to be another way. Some other non-life threatening emergency to draw Knox away from his computer in a rush without logging off and to distract the others as well. But what that might be, I have no idea.

For the rest of the morning I sit contemplating any and all alternatives. Doug doesn't return to his desk and it really starts to worry me. I'd be glad if he's deathly sick and went home but for some reason I can't picture it. He's one of those creepy workaholics. I wouldn't be surprised if he got the flu, fever, and broke his leg and still showed up to correct typos. Him not being here is a bad sign.

At lunch time, I make a beeline for the elevator as usual. I press the button and the second the doors open, I find a meaty arm blocking my way. Knox leans in from the side.

"Why don't you come to the cafeteria with me instead?" he says.

"I can't even go out to get lunch?"

"You know the situation."

Right. I'm on lockdown for my own protection. What a joke.

He lets me into the elevator and I fight the urge to roll my eyes. "You know the cooks hate us, right? They have a thing about werewolves."

"It's fine. Come on."

"If they spit in my soup, I'm blaming you."

He laughs as if it's a joke, but it's really not. I've heard stories from the others and witnessed it firsthand myself. That's why I don't eat in the cafeteria. They're about as friendly and hospitable as Milton.

We ride the elevator down two levels to the cafeteria. There isn't a crowd yet but people are starting to filter in from the stairwells and elevators. Half the floor is one giant open eating area while the rest houses the kitchens. Knox pays for both our lunches—a friendly gesture that he refuses to be repaid for—and we load up our trays from the buffet. Knox orders a bowl of soup despite my earlier warning and the grouchy cook slops a ladleful into a bowl so it's a bit messy before handing it over. What a jerk. At least I don't think she spit in it.

Knox smiles, takes the bowl with soup sliding down the sides, and says, "Thank you."

He turns away and I follow a few steps before pausing and watching the cook get the next person in line a bowl. It's Karen, Knox's cubicle mate. The cook carefully ladles the soup and even wipes off the edge when she dribbles a bit before giving it kindly to her customer. When the cook catches me staring, I don't bother to pretend I didn't see. Her cheeks go red but she returns my glare with a frosty one of her own.

"You know—" I start, ready to unleash my anger on this stupid person, when Knox wraps his hand around my upper arm and drags me away. I rip out of his grip, slopping a bit of my juice.

"Take a seat," Knox says using his commander voice and leaving no room for argument.

Fuming, I take a seat as far away from everyone else as I can near one of the windows. I practically slam my tray onto the table while Knox calmly takes the seat next to me on the small table.

"You need to calm down," he says.

"You know I don't like coming here," I snap.

He ignores his food and elects to pin me with that critical gaze of his. "You're really wound up."

"You don't say."

"It's not really your style."

Instead of replying, I drain my cup of juice. Knox is unrelenting though. He pushes his tray to the side so he can rest an arm on the table and angle himself towards me.

"Hawk."

I don't give him the courtesy of looking at him. "What?"

"You need to talk to someone about what's going on with you."

"You're right. I'll call my sister." I slap a hand to my forehead. "Oh, that's right. She's out killing hydra and doing the job I should be doing. Maybe I should call my friend Jefferson—oh, wait. He's busy too. Let me see . . . who's left? Hmm, I guess that's it. Unless you can suggest a good therapist."

"That's enough," he says sharply. I nearly flinch at his tone. It's the same one he used when he trained me during Spartan boot camp. Heat rolls off my face.

"You can't keep going about your life carrying something like this with you," he says.

"I've been doing it for over fifteen years," I mumble. "How long have you been a werewolf again?"

"Seven years. And before that I was a black man growing up in Minneapolis. I know exactly how it feels to grow up with the burden of people's prejudices always on your back and in your face."

I swallow and can't meet his eyes, not out of anger but shame.

"I know what it's like when people judge you for what you are or look like instead of who you are. None of them will ever truly understand what that feels like to be in our shoes. You can fight them every day of your life but no matter what you do, some people will never relent their misguided preconceptions."

"So you just stop fighting?" I ask quietly.

"I don't give them reasons to confirm their prejudices, and that is a battle all in itself. It can be hard to be kind to people when they think of you as something less than human. But do you know why I do it?"

"Why?"

He doesn't say anything until I finally meet his eyes.

"Because the only person's opinion that really matters is my own. I know who I am. They don't and I won't let their fears and hatred stop me from being the best possible version of myself. Do you understand, son?"

I nod mutely and lower my eyes to my plate of fries, fish, and mashed potatoes.

"I understand your anger, I really do," he continues and pulls his tray back towards himself. "Neither of us wants to be here since, as you said before, we're men of action. But tell me, could you very well with a clear conscious go into the field when you know there is a monster out there that could make you attack your fellow agents? Could make you turn on your friends?"

Ever so slowly I shake my head.

"This isn't forever and it's not about us. It's not about what we want. It's about protecting our own. So, we'll stay here and suffer through typos and Milton. Because the truth is, Hawk, we *are* dangerous—to ourselves and others—and if staying on the sidelines means I can't be used against my comrades, then I'll take a knee. That doesn't mean I like it and it sure doesn't mean I want to stay here, but I'm going to do it. Do you understand?"

I clear my throat. "I do. I get it, I really do."

"You aren't alone in this." He claps a hand on my

shoulder. "Bottling it up and keeping it to yourself isn't doing yourself or anyone else any favors. So, talk to me. Get it off your chest."

For a moment, the path before me wavers and splits in two.

I could tell Knox everything here and now. I could tell him about the serum and what it's been doing to me. I could tell him about Phoenix and a possible cure looming on the horizon. He's still fighting for the werewolves but in his own way. Maybe if I told him, he'd help me find Erebus himself. We'd be a team—we'd be Spartans again fighting the good fight. The end of that path is uncertain and could either be a great step forward or the breaking of everything.

Then there's the other path. I keep silent about my secrets. I don't tell my mentor the pain I've been struggling with ever since I started taking the serum again. Knox would remain in the dark and I would continue to seek my own answers behind his back. That path lies with Genna and the werewolves she's freed. This path, too, is uncertain.

When did my choices boil down to two things so monumental that either way is sure to decide my fate for the rest of my life?

I want to be able to trust Knox with the secrets I've been hauling around. Perhaps if he knew the whole truth . . . if he just *knew* the reality of the serum . . .

"You can talk to me," Knox says in a calm, reassuring manner. His hand stays on my shoulder to make his presence doubly known.

My resolve starts to melt away like hot wax. How desperately I want to have someone to talk to in this moment and know I can rely on. I'm sick of being afraid to share my burdens. I'm sick of feeling trapped within my own skin. Knox is a fellow warrior and werewolf. He'd understand. He has to.

I roll my lips and my fingers shake a little as I rest them on the edge of the table. I don't have a clue how to even start this kind of conversation.

"I'm tired." I decide starting at a simple point is the best way to go. "I'm tired of... well, all of it—feeling useless, the distance everyone here keeps, the distinct lines between us and them as if we didn't all come from the same place to begin with. I'm just... tired."

Knox nods and at last removes his hand from my shoulder. "I feel it too. It wears at you, dulls your edges. It can turn you bitter quick if you let it."

"How do you deal with it?"

"Find people to give you the support you need so you won't be smothered by everything. It's tough going it alone. It's tough even when you have support, but there's strength in numbers. That's one of the reasons the Spartans are structured in teams. There are no lone Spartans. And if there's ever anything you need, you come ask me. I don't care if it seems too small or too big, you ask me. I've got your back. No matter what."

This is my moment. The words sit on the edge of my tongue. I could tell him about the seizures and ask about Erebus. Knox could get the information for me and I would never have to go behind his back to do it. The thoughts linger in my mouth but I can't seem to get them out. I'm not sure what holds me back—cowardice or caution. I've never told anyone about the seizures except Genna and only because she was witness to it. The thought of telling Knox—

my teacher and childhood hero—twists my gut. Would he think me weak, a thing to be pitied? I don't think I could stand that.

Or he could realize the other half of my predicament. My inability to stomach the serum. He's called us dangers to ourselves and others before. He's made that plain. If he considered me a threat in the slightest to myself or those around me...

No. I can't tell him because I know exactly what he would do. He'd do his duty and protect the people, even if that meant sending me to the Fields.

And that—that is somewhere I will not go.

"I appreciate it, Knox," I say quietly. "I'll let you know if anything comes to mind."

He gives me a rare encouraging smile and starts on his lunch. I stare at my tray for a good long while before making a show of eating. It takes a great deal of effort to chew the tasteless meal and swallow past my dry mouth.

We're quiet throughout the rest of lunch. The cafeteria grows louder as others come in but we leave before it gets too crazy. When I return to my desk, I feel stiff and heavy with everything on my mind. Knox has thrown a wild card into the middle of my plans. Everything in me feels wrong and I wage an internal debate for the umpteenth time about who I am, what I'm doing, and what I ought to do next.

I'm in the middle of this haze when I realize the pain in my veins recedes and warmth tingles in my fingers. For a frightened second I think I'm getting seizure symptoms before I realize I'm more clearheaded than I have been in a long while. Swiveling about in my chair as footsteps approach, I expect Doug to have at last come in to work but who I find standing there instead nearly stops my heart.

As Phoenix unexpectedly appears with a bright smile and bags under her eyes, I freeze in my chair as I'm slammed by one part undulated happiness and one part absolute terror.

My twin sister is here!

But why is she here?

And then that sharp taste of dread...

Does she know?

24

Phoenix

I wouldn't say Hawk is especially "thrilled" when I show up at his work place out of the blue. I want to surprise him and make his day but when I sneak up to him at his cubicle tucked into the back end of nowhere, he goes a bit pale and freezes.

"Hi!" I open my arms wide. It takes him a few seconds to get over his shock, stand, and give me a hug. I try to ignore how worn he looks, how strained and tired. When we pull apart, I note the bruise-like shadows under his eyes, the creases in his face, the strands of white hair peeking out at his temples.

"I had no idea you were coming," he says at last.

"Yeah, I wanted to surprise you. So . . . surprise!"

"But—I thought you were off killing hydra."

"We've been granted a week of leave to clear our heads, rest up, that sort of thing. So, I got on the first plane I could to Seattle." I give him another hug. "It feels like ages since I last saw you."

He sighs and pats my back. "It's good to see you, Fifi."

Standing here with my arms around my brother, it's easy to sense the war raging inside him—one part werewolf disease, one part serum. I let my essence surge around us like a cloud of warmth to ease the conflict and save him from the pain I know is there. He sags in my arms as his muscles unwind.

"It's *real* good to see you," he whispers.

I want to smile, glad I can help him once again with my presence since the pendant clearly hasn't been enough, but I can't ignore the fact that he's been dealing with this pain on his own while I've been away.

Someone clears their throat behind us. "Ah-hem."

Hawk and I pull apart to see who it is. He's a pudgy man stuffed into a suit with a huge watch on his wrist. He's eyes appear enlarged behind his extremely thick glasses and his too thin lips are made even thinner as he purses them at me.

"Can I help you?" I ask.

He puffs up as if trying to appear intimidating, but considering I've spent the last two months taking on hydra, it's a pretty poor show. I give him a flat stare to make sure he knows just how unimpressed I am.

"This area is for employees only," he says in a clipped tone and higher pitched than I expect. "How did you get up here?"

"Your security guard let me in."

"And *who* are you?"

"Spartan Phoenix Mason with advanced specialist Team Sierra."

Whispers and murmurs break out behind the shelves—clearly the rest of the office workers are listening in. I'm not in my Spartan gear—just normal cargo pants and a plain t-shirt—but I stand upright and stern in sharp comparison to this rude little man.

The man's eyes glance between Hawk and me, sorting things out for himself.

"And who are you?" I ask.

"Milton Podge. I run this office."

"Hmm." So, this is the cranky boss Hawk's complained to me about. I can see why he doesn't like him. "I was hoping Hawk could skip the rest of the day. I'm on a short bout of leave right now."

Milton's nose makes an odd twitch. "Unfortunately, despite the circumstances, employees are not allowed vacation hours without proper prior notice."

"It's okay, Phoenix," Hawk says quietly behind me. "I can catch up with you after work."

I don't bother to drop my tone when I say, "Seriously? There's no sort of exception? I've been off fighting level five monsters for two months straight and you can't let my brother go for an afternoon so I can spend time with my family before I head back into the bloodshed?"

Someone beyond the shelves whispers, "Shots fired."

But Milton doesn't back down. "I'm afraid I don't make the rules. I just follow them."

Hawk puts a hand on my arm. "I'll meet you later."

I give Milton a dark look before turning to my brother. "Call me once the rules say you can go."

He gives me a small smile and I budge past Milton on my way out. Murmurs and not so quiet talk follow me as I make to exit the cramped office space. Then a giant steps into my path just as Charlie appears out of thin air at my side. Gasps follow his sudden appearance but I don't flinch and neither does Spartan Knox who I've run into.

"Spartans," he says and we each shake his hand.

"Sir. How's office life treating you?" I ask.

He bobs his head to the side. "I'd much rather be out in the action. I've been keeping track of Sierra. You're doing impressive work."

"Thank you, sir," Charlie and I say in unison.

"How's Hawk been?" I ask.

The Spartan's eyes travel to the cubicle trapped in the corner. "He's been having a rough go of it. Didn't like having his wings clipped before he even had a chance to fly."

"I'm pretty sure anyone would feel the same in his position."

"Grounding the werewolves was necessary." He leans in closer. "I heard what happened at Werevine."

My brow cinches into a frown. "A lamia was behind that, no doubt to keep pressure on the werewolves while the lamia and their friends cause their own chaos elsewhere."

He shrugs. That's one thing I've never understood about Knox. During training, he seemed so passive about werewolf issues as if they deserved everything they got—despite the fact that he himself is one. Heat colors my cheeks and I find myself getting angry at the thought of it.

Charlie must sense pending danger because he nudges me with his shoulder. "So, Hawk's not coming?"

"No. Mr. Stupid-pants won't let him leave until the work day's over."

"Of course, not after what happened," Knox says. "He can only go out later if you two stay with him."

I openly stare. Has the situation gotten so bad that werewolves can't even go off by themselves to live their lives without supervision? Why didn't Hawk say anything about this particular condition? Why hasn't *anyone* said anything about it?

Charlie tucks his hands into his pockets and rocks on his heels. "We might as well check out the local bookstores for the time being. I've been dying to visit the library."

Spartan Knox nods. "Make sure to head to the Fremont Troll."

"That's where the Nympharum Library is, right?"

"Yeah." He gives us directions and we say our hasty farewells. Charlie is practically chomping at the bit to get going. I drag my feet and cast one last backwards glance towards my brother's hidden alcove wishing things could be different. We head out and catch a ride on metro transit. Charlie can't sit still and stands grasping one of the poles while I take a seat and stare blindly out the window.

"You okay?" Charlie asks part way through the ride.

I shrug. "Yeah."

"You sure?"

I turn away from the window and he slides into the seat next to me.

"Hawk just seems so . . . distant," I say. "Forlorn, I guess. And he can't go out unsupervised? It's ridiculous."

"Hmm."

"That's it? That's all the advice you have for me? Where are your words of wisdom?"

He raises an eyebrow. "I didn't know you relied on me for such things."

"Of course I do. Don't be stupid."

He straightens in his seat and dons a smug sort of smile. I roll my eyes.

"Well," he says and massages his chin. "I'm sure Hawk needs time to adjust and the situation isn't helping. Whether you like it or not, he might be jealous of you."

I gnaw on my lower lip and fiddle with a rip in the seat in front of me. "You think so?"

"Nix, he's been stuck in a cubicle after training for a year to be a Spartan. Yeah, I think he could be jealous."

He's right, of course, even though I don't want to admit it. It's not fair—any of it—but there's nothing to be done about it. Nothing, that is, until I can become a cure. Then Hawk will never be segregated like this ever again. There won't be a dark hold over him and the other werewolves. They'll be truly free for the first time in their lives since being bitten. I like thinking of it. It makes the consequences upon myself easier to bear. In fact, I like it so much that I think on it for a long time as I stare out the window without really seeing the city.

I glance back at Charlie at one point. He has his head cocked to the side and is watching me intently.

"Why do you always do that?" I ask, unable to contain myself.

"Do what?"

"Stare at me like I'm—I'm some sort of prime specimen for your studies or something."

"Because you *are* a prime specimen."

My cheeks blaze.

He blinks as if realizing what he just said, coughs into his hand, and then gives a loud laugh. "Ha! I knew I could make you blush."

"Unicorn," I grumble and look pointedly away but catch his own cheeks growing red in my peripheral vision.

"Hey, you're always saying that kind of stuff to me," he says with a shrug. "Just thought I'd return the favor."

"Well, it's actually true when I say it," I mutter under my breath.

He scoffs. "Hardly."

I shift in my seat to give him the full intensity of my glare. "You calling me a liar?"

"Phoenix, *please.*" He rolls his eyes. "No one actually calls someone 'really, really ridiculously good-looking' unless they're mocking them."

"*Seriously?*"

"What?"

"That was *true*, you idiot."

He throws up his hands. "You never made that clear!"

"How many times do I have to call you more handsome than a thousand stars until you believe me?"

He crosses his arms over his chest like a stubborn six-year-old. "You've never said that."

"Well, it's true. You are more handsome than a thousand stars."

His face turns puce. "I'm going to port to the other side of the bus."

"No, you aren't."

"You're absurd, you know that?"

I grin. "No, *you* are, you devilishly handsome man."

"Stop it."

"Okay, fine." I give a dramatic sigh and sit with my chin propped up in my hand. "I'll just have to settle for staring at you. I could stare at that perfect face all day."

He glowers at me and returns my stare evenly. "Fine."

"Fine."

So I continue to stare but he doesn't look away. It starts to feel pretty weird. I've never held someone's gaze for this long. It's almost too . . . *personal* somehow. A few times I almost burst out laughing and Charlie looks like he's liable to do the same. But I'll be darned if I look away first since it's become a challenge. *Pixies*, he's not going to look away either, is he? Why do I always so bluntly tell him how good looking he is? Isn't that weird? He probably thinks I'm some kind of obsessed stalker. What's wrong with me? Embarrassment creeps up on me and my whole face feels like it's on fire.

At some point his expression relaxes and changes back to that studying look of his. The urge to look away is strong but I clench my hands in my lap and keep steady.

"Can't take the pressure?" he says with a hint of a smile.

"I'm totally winning this thing. I don't know what you're talking about."

"You could always look away."

"You first."

"Do you know you have just the faintest bit of gold rimming your pupils?"

When I squirm a little in my seat, he laughs but then launches to his feet. "Crap!" He grabs my hand and yanks me out of the seat to dash down the aisle. "We've missed our stop."

Indeed, I didn't even notice the bus had stopped and began to pull away. The driver looks irritated as he jerks to a halt again and lets us off. We giggle to ourselves—which is a really odd sound coming from Charlie—and walk along the sidewalk to the bridge where the Fremont Troll will be hiding beneath.

Once our giggles subside, Charlie swings his arms looking completely carefree and lets out a long exhale.

"I'm glad you're my friend, Phoenix," he says. "I never used to have this much fun."

"What? You? Not have fun? I'd never believe it."

The joy in his face subdues. I guess that was the wrong thing to say.

I nudge him with my shoulder. "I'm glad you're my friend, too. Apart from my brother, I never really had *close* friends."

"Probably more than me," he says.

I glower at him. "Don't turn this into a competition too. Let's not out depress each other. That's much less fun."

"Right." He rolls his shoulders. "Okay. Fun. Then let's go find us a secret library."

"Let's."

We reach the bridge and walk down the steep incline to the culvert below. A massive troll of cement looms with a car in its fist. There are tourists here climbing on it and taking pictures with their friends. Charlie and I watch as we stroll by to the other end of the culvert. There's a near blank stretch of cement apart from a small patch of graffiti—a gryphon spray-painted in blue. Charlie and I lean against it nonchalant and whisper under our breath, "Nympharum."

The air wavers around us and two seconds later we see

versions of ourselves—illusions—walk away and out of sight while the wall behind us becomes corporeal and we lean back through the illusion out of sight. The wall reforms behind us and we find ourselves in a down sloping tunnel illuminated by bioluminescent streaks in the ceiling above. I have to blink a few times to adjust my eyes but once I'm accustomed to the low light, I let out a gasp of awe.

Beneath the beautiful bioluminescent lines etched in swirls and whorls on the ceiling stand two sentinels at the entrance to the library. At first glance they seem like figures carved out of wooden pillars to support the tunnel but then I notice the eyes glow and blink. Nymphs in their full tree forms to guard the way inside. One of them giggles as I study them over long, but they're fascinating. I don't see nymphs like this very often.

But Charlie's already past looking at the nymphs and hurries down the flight of steps etched with pale blue light in the stone. I follow after him but take my time enjoying the intricate carvings, the strange light, and an oddly sweet fragrance on the air. The steps go on forever deeper and deeper into the earth.

"*Come on*," Charlie says at the bottom of the stairs and waves me on urgently as if the library's going to vanish because I'm too slow.

I pick up my pace and my jaw drops when I reach the bottom. I mean, I see magical stuff all the time and it's awesome, but this place is beautiful.

The library unfolds before us like a—well, calling it a cavern sounds so harsh and ugly. It's more of a carefully crafted, enormous hall supported by pillars at regular intervals. Like the entrance and stairs, everything from the ceiling to the pillars, to the stone shelves, down to the tiles we stand on is engraved. Everything is made to look like the stone took root here and branched out in spectacular fashion to house the hundreds—maybe thousands—of bookshelves. They stand in neatly arranged rows separated by little streams where water sprites play, comfortable chairs for reading, and little braziers where I spot fire sprites dozing. Nymphs of all shapes and sizes loiter between the shelves, some more humanoid in appearance while others are like the guardians at the entrance and have taken root—literally—in various spots of the massive hall stretching as far as I can see.

Movement overhead catches my attention. What appear to be large, glowing dust bunnies float through the air. As I watch, one wafts directly to me. I hold out my hands and a second before it touches my palms, it transforms into a tiny, baby fox. It's possibly the cutest thing I've ever seen in my life.

"Familiar spirits," Charlie murmurs beside me and watches the progression of the others still floating along on some invisible current round and round above the library.

The kit—soft fur, adorable face, and tiny paws—looks at me with glowing eyes.

"Can I help you find something?" it says in a voice to match its size.

"I . . . gosh, you're cute. Is it okay that I say that?"

The familiar giggles with the voice of a child.

"How big is this place?" Charlie asks with a sharp look to me as if I'm wasting his precious time. Forgive me for enjoying a small bit of innocence.

"The Nympharum Library has the largest collection of

magical books in North America. We have books on history, dragons, ancient family trees, art, and many languages as well as fiction, memoirs, and more. Can I help you find something?"

"Family trees?" I ask. "Any on the Constantines from Romania?"

"Oh, yes!" it squeaks. "We have a genealogy of their lineage dating back to the last great war."

I'm immensely curious. I know they were a bunch of werewolf hunters but they're also my family—my history. I know so little about where I come from. If I'm going to spend some time here, I might as well take a look.

"Shall I show you the way?" the kit asks.

I turn to my friend. "Charlie? What do you want to find?"

He spins slowly on the spot as he soaks it all in. "Where do I even start?"

"Do you have a favorite book or topic?" the kit asks. "We can recommend others."

"*Pride and Prejudice*," I say quickly and Charlie glowers at me. I grin. "Oh, he's been reading it forever."

"We have a large selection of historical romance novels," the kit pipes up helpfully and I stifle a laugh at the look of death Charlie gives me. "Perhaps you would like to try *Fur and Claws* or *My Fair Dragon*."

"*Actually*," he says crossly. "I wouldn't mind seeing what you have on IMS authors."

"Oh!" the kit trills. "My friend can help you."

He makes a shrill cry and another mote of light floats down and transforms into a rather severe looking bald eagle that lands on Charlie's outstretched forearm.

"IMS authors?" the eagle says in a deep tenor that makes me think of an aging professor in the midst of a history lesson. "Yes, we have memoirs from J.R.R. Tolkien and C.S. Lewis if you're interested. Both outstanding chaps, wonderful agents, and spectacular authors if you want my opinion."

"I've heard real interesting things about those two," Charlie says as he absently walks away with the eagle. The two chat back and forth until they become lost amongst the shelves.

"Shall we find the genealogy on the Constantines?" the kit asks.

"Oh, yes. Please."

"Follow me!" It hops up and trots through the air as if on some invisible walkway.

I follow the familiar deep into the shelves and halt before a series of very old books. A pedestal stands nearby with a stool. The kit points to a particularly large, leather bound book that I tug off the shelf and lay on the pedestal. I take a seat and open the crinkly pages to find colorful, embellished text. The kit perches on my shoulder, its weight featherlight, and we read together.

It's an odd feeling looking at the long list of names, each one accompanied by their deeds in life and descriptions of their death. Several of the first chronicled helped during the last great war alongside the majestics. A woman named Gavrila was even an aide to Terra. Wow. Who knew? Then I had an ancestor famous for killing thirteen werewolves in a single night. One man named Albert had no notable deeds but was listed as killed "by his own sheer stupidity." I flip through the pages until I reach the end. Things turn bloody fast. Family members get killed off in droves with horribly colorful descriptions like "ripped apart by werewolf" or "dragged by werewolf to den and shredded into pieces." I gulp and stop reading the descriptions altogether and read only the names.

There. Right at the end. *Mary Constantine.* Mom.

Specialist Jaeger had told me I was a Constantine but only now, seeing my mother's name at the end of this book, does it really hit me. Werewolf hunters. That's my lineage. That's where I come from.

There's a brief description of how the remnants of her family came to the Americas and she was born in Virginia. She then married Robin Mason, a fellow IMS agent, and they had two children. I run a finger over my name and Hawk's. I can't believe we're in here.

"Someone keeps updating this thing?" I say out loud.

"Of course!" the kit squeaks. "Knowledge is too precious to waste. It must be recorded."

There are several heroic deeds listed under my mother's name—aided in subduing werewolf activity across the Midwest, worked as a specialist in the IMS as a werewolf tracker, saved the Prime Minister of Canada as part of a special joint task force—"Holy cow, Mom"—and the list goes on. She apparently led a very successful career in the IMS, most of it hunting werewolves.

I think that's it, but then I flip to the last page just to see if I have any relatives still alive out there somewhere, and discover a page with a record of me on it.

Phoenix Mason (Constantine)

Valorous Record: Successfully apprehended the alpha werewolf. Currently enlisted with the Spartans.

Death: —

"Geez, they *really* keep this up to date. I wonder—"
Hawk Mason
Infected.

And that's it. There no a valorous record. It's as if he's not worth the effort, forgoing even a Constantine in parentheses at the end of his name.

"Who updates this?" I ask angrily.

The familiar hops down and touches a paw to the page. "A resident genealogist updates the family histories periodically."

"What a prick," I mutter.

The kit tilts its head to the side trying to catch my words. I clear my throat and hastily close the book. The familiar bounds back to my shoulder. Maybe one day this book will say "Valorous Record: cured all werewolves" and Hawk will finally get the recognition he deserves. Then again, maybe my death will also say "cured all werewolves." Is that what it'll take? Even so, I've resigned myself to this path, no matter where it takes me.

"Is there something else I can help you find?" it asks.

I stare blankly into the distance. I'm supposed to be enjoying my time off but I'm making a bad show of it at the moment.

"Do you have anything *fun*?" I ask.

The kit chirps and its fur ruffles as if it can't contain its excitement. "I'm so glad you asked! Follow me!"

It trots away through the air and I walk in its wake. We head deeper into the library until we reach an area brightly lit with false sunshine from the ceiling to illuminate a spacious area between the shelves. There are no seats here but an interesting ring design on the floor of red and gold swirls. The kit bops along to a shelf full of thin but colorful volumes.

"Pick one!"

I look for the titles but there are none. There are only what appear to be musical notes on the spines and covers. When I page through a bright blue one, I find there's also nothing inside.

"I don't get it."

"Watch." The kit sings a single beautiful note. The book comes to life at the sound, and words—no, lyrics—appear on the pages along with drawings that color themselves in and move. I've never seen or heard of books like these before.

"They're musical stories," the kit says helpfully. "Created by the fauns and nymphs for interactive storytelling. Go ahead."

"What?"

"Sing! That's how the magic works." The little fox nods encouragingly while it hangs in the air across from me.

"Oh, boy." I clear my throat, quickly look around to make sure there's no one too close nearby, then read the first line with a few random notes I make up on the spot. "*Over hills, across the seas, through the desert, above the trees.*"

As I sing the lines, light escapes from the book, wind moves around me, and I can smell the sea, feel the heat of the desert, and hear the rustle of leaves. I stop for a moment and the magic of the book pauses as I do.

"Oh, cool," I say under my breath and keep singing softly. "*Starlight shiiiiiines. Starlight shiiiiiines.*"

The lights darken as mist surrounds me and pinpricks of light appear like the night sky has dropped in. I giggle and reach out to touch a star. It glows even more brightly.

"*Through darkened night comes moon divine. How it shiiiiines, moon diviiiiiine.*"

And indeed, through the black mist a radiant full moon appears. There's no other word for it—this is *magical*. I keep singing and night gives way to beautiful dawn, I move across seas, visit mountain peaks, and fly with gryphons. I wonder what other song books are here. What scenes do they create? What worlds do they explore?

I wonder . . . I wonder if I'll ever be able to enjoy something like this again. After I turn myself over to the labs, will I ever be able to return here?

As if the book senses my distress, the images fade out of existence as I stand there silent. The ink and images on the page ever so slowly vanish with no singing to sustain them. The world suddenly feels awfully gray. Somehow it feels . . . fateful. Like an echo of what's to come.

"Why'd you stop?"

Charlie comes up behind me, the eagle familiar on his shoulder. It hits me then, the people I'll be leaving behind too. Not just Hawk, but Charlie, the team, Jefferson, everyone. A hollow ache opens in my chest.

"This is all worth it, isn't it?" I say quietly. "What we do. The sacrifices we make. The sacrifice I need to make . . ."

Charlie steps forward and takes the book from my hands to examine the empty pages.

"I mean, I'm going to turn myself over no matter what happens," I continue, realizing I need to get this off my chest. "But I just—I'm scared. Maybe I shouldn't be but . . .

what if . . . what if I never see the people I care about again? What if I don't see Hawk? Or you? What if they need to bleed me dry for a cure? What if I—"

"Don't you dare say die," he says sharply. "Don't you do that."

"But—"

"If some lab tech or IMS authority thinks losing you is worth it, you know damn well the rest of us won't stand for it. *I* won't stand for it. I'd find you. I'd save you."

It suddenly becomes very difficult to breath beneath that intense stare of his. He closes the book, steps forward, and wraps a calloused hand around the back of my neck, faces so close our breath mingles.

"You are *not* alone, and you never will be." He stays that way until I nod once in understanding.

When he steps away to open the book, the air comes rushing back into my lungs.

"Now, I'm going to finish this book," he announces and clears his throat. "It's too cool to let it go to waste."

And he does. His beautiful voice fills the space between the shelves and the book comes alive once again. I've never heard him sing solo. I have a feeling he only does it when he's truly alone. But I'm here now. And I could listen for ages. As stars, clouds, and night skies whisk around us, I step forward and rest my head on his shoulder. I close my eyes to commit that voice to memory. This is something I never want to forget—or let go.

25

Hawk

I make my way to Knox's desk five minutes before the end of the day. Before he even turns around to talk to me, he logs off and then swivels about in his chair to give me his full attention.

"Mason," he says.

"Sir, I'd like to go spend the evening with my sister but I know there are restrictions on me right now." I hate having to ask for something like this. A normal person would be able to walk out the doors downstairs and do whatever they pleased. But no—I'm a grounded werewolf who has to ask permission to even go spend time with family.

Knox folds his arms over his chest. "There's not an issue with you spending time with your sister and Jaeger."

"Really?" Thank goodness.

"Both of them being Spartans from Team Sierra certainly swayed minds in your favor."

Oh. That makes me less enthusiastic then. So, if my

family was made up of clerical workers or lawyers, they wouldn't have let me off the hook for the evening. Phoenix and Charlie are Spartans so they can *secure* me or any threats or whatever. I'd really like to start a fight with someone but I clench my hands and take it for what it is. I have permission to get away from these stupid people for a while.

"Enjoy yourself," Knox says and starts gathering up his things.

"Thank you, sir," I mutter and run to grab my jacket and wallet.

I'm already waiting at the elevator by the time the clock strikes five. There's a mad rush for the exits but I'm at the head of the line. A second after I shove the glass doors open and step onto the sidewalk, I hear Phoenix holler for me.

"Hey, ginger!"

She jogs up with Charlie on her heels and sweeps me into a hug. The aches in my bones that have been lingering since her absence melt away in the warmth of her embrace and magic. The angry parts of me settle and the tense muscles throughout my body relax. When we pull away from each other, her hands linger on my shoulders as if very unwilling to part in any manner.

"You look peaky," she announces. "You could use a good meal. Doesn't he look peaky, Charlie?"

"Help us all, you're sounding like Theo's grandmother."

"I don't really see the problem with that," she says and lifts her chin. "Where do you want to eat, Hawk? My treat. Anywhere you want."

"Be careful with your generosity when it comes to food and me," I say with a smile, finding it easy to smile for once.

"I know but I don't care. I haven't seen you in ages, dang it. I do what I want."

Yeah, I'm sure she does—whereas I have to ask permission to hang out. I clench my jaw for a second and let that thought wither away. Now's not the time for feeling grumpy and gloomy. There's no point wasting this opportunity of freedom and relaxation.

Phoenix and Charlie wait for my response with patient smiles. Pixies, it's good to see them again. Heck, it's nice just to have people that see me for me.

"Anywhere?" I ask slyly.

My sister rolls her eyes and hauls on my arm. "*Yes*. Now pick somewhere, I'm starving."

At her insistence, I finally choose a seafood restaurant near the beach. As we walk to our destination, we talk about light and ordinary things—the people we've been working with, the current weather in Seattle, their flight over here, and thoughts about how to spend the rest of the week they have free. We reach the restaurant and manage to get a booth straight away with a view of the waves in the harbor.

When I ask about Theo's grandmother they mentioned, the conversation steers into work.

"Well, we stopped at his family's home after that fiasco at Werevine," Phoenix says around a mouthful of biscuit appetizers. She shakes her head and the light dims in her eyes. "That was . . ."

Charlie nods in silent agreement about whatever "that was."

"So?" I prod. "What happened out there?"

She surveys the area around us and drops her voice. "A lamia called Iota was leading a bunch of werewolves to attack the facility. They claimed they were holding the place hostage until the IMS told the truth about the serum." While Phoenix holds my gaze, Charlie avoids looking me in the eye altogether and rips a biscuit into small pieces. My brow lowers in a frown. "Maybe part of it was true. Maybe some of them *do* know about the bad reactions, but I doubt they would have ever gotten that far without the lamia egging them on to put the target back on the werewolves."

I blink and the air goes out of the room. She flat out acknowledges the truth of the serum with Charlie right here. And the way he's avoiding looking at me—

"You told him," I breathe.

Phoenix goes red in the face which is answer enough. My jaw drops and heat crawls up my neck as I realize she told my secret—my terrible, potentially life-ruining secret—to someone else. I don't care if it's Charlie. She told someone when I haven't breathed a word about her abilities.

"You—"

"I can explain," she says quickly. "During one of our missions, I screwed up. My team, they—they found out about me."

"Wait, did you tell your entire team?" I hiss between clenched teeth. "How could you do that? Why?"

After all the debates we've had, all the things we've both done to hide that devastating secret, she went and told five strangers the truth about me? About what the serum does to me and what we've both done?

"Hawk, calm down," Charlie cuts sharply across my rising anger. He holds one hand out towards me across the table—the other he rests on Phoenix's shoulder and I see her visibly relax under his touch. "It's okay."

"How can you possibly say that?"

"Because you can trust us," he says. "Not one of us would sell you out. We haven't said a word to anyone."

"Why not?"

"Because you're Phoenix's family," he says as if that clears it up. "We agreed not to say anything. And don't blame Phoenix. She was cornered into telling us everything. We . . ." His eyes flicker to her. "Well, some of us weren't so willing to let it drop. And I can tell you, she was ready to bolt or stop us the second any of us looked like we might do something about it."

My sister's mouth tightens and she shoots a look at Charlie. He meets her eyes and something passes between them. I don't know if they even realize the tension they create around and between each other. Not that I care at the moment.

"You—but if you know—"

"We know the endgame here," Charlie continues. I'm surprised Phoenix has stayed quiet for as long as she has without interrupting. "We're going to respect both your wishes until that time comes."

"The endgame," I repeat. The words sound so very final.

"A cure," Phoenix says at last, somewhat subdued. "Look, can we . . . can we just enjoy what time we have here? Please?"

I keep my fists clenched under the table and breathe heavily through my nose. After everything, I still can't believe she told them about me even if they did find out what she can do. But when I look to Charlie, he bobs his head as if to say everything is fine. No one's going to burst in here to haul me away. It really starts to sink in then.

Charlie knows. Other people know, and I'm still here. Maybe . . . maybe I should have told Knox about everything after all. Then I remember *I* had considered telling him not only my side of the story but what Phoenix is capable of as well. I had been willing to betray her secret just as she did mine.

The tension seeps out of my shoulders and my fingers lose their death tight grip. As I uncoil, the pair across from me do the same.

I clear my throat. "Right. Fun. Happy times. I can do that."

Phoenix smiles uncertainly. "We remember how to do that, right?"

"Well, I don't know. Has Charlie *ever* had fun before? Does he even know what that is?"

Charlie rolls his eyes. "Har har."

The atmosphere immediately warms between us and the argument mere seconds ago is pushed aside.

"Don't worry," my sister says and nudges her teammate with her elbow. "Theo and I have been showing him the finer things in life—like appreciating a well-timed fart."

A smile finds its way onto my face and I lean back in the booth stroking at my invisible beard. "Ah, yes. The well-timed fart. A classic. Has he yet been introduced to the highly professional 'pull my finger' gag yet?"

He chooses a bad moment to try to take a drink of his pop and practically chokes on it.

"His education hasn't advanced so far yet," Phoenix says, taking on the air of a sophisticated professor and waves one hand dispassionately. "I think it's time he learned the subtle art of bubble making with a straw, however." She levels a critical eye at Charlie and pulls her drink towards herself. "Pay close attention."

Then she blows into the straw and creates loud bubbles in her drink. Charlie goes red in the face and glances around him as if we're going to get hauled out of the restaurant.

"Geez, I forgot how you two get when you're together," he hisses and tries to take Phoenix's drink away from her. She starts giggling madly and keeps on making bubbles.

"Superb demonstration!" I say and lightly clap my hands. "Now watch a true master."

Charlie looks like he wants to hide under the table as Phoenix and I loudly make bubbles in our drinks like a couple of five-year-olds. But then Phoenix starts laughing, I start laughing, and soon even he begins to laugh.

We are a bit mad, I know that, but I think we both decided a long time ago that if we enjoy something—even something childish—it's okay if other people don't understand or approve. I know Phoenix can be easily embarrassed given the right circumstances, but with me around, her barriers drop. So do mine. Life's too short to pretend we don't find silly things like this funny. The world's too full of darkness to not enjoy the light you find.

The three of us mess around but make sure to be extra polite to the waitress so they don't kick us out or anything. After our bellies are full of delicious food, we take a walk and babble about goofy things. Despite the fact the beginning of our outing got a little rough, there's a lightness in my chest that keeps expanding the longer I'm with them. Part of me expects Charlie to give me funny looks since he now knows my trouble—or at least part of it—with the serum. But he doesn't. We're pals like we were during Spartan training as if nothing's changed. That, and he seems far too preoccupied with whatever Phoenix is doing to spare me haunting glances or anything.

Eventually we stop to catch a movie and toss popcorn at each other during the superhero flick. For a short while I forget the two paths that lie ahead of me. I can ignore the pain in my body that's been reduced to an ache. I can relax.

At the end of the movie, Phoenix suggests hanging out at my apartment.

"No, no. I spend enough time there already," I say and wave her off. The truth is, I don't want her to see my depressing apartment and the mess I've made of it. "Why don't we party where you're staying?"

"Whatever works."

I expect to head for the IMS apartment complex—which reserves rooms for agents moving in and out of the area—or even for one of the smaller hotels. Instead, we meander over to one of the most extravagant hotels in the area complete with a fancy chauffeur outside, parking attendant, and butlers waiting at the elevators. We move through the double glass doors and I let out a low whistle. A vaulted ceiling reaches way above my head inlaid with patterns of gold and green. A fountain tinkles in the middle of the long foyer and a man with a very twirly mustache stands at the check-in counter.

"I didn't realize they were paying you guys so well to afford a place like this," I say.

"They aren't," Phoenix responds and leads us to an elevator. "Charlie paid for it."

I turn to Charlie with a slack jaw.

He sticks his hands in his pockets and shrugs. "My parents left me some money when they died. And I figured why not. We've been sleeping on the floor of the Osprey long enough. A little self-indulgence sounded pretty good."

Huh. So either Charlie seriously splurged or . . . his parents left him with a lot of money. I think on that for a moment. I never really took it into consideration the quality of his clothes. I know firsthand how nice they are after he loaned me some for a while after the Moose Lake Field Office blew up along with our clothes. I'm betting Charlie doesn't splurge. He buys quality and leaves it at that without waving his money around. I like that about him. He stays down to earth when he could have bought himself a place of luxury instead of slumming it with the rest of us.

The elevator dings on the twentieth floor and our footsteps hardly make a sound on the plush maroon carpet. We pass a vending machine, an ice machine, and finally reach the conjoined suite they've rented out. I snort when I realize that but Phoenix looks at me as if she has no idea what's going on. Charlie gives me a flat stare.

The room is huge and despite there being a king sized bed in here, it doesn't feel cramped in the least. There's a mini bar, a giant television, an enormous bathroom—

"Good grief," I say as I take in the lush trappings. "I don't think I've ever been in a room this nice."

"Make yourself at home," Phoenix says.

Charlie opens the door that connects their two rooms. "I'll be right back."

I take a seat next to Phoenix's duffle bag on the bed and run my hands over the covers. Silky smooth. My sister pulls off her ponytail holder with a groan and threads her fingers through her hair before falling flat on the bed behind me with her face in the blankets.

"Long day?" I ask.

She mutters something unintelligible with her face squished into the bed.

"You know, it helps if you lay in a position so you can actually breathe. Don't suffocate on me."

With another groan, she rolls onto her back dramatically with arms spread wide.

"It's been a long couple of months." She blows a few stray hairs out of her face and sighs. "It's been weird not having you there."

I drop my gaze to my hands. "Yeah."

"I've missed you, Hawk."

"I've missed you, too."

"You know, our birthdays are coming up soon."

I gasp. "What? Why didn't anyone tell me?"

She grabs a pillow and launches it at my head. I dodge with a laugh and it tumbles to the floor.

"I don't know if I'll be able to come be with you on the day," she continues. "We've never been apart for . . . for that."

Our birthday—and anniversary of our parents' deaths. Yeah. I bet most people don't get to claim that. I bet their birthdays are full of joy and excitement and cake. Ours involve a lot of pretending we're okay.

"We can always call or something," I say quietly. "Live chat."

"I guess."

To be honest, our birthday and that horrible anniversary haven't been taking up my thoughts at all. Perhaps I should care more but I haven't had time to between navigating treacherous waters and keeping myself from drowning in the pain of the serum.

Phoenix eventually pushes herself upright and slouches into the bathroom. When the door clicks and I find myself alone, my eyes dart to her duffle bag as a spark of inspiration hits me. Before she or Charlie have a chance to reappear, I slip out into the hallway, dig some cash out of my pocket, and buy six different candy bars and chips from the machine outside. I tiptoe back into the hotel room and quietly unzip her bag to find ideal hiding places for the candy. I haven't had an opportunity to do something like this in a while. I hope when she discovers these surprises later, it'll make her day.

There's a black armored suit in here that I stop and ogle for a moment, running my fingers over the textured scales of it, before moving on and hiding a chocolate bar in her sock with a silent laugh. I shove some sweets into a side pocket, tuck more chocolate into one of her shirts, wiggle sugary goodness into the plastic bag with her shampoo, and—

Something metallic sticks out of a hidden pocket at the bottom where I had been hoping to slip in the last of the candy. My fingers grasp the edge of the magazine clip for a .45 and pull it out.

Red bullets stare me in the face.

My fingers accidentally skim the wolfsbane-coated bullets and burn where they make contact. I drop the magazine onto the bed and lurch to my feet, stumbling away from that—that wretched *poison*.

Roaring fills my ears and my world begins to splinter apart.

Everything has been depending on Phoenix being the cure. And yet here and now when I need to believe that the most, I find her toting the weapon of my annihilation.

I can't breathe. I can't think. I grab at my hair and a thin, wheezing sound escapes me.

The bathroom door opens.

Phoenix's eyes lock onto me, widen in alarm, and then spot the magazine on the bed. The blood drains out of her face which tells me everything I need to know.

She had planned on keeping that store of wolfsbane bullets a secret.

"W-what—where—how did you?" she sputters.

"What are you doing with that?" I say loudly and jab a finger at the magazine.

"I can explain—"

"What the *hell* are you doing with that!" I shout. Whatever leash of control I had is gone.

"I wasn't planning on using them," she says calmly and holds her hands out towards me as if attempting to soothe a wild animal. "It was just a precaution—"

"For killing a werewolf," I snap. "For killing someone like me."

"I would *never*. You know that."

"Do I?" I practically spit. Her head snaps back as if physically struck. "How did you even get them? They're illegal. You must have really wanted to get your hands on those."

"It's not like that."

"Then tell me what it's like!" I roar and clench my hands into fists at my side.

A door bangs open behind me.

"What's going on?" Charlie demands and ports into the open space between the two of us to act as a human barrier.

I focus my sights on him. "You knew about this too, didn't you?"

"What?"

I point to the magazine and he picks it up. His face goes slack before his eyes harden.

He holds it out towards Phoenix. "Where did you get this?"

"I..."

"Did you get it from *him*?"

She swallows and looks desperately between the pair of us now united in anger against her. I can't believe this. The person I trusted the most—

When she doesn't immediately respond, Charlie demands, "Did you get this from my uncle?"

"He gave them to me," she says breathlessly and clutches a hand in the fabric of her shirt above her heart. "I only kept them to use against Dasc. I should have told you."

"You *never* should have taken anything from him," Charlie snarls and whips the magazine onto the bed where it bounces and hits the floor with a heavy thud. "I can't even look at you right now."

"Charlie, *please*—"

"With everything you can do, that's the route you decide to take? You're a coward. You're just as bad as he is," he says then turns away and disappears. The door to his suite slams shut.

Phoenix's face is so pale she could be a ghost.

"How could you?" I go on and take a step closer, fingers clenching and unclenching. "Do you have any idea what

I've been through the last few months without you here? I've been ostracized, shuffled into a corner where no one wants to look, and put under the heel of the serum. Do you realize the pain I've had to endure every single freakin' day?" I turn and shove her bag off the bed with as much force as I can muster. "Do you have any idea how alone I've been? How abandoned?" I grab the lamp next to the television and hurl it across the room where it shatters. "And you know the one thing I held onto to get me through all that crap? You!"

I jab my finger in her face and she stops breathing altogether.

"I trusted you! My sister, the big hero. The one to be the cure. And that's what you decide? You'd rather blast us away than even try?"

"No! I'd never."

"If you never planned on it, then you never would have taken those bullets," I snarl.

A tingling enters my fingers and I can sense the impending seizure as the world becomes too stark, too bright, too loud.

"Hawk, I never meant—"

"I don't care."

I stumble to the door and wrench on the handle.

"Don't leave like this," Phoenix demands behind me.

"I don't take orders from you. Don't call."

I shove the door open and slam it behind me. A few guests have gathered in the hallway at the sound of our fight and a security guard approaches from the other end of the hall. I hurry to the elevator and the doors shut before I can be stopped. My head feels like it's floating away from my body and I hardly manage to hit the emergency stop button before I lose myself completely.

Seconds, minutes, or an hour might have passed by the time I finally come round on the floor of the stopped elevator. My shoulder hurts, one of my ankles smarts, and it takes forever for the world around me to fall back into place. I cough past grime in my throat and blood speckles the carpeted floor.

Slumping back onto the floor, exhaustion takes me—not only physically but emotionally.

I realize I'm at the end of my rope and the only thing left is to fall.

That's when the tears start. They bubble up from my core and I shake with the force of sobs ripping out of my throat.

Empty. That's what I am.

There's nothing anymore. No hope. No happiness. Nothing.

Reaching the bottom of that dark pit and seeing only darkness around me, I realize there is nowhere left for me to go.

The only path is to walk through the darkness.

Struggling to my feet, I hit the emergency stop again and ride the elevator to the ground level where I'm promptly thrown out by hotel security.

I don't go to my apartment. There's only one place I can go.

The streetlights guide me to a general store. Knowing I must look a wreck from the way people's faces turn alarmed when I walk by, I grab a cart and sluggishly walk the aisles finding exactly what I need. I get an odd look from the cashier when I check out—fake spiders from the Halloween section, a whoopee cushion, cheese powder, clear nail polish, a number of other miscellaneous props for my mission tomorrow and—

Peanut powder.

26

Phoenix

To say things couldn't have gone much worse is an understatement. Charlie and I head out of Seattle the morning after next. I try to see Hawk but he's not at his apartment. I try his work place next but I'm told he's not available. All the while Charlie avoids me like the plague, hiding at the Nympharum Library until we leave. It hurts. Everything about this hurts, and I wish I had never taken that magazine of wolfsbane bullets from Specialist Jaeger.

And Hawk isn't the only one angry—no, angry is too small a word for what my brother feels. Charlie only talks to me in short, clipped sentences since he's mad I took anything from his uncle and never told him about it. I don't know how to fix this. Maybe it's something I can't. It's a brutal blow. On the flight back to Minnesota, I try listening to my parents' old song to cheer me up but it does nothing except remind me of what I've done.

In Minneapolis, Charlie and I are quick to part ways even though we're both heading north. We split into two different taxis. He's heading to Duluth to meet Melody and Alona—both back from their own quick sojourns—at the Blue Comet while I make for Moose Lake. It's past time that I check in on the city that transformed me into what I am today. Also, I don't know where else to go. Theo's still with his family. He invited me to stay a day or two but I don't want to be around that many people right now. John won't be flying in until tomorrow to meet us at Camp Ripley. I finally got in contact with Jefferson but he's off on another lead searching for Genna after a very short stint in the penitent cells—five whole minutes—for his altercation with Specialist Jaeger. He's too preoccupied to meet up. I'm on my own for this one.

While en route, to keep myself entertained I text Theo and we chat back and forth about what recipes he thinks I'd be up to the task of attempting. He offers to teach me the basics and even have his grand-mère show me a few things. It distracts me from Hawk and Charlie's anger if only for a little while.

When the taxi finally takes the exit ramp to Moose Lake, I'm hit by a wave of nostalgia. I remember how very unimpressed I was with the city when I first came here. But then the place grew on me and Jefferson made it a home. I stare out the window at the familiar buildings. This used to be my territory. I protected these people. How have things changed since I've been away?

The taxi stops at the hotel on the edge of town and my ride waits for me on the far side of the lot. Deputy Graham leans against the side of his squad car with arms crossed, legs crossed, and his wide-brimmed hat pulled down low as if he's taking a nap while waiting for me. But the second I step off the shuttle and start walking towards him, he stands straight over six feet tall and tilts back his hat with a finger to give me a wane smile.

"Been a long time," he says when I approach.

"It's good to see you, Deputy."

"It's Jared to you."

He wraps me in a hug and I'm nearly lost in his long arms and thick chest. I pull back with a sad sort of smile and really look him over. He's hardly changed—chin-length hair, array of stubble on his face, and gentleness in his eyes. But there are differences. He seems thin, perhaps drawn. Or maybe I'm putting too much thought into it.

"So, how was your trip?" he asks and pops open the trunk for me. I dump my bag inside next to the arsenal he has stored in here.

"Fine."

"That's a pleasant word for not so good."

"Why would you say that?"

He bobs his head to the side and moves to the driver's door. "Call it a gut instinct. You look like crap."

"Thanks."

"Come on."

I slip into the passenger's seat—which is a little cramped with his computer and whatnot up front—and we head into town. He's quiet but I don't mind. I'm too weary for small talk. Everything looks mostly the same. Minor things have changed and there are obvious repairs from a major flood in the area I happened to miss while away at Spartan training.

"How's the new field office doing?" I ask.

He shrugs. "Well, no one's really been charmed by the agents that came to replace Jefferson and you lot. Granted, it's hard to be charmed when our lives have been disrupted so much by the werewolf regulations."

Right. That. I haven't spent much time with werewolves in a normal setting lately. I know they booted the agent werewolves from field duty and tightened up restrictions for the civilian werewolves, but I haven't seen it firsthand. Deputy Graham fills me in on what Moose Lake has endured. Curfew hours, unable to meet in groups, mandatory testing on a weekly basis, and harsher punishments for minor infractions. Then, on top of that, keeping it secret from everyone not in the know.

"I tried applying to the IMS a few months ago," Jared says when we reach his house and puts his squad into park. "Thought I'd have a better chance of finding my sister that way."

"And?" I ask even though I already know what he's going to say.

"They rejected me right off the bat because of what I am. Said they can't take the risk. I'm not surprised, though, considering the extra precautions they already put on me."

Extra precautions? "What do you mean?"

"Because of my job as a deputy. I'm more dangerous since I'm in a position of authority and have access to resources normal people don't. That, and the fact Rosalyn is my sister."

"I'm sorry."

He shrugs and runs a hand through his shaggy hair. "It is what it is."

"Maybe someday . . ." I swallow and look down at my hands. "Maybe someday that'll change."

"Maybe, but I'm not holding my breath until then."

We get out and he carries my bag in for me like a gentleman. He gives me a very quick tour of his house and offers me the guest room that had once been Rosalyn's. It's mostly bare except for a log-framed bed and painting of a bear.

"I really appreciate this, Jared."

"I was surprised when I got your call, to be honest." He leans against the doorframe. "Thought you'd be spending your spare time with your brother or that team of yours."

"Yeah, me too," I mutter and clear my throat. "Things have been . . . complicated."

"Hmm. Well, if you need anything, let me know. I'm working the night shift so I'll be heading out in a couple of hours."

"Since you offered, could I borrow your car for a while? I'd like to drive around and see the area again. I'll fill up the tank."

"No problem." He digs in his pocket and tosses me the keys. "The sedan's in the garage."

"Thank you."

"It's the least I can do for Moose Lake's hero."

Right. Hero. I can't seem to swallow that title when my stomach already churns enough with guilt. If I was a real hero, I would have turned myself over already to the IMS labs despite everyone's insistence and my own inclination to protect myself first and foremost. As if my desires are more important than the lives of the entire werewolf population.

I realize I'm brooding because Jared hunches somewhat to watch me with concern. With a fake smile, I move past him and to the garage. The beige sedan rumbles to life and I start my reunion tour of the city. I'm not much of a people person but I make sure to catch up with as many people as I can. I'm not sure what I'm expecting or what I'm searching for, but in my gut I feel like I need vindication. I need to see firsthand what the werewolves are going through.

Mr. Wick is out on his farm taking care of his cows and chickens. He's happy enough but he's been in better spirits. Apparently the new field agents in the area have been hard on everyone and even suggested he might have territorial issues because of his farm. It's stupid. Mr. Wick is one of the most generous people I know and is always willing to help others, even granting use of his land for our previous werewolf games.

The story is the same everywhere I go. Life's been difficult for the werewolves. I discover a lot of the high school graduates stayed in town instead of going to college or moving away like many of them wanted to. The IMS grounded them so to speak, not wanting their influence to go to heavily populated areas. I find Ben holed up in his house taking online college courses, trying to make the best of it, and tells me more than a few times that he's currently dating one of our classmates. But his life feels stunted. As do so many others. They can't even meet for Werewolves Anonymous anymore to vent their grievances. The IMS deemed it dangerous for werewolves to congregate so if they have any concerns, they're supposed to meet one on one with the field agents who always seem too busy to take anyone's complaints.

Frustration building in my chest, I visit the field office itself. They've built a modular home on Jefferson's old lot. It feels out of place and too orderly to replace the rugged cabin that had been patched up with duct tape. When I arrive, I find three agents working busily at their computers and am told the fourth is out making the rounds. The tiny man, willowy woman, and freckled senior agent seem excited to meet me but I discover it's only because they want to vent to someone who knows the area, thinking I might share the same opinion on the residents. But I don't. I know Mrs. Ferguson can be a bit anal about things but she's fiercely loyal and protective of her son—traits they dismiss. And they think Mr. Wick is a bit of a simpleton, instead of the generous spirit he is.

It gets to the point where I blurt out angrily, "They're *people*."

They exchange looks amongst each other as if I'm crazy and the tiny man says, "They're werewolves."

"And you're an idiot."

"Excuse me?"

"Treat these people better, or so help me—"

"Are you threatening us?" the senior agent growls and locks his arms over his chest.

I level such a frosty look at him that he swallows. "I kill hydra on a daily basis. I don't make *threats*."

None of them respond but I've had enough of this place. I know the kind of people that won't listen no matter how much I argue. So I move on and take Jared's car on a loop through the city streets to see how things have changed and to give myself time to cool down. The trees are on the verge of changing color and there's a pleasant coolness to the air. I stop at the city park for a while and watch the lake as kids run around the playground. I'm anxious and unsettled and realize I'm stalling before heading to the last place I mean to go. There's one person here that I owe it to.

I run my thumb over the faint scar on my forearm where sharp wolf teeth once tore into my flesh. It doesn't have the silver sheen as a normal werewolf bite and has faded to be hardly noticeable. For such a significant thing, there's hardly any trace of it. The bite that really set things in motion for my life.

Knowing I can't put it off forever, I finally walk out of the park and drive to a house at the end of a long dirt driveway. An old Buick sits in front of the wide porch and light streams from a single window. I wait in the car after turning off the engine and stare at the window thinking of happier times. I'm not sure what finally gets me to move but move I do. Up the porch steps, to the door, and—after a deep breath—press the doorbell.

Thirty seconds pass as I linger in front of the door. I understand if she doesn't want to see me. Maybe coming here was a waste of time. I allow another thirty seconds to pass before I make for the stairs. Just as my foot touches the top step, the door creaks open behind me.

"Phoenix?"

I turn around and see what's become of my friend. She's stick thin, cheeks sallow, eyes dull, streaks of blue in her hair, and sporting a pair of dark wrist cuffs to match her black shirt. The year and change that's passed since I last saw her hasn't improved her disposition. And to think, when I first met her she sported fandom t-shirts, loved pink, always had a bounce in her step, and hardly ever wore a frown. This is no longer that girl.

"Ashley." I don't know what to say or do next. Somehow I'd like to make amends, perhaps even tell Ashley the whole truth about everything, but I don't know how.

"It's been a while," she says.

I nod mutely and roll my lips together.

"Why are you here?"

"I . . . I want to talk," I say.

She studies me for an eternity, blinking slowly. Then she pushes the door further open and steps aside to allow me entrance. It's a start. I walk across the porch and enter the foyer.

Her house has certainly seen better days. I don't think the place has been dusted in ages, there are papers littered everywhere, and pieces of furniture are randomly missing, like the sofa and television stand. The place is askew and so unlike the time I had once stayed overnight when it had been clean, organized, and homey. There's no sign of either of her parents and the whole place puts me a little on edge. It's not right.

Ashley leads me into the kitchen and gestures silently to one of the stools at the eat-in counter. I take the offered seat and watch as she takes a steaming jug of water out of the microwave and pours it into two cups before mixing in hot chocolate, creamer, and a dash of cinnamon. She puts one in front of me and stands on the opposite side of the counter with her own.

"Thank you," I say quietly.

"I was in the middle of making some anyway," she says

and shrugs, absently stirring hers with a spoon. "It's an old family recipe."

It does smell good but I don't have much of an appetite at the moment. Part of me desperately wishes I had one of my teammates or Hawk with me here for this, but the other part of me knows I can only do this alone. I may not be the best with words but they're my words to offer and I know they'll be true.

Before I can say anything, whether it be an apology or explanation, Ashley says, "You've been gone a long while. Where've you been?"

"I, uh . . . passed my exams to become an agent. Then did more training and I've been working as a Spartan with my team." Her eyebrows rise and I clear my throat. "It's like special forces for us."

"Oh."

"Yeah."

Well, this isn't going terrible but it's certainly not as poignant as I had pictured it in my head either. If this was a movie, I'd now make a heartfelt speech and win back my friend, we hug, and it's beautiful. But I'm awkward and no movie star.

"So . . ." I clear my throat for the third time I think since I got here. "What about you? What have you been up to?"

She takes a long slow drink from her mug. I do the same so I don't just sit here staring at her. The hot chocolate *is* good. There's a bit of a quirky aftertaste but I think that's the cinnamon or maybe the creamer's expired.

"I got a job at the grocery store," she says without looking up. "To help out, you know, since it's hard to leave here. I've been looking into taking online college courses."

"I hear that's what Ben's been doing."

She smiles. "He's the one that talked me into it. He's a good friend."

"Yeah, he is."

She takes another long drink and I do the same.

"Did you want to talk about anything in particular?" Ashley asks.

"Well . . . yes." I rotate the mug in circles on the counter to keep my hands busy. "I know I've said it again and again, but I'm sorry about everything that happened, Ashley. We didn't part on good terms and I regret that, I really do. And I'll never forgive myself for not protecting you better and stopping that werewolf from biting you. You were a good friend, Ashley. I should have been a better one."

Her dull eyes widen but her brows draw together. She looks distressed. Did I say the wrong thing? *Pixies,* I always say the wrong thing.

"Look, I—I'm not asking for you to be my friend again. I just wanted to do what I could to mend the bridge, so to speak."

"How?"

I exhale slowly through my mouth and take another long drink of the hot chocolate to give myself a moment to bolster my courage.

"By telling you the truth," I say. "You deserve that."

And so I do. I do my best to explain my own secret and Hawk's as well. I want her to understand because I've realized I'm running out of time. I've agreed to go to the labs once I'm ready and once that happens, I don't know if I'll ever get the opportunity to do this ever again. As the secrets pour out, of how Hawk reacted to the serum, my own abilities, the reasons to keep it hidden, and even the truth about Duke, Ashley remains quiet as I struggle through it. My body grows heavy as I lay everything out on the table and watch the silent tears run down my old friend's face. When at last Ashley knows everything, a dour silence fills the house. I stare at my mug, unable to gather the strength to take another drink.

"I guess what happened makes sense now," Ashley says at last, her voice surprisingly steady and calm. The Ashley I once knew was very good at making exaggerated reactions to everything. "Except for Jason. You could have protected him. Why didn't you?"

I'm tongue-tied and not really able to offer anything in response. Hawk had questioned me the same after Jefferson and I took Jason into custody. I should have. I should have done more then, but I'm going to make up for it now. Soon. As soon as my magic reaches its peak, I'll go to the labs. I'll do whatever it takes to put an end to the werewolf disease.

"He died, you know," Ashley continues.

Shock reverberates through me and I can't form the words to reply. He *died*?

"Killed himself in his cell. Did you know he was kept in a cell? I didn't." The expression on her face hardens and she balls her hands into fists on top of the counter. "I found out not too long after my father died."

There's a hollow ringing in my ears and I make no move to reach out to comfort her. I'd like to say it's the shock holding me firm in place but only then, when I see the hatred simmering in Ashley's eyes, that I understand. I can't move. I literally can't move a muscle. She put something in the hot chocolate and I missed it. I'd been so focused on the fact that she invited me in and on spilling my secrets that her own slipped by me. I'm paralyzed and only remaining upright in the stool by my elbows propped up on the countertop.

What has she done?

Another tear slips down her face as she glares at me with such intense hatred. "I thought that was the worst of it. How could things get any worse, right? My father dies from a heart attack, I find out my boyfriend's killed himself, and as if that wasn't enough, my mom—" She hiccups back a sob. "—got attacked by a rogue werewolf that hadn't taken the serum. She didn't make it."

Silence fills the expanding void in my mind. No. This can't—this can't be true.

"How much bad can someone experience in a lifetime? How much pain? I can't do this anymore, Phoenix. I can't. I won't." She leans in close and I can't move a muscle to lean away or flinch when she prods me hard with one finger right in the chest. I can still feel pain, I just can't stop it. She pushes me hard enough in the sternum that I fall backwards off the chair and my head cracks on the wooden floor. I'd cry out if I could, put my head in my hands, but I can't. There's nothing so terrifying as being completely helpless. I'm at Ashley's mercy and there's nothing I can do about it.

She stands over me, my eyes blankly staring up at the ceiling.

"This is all your fault," she snarls. "But I'm going to make things right. She told me the truth about the IMS, about you, about the werewolves."

She? Who?

"They want to wipe us off the map, but we're going to

fight back. They already think we're monsters, so we'll *be* monsters. Werevine was only the beginning."

Werevine Pharmaceutical. She had a part in that? Then this "she" Ashley's referring to . . . oh, no.

Ashley gets on her phone and makes a quick call. "She's here. I have her. You better hurry."

The werewolves at Werevine weren't alone. They had a lamia amongst them. We killed Iota but there are always more lamia. There will always be thirteen. I won't be at the mercy of Ashley for long. Something far, far worse is coming.

I'm alone. I have no backup. No one knows where I am. It's difficult not to panic despite my Spartan training. I'm utterly defenseless. Despite urging my limbs to move, they lay frozen and crooked on the floor as Ashley hovers over me. I try to push out my magic but it's so sluggish. There's only one hope for me. Scholar's pendant is still tucked safely away beneath the collar of my shirt. I try so, so hard to wrap my magic around it and alert Scholar that I need help. She could contact someone and send help. She could let my team know I'm in trouble. But using my magic is like trying to spread cold molasses.

I don't know if it works. I don't know if I get the message to Scholar even though every cell in my body screams at that pendant.

But I've run out of time.

I hear the door creak open and footsteps saunter towards me. Ashley backs away so the newcomer can take her place. The slit eyes of a snake watch me with amusement and black hair brushes my face when she bends down to inspect me even closer. Her smile reveals her sharp teeth.

"Hello, darling. Did you miss me?"

Epsilon.

Terror. Sheer terror is what runs through me as Epsilon—the lamia that got away—drags me by my wrists into the middle of the living room. Strands of my hair catch and rip out of my scalp. My head thunks on the hard floor. But there's not a damn thing I can do about any of it. The overhead light shines brightly into my eyes and I can't blink against it.

"Ah, that's better," Epsilon says somewhere to my left.

"What now?" Ashley asks.

How on earth did Ashley ever become involved with the lamia?

"Now, I get what I came for," Epsilon says.

Her shadow falls over me as she blocks out the light. She hunches down low with her hands planted on her knees to leer at me. She brings up one of her claws, looks at it as if inspecting for dirt, then ever so slowly drags it from my temple to my jaw. The pain is sharp and immediate but I lie helpless on the floor, unable to defend myself in the least. Epsilon seems extremely pleased by this because her sharp smile grows.

"Excellent. I was afraid you might have some resistance to medicinal applications but it looks like your tricks only work on magic, don't they? What a pity."

She roughly takes my chin in her hand and leans in so close I can feel her breath on my face. "I want you to be awake for this. It's ever so boring when people are unconscious. I want you to feel this. I want you to know how helpless you are. How helpless I felt when you aided in killing my sister Zeta."

I've been in bad spots before but . . . I can't see a way

out of this. If ever there had been a bleak moment before, this takes the cake by a long margin.

Epsilon makes another line down my face beside the first one. She laughs as I grimace inwardly.

"I could do this all day," she says. "Take one piece of you at a time. Slow. Ever so slow."

"You said you weren't going to do that," Ashley says from wherever she's watching. She's *watching* me be clawed up by this monster.

"That's true," the lamia says and gives a dramatic sigh. "I can't waste too much of her blood. I need it. Bring my bag."

Footsteps and then Ashley appears over Epsilon's shoulder with a duffle. I can't see what happens next when the lamia sets the bag next to me and pulls something crinkly like soft plastic out. A few seconds later, a needle is shoved none too gently into my arm.

"Waste not," she says in a sing-song voice.

I've been so worried about the IMS labs but I'm going to be bled out right here. Everything I've been through will have been for nothing. Epsilon could kill me in a second but she wants my blood. She must know its value. Maybe with it she and Echidna could take the werewolves off the board. Or maybe . . . I think of Scholar's plight—a majestic dragon weakened greatly by the werewolf disease in her blood. But Scholar wasn't the only one bitten. Echidna had been bitten by Dasc himself. What if she's just as weakened as Scholar? What if the lamia plan to use my blood to try to cure Echidna?

"I've been so impressed by your work," Epsilon says as she holds up a bag that begins to fill with my blood. "I've been watching you chase after those hydra and studying you, naturally. Such power in such a pathetic, mortal body. Useful though. Had to kick it up a notch to elevate your levels. I'd say you're close to peaking. Had to make sure you were as powerful as you could get."

Please tell me it isn't true. Did Epsilon send in those hydra for me? To work my powers up into a lather? No. She can't have. She wouldn't. There's more to the plan. There has to be.

She picks up my arm not currently being drained and plays with my forearm. "I see you've healed up after helping Terra escape from Underground. Speaking of which . . ."

Epsilon sniffs at the air, trails a claw down my throat and carefully lifts Scholar's pendant up by the chain. She clicks her tongue then rips it from my neck and hurls it across the room. I feel as if I've lost my life vest while lost in the middle of the ocean.

"How much longer?" Ashley asks.

The lamia snarls in her direction. "You're impatient."

Time passes as Epsilon continues to gloat over my motionless body. But as one bag is changed out, then another, the world starts to dim. The light overhead burns into my eyes but I feel as if I could drift away into a nap.

"We should give it a try," Ashley says. Her voice sounds strangely muted.

My vision blurs and I can hardly make out what's going on. Epsilon takes a small sip from one of the bags of blood, hisses in displeasure, then extends a hand towards Ashley.

A moment passes by.

"I don't think it's working," Ashley says. "You said you could cure me!"

"I said I'd give it a try. And so I have."

"What about her? We should—I don't know, let her rest up and try again."

"Or not."

There's a quick blur of motion, a click, and then the deafening bang of a gun being fired. A heavy thud follows. Ashley. No, no, no.

I'm fading fast as Epsilon returns to block out the light.

"I think we're rather close, don't you?" she says. The next second she swivels her head towards the bay window with a snarl.

"Close enough," she says through gritted teeth. She's just a blurry blob to me. I'm so dizzy. She brings the gun up so it's aimed at my forehead.

And fires.

27

Hawk

I walk into the office with various prank devices hidden in my lunch bag. It's stuffed full of ingredients to cause havoc if timed and executed properly. There's no longer any hesitation left in me. I keep my eyes open and prepare for what's to come. This is no longer my work place. It's a mission.

I'm a monster. I can't deny it anymore and I can't keep hiding from it. Maybe the people who have been afraid of werewolves all along have known the truth. There's darkness inside each of us we can never truly escape. Genna's offered an avenue for salvation, though, and I intend to see it through. No matter the cost. I'm not turning back now.

Half way through the work day, I set my string of "incidents" in motion to cause the right level of chaos and confusion that's going to be necessary.

Finding Erebus starts with a whoopee cushion.

Milton comes storming out of his office waving the thing around, his face the color of a beet.

"Who put this under my chair?" he demands and garners everyone's attention.

I slowly rise out of my chair and move away from Doug who's returned to work at last. Not that I care. He's a nuisance I'm going to be rid of soon enough.

And while the rest of the office might have ignored me or not given me the time of day, I've been watching them for months.

The whoopee cushion is a match for the one Nate keeps in his desk drawer. I see him open the drawer to make sure someone hasn't taken his for this prank. Right on cue, he lets out a screech as he finds the fake spiders I put there earlier. His panic jars the people next to him and draws Milton their way. I move closer to my target with the cover of seeing what's going on. Others rise as well and start whispering amongst each other. Good. I want bodies up and moving around.

As I pass the first set of cubicles, I slip a dose of cheese powder into the open cup of orange juice on Dylan's desk and move on towards the water cooler. He takes a drink moments later and spews it on his desk causing yet more alarm. I get myself a small cup as Milton tries to sniff out who the prankster is. Moving inconspicuously backwards, I set the small cup on the top of the copier and tip it into the mechanism before setting it to copy a stack of paper left nearby. Four more steps and I swing into the cover of the break room just as something sparks in the copier and it makes a horrid smell. Someone notices and draws more attention.

Each of the distractions I've arranged pull groups of people in one direction then another and another, stirring up confusion and chatter. Milton's angry voice sounds and when I hear the air horn go off by Vicky's desk that I had attached to her phone, I know that's the signal to move in. When I step out of the break room, sure enough there is hysteria brewing all over the office. People's eyes are on Vicky, on Milton, on the copier smoking, and Nate trying to explain away the whoopee cushion. In the middle of it, Knox remains by his computer with Karen on his right. Karen's in the middle of eating her cupcake while she watches the show. Any second now...

She gasps and drops the cupcake onto her desk. Guilt twists my gut as Karen begins frantically digging through her drawers looking for her Epi-pen.

Knox notices immediately. "Karen?"

The second he realizes what's going on, he lurches out of his chair to help her find the Epi-pen. The second Knox slips around the edge of his cubicle, I slide into his spot.

He's still logged in.

My fingers fly and open up the file search.

Erebus.

One record found.

"Someone call 911!" Knox shouts. "And find me Karen's Epi-pen!"

The chaos only intensifies and panicked voices add to the din the copier is making.

I open the file record and page as quickly as I can for the information I want—past a physical description, list of offenses, something about a French warrant, and at long last where he's currently being held.

The Fields—solitary confinement.

The air leaves my chest. I hastily close the search and delete the search history. I've got maybe two seconds until Knox spots me here.

I swivel about and prepare to act as if I've just found Karen's Epi-pen when a hand closes around my wrist and I'm wrenched about to face—

Doug gives me a menacing smile, rips the Epi-pen out of my hand, and taps Knox on the shoulder with it. The Spartan whips his head about and freezes when he sees Doug holding onto me and the Epi-pen in his hand. Anger flashes in his eyes before he takes the pen and injects it into Karen's leg.

I can't get enough air as the world spins. I've been caught red-handed. The second Knox is done making sure Karen is okay, his attention is going to turn to me.

But I have the information. I have everything I need. Just one thing stands in my way.

"You're going away where you'll never see daylight again," Doug says softly as if thrilled by this turn of events.

I've already come this far. There are no other options.

I wheel into Doug's chest, buck my hips back, and while keeping a hold on his arm, throw my weight forward. Doug flies over my shoulder and slams into Knox's desk with a tremendous crash. Shouts ring out but I'm already in motion. I bolt to the emergency stairwell and hear Knox shout at my back. Adrenaline floods my veins and every sense goes super sharp. I'm a trapped animal and I know it.

The door screeches as I fling myself into it and leap down the segments of stairs two floors before racing through the cafeteria and taking the elevator on the far side. It moves about twenty seconds slower than I need it to.

"Come on come on come on come on—"

The doors open.

I fly out as alarms ring through the building. At the bottom of the steps and blocking the entrance, I find Jerry the guard and a gang of his friends waiting. I barely dodge taser wires shot at my chest and slide down the stairs to avoid another pair. My leg hurts from the odd maneuver but I can't let it slow me. I grimace through the pain and come up directly in front of Jerry.

They might be good security guards but they're no match for a Spartan.

Jerry's on his back in two seconds flat, the next guard finds his own taser used against him, the third manages to block a single blow before crumpling from a kick to the back of his knee, and the fourth gets flipped behind the guard's desk.

Then I'm running again.

Things could have gone better, that's for sure but I anticipated something like this happening. I came prepared. The glass doors groan from the force of my shoulder plowing into it. Around the corner, I've got a rental car waiting for me that I parked there this morning. I just need to make it to the woods and then I'll have a fighting chance of making it out.

Erebus is at the Fields. Genna will know how to get to him. I need to get the information to her.

I'm fifteen feet away from my getaway vehicle when I feel the tingling start in my fingers.

No, no, no, no. Not now.

Panic grips my spine. If I have a seizure now of all times—

The sun grows too bright, the sidewalk moves in front of me like a treadmill, and the buildings cave in from the sides.

I can make it. I'm so close.

I stagger to the car and manage to get the door open.

Almost. Almost there—

My mind empties and I'm partway into the driver's seat when I lose myself.

The world slips through my fingers, indescribable and surreal.

Coming back to is a painful process of fear, confusion, and panic welded together. It takes a long time for my eyes to adjust and my mind to clear.

When at last I come to my senses, I find Knox standing over me—bio-mech gun drawn—and realize I've failed.

I *failed*.

Knox hauls me partway up none too gently. I'm light-headed and woozy. I wince and reach a hand to my head to find blood there. And on my arm. Everything hurts inside and out.

"Don't move," Knox growls. "You're under arrest for treason, sedition, and plenty more, I'm sure. Under the provisions of the Dragon Pact, you may be held without representation for an indefinite period of time."

My brain goes numb and the world fades away as Knox drags me to my feet, brings my hands behind my back, and cuffs me.

"Under Federal Title 51, any human rights afforded to you have been temporarily suspended . . ."

I was so close. So close and then the serum screwed everything up.

"... Penalties will be decided at a later date and time..."

The real kicker is that I have the information. I know where Erebus is.

"Do you understand what I've just explained to you?"

I nod vaguely and he turns me towards the building.

Onlookers stop to gap but Knox hurries me indoors away from the gawkers. But there are plenty of gawkers inside too. They silently form a corridor for Knox and me as we head to the elevator. The ride up is silent and heavy. I stare blankly at the doors in front of me. What have I done?

"I can't express how disappointed I am in you," Knox says quietly right before those doors open again.

Disappointment. Yeah, I know the feeling well. Disappointment in myself, in the world, in the people closest to me.

We emerge at our floor. Milton waits for us tapping his foot. The people I've spent the last few months with stare or avoid eye contact as I'm marched into Milton's office and forcibly sat down in a chair.

"Get the nurse," Knox commands Doug who followed in behind us. Doug obediently slips away and returns moments later with the wrinkled old woman who's stationed in the building to keep an eye on the werewolves.

"What happened?" she asks as she sees the blood from my scrapped arm and the throbbing spot on my head.

"I don't know," Knox answers, beefy arms crossed over his chest and towering over me making it very clear there's no chance of running again. "He might have slipped getting into his getaway vehicle."

"It was a seizure," I say quietly. "I didn't slip."

"A seizure?" The nurse frowns. "I don't remember anything of the sort in your medical records."

"That's because it's not."

"It doesn't matter," Knox says loudly over us. "What matters is—"

"Of course it matters," I snap and match his volume. "It matters a hell of a lot more than you think it does."

Knox levels that commanding stare at me but I don't care. I'm done, I know that. What's the point in pretending to be a complacent suck up anymore? Let them know exactly why I did what I did. Let them know the truth for once in their miserable lives.

"You don't get to talk to me like that, not after what you just did," Knox says.

"How about I don't give a damn! You're a blind, simpering fool who doesn't give a crap about the people who are the victims in all of this!" My throat strains with how loud I yell. Let the whole office know. I *want* them to know. "You turn a blind eye to what the werewolves are subjected to because you think they deserve it. Did any of us deserve to be bitten? Become unwilling victims of our circumstances? Do you have any idea what the serum does to people like me? Those seizures are because of the serum! You and the rest can deny it as much as you like but it's no cure, and it's a living death sentence to those that react to it like I do. I've been living in fear my whole life because of that drug. And instead of helping the people made sick by it, the IMS throws them into a black hole because dealing with it would just be too damn hard! I won't apologize for doing what I had to!"

I'm practically wheezing and silence echoes in the empty spaces after my speech.

Knox doesn't even blink. "So leading the werewolves right into Dasc's arms is preferable?"

"What?"

"Doug followed you that day, remember? And your story never added up for me. Then there's something else."

Doug suddenly appears from behind me. "I dug into your medical history. There's a lot of inconsistencies that were patched up by Aaron Wallowitz, someone we already know is a traitor. How long have you been off the serum?"

"I—that's not—"

"No more excuses," Knox says. "Tell us everything you know about Rosalyn Graham and her co-conspirators, Genevieve Barnes and Aaron Wallowitz."

The air goes out of my sails. "I don't know what you're talking about."

"Oh, I think you do. Tell me what you know, where they are, what they've been doing, and I'll try to help you."

I swallow and my eyes rest on the blood on my arm that's still oozing from a long scrape I got somehow during my seizure. Probably from the cement sidewalk. Genna's words come back to haunt me—if given the choice between my sister and the location of the compound, what would I do? Now I truly understand her precautions. Knox isn't threatening Phoenix in this—yet—but I also can't give them a solid answer even if I wanted to.

"I think I'm done talking," I say quietly.

"Are you sure?"

"I'm sure."

Knox gestures to the nurse and she begins cleaning the

cut on my arm and inspecting whatever I did to my head to make it throb so much.

It's over. I tried to play the game and lost.

While the nurse patches me up, the others discuss the next steps—my fate. Eventually Knox gets permission to have a transport come pick me up to send me to the Fields for assessment. Milton argues to send me straight to the penitent cells at a nearby facility but Knox argues against it. Perhaps some part of him believes me about what I said, that the serum isn't without its flaws.

Then Doug speaks up. "If I may, I have additional information about Hawk's recent activities. During my research into his background as you requested, I discovered correspondence between him and the assailants of Werevine Pharmaceutical."

My head snaps up and the nurse makes a small sound. "What?"

Doug ignores the interruption. "He gave them blueprints of the building using his IMS clearance and aided them with information on IMS protocol."

"That's a lie."

"In addition," he continues a bit louder. "It appears he and these other werewolves were coordinating assassinations of several directors, including Director Knox, sir."

"That's a lie!"

"Give me the proof," Knox says and doesn't look at me.

"I have it here." He pulls out a flash drive and plugs it into Milton's computer. The three of them hover in front of the monitor but I can't see a thing. The longer they look at whatever false documents Doug is showing them, Knox's face turns more and more rigid to the point of being frightening. When he finally lifts his gaze to me, the man I once called a mentor looks like he could kill me right then and there.

"It's a lie," I say breathlessly. "I'm being setup."

"But you don't deny using my own credentials to access classified records."

"I—no. I—"

"Then why should I believe a word you say?"

"Knox, *please*. I have nothing to do with any of that. I would never— "

He straightens to his full height and towers over everyone in the room. "Get him ready for the transport."

Two of the security guards I laid out earlier yank me to my feet.

"He's lying!" I shout and strain against the hold on my arms. "I didn't help with the assault or—Knox, please! What I did, I did to help the werewolves. I would never attack the directors!"

But my pleading falls on deaf ears. None of them look at me. Well, none of them except for Doug with a smug smirk he manages to hide from the others. He walks to the door as I'm hauled out.

"Hawk," he says and turns part way towards me. Knox and Milton turn away and my guards are focused on hauling me to the elevator.

So I'm the only one who sees when Doug's eyes go completely black—whites and all.

"You should've been more careful," he says.

And in a blink, his eyes are normal again. Dull.

Not human. A monster. Hiding right in our midst this entire time.

"What are you?" I breathe.

Doug smiles and walks away.

"What are you?" I shout after him. My heels catch on the carpet as I flail trying to break free. "Knox! Look at Doug! He's not human! You have to check him! *Knox!*"

But I'm ignored wholeheartedly by everyone.

Except my guards, one of which hits me hard enough on the back of the neck that I blackout.

The world swims back into focus with my head pounding harder than ever. I find myself sitting in the back of a van, hands still cuffed, ankles now cuffed as well to my seat, and a chain leading between the two. They're a special make, so even if I shifted they would hold. The last time I saw a pair of theses cuffs, they were being used on Dasc.

Directly across from me sits Knox in all his cold fury, flanked by four guards with bio-mech rifles.

The van rocks as it starts to move.

There's no way out. No friends to help me. No escape routes to take. The only thing I have left are my words which I doubt will count for much of anything.

"I would never attack your brother or any of the directors," I say. This is my last chance to appeal. "Yes, I'm guilty of using your account, because my only hope for myself and the rest of the werewolves is finding a cure."

"And you couldn't just share something like that with the IMS?"

"No. Because of Jason Marsden. Because of every werewolf dragged to the Fields. Look up Jason and tell me if you think he deserved what he got."

"So Dasc is a better option."

"No. I told you, I'm not working for him and I never

will. This is about the werewolves. Our kind. And the only way we're going to make it is by being free of both the IMS and Dasc."

"Do you know what you sound like? An anarchist."

"That's not—" I shake my head. "It's not about rejecting authority or any of that crap. It's about doing what's right. But I'm telling you, that nonsense about attacking Werevine and assassinating the directors is a bunch of lies. When Doug talked to me when I was being hauled out, his eyes went black. He's not human. He's some new monster that's been hiding right under our noses."

"I'd love to believe you, Mason. I really would."

My heart falls deeper into the pit it's found itself in. "But you don't."

He shakes his head. "I can only hope you get the help you clearly need."

I bow my head low enough so I can put my face in my cuffed hands.

We rumble on in silence and I dread what comes next. Not only being confined, but being useless. What can I do behind bars and trapped with the other poor souls injected with the serum? Will I go mad like Jason? Will I put an end to the agony when it becomes too much? I don't know. I honestly don't know.

Minutes pass, half an hour, maybe an hour. No one says anything.

Then—

The driver shouts. "OH, SH—"

The tires squeal, I lurch hard against my chains, and the van leans precariously to the side. Then we're rolling. Bodies are flung this way and that. I'm clocked by things flying in the open space of the van. The only thing that keeps me put apart from the seat belt are my restraints that bite into my wrists and ankles painfully as I'm wrenched about. Everything is a tremendous crush of sound until the van wobbles to a halt and my head spins.

The reek of gas and oil fill my nose along with blood and burnt rubber. My eyes can't seem to focus as I hang partway suspended out of my seat with the van on its side. Below me the others are struggling to reorient themselves.

My ears ring but I hear another crunch of metal. The backdoor is wrenched open and the barrel of a gun peeks into the open. Three bio-mech pulses fire into the van. Three of the guards slump where they ended up in the rollover. Knox and the remaining guard are in a tangle trying to get at their weapons when one more pulse knocks them both out.

I manage to cock my head enough to see a dark figure squeeze in.

"*Genna.*"

It's really her.

"Are you hurt?" she asks.

"You came for me." My head continues to swim and everything is some sort of wacky dream.

"Yeah, and we're getting out of here as fast as we can if we want it to make any difference." She steps carefully over the bodies and wreckage inside the van to inspect my restraints.

"Knox has the keys," I say, still in awe of her presence here. "I thought I was alone."

"You were never alone, Hawk."

She starts digging in Knox's pockets until she has the keys in hand. Four clicks later, she braces my body with her own as she undoes the seat belt and I fall out. I crumple, my body a wobbly mess.

"Steady there," she cautions and helps me out the open door into fading twilight.

Rosalyn's there as well as Witty, both armed—*not* with bio-mech guns—and watching our surroundings on a forested road. I don't have a clue where we are.

"I'm so glad to see you guys," I puff and brace my hands on my knees. As if in response, Rosalyn slaps a gun into my hand when I rise back up.

Witty does a happy little jig and skips over to inspect the van. "I managed to track the GPS of the van once we found out you'd been arrested. I'm just glad this worked! Now we can finally—"

Like a flash of lightening, Knox appears behind Witty and wraps his head in a vice grip. One hand holds a gun—bullets, not safety pulses—to Witty's temple. How did he—

The other guard. He must have been shielded from the bio-mech pulse by the other man's body and pretended to be unconscious, waiting for an opportunity to strike.

"Drop your weapons," he orders.

"You just don't go down, do you?" Rosalyn drawls, her gun already aimed at Knox's head.

I draw up my own gun but put a hand out towards Rosalyn. "Don't."

She bares her teeth and Genna remains silent beside me, her dark eyes assessing.

"None of you are walking out of here," Knox continues. "The question is whether or not you'll be in pain"

"That's a lousy line," Rosalyn says. "I'm hardly intimidated.'"

"Shut up, Rosalyn," I growl.

Genna speaks up. "You wouldn't. You won't kill Witty."

Any other day I think she'd be right. But now, there's no hesitation in Knox's face. I know this man. I trained under him for a year. He's a loyal soldier and a good man—but he's also the Frost Wolf. A savior to some and the devil to others. In this moment, he's the devil.

"Remember what I told you," I say. "Check Doug and read the file on Jason Marsden. And please try to remember that I didn't want to do this."

I fire.

Knox shouts as the bullet goes through his trigger hand and out his shoulder. The important thing is, he'll live. The second he drops the gun, Genna swoops in like a shadow and hits Knox square in the jaw. He collapses but isn't down for good. Genna hits him in the chest with a bio-mech pulse and he falls unconscious.

Then I realize she could have pulsed him down at any time.

"You let me shoot him," I say aghast. "*Why?*"

"With a pulse, he still could have shot Witty on a reaction pull. But I know you have excellent aim."

"So . . . not a test."

She ignores the question and grabs Witty's elbow to keep him upright since he seems liable to fall over. "Shake it off. You're alive."

He bobs his head but his eyes remain unfocused.

"Well," Rosalyn says with a sigh. "I hope this wasn't a supreme waste of time. I sure hope you got arrested for a reason, Hawk."

"It'd be *real* easy to shoot you too, Roz."

She gives a sarcastic bow. "Good to know I'm doing my job right."

"*Enough.*" Genna's voice cuts sharply across the both of us, and she looks to me. "Did you, though?"

I nod. "I got the information. I know where Erebus is."

"Finally," Rosalyn mutters.

"And Merlin knows exactly where he is too."

Genna's expression hardly gives a trace of surprise but she's always been good at hiding her reactions. "Don't tell me..."

"He's at the Fields."

The same place Merlin once escaped from. Erebus has been there the whole time.

28

Phoenix

I hear the thunderous gunshot but the impact never comes. One second I'm alone facing death at the end of a barrel. The next, a figure is hunched before me and staggers when that gun fires. Still unable to move, I watch as the two dim figures struggle and a body falls next to me. There's the sound of shattering glass, hisses, a throaty caw, and wet, labored breathing.

"Don't be dead."

It's Charlie. Charlie took the bullet. It's Charlie lying next to me bleeding out. It's Charlie who presses shaky fingers to the side of my neck looking for a pulse. I want to shout, I want to burst free of my body, I want to save him. But I can't. I can't!

"Don't be dead." He repeats it over and over again as his voice weakens and eventually falls silent.

Although inside I'm screaming for freedom from my

useless body, the world grows ever dimmer. Epsilon took too much from me. I don't know how much longer I'll last. I don't know how much longer Charlie will either.

Wings brush my face and a second later there's another set of fingers checking for my pulse. I hardly catch Alona's words. I think she says something to me, or maybe she's on the phone, but I'm too far gone. At some point I'm conscious of being moved but that's it.

When I come to again, it's very slowly. I blink a white ceiling into focus. A sheet covers me up to my chest, I'm aware of a needle in the back of my hand, and the beeping of a monitor nearby. My eyes burn, my tongue feels thick and heavy, and my body aches. I'm not able to do much but I manage to see the bag of blood hanging beside me along with an IV replenishing what I've lost. A small tube is tucked around my face under my nostrils giving me oxygen.

I feel wretched and not just physically.

Charlie. Ashley. Where are they? Are they . . . are they . . .

My hands curl into fists—the most movement I've been able to achieve so far. Then deep in my core, my bones, every last part of me burns with a seething fire. Furious is too small a word for what I feel. The strength of it changes me into something new and deadly. My body arcs as a pulse like a bio-mech gun explodes out of me. The equipment around me shudders as it's pushed by the force of my rage, the heart rate monitor beeps wildly, and dust sprinkles me from the ceiling tiles.

"You're going to make yourself worse," Alona scolds.

She appears at my side a second later and grasps my hand. Weak once more, I go limp and fall short of breath.

But the fire continues to spread through me as if my body is burning away its weaknesses and preparing to destroy everything around me, including myself. I've felt a shift like this before when Hawk almost died at the hands of the lamia. Some deeply seated part of my magic has changed. The last time it felt like a call to arms in my bones—this time it feels like a volcano about to erupt. I'm angry. I'm *furious*. But above all, I'm terrified.

This is my fault.

"Charlie," I breathe. "Where is he?"

Her dark eyes soften. "He's in surgery. Melody's waiting by him for word. Theo and John are coming here as fast as they can."

I close my eyes that smart from being so dry. "How bad?"

"Things could have been worse if we didn't have blood supplies for the team on hand. You'll be okay once the paralytic agent wears off. But Charlie . . ." She squeezes my hand. "He took a shot to the chest. A nurse keeps coming out from surgery to keep us up to date. It's been rough but he's hanging in there. He's a fighter. He'll pull through."

He wouldn't be in this position at all if I had turned myself in ages ago. He took that bullet for me. There's a cold, dark void in my chest where no light can touch and it grows the more I think about losing him.

"And Ashley?"

"She didn't make it. Epsilon shot her in the head."

Oh, God. The person who's probably suffered the most and—I can't fix it. I can't undo this terrible end. The void grows.

"What happened in there?" Alona asks.

I blink several times as my eyes start to swim. "Ashley drugged me. I wasn't careful enough. I walked right into it."

"That's sort of the point of a surprise attack, Phoenix. You aren't supposed to see it coming."

"I should have."

"Tell me what happened next."

I swallow past my dry mouth. "She was working with Epsilon. She must have told Ashley she could cure me if they had me. Epsilon drained me out, tried a taste on Ashley, but then..."

Rivulets run down either side of my face. Alona squeezes my hand more tightly.

"Scholar warned me," she says softly. "She knew you were in trouble. We came as fast as we could. Charlie was beside himself. We were supposed to go in together but he saw Epsilon draw that gun on you and—"

"He should have ported her away or—"

"There wasn't time. He would have needed to port in, then port again. One more second would have meant a bullet getting put in your head."

My face twists up and I try to turn my head to hide the obvious pain written across it. "I—he—"

"Nothing we do can change what happened. He made his choice."

"He shouldn't have."

"*Hey.*" Alona says it so sharply that I look up again. She's exceedingly cross. "If you want someone to hold you hand while you go 'woe is me,' then wait for Melody to get in here. But I'm not taking any of your martyr crap. Don't belittle Charlie's choice to save you because you know very well you would have done the exact same thing in his position. Yeah, Charlie's in the tough spot. It sucks. It's terrible. But instead of saying your places should have been exchanged, respect what he did. Thank him. Make it an act worthy of you."

I blink back my tears, stunned. She releases my hand and rolls her neck around her shoulders.

"I'm going to check on Charlie," she says. "In the meanwhile, pull it together. We need you, same as you need us."

She walks out of the room and I'm left to mull over her words. Alona has a terrible bedside manner but . . . I don't need someone to hold my hand. I've been hand-holding for a while, I realize. My team wanted me to head to the labs as soon as they found out what I could do, but they held my hand as I confessed my fears and let them stop me. I've kept myself sheltered. Sure, I've used my abilities to help my team, but only to such an extent that they go unnoticed by anyone else. Perhaps I've needed a stern talking to. First Hawk, now Alona.

Epsilon said my abilities were "close enough." Maybe close enough should be good enough for me too.

Alona returns in short order with news that they've stabilized Charlie. I only nod in relief. I don't trust myself to speak. A nurse comes in shortly after to check my vitals, give me some eye drops, and see if I need anything. Once she leaves, I gesture weakly to Alona and she scoots her chair forward to prop her feet up on the side of my bed.

"What about Epsilon?" I ask quietly.

She works her jaw and crosses her arms over her chest. "Got a taste of Charlie's blood and ported out of there. I chased her down a ways before she disappeared. There's a massive man hunt for her."

She got away. *Again.* That's three times now.

The next time I come across her, I'm going to rip her head clean off.

"What now?"

"Now?" Alona shrugs. "You rest up. Charlie gets better. The rest of us stick around to guard your sorry butts until they call us out. You can give your full report once John and Theo show up."

I roll my lips together, enjoying the sensation of simply being able to move. "Okay."

"In the meantime . . ." She digs in her pocket and pulls out Scholar's pendant. "I thought you might want this back."

I hold out a shaky hand and she lays it in my palm. It beats faintly against my skin so I curl my fingers around it as if to soothe its anxiety at my own distress.

My gaze drifts to Alona. "Thank you for saving me."

"You're welcome."

She folds her hands over her abdomen and settles in to stare out the windows and glance periodically at the door—my guardian. I do my best to sleep but there's so much running through my mind that it's nearly impossible. I keep experimenting with moving my limbs and rolling my head back and forth on the pillow as the poison in my veins slowly wears off. Eventually I'm able to sit up and remain so simply because I can.

"So, what are you going to do now?" Alona asks.

"Sit here."

"I meant—" She cocks her head to the side and the silky

dark strands of her hair fan out across her shoulder. "I felt that burst when you woke up."

I coil my hands in my lap and keep my eyes on my calloused fingertips. "Yeah."

"That was different."

"*I'm* different."

"So what does that mean?"

I meet her piercing stare. "It means I stop running. I'm done hiding."

"You think you're powerful enough?"

My brow draws together. "Close enough. Are you going to try to stop me?"

"No." She taps a finger to the pendant still cupped in my palm. "But Scholar might if *she* doesn't think you're ready. Once you go, there's no turning back."

"I know."

"Are you prepared for that?"

"No." I take a deep breath. "But I'm going to regardless."

She gives a single silent nod. We remain that way sitting in the dim room, when two people burst in—Theo and John. They made it. Theo practically sprints to the other side of my bed to give me a hug. John stands beside Alona and lays a hand on my shoulder.

"How are you?" John asks.

"I've been better."

"We picked up your stuff," Theo chimes in and points to my duffle slung over John's shoulder. "And let Deputy Graham know where you are. He said he'd come but he's helping with . . . *stuff* right now."

John gives him a long sideways look when my face

burns and I'm sure my cheeks must be a deep shade of red. Meaning the deputy's dealing with the crime scene left behind. With Ashley.

"We just checked in on Charlie too," John says.

"And?"

"They need to keep a close eye on him for the time being but things are looking up."

Theo gives me his best smile. "It's going to be okay. We're going to be fine."

Right. I wonder what it's like to be so optimistic all the time.

John takes a seat on the armrest of Alona's chair and Theo sits on the other side of my bed against my legs.

"All right," John says. "What happened, Phoenix?"

So I tell them. I tell them of the journey that led to Ashley's house—all of it including Duke and Hawk and the remaining secrets I've kept—because they deserve to know. This charade is coming to an end anyway. Then I lay out Ashley's trap, her reasons for doing so, and explain why Epsilon was there. When I finish, Theo paces at the foot of my bed, John stands stoic as usual, and Alona remains seated with her fingers templed together.

"How do we handle this?" John asks.

"We don't," I say before anyone can come up with some grand excuse for why Epsilon captured me and drained my blood. We probably could come up with something but I don't even want to think about that lest I be tempted. "I'm not going to hide anymore."

"Are you sure?"

"Don't give me another out. I don't deserve it. I've already taken too many liberties as it is," I say. Alona gives me a sharp look but I shake my head. "I'm not saying 'woe is me.' I'm taking responsibility. I appreciate what all of you have done. Truly. You protected me and my secrets even though you had no reason to."

"We had reason," Theo interjects and plants his hands on the end of the bed. "We're a team. We're family."

My eyes smart and I blink furiously. "I'll write the report myself and make sure nothing is reflected poorly on you. I—I'll do it tonight."

"No, you won't." John gives me his most severe look with arms crossed and feet firmly planted. "Phoenix, if you're going to turn yourself into the labs, then you do so when you're well and on your own two feet. Don't give anyone ammo when you're down. You go out like a warrior, not a woman throwing her chips in."

"But—" I start but the others nod in agreement with John's sentiment. "They'll be expecting a report on what happened."

"And I'll delay it for as long as I can," John says. "When you're better, you walk it straight in to Director Knox. If there's anyone in IMS command I trust completely, it's him."

On that we can agree.

"And you have to say your goodbyes to Charlie before you disappear," Alona adds. "He'd kill us if we let you go without telling him first."

I swallow. He's not the only one I need to say goodbye to. Somehow I need to make things right with Hawk, then say a few words to Jefferson, my team, Celina and Doocan, and send a message to Scholar at the last possible moment so she can't stop me. And that's it. Then I'll go to Director

Knox, explain everything, and go to the labs without any resistance where I'll most likely spend the rest of my life locked away. Too valuable to lose.

As I think of the words I'll need to say, Melody swings into the room looking pale.

"He's out of surgery," she says without preamble. "They've moved him to the ICU."

"Can we see him?" I ask.

"They'll let us in as long as we stay out of the way of the nurses and doctors."

Theo lets out a single humorless laugh. "How'd you manage that? They never let people in."

"They'll let us in," she says, a dark glimmer in her eyes.

I immediately try to work my way off the bed before I find the whole of the team blocking my way and telling me to take it easy. Theo rushes out and gets me a wheelchair—followed in by a nurse asking what on earth we're doing as I need rest. Melody and John help me into my mobile transportation as Alona drags along the stand with the IV and blood bag. Everyone is equally stubborn with the nurses who try to stop us from going to see Charlie and eventually they let us through.

Theo wheels me in and as a group we crowd around Charlie's bedside. When I lay eyes on him, I can't breathe. He's got a tube sticking out of his mouth to breathe for him, a thick mass of bandages sticking up underneath his hospital gown, blankets pulled up to his waist, and a steady morphine drip going into his arm. I'm so focused on him, on the trauma and despair, that I don't even notice the nurse lingering by the monitors at his bedside.

"How's he doing?" John asks on everyone's behalf.

The nurse folds her hands together and talks in a soft voice. "He lost a lot of blood. The supply your agency gave us saved his life. He's stable at the moment but his condition is fragile. We'll keep a close eye on him and keep him sedated until his condition improves. I realize this is a difficult time, but I must ask you to please wait outside the room in the waiting area."

"Please, we'll stay out of the way," Melody pleads.

But the nurse is having none of it. She escorts us out of the room but we don't give up that easily. If we aren't allowed in the room, then we'll stake out the hallway—which we do. Theo rounds up chairs from somewhere and forms a line for Charlie's guard. We sit silent and lost in our own thoughts. Melody paces back and forth, muttering something under her breath and never taking her eyes off Charlie's door.

I test my limits once again by slowly rising out of the wheelchair and holding myself steady with the metal IV stand. I move into Melody's path so when she turns to pace in the opposite direction, she has no choice but to stop. She halts, eyes swimming, and I weakly wrap my arms around her.

"We're going to be okay," I whisper. I say the words as much for her as for me.

Melody melts into my hug and holds onto me so tight it hurts. I continue to whisper encouragement to keep up her spirits and chase away my own doubts. Then Theo's arms are around us, then John's, then Alona's. It's a long time before any of us break apart.

The night drags on and I settle in the wheelchair as a nurse comes to click her tongue at me, change out my IV, and check my vitals once again. She brings us blankets a little while later and I tuck my knees up to my chest to rest curled up in a ball. John bundles up his blanket for a makeshift pillow, Alona falls asleep with her head on Theo's shoulder, and his head against the wall as he snores softly. Melody continues to pace until she too takes a chair to get some shut eye. I slip in and out of dreams and nightmares waiting for this terrible night to end.

When I fully wake, I'm back on a bed with a blanket draped over me. Theo lingers outside the door to my room but takes long strides to my side when I sit up.

"Morning, sunshine."

I rub the sleep from my very, *very* tired eyes. "Any word?"

"They were able to remove the tube so he's breathing on his own."

"Why did I get moved?"

He gives me a sad smile. "You were hurt too, remember? You needed better sleep than what you were getting in that wheelchair."

"Right."

"Hey, Phoenix?"

"Yeah?"

Theo takes a seat on the edge of the bed and takes my hand in his. "I just wanted you to know that I think you're incredibly awesome, *mon chéri*. No matter what happens next—" He makes a face like he ate a lemon. "Sorry, no. That's too depressing. Let me start over. Phoenix, you make life awesome with your explosive punches and magicalness. The end. No sad goodbyes, okay? I don't believe in them."

I smile and place my other hand on top of his. "Thank you. And . . . *au revoir*."

He grins. "*Au revoir*. But not quite yet. Breakfast. Healing. All that good stuff first."

He helps me off the bed and tucks my hand into the crook of his arm to guide me to the cafeteria. We meet John there as well. Melody and Alona are waiting by Charlie's room. We're not leaving him alone at any time. Theo, John, and I gather up breakfast, pile it on a couple of trays, and bring it to our row of chairs to continue our waiting game.

Melody's pacing again but has a phone to her ear this time. "Of course, director. The report is coming. We'll have one of our own bring it straight to you once we're ready." Her eyes latch onto me briefly. "I understand that but we'd appreciate a minor delay. Yes . . . yes. Thank you, sir."

"So?" John prompts.

"The report is officially delayed," she says and tucks the phone into her pocket. And now we wait."

In the meanwhile, Melody brings me her tablet so I can prepare messages to my friends on a delay to be sent a week from now at which time I hope to deliver my secrets up to the director. I don't want anyone to try to persuade me out of it. The messages I prepare for Jefferson and Hawk are by far the longest and also the hardest to write. I plan on calling them both just before I give myself up but I wanted something more waiting for them too. They deserve more from me. The day draws on and the others do their own paperwork, patrol the hospital, and keep in touch with the teams hunting Epsilon.

Eventually we're allowed in to Charlie's room itself and the others give me the chair at his bedside while they rotate in and out to keep an eye on the area. There's no telling if Epsilon will make another go at me or do further harm to Charlie. Around dinner time, Theo goes to grab food so Melody and I are left alone in the room as Alona and John do guard duty outside. I'm feeling better but all of us look worse for wear. Melody's hair is frazzled and she keeps toying with Charlie's leather bracelet from his bag of belongings.

It's agonizing waiting for someone to wake up. I need him to wake up. I've decided to wait not only until I'm feeling well to meet with Director Knox, but when I know Charlie is okay and Hawk is safe. Hawk's safe enough where he is even if he doesn't like the current situation, but Charlie . . . I'll wait for Charlie. So, I stare at his pallid face waiting for him to wake up. He looks peaceful—apart from the fact he's lying in a hospital bed with a thick bandage strapped to his chest and pale, bruise-like shadows under his eyes. He's got a bit of scruff starting to come in too. Even with our hectic missions, he made time to shave so it's the first time I've seen him with stubble. The five o'clock shadow makes him look even more handsome actually. I wish he'd believe me when I tell him that.

But that's part of Charlie's personality, isn't it? He never thinks he's good enough. He'll join in word play or act superior at times but there's so much doubt and sorrow heaped on his shoulders. And he took that bullet without a second thought.

"I never regretted it, you know," Melody says from the other side of Charlie's bed.

I tear my eyes away from his face. "What?"

"I never regretted saving my friend's life even though I

lost my skin and magic. Some sacrifices are worth it. Some *people* are worth it."

I get what she's saying but it doesn't really make me feel any better.

She walks around the bed and pushes a worn book into my hands. It's her copy of *Pride and Prejudice* she had been forcing Charlie to read.

"I've heard it helps if people talk to you when you're in a state like this." She nods to Charlie. "It might do him some good."

She pats my shoulder and says some excuse about going to the bathroom before she leaves. I thumb the weathered pages of the floppy book and find Charlie's bookmark—a receipt from a library—near the end. I crack it open and start reading from the top of the page in a soft voice. The characters are mostly familiar to me from the time Melody had us watch the film adaptation so I get the general gist of where I am in the story.

"*I have been a selfish being all my life, in practice, though not in principle. As a child I was taught what was right, but I was not taught to correct my temper.*"

I don't know how long I keep reading out loud but I continue to do so because I hope Charlie can hear me. He's not alone. There's someone watching over him. There's someone that cares. He needs to know.

"*I love him. Indeed he has no improper pride. He is perfectly amiable. You do not know what he really is; then pray do not pain me by speaking of him in such terms.*"

I pause, my throat feeling dry, and look around for a cup of water.

"Why'd you stop?"

I gasp and leap out of my chair at the sound of Charlie's weak voice. His eyes are open and fixed on me. I lurch forward and grasp his hand.

"You're awake!"

"Yeah," he croaks. "Ow."

My eyes water as I beam at him and don't care to stop the tears that escape. "You scared us. I was terrified that you'd—" I swallow and shake my head. "But you're awake. You're okay. You're going to make it."

"And you're alive," he says on an exhale and closes his eyes again. "Thank God."

I squeeze his hand and lean in closer. "Thanks to you."

"When I saw you lying on that floor . . . I thought I was too late again. I thought you were dead, Phoenix. Do you have any idea what that did to me?"

His pale green eyes pin me where I stand leaning over him. The weight of it settles on me and I slowly sink back into the chair but keep my hand wrapped around his on top of the bed.

"I've been too late before," he continues in a rasp. "I never told you."

"Shh, Charlie. You should rest." I look around for a cup of water again. He sounds like he could really use one.

"I need to tell you."

"Charlie . . ." I worry my lower lip and let out a slow breath. "I already know. Your uncle told me what happened to your parents."

He blinks fast and a single tear slips down his cheek. "You didn't say anything."

I avert my eyes as my face grows hot. "I shouldn't have known. I should have waited for you to tell me, and I didn't want you thinking I violated your privacy . . . which I did. I'm sorry."

"You still don't know. I never told my uncle everything."

"What are you talking about?"

He blinks rapidly and the heart monitor beeps increase in pace as he takes a stuttering breath. "I—I knew what my mother was. I knew she had become a werewolf but I lied. I said I didn't know what happened." His voice cracks and rends a tear in my heart. "If I had said something, if I had done more, I could have stopped her from killing my dad."

He sucks in a sharp breath and winces. I lean in closer, wishing I could do something to mend his pain.

"They told me they were just going to trap my mother and fix her," he continues hardly above a whisper. "Then everything happened and—I was too late. She killed my dad but . . ."

"She was still your mom," I say quietly.

He nods and moves as if to brush away the tears on his face but can only lift his arm partway before the IV snags and he lets his arm fall.

This is it. This is why Charlie can teleport through space and time. He's never been running away. He's always been rushing to save the day—to be there in time to save a life. It also explains why his feelings about werewolves are so twisted. The disease made his mother worse and drove her to become a true monster. And yet . . . he still loved her.

"I said some horrible things to you," he whispers. "And I was almost too late again. I should have stayed with you."

"But you were right. I never should have taken those bullets from your uncle. I should have focused on healing, not killing, but I lost my way. I let my temper get the best of me." I clear my throat and study the back of his hand. "Charlie . . . I . . ."

As if knowing exactly what I'm going to say, goodbyes and all, he says, "I can't lose you."

My chest caves inwards as I see the desperation coloring his face, the worry in his eyes, feel his grip on my hand. How many times has Charlie been left behind by the people he cares for? His parents, his uncle, his friends. And now I'm about to do the same thing. I hate it. I hate every part of it and yet . . . I know this is the right thing to do—even if it hurts so much to do it.

So I don't say goodbye. I don't give him the speech I've been preparing in my head for this moment. I stand, smooth out the blankets at his side, and carefully clamber up onto the bed next to him. Being ever so aware of his injury, I curl up against his side, rest my head beside his, and keep his hand in mine.

He doesn't say anything but tilts his face to the side until his cheek rests against the crown of my head. I think of what I'll miss when I head to the labs, I think of the words I'll leave in a letter for Charlie when I go, and I think of how much I'll miss him.

"I don't want to lose you either," I whisper.

29

Hawk

It takes two full days for the reality of my situation to sink in.

I'm a fugitive wanted by the IMS.

I shot Knox.

And in the chaos that ensued, I lost Scholar's pendant with Phoenix's blood that kept the peace between the serum and werewolf disease battling in my blood.

But most importantly, I'm no longer taking the serum.

The pain evaporates more each day I'm free of it. Yet as the pain vanishes and Phoenix's power isn't there to soothe my wild side, I can feel the other half of me growing stronger. I've never truly felt it until now. All my life I've had Phoenix's boon to keep me on the straight and narrow. With her far away and her magic gone, the itch I have on the back of my neck grows into an animal of its own. I can hear it growling in the back of my mind, willing me to go wolf and be truly free—not only of the IMS and the serum, but myself.

More than ever I feel a connection to the other werewolves around me. I'm keenly aware of Genna, Rosalyn, and Witty at all times as we hide out in a motel in Nevada. There's an ache to shift that's almost impossible to ignore. I've been white knuckling it for the last day.

"We could lock you in the bathroom," Rosalyn suggests. "Let you get it out of your system."

"I can handle it," I say through clenched teeth.

She rolls her eyes and says to Genna instead, "If he can't control himself, he's going to be a liability in any fight ahead of us."

Before I can do anything that I want to—like punch Rosalyn—I stride off and out the door. A hot, dry wind blows into my face outside. The sound of crickets is loud around this desert way station. As soon as I told Genna that Erebus is at the Fields, she brought us here—close to our target without drawing attention to ourselves. She knows where the facility is because Merlin told her, but the place is a fortress. The only person known to have escaped is Merlin himself but so far he's refused to come help us or even tell us what he knows of the facility. The last day has been Genna exhausting herself on the phone trying to convince him otherwise. Whatever happened to Merlin in that facility must have been terrible if he's loath to even be in the same state as it. Which obviously presents a problem since he's supposed to be our in and out for accessing the facility.

Then there's the other question we keep asking ourselves. What is Doug? What is his plan? Whose side is he fighting on?

So, here we remain, sprawled in the heat of the motel under a dry Nevada sun.

The stars shine bright in the heavens overhead. I don't know if I've ever had so clear a view of them. And it's so dry. Seattle was always wet and Minnesota wasn't much better. It's a change of pace, and I'm determined to be distracted by it at this point. Anything to keep my mind off the snowballing whirl of problems.

I do a tour around the motel and find Witty standing off by himself staring at the stars, a bemused smile on his face.

"Well, I'm glad to see the weight of the world isn't burdening your shoulders," I say as I join him.

He chuckles. How can anyone chuckle at a time like this?

"You know, some things seem so small after you've learned how to truly appreciate your life," Witty says. "Like constantly worrying. I mean, I still worry, but not all the time. I trust Genna. She'll figure things out."

I watch him out of the corner of my eye. He's not the same Witty anymore. This is a side of him I've never seen.

"Take the night sky," he says and gestures to the velvety darkness above us. "Did you know I never got the chance to star gaze before? I was always in Underground, nose to a computer screen." He takes a deep breath of the wind whispering in our faces. "It's so beautiful."

I've never heard him speak so openly before without restrictions on himself. He's usually apologizing or correcting himself or overthinking what he's said.

"You've changed," I say quietly. "More sure of yourself, I guess."

"After I left Underground, I found a part of myself I thought I had lost a long time ago."

I nod. "Your legs."

"No. Not my legs. I mean, being able to use my legs is—"

He gives a hearty laugh and claps a hand on my back. "Being able to run is *great*. But that's not what I'm talking about. I found my courage again."

"I think you had plenty of courage before," I say but he shakes his head.

"I was always afraid of what people thought. I was too timid. Not that I'm *not* timid anymore but, what I mean—the most courageous thing I ever did was protecting you and the whole serum thing."

"Thank you, by the way."

His broad smile is so full of life it's almost a wonder. "But that was . . . a glimpse of myself that I was afraid to explore. But when I got out and was turned—" He says it with no hesitation or shame. "—I rediscovered that part of myself. The wolf made me strong but didn't magically heal my legs overnight. I had to really fight for it but I found I had the courage to fight for it. I had the courage to fight for myself. To me, the werewolf curse isn't a curse. It's—well, it's like it amplified a part of me. It scared me at first but then I embraced it. Genna said she's never seen someone take control of themselves so quickly."

Heat crawls up my neck. I've been a werewolf for over fifteen years and I still can't manage it—not without my sister anyway.

"How?" I breathe and don't bother to keep the desperation out of my voice.

Witty squints a bit, crosses his arms over his chest, and looks like he's thinking hard. "I have a theory. I've talked to Genna and Rosalyn about their own experiences to gather data as well as plenty of the werewolves at the compound."

"I'm not surprised."

"Everyone's stories are different and yet the same. For Genna, controlling her wolf half meant using its strength as her own to become something greater than herself." That sounds deep. He's really put a lot of thought into this. "For Rosalyn, it was a matter of embracing her vicious side to become better than everyone else."

"Yeah, that sounds like her," I mutter.

"The other werewolves in the compound had different experiences as well, *but*—" He holds up a finger for emphasis and faces me. "There was one common factor throughout."

"Which was?"

"Acceptance."

I swallow and let that sink in.

"I think that's why I handled it so quickly," he says softly. "Because I had already accepted it before I even became a werewolf."

"And what? You're magically cured?"

He shrugs. "It's not a cure. I still get bloodthirsty, but I've never lost control of myself. I can focus. Because I faced the darkness inside—that everyone has—and accepted it."

Darkness indeed. "I accepted my fate a long time ago."

He shakes his head. "No, I don't think you ever did, Hawk. You've always been trying to fight someone else's darkness but the reality is, the darkness is your own."

With one last clap on the back, he leaves me in silence and walks back to the motel.

I'm left alone with the warm breeze in my face and a dry mouth. It becomes very difficult to swallow. Alone in the night beneath those twinkling stars, blinking against raw epiphanies, I let the tears run down my cheeks unabashed.

All my life I've been fighting against this *thing* buried

deep in my chest. It's full of anger and hatred and violence. This thing of malice waits in the darkest corners of my mind but is always there. Most of the time I can push it to the side or pretend it doesn't exist but it's there. I blamed the werewolf disease for it. If I wasn't a werewolf, I was sure I'd be happy. But there were times when the anger got the best of me. It would come out as an ugly thing with harsh words and meaner actions, and I would blame it on the magic in my blood.

Not once—not *once*—have I ever considered that all the built up rage is from me.

Amplified, Witty said.

The werewolf disease didn't create the monster inside me.

It just brought out what was already there.

My throat grows ever so tight and I run a hand beneath my nose. I linger out under the stars and really study the beast coiling inside. It has fangs and fur but beneath I see my rage of being caged, of being wronged, or being thought less of because of what I am. I poke and prod at it until the pain grows and grows. I let it wash over me as I realize who I am.

And find my own courage to face myself.

I stagger back to the motel room and have difficulty opening the door. It's late and only one lamp is left on. Rosalyn and Witty have already fallen asleep on the two beds inside.

When Genna sees me, her head jerks up sharply and she rises from the chair at the small table where she's been busy thinking and calling Merlin all day. She tiptoes over and kneels down to my height.

It's only then that I realize I'm no longer a man. But I am me.

Genna puts her hands on either side of my furry muzzle, fingers lightly massaging my ears, and brings her face close.

"Welcome to the pack, Hawk."

⁓

When Merlin finally shows up on the fourth day, the first words out of his mouth are, "I won't do it."

"Here we go," Rosalyn mutters.

Genna immediately launches into a speech about how we need Merlin, he's our best chance of success, and we can't do this without him. As they've been doing for the last few days over the phone, they argue back and forth. Merlin is absolutely adamant about not stepping foot inside the Fields again. Whatever happened to him in that facility has him terrified. Despite his power, this place has him running scared.

I sit on the edge of one of the beds watching the encounter with my elbows perched on my knees. I'm obviously concerned about the current situation but a tremendous burden has been lifted off my shoulders. While Genna has been attempting to get Merlin to come here, I've been out in the heat of the desert practicing shifting back and forth with Witty and Rosalyn looking on to make sure I'm "not a liability." The difference between now and the entirety of my life up until this point is astronomical. The bloodthirsty compulsion remains but now that I've accepted it, embraced it, it doesn't control me.

As Genna once put it, I had to become meaner than my demons.

It's the strangest feeling not being afraid of myself.

Now Merlin's arrived, and with his presence comes the bite of the serum since it comes from his veins. I can feel it sliding under my skin like an invisible pair of hands wanting to leash the beast slumbering inside, but it doesn't hurt me anymore. I don't like it, and I never will, but it's almost as if Merlin's power no longer has an interest in tormenting me since I've reined in my own inner demons. I've been trying not to cry with joy for the last several minutes.

It's also made me realize something else. The werewolves stuck in the Fields are never going to experience this sort of freedom within themselves. There's no one to show them the light as it were like Witty did for me. The people holding them don't understand what's inside or how to "fix" them. Even if the primary mission is to find Erebus to seek out a cure, I'm determined to free those trapped inside.

"I WON'T GO!" Merlin thunders and the entire motel shakes. Even a few car alarms go off outside.

Well, that's one way to snap me out of my reverie.

Silence falls over the room and even Rosalyn looks daunted.

"You don't know what it was like," Merlin continues in a pleading voice. He stands bowed and withered as an old man, hands frantically tugging at his very long beard. "I went in there willingly all those years ago and *they drained the life out of me*. I couldn't escape. I couldn't get free. I was trapped like an insect under their grimy hands! I won't be ensnared by their traps again. Not ever. Not for anyone or anything."

"How did you finally escape?" The question leaves my lips before I can stop it and everyone's eyes pin me where I sit.

Merlin slumps onto the edge of the bed next to me. "One of the nurses took pity on me. She wouldn't draw my blood like she was supposed to or at least less. It wasn't much but it was enough. I broke the locks and escaped through a tiny air duct. Running through the desert afterwards nearly killed me." He wets his lips and stares at his wrinkled hands. "Do you have any idea how it feels to be trapped like that? Without the power to set yourself free?"

"I do. And that's exactly why we need your help, Merlin. Every single werewolf on the planet needs us to succeed here or they'll live out their lives feeling the exact same way you did in there. Trapped and powerless to escape their circumstances."

Merlin shakes his head. "You can't ask me to go back there."

"Then what exactly is the point of you?"

The air grows heavy around me and Merlin's eyes turn sharply on me. "Excuse me?"

"You have such amazing power but you're just going to waste it hiding away and doing party tricks."

"Hawk," Genna cautions from her spot at the table.

But I'm done with mincing my words and playing nice. I've been doing it for far too long.

"You drank a dragon's blood to get that power. You're the only person who can help us but you're going to sit on your hands while the world suffers?"

"I did my own suffering," Merlin growls. The lamp behind us, a few pieces of trash, and a pillow start to rise on their own in the wake of the Magus's anger.

"Oh, I'm sure you did, but do you also know how many people have suffered *because* of you?" I gesture with one hand to him in disgust. "Your serum isn't a gift, it's a chain. The magic in you stems from your own personality, so what twisted thought in your head made your magic become some kind of mind control on those around you? You just *have* to be in control of everyone and everything, don't you?"

The bed shakes beneath me and soon the walls are trembling too as Merlin gets to his feet. The others stand in alarm and shoot me sharp looks for stirring up this bit of chaos.

"Shut up, Hawk," Rosalyn snaps.

"Don't talk about things you don't understand," Merlin says. His voice sounds amplified and reverberates in my ears.

"Then enlighten me!" I shout. "Stop hiding the truth! I know what your magic feels like, so don't lie to me. I also know what protective magic feels like from my sister. But that's not you. Your magic is like some invisible prison to cage us and—"

"I had to or he would have killed everyone!" Merlin thunders back. There's a whirlwind of sheets, pillows, wrappers, and lamps whizzing around us in his fury. I have to duck a few times to avoid getting smacked in the face.

"Who are you talking about?"

"ARTHUR!" His face has gone beet red and his arms shake as he clenches his fists at his sides. "He was like a brother to me! And there was nothing I wouldn't—that I *didn't* do—" He throws out a hand and a picture frame whipping by him explodes into dust. "You want to know who I really am? Then let me tell you the truth about Mordred and Morgana. They aren't fairy tales. They aren't myths. They were real. And they ruined everything Arthur and I worked so hard to build. Because Mordred—the one you call Dasc—bit him and changed him into . . . into a . . ."

"A werewolf."

Sweet majestics.

"That's right. Mordred, son of Morgana the great witch, turned Arthur into a beast."

Which makes Morgana . . . Echidna, Mother of Monsters. Holy—

"I had no choice!" Merlin shouts but there's a quaver in his voice. "There's no cure for the werewolf disease. I had only one hope and I did whatever I had to in order to save him from himself. So I went to the Worldly Queen. I drank of her veins. Then I *stopped* him from being a monster."

Everything falls into place—Merlin's control, the serum, everything. Of course Merlin's magic would have become what it did. He was never about to accept what Arthur had become. His only thought was to control the beast.

"I gave up everything," Merlin sobs. "And it still wasn't enough. Arthur disappeared. The kingdom crumbled. My friends died around me. I've been trying to atone ever since but it's never been enough. *I* have never been enough. And I never will be."

The objects around the room begin to fall lifeless in a circular heap.

"You cannot ask this of me," he says quietly. "I have sacrificed and given enough for one lifetime." He walks stiffly to the door. No one moves to stop him. "I wish you the best of luck, I really do."

I take a step towards him at the same time Genna does.

"*Please*, Merlin," she says. "One more time and no one else will ever have to endure such tragedy as you did."

He doesn't turn around. "I've told you everything I know to get you inside. The rest is up to you."

Then he walks out the door and vanishes.

A beat of silence passes. Then another.

Genna's fist flies out of nowhere and she punches me in the face. I stagger away from the blow and hold a hand to my throbbing cheekbone.

She snarls at me, "He's not the only one who's sacrificed everything."

I blink. Stunned, I don't know what to say. The weight of what I've done sinks in. I pushed our best chance of succeeding out the door.

I work my lips a few times but Rosalyn shoots me a sharp look and says, "Don't talk."

Witty walks over on wobbly legs. "What now?"

The three of them exchanges glances and Genna looses a heavy breath.

"We press on," she says. "Merlin gave us the way in. It's up to us to succeed. Are you with me? All of you?"

Witty immediately puffs out his chest. "Of course."

Surprisingly, Rosalyn hoists her chin and says, "Always."

They look to me. I swallow my pride and realize this is it.

"Let's do this," I say and know my fate is sealed.

With the path ahead of us uncertain yet clear, we go about our preparations. Genna's already come up with a secondary plan in case we didn't get Merlin on board. He gave up his knowledge of the layout and exits so we have some bearing but it might not be enough.

"I'm still angry at you," Genna says as we load our bags into the back of a plain white van that Rosalyn procured.

"But to be fair, I don't think Merlin was ever going to come along no matter what. We still have a shot of getting Erebus out but as for the rest..."

My heart pounds in my ears. "We have to try."

She slams the back door shut to face me with eyes glinting. "And what exactly will we do, hmm? Without Merlin's help, how do you propose we get them out of there in one piece without being arrested or killed?"

I drop my gaze. "I don't know."

She huffs and plants her hands on her waist. "Well, at least Merlin can keep an eye on the werewolves we've already freed in case worst comes to worst and we don't make it out of the Fields. Even if we pull this off, we might not be alive for much longer than that."

"Why do you say that?"

She pins me with those dark, stormy eyes of hers. "I was supposed to report in to Dasc a day ago. He'll figure out what happened soon enough."

My heart stops. "What?"

"We aren't just running from the IMS at this point. He'll be coming for us. That's why we have to make it to Erebus before he can stop us."

"But what about finding the other compounds? I thought you needed Dasc for that."

She lifts her face to the sky. "I took a gamble on you and a cure. If I've just damned those other compounds by losing Dasc's confidence... then I guess I'm damned too."

I swallow and try not to give it too much thought. I should have known. None of them seemed overly concerned about reporting in to Dasc or anything over the last week. Genna's cover—the one she released Dasc for in the first place—has been blown. Because of me.

"I'm sorry," I say quietly. "For everything."

"There's always risk in whatever I do," she says. "Let's just make it count."

There's no arguing with that. If there's ever going to be salvation for the werewolves, this is it. Find Erebus, rescue him, and through him locate the Magi.

"We can do this," I say.

Genna smiles. "Was there ever any doubt?"

It's with that bravado that we all clamber into the van and head out. The ride is silent and long as each of us prepares mentally for the mission ahead. Win or lose, this will change everything. We know that. But the stakes are too high for us to fail. We *have* to succeed.

The night slips away from us and it's three o'clock in the morning when Rosalyn finally brings the van to a halt in the middle of the desert. Without uttering a word, we climb out of the van, check our tan clothes and equipment, then leave the van behind to start walking across the rocks and sand. The sky is clear but it's almost a new moon so there's little light to see by. Once a good ways out from the road, we pause and shift into a pack of wolves. My eyes and senses adjust rapidly to the change. I'm in control but more aware.

It's time.

Genna leads our single file line through the desert, eyes looking up at the stars every so often to lead the way. We trot for miles circling wide of where we know the entrance to the facility is. According to Merlin, there's a huge landing pad and entrance shielded by an illusion but the majority of the compound is beneath the desert. It's a sprawling complex which is going to be an issue in itself. We don't know where Erebus is located inside and trying to sneak or fight our way to him will be tough enough. Then there's trying to escape.

Relax, Hawk. Breathe. You've trained for this.

Funny—I don't think the IMS ever anticipated a Spartan using their training against the very people that trained them. Such a thought would have felt bitter a few weeks ago. Now I find it doesn't bother me nearly as much as I expect it to.

We move at a steady clip but cautiously, skirting patrols and sentries. Either we do this right or we don't do it at all. Our luck holds out and we manage to reach the hidden entrance undetected. It's not much of an "entrance" really. It's quite possibly the smallest duct I've ever seen in my life and it's so well hidden in a scrub of brush that it would be impossible to find if we didn't know where it was. The grate itself blends seamlessly into the ground but the sand shifts away from it as it cycles the air. Staying low, we make sure we're clear before Witty shifts and hauls out his laptop. It's show time.

He sprawls out on the ground while the rest of us watch his back and gets to work to deactivate the sensors inside the duct. It doesn't take him long. Thirty seconds later and he has the grate free. Genna shifts into her human self and slips into the small opening first. It's a good thing we're each pretty slim or this part would be extremely difficult. As it is, I don't fancy squeezing myself into a duct and army crawling a long ways. But such is my luck. I shift and crawl into the duct after Genna. Witty is next with Rosalyn as our rear guard. We don't say a word, we just do—it's almost like working with Spartans.

My elbows and knees ache from the awkward position and very narrow space in which I'm forced to crawl. Sweat gathers on my forehead and I begin to pant. The duct continues on forever and we stop to rest two times for Witty's sake when his legs start to tremble. He may be able to use his legs again but after having been atrophied most of his life, they can't take a lot of abuse yet.

When at last the air feels too stuffy and we've been crawling for what feels like hours, Genna brings us to a halt. I cock my head and hear muffled voices outside the confines of the cramped space. We're definitely a ways into the facility. Accordingly to Merlin, if we get out through the third vent we come across, we'll end up in a lab with a terminal we can access to find Erebus. We move more slowly, aware of every sound we make and every sound below and beyond.

Vent number one. I can hear howls faintly in the distance and cries of pain.

Vent number two. Through the slits I spot a couple of men in lab coats talking over coffee.

Genna holds up a closed fist as she reaches the third vent. She remains motionless as she watches the room below. A minute passes, maybe two, before she quietly pulls out a tool from her pocket to undo the fastenings on the vent cover. Ever so gently, she lowers the cover and keeps hold of it as she maneuvers herself down through the hole. Once she's hanging, I grab the cover to keep it from falling and she lands lightly on the white floor below. At her signal,

I follow after her as Witty then holds onto the cover next and puts it back in place for the time being. He and Rosalyn are going to stay right where they are until we have a better idea of what we're up against and where we are.

The room we find ourselves in has a very sterile quality to it—everything is white from the ceiling to the floors, and there are medical instruments in meticulous rows on a steel rolling table beside a gurney with restraints fastened to the side bars. Charming. I'd like to get out of here as soon as possible lest I become strapped to one of those gurneys but I don't need to say a thing. I can see it in Genna's eyes—dark and terrible loathing for what she sees around her. But there's no computer here like Merlin said. They must have moved stuff around.

In the distance, cries of pain and desperate howling continues.

What sort of nightmare is this?

Genna and I form up silently at the door. There's a small window up high in the door and through it is a long white hallway, empty at the moment. We don't have much to go on here. Merlin never saw much of the facility itself, just his own room and the hallway which they shuttled him through to the lab. The rest is a disaster waiting to happen. Wandering around would be pointless and would get us caught in no time. Our best chance is to catch someone alone and get them to talk. Our best chance but an awful risk at the same time.

A pair of scientists rounds the corner in stereotypical white lab coats. I lean back out of sight and motion to Genna.

"Take them?" I whisper. She's leading this mission. It's up to her.

She nods so we wait at the ready. The pair of men stride along. The second they're past, Genna opens the door and we slip into the hallway like shadows. Before either of the men have a chance to realize what's going on, we're upon them. Arms locked around their necks and hands clamped over their mouths, we drag them back into the room and shut the door.

"Cooperate and no harm will come to you," Genna says at the ear of her captive. "Make a sound to alert others and it's the last thing you'll ever hear. Nod if you understand."

He does.

She loosens her grip on his mouth but not around his neck. Thankfully, she's put the fear in him and he doesn't make a sound. These are just scientists, not soldiers. Middle-aged, one stick thin and the other a bit pudgy. They aren't prepared for something like this.

"Is there anywhere you're supposed to be right now?" she asks.

"We're doing the rounds on our patients."

"Where's the nearest computer terminal to access the system?"

"At the end of the hall to the right. There's a nurses station."

"So it's manned."

"I don't know. People come and go to use it."

Genna meets my eyes. Dangerous, but what other choice do we have? I notice she's not coming directly out and asking where Erebus is. The less anyone knows the better, even if it might be an easier route to take. It could easily backfire on us if these two get loose.

"What sort of security measures are in this place?" Genna asks.

"I . . ." She squeezes her arms a bit more tightly about his neck and his eyes bulge as he claws at her arm. "Badges," he chokes out. "At every door. And codes for patient rooms."

So we need badges and patient room codes. Luckily, each of the men we've captured have a badge a piece. Not so fortunate, they're photo IDs. If someone is actually paying attention, it'll be pretty obvious we aren't them. If our luck holds, that'll be something.

The man in my arms struggles as I grab his badge and inspect it more closely. From a distance someone might be able to mistake him for me . . . if they're a bit near-sighted and old. And can't make out red hair. I look to Genna but it's clear the apparent obstacles are not changing her mind. We're doing this one way or another. She nods to me and hits both men with a blast of her bio-mech gun. The pair slump to the floor and we immediately start stripping off their lab coats and shirts. While we do so, Witty and Rosalyn clamber out of the air duct.

"Only two sets of clothes," Rosalyn points out and stands over my shoulder with a sour look.

Genna bunches up the coat and shirt in her hands and thrusts them at Witty. "You take one. You're our computer expert. We need you to get to that terminal."

Before anyone can suggest otherwise, I keep a firm grasp on the other set and say, "I'll be the second." Both girls level piercing gazes at me so I flash the badge at them. "Do either of you look like a Donald? I'll protect Witty and I can talk myself out of anything."

"Smug," Rosalyn says yet somehow manages to look proud.

"And true."

I strip off my tan shirt and swap it for the white one along with the coat as Witty does the same. The clothes are a little big for me but Witty's look to fit. We make sure our badges are attached to the pocket of our coats and then at the all clear from Genna, step out into the hallway for the real test. I keep my steps unhurried and Witty matches my pace. I'd love to be running but that would sort of be a dead giveaway. My heart thunders in my chest but I do my best to keep my muscles loose and relaxed.

It's a long hallway but we don't meet anyone else. We reach the first intersection where there's a nurses station just as our buddy said—a single corner desk with a phone and computer for easy access. For our next bit of luck, there's no one currently here.

"Work your magic," I say quietly.

Witty slips around the desk to the computer. I remain vigilant beside him, one hand braced on his shoulder as I also keep an eye on what he's doing. He plugs a USB flash drive into a port and the show begins. His fingers fly and he mutters nonsense under his breath as he opens black windows with white text filled with code I don't understand. But whatever it means, it must make sense to him because before long he's out of the black windows and into what looks like a program tracking the patients in the facility.

Just as footsteps come up the hall. Witty's muscles lock up under my grip and he gives me a frantic look.

"You're tech support," I whisper at his ear. "You know

how to play that part. Don't be shy. And I'll play the stupid person asking you what you're doing."

Easy enough.

The footsteps come closer and I worry as sweat gathers on Witty's brow. Before those footsteps reach us, I start to talk to make sure it doesn't seem like we're picking up a conversation the second someone shows up.

"I swear, I don't know what button I hit," I say and give Witty's shoulder a squeeze. He's in safe hands. "Should I have tried turning it off and turning it back on again?"

"That wouldn't have helped," Witty mutters but a little louder than he probably would if it was actually just the two of us. I give him a wide smile.

"But you can fix it, right?"

"It's going to take me a bit. You really screwed this thing up."

"Great."

The footsteps turn the corner and reveal a very tall man with wide shoulders. He's in a white lab coat same as us but it stretches tightly over his chest. He looks more the type to hold patients down during . . . whatever it is they do here. He stops, looks at us both, then approaches the other side of the desk to wait.

Challenge number one. You were born for this, Hawk old boy.

"Sorry, it's going to be a bit," I say and gesture with my free hand to Witty. "I, uh . . . well, I'm not sure what I did actually."

"You somehow deleted the algorithm on the passcode," Witty growls.

"I have no idea what that means."

As we talk, Witty pulls up schematics of the building while running a search for files on Erebus.

"It means no one can log in until I fix it," he says.

I smile at our new companion. "Like I said, it's going to be a while."

"Well, it better not be too long," he says and glances at a flashy watch on his wrist. "The inspection's starting in less than an hour and we need to finish our rounds before Draco gets here."

It's quite the effort to keep that benign smile on my face. Draco's coming. In less than an hour. There's a pounding in my ears and Witty goes pale. The man's eyes latch onto that and he frowns. Instead of ignoring Witty's reaction and making it more obvious, I clap Witty on the back.

"It's okay, don't sweat it," I say. "I'm sure you won't have to deal with him again."

The man points between the pair of us. "You've met Draco before?"

"Oh, yeah. Right in the middle of a tech crisis no less. Our pal here was sent in to help." I shake Witty's shoulders for emphasis. "That dragon has a temper."

"So, I've heard." The man relaxes again but—seriously, he needs to go away.

Surprisingly, Witty comes to the rescue.

"It's hard to work with you two talking," he says in a flat tone and keeps clicking away on the keyboard.

"You might as well find another computer," I say quietly to our buddy. "I'll stay here and keep people clear. You do *not* want to see him when he's angry."

Witty levels such a glare at me that I want to clap and give him an acting award.

At long last, the man gets the hint and walks down another hallway in search of a computer he can use. As soon as his footsteps disappear, I lean in close to whisper, "You did great, pal."

But Witty shakes his head. "I looked up Erebus, I looked everywhere..."

I look at the screen and see a schematic for the entire facility. It's then that I realize why this place is called the Fields. There are fields of cells—cells upon cells upon cells, hundreds, maybe thousands—hidden beneath the sands of Nevada. Smack dab in the center is a large room labeled "portal."

Now the color goes out of my face. "Please tell me he's here."

"Transferred three days ago," he says weakly. "On outstanding warrants from France."

France.

"To some place called... *Maison Bêtes de Gévaudan*. Did I say that right?"

He's not even in the same country.

"What do we do now?"

We... what on earth *can* we do? Our target is gone. If we can even get out of the States, we'd have to somehow get into France which is currently on lockdown. Then find this *maison*... place... thingy. Everything—sneaking onto Knox's computer, getting arrested, breaking into this place—has been for nothing.

"Are you absolutely sure?" I ask.

He nods and pulls up the record of the transfer order along with the detainer signed by the French *Spartiate* that took him. He's gone.

"I am not leaving here empty-handed," I snarl.

Footsteps sound nearby and I look up to see who it is. I catch sight of the same man that approached us earlier quickly turn about and walk away from us. My eyes narrow on the spot where he vanished before scanning the hallways around us. Something's not right.

"Witty." I pat him softly on the back. "Get back to the duct. Go quietly."

His eyes widen and he frantically looks around. "What is it?"

"I think we've been made. Go."

He immediately gets up and walks a bit too fast to be inconspicuous. I move a bit more slowly after him to check the ways behind us. There's no one. I catch up to Witty as a pair of guards round the corner up ahead. I grab Witty's arm to pull him to a stop.

"I forgot my badge," I say loud enough for the guards to hear. "Let's go back."

We turn around—my heart pounding in my ears—and walk as casually as we might away from the guards. Passing through the intersection of the corridors, I'm about to take another hallway when more guards appear. We move to the next but then there are more guards and more until they block every exit. As they come closer, they draw their bio-mech guns.

Alarms sound through the building.

We have to run.

"Hawk Mason!" a familiar voice shouts from the hallway on my left. My heart plummets into my stomach.

Swiveling about, I find Spartan Knox standing alongside the guards with his arm in a sling. The breath leaves my body and I can feel the bars of a cage closing in around me. I tried to cover my tracks but they must have found out who I was looking for when I got into Knox's account. Perhaps we thought too highly ourselves to believe we could infiltrate the Fields and find our target. Now Erebus is gone and we're trapped.

I won't give up without a fight. My fingers twitch and drift to the back of my waistband where a bio-mech gun rests against the base of my spine.

"Come quietly, son," Knox says.

"I'm not your son."

If we could get to one of the hallways and not in the open of this intersection, we might still have a chance to make a run for it. I can take on a pack of guards myself. Maybe I can at least be a distraction so Witty can make it out and let Genna and Rosalyn know where Erebus went.

"I don't know what crusade you're on," Knox continues, trying to talk me down. "But this isn't the way. I can help you. But you have to let me."

"Like how the IMS helped Jason Marsden?" I respond while keeping an eye on the surrounding guards. They haven't fired even though that would be the easiest way to end this standoff. We're at their mercy right now. I can see Witty shaking out of the corner of my eye. "Did you look into him like I said?"

"I did."

"And?"

"What happened to Jason was tragic. I won't lie, things could have been handled better. And the IMS *will* do better. I promise you that."

"Are you making that promise? Or is the IMS? Because the promise of a werewolf doesn't mean much to them. We both know that. And you know this is wrong but you'll just stand back and let it happen. I'm not willing to do that. No matter what it takes, I'm going to free the werewolves from this nightmare, even if that means working against the IMS."

He doesn't say anything for a long moment and I know. Even if Knox is telling the truth and wants things to change, they won't. Not with Draco in charge and people that think the same as him in positions of leadership. The status quo will never change until we force it to.

"You aren't going to back down, are you?" Knox says. The disappointment in his voice is plain.

"I can't."

Knox raises his hand and gestures to the guards beside him. Just as they fire, I throw Witty and myself to the ground to avoid their blasts. The hairs on the back of my neck stand on end as the pulses pass within inches. Before I can get to my feet to make a break for it, a fight erupts down the nearest hallway. I grab Witty's sleeve and yank him up to run out of the intersection through the bio-mech barrage.

Dashing into the hallway leading to the duct, I almost trip over a few unconscious bodies on the floor. The last man of the group crumples to the floor, leaving Genna and Rosalyn standing fierce above them.

"Come on!" Genna shouts.

The duct isn't too far, but even if we reach it, the guards

will be only steps behind us. Unless we can find another exit, we won't escape.

Guards appear at the other end of the hallway. Genna, Rosalyn, and I open bio-mech fire as we scrunch up against the walls or go low to avoid the answering pulses. But there's too many. I check behind us and find that way also blocked, Knox standing in the background as the guards surge towards us.

Trapped again.

"Drop your weapons! Hands behind your head! On the ground!" The commands blur together in an angry swarm of shouting from the guards.

There's nothing we can do. There's too many of them.

We drop our guns, put our hands behind our heads, and slowly sink to our knees. The guards advance and my last hope shrivels in my chest.

Everything was for nothing. None of it changed anything.

And I'll be subjected to the serum again.

Jason bleeding out in his cell flashes before my eyes.

No. Not like this.

A booming explosion sounds from somewhere in the facility and the lights flicker overhead.

"What the hell was that?" one of the men shouts.

Another explosion follows it along with shouting in the distance. What the—

Dust falls from the ceiling as a third explosion shudders through the floor beneath me. Some of the guards keep their eyes on us but the rest are looking up and down the hallways. Shouts pass commands and a group breaks off to run in the direction of the noise. They don't get far before something strange happens. Every single guard in the hallway freezes like twitchy puppets. On stiff legs, they form two orderly lines on either side of the hallway, turn about to face each other, and then aim their bio-mech guns at each other.

Their confusion is evident as they shout to each other.

"I can't stop my body!"

"What's going on?"

"Don't shoot me!"

"What's doing this!?"

Then without warning, a sharp wind blows through the hall as they all fire and the two rows of guards collapse to the floor.

In the stunned and confused breath of silence, I rise from the floor. Myself, Genna, Rosalyn, and Witty are the only ones left conscious. When the last guard falls, a glimmering light sweeps in from the other end of the body strewn hallway.

Merlin—truly the magnificent—appears in a blaze of white light. It shines from the depths of his eyes, flows off his white robe, and flashes like sparks of lightning from his long beard. He even holds a gnarled staff in his hands with a gleaming green gem nestled in the top.

He walks to one of the bodies near his feet and soundly clunks the end of his staff on the man's head.

"I never liked you," he says and his voice booms.

"Merlin!" Genna cries. I've never seen her so relieved before. "You came!"

"Hawk was right," he says gruffly and gives me a singular nod. "And I've wanted to destroy this place for ages. Let's make a mess, shall we?"

"Wait!" I jog up to him along with the others. He's

amazingly cool right now and yet also a bit hard to look at. I feel like I need to shield my eyes. "Draco's coming soon. We have to get everyone out of here."

"The wolves," he says as if to himself and strokes his long beard. "And go where, my young ginger friend?"

"Anywhere is better than here." In a spur of brilliance, I remember what I noticed on the building schematic earlier. "There's a portal in the center of this place. If we can get them there . . ."

Genna lays a hand on the blazing wizard's arm. "We can send them to the unknown."

I blink. "What?"

"Canada," Rosalyn says softly and her voice is nearly drowned out by the alarms going off in the building. "Our old home."

"The compound in Seattle isn't big enough, not since we stuffed it with more wolves from the Watch Guard," Genna explains. "But we can make the old compound work and we won't be found there. Merlin, can you do it?"

He nods. "We must congregate at the portal and I will draw them to us. Follow me."

I expect him to lead us down the corridors but he faces the closest wall, points the end of his staff with the gem towards it, and blasts it asunder in a hail of debris and plaster dust. I throw up my arms and close my eyes to shield myself from the blast.

Witty coughs and rasps, "A little warning next time? Please?"

With the way clear straight through the wall, Merlin strides ahead and obliterates another wall as if it's nothing. Blinking against the cloud in the air, we hurry after him. Well,

I guess no one can expect where we're going to show up since we aren't using the usual means for getting around this place. Merlin must know exactly where he's going because he hardly even pauses in his march through the facility. Any guards or scientists we meet, he either blasts away or has them shoot themselves with their bio-mech guns.

I've seen the power of Blessed. I've seen the power of a majestic class dragon.

But a Magus—it's a thing all its own.

We at last reach the doors to the portal room. Merlin points that mystic gem of his and the dragon's barrier practically melts away. One more blast and we're through.

The room is a large dome with a black arch in the center up a few steps almost exactly like the one in the middle of Underground. The black stone is etched with golden dragon script that gives a faint glow. The air around it shimmers with an odd bluish light. Merlin walks to the base of the first step then stops and slams the end of his staff into the floor where it remains standing upright. He tilts his head back, raises his arms to either side, and closes his eyes.

"Guard me," he says. "This will be tasking enough as it is without interference."

Genna gestures to us and the two entrances to the room. Rosalyn and Witty head for the north one while Genna and I converge on the south that's smoking slightly from Merlin's blast. A tingling sensation crawls over my spine and I glance at Merlin as light radiates off him. I don't have the faintest clue what he is anymore or what he can do. He's a terror unto himself. No wonder people remember the stories of Merlin.

"Here they come," Genna says under her breath.

And they do. Waves and waves of guards and personnel trying to stop us. But this is what I trained for. I've been craving combat for months and at last I'm able to unleash myself. My shots find their marks, my punches meet my opponent's pressure points, and my feet remain swift and sure. I'm good at this, I always have been. It's a routine varied with calculations and instinct. It's a dance.

Next to me is Genna, a whirlwind of precise fury and chaotic energy. Now more than ever I feel a kinship with her in the midst of battle and revolution. She knows who I am and what I am and has never shied away. She's my friend. She's my comrade. She's my pack.

Genna holds out a hand during a lull in the fighting. "Watch yourself. Here they come."

Like wolves on a scent, the ragged and tired prisoners come rushing through the hallways. Genna and I stand back as they flock in droves to the chamber. I don't know how Merlin did it but he's busted them out and guided them here.

It's a miracle.

Yet also terrifying.

Some come crying, some shouting in anger, others with no emotion whatsoever on their faces. One by one they filter into the room from our entrance and from the northern one as well that Rosalyn and Witty defend. In fact they keep swarming in until the room is full to bursting. A few guards manage to slip inside and fighting breaks out in the center. Genna and I muscle our way to the brawls and knock out the guards.

We're doing it. I can't believe it. We're—

A roar shakes the very foundations of the facility and reverberates in my head. Everyone freezes and a deadened silence falls.

That's the roar of a very angry, very powerful, majestic class dragon.

Draco's arrived earlier than expected.

"Merlin!" Genna shouts. "Whatever you're going to do, do it now!"

He picks up his staff and holds out a hand palm first towards the center of the archway. His light dims and the air shimmers more brightly in the portal.

Then nothing happens.

Genna and I shove our way to Merlin's side. "What is it?"

The blood drains out of Merlin's face. "There's . . . not enough juice. Not for this many people."

Rosalyn stomps over to us practically spitting. "Why didn't you say anything earlier?"

"I was busy being magnificent!"

"I'm going to wring your sorry—"

Another roar thunders overhead. I swear it's even louder this time. Draco has to be right on top of us. We have seconds to make a getaway.

"Do something!" I shout. Panicked voices echo behind me. "Do anything!"

Merlin rolls up the sleeves of his robes and sucks in a long breath. "This is going to hurt."

He tips the staff closer to the archway until the gem touches whatever magic is trapped within and shines like a beacon. Vibrations in my ears drown out all other sound, even that of Draco's ferocious roars. The air around me suddenly has a frosty nip to it and the hairs on the back of my neck stand on end. I grab Genna's hand and look to the ceiling as bits of stone sprinkle my head.

I can feel my body being tugged towards the apex of that portal as the ceiling crumbles amidst screams. Long talons shred apart the stone and cement. Large chunks give way and crush the few unfortunate souls standing directly beneath. The smell of blood fills my nose and my eyes water.

The last thing I see of the Fields is Draco's elongated snout pushing through the gaping hole above me, his deadly teeth, furiously bright eyes, and a spout of fire.

Then we vanish.

My lungs compress and my breath leaves me. My muscles go limp for a moment and I fall to my knees on a dusting of snow and hard, frozen earth. Cold air engulfs me, bringing out goosebumps.

Canada.

Merlin sways on his feet. "That . . . hurt . . ."

He coughs and blood burbles out of his mouth before he crumples into the snow.

30

Phoenix

When I leave the hospital, I do so silently and in the early hours while Charlie is still asleep. When he wakes, he'll find a letter at his bedside along with Scholar's pendant. It'll protect him now, and I can't risk Scholar coming after me if she's able to somehow sense where the pendant is. I've cut the lines of my safety net. There's no turning back.

Goodbyes are shared with the rest of my team. I pass each of them individually on my walk out. Theo gives me a hug and small piece of chocolate cake for the road. Alona gives me a proud nod, stoic as ever. Melody wraps me up in her arms so tight it's hard to breathe, but then she too lets me go. John waits for me out in the parking lot. I expect him to say goodbye too but it turns out he's adamant about going with me to see the director.

"No Spartan goes it alone," he says and that's that.

John takes the wheel as I brace myself for the phone

calls I'm about to make. I've prepared speeches in my head but I've never been good at making them.

I dial Jefferson's number first.

"Phoenix?"

"Hey, it's me."

"How are you? Melody sent word about what happened. I've been worried."

I close my eyes and take a deep breath. "It was a wake-up call, that's for sure, but I'm okay. And Charlie—well, he's recovering. He should be okay too."

"Any word on Epsilon?"

"Not yet."

"I'm sure they'll find her soon."

"Yeah."

"So, what's up, kid? Why the call? Have anything new for me?"

Here's the moment I've been dreading. "Jefferson, when I said the attack was a wake-up call, I meant it. You might not know all the details, but Ashley was directly involved. This escalated out of control because of the pressure put on the werewolves. I've been biding my sweet time while lives have been ruined. It's time I put an end to it."

"Phoenix..."

"I'm done hiding."

"You better not be saying what I think you're saying," he says, his tone sharp.

"I'm going to Director Knox to explain everything. I don't know what'll happen next and I don't know when I'll be able to contact you again."

"Phoenix, wait—"

"I've done my waiting. Too much of it."

"*Stop*. Listen to me," he says urgently. I do my best to keep calm and not be persuaded by his mounting panic. "You go in there and you'll never come out again."

"This was always the plan, you know that. I appreciate everything you've done for me."

"You're not ready!"

"I'm close enough to ready. I've made up my mind. I'm going through with this."

"Don't, please. I've already lost one daughter."

I almost choke on my next words. "I might not have known my father, but I'm glad I had you as a dad. Take care of Hawk for me."

"Phoenix!"

"Goodbye, Jefferson."

I hang up before he can say anything else. My heart's already breaking enough as it is. I can't bear to hear his pain. And I know the next phone call is going to be even worse.

I dial Hawk.

The phone rings and rings but he doesn't pick up. I reach his voicemail, hang up, and try again. I do this three times without success. Either he's away from his cell or not picking up on purpose. But I've run out of time. Minneapolis surrounds us and we'll be at Underground soon. I call one more time and wait for his message to leave a voicemail. It beeps, and I wet my lips before I begin.

"Hawk, it's me. I wanted to talk to you in person but I'm out of time. I wanted to say . . . to say I'm sorry. You were right. Maybe I have been a coward. I never should have taken those wolfsbane bullets. I hope someday you'll forgive me. If you try to call me back, there's a good chance

I won't answer. I'm going to the director. I'm going to tell him everything. Maybe I'm not quite ready to be the cure for the werewolves, but I can't sit on my hands anymore. I don't know what'll happen but I expect I'll be out of touch for a while or . . . well, I don't know."

I swallow and pinch the bridge of my nose. "I just want you to know that I've never been ashamed to be your sister. You were never a burden or luggage or whatever you might think. Being your twin is, and always has been, a privilege. I love you, dog breath. Nothing will ever change that. So this is goodbye, I guess. So . . . yeah. Goodbye."

I hang up and slump in my seat, eyes glued to the trees alongside the road as we pull up to the power park.

"Are you okay?" John asks.

"No."

We don't speak again as we enter the power park, take the long chutes into Underground, and walk through Merchant Square and the colonnade. I've prepared myself as best as I can for this encounter. Everything I've endured has been leading up to this. I wonder how long it'll take to make a cure—because after everything, this better work. Will the director have me escorted to some hidden facility straight away? Will my fears and Jefferson's warnings be proven wrong?

Or will Draco show up to take me away?

I swallow my fears and keep my head held high as John and I enter headquarters and pause before the receptionist.

"We made an appointment with Director Knox," I say before she can ask.

"He'll be with you as soon as he's out of the emergency council meeting. Please take a seat."

Emergency council meeting? What's happened?

John takes a seat on the cushioned bench but I can't stay in one place. I stand beside him, shifting from one foot to the other, occasionally pacing, and worrying my bottom lip. I had hoped we'd be able to go straight into the director's office once we got here. I don't do well with waiting. The clock ticks out the slow minutes until the receptionist's phone rings. She answers then gestures for us to go on in.

I walk side by side with my Spartan leader and mentor. I'm glad he came with. His presence is reassuring. We walk up the stairs, down the hall, and pause outside the door to the director's office.

"Are you ready?" John murmurs.

I nod and knock on the door before I'm allowed to change my mind.

"Come in."

We march inside and find Director Knox standing behind his desk, an open folder in his hands. He looks frazzled. It's not a common thing for him.

"I must say I'm surprised you stayed in the lobby and waited to be invited up," he says and slaps the folder onto his desk. "I thought you'd march in here like you usually do."

I fight the frown trying to work its way onto my face. "No, sir."

"I guess you've learned some control being with the Spartans." He sighs and takes a seat, gesturing for us to do the same.

"Is Draco around?" I ask, feeling the need to confirm that the majestic dragon is far away at the moment I reveal my secrets.

"He's out dealing with the situation, which is why I

assume you're here. Although, I don't know how you managed to hear about it. Unless . . ." He sets his forearms on his desk and looks me over with a critical eye. "Did your brother contact you?"

I blink. "What?"

"Phoenix, I need you to be honest with me."

"No, he hasn't contacted me. I was trying to get ahold of him but he wouldn't pick up. Sir, what's going on?" Is Hawk in danger? What happened to him after I left Seattle? If he's in trouble now of all times . . .

His eyes narrow for a moment before he leans back in his chair. "So, you don't know."

"Don't know *what?*"

"I'm sorry, but Draco left specific instructions you aren't supposed to know. I can't tell you."

I launch out of my seat. "You're the *director*. Sir, if something's happened to my brother—"

"Mason, sit down."

"Sir—"

He jabs his finger at me. "This is exactly why Draco didn't want you to know. You don't listen."

Glowering, I promptly sit again and wait. He looks like he's really struggling not to roll his eyes or shout at me, but I don't care. I was prepared to turn myself in, I really was—but that was before this. If Hawk's in danger somehow . . .

Director Knox straightens and smooths out his lapels. "If you didn't come here about *that*, then why are you here? The message left for me said it was extremely important."

Well, now what do I do? I look to John but he doesn't give me any indication of his opinion. This is my choice. I study my hands, think fast, and debate with myself. Hawk has always been my number one priority. He's my brother, my twin. But how many times has it backfired in my face when I'm so focused on my family and pay no heed to everyone else around me? What about Ashley? What about Jason? What about the werewolves? Will I always keep putting this off because there's a chance Hawk could be in trouble?

Hawk doesn't need a babysitter. Whatever's happened sounds bad—especially if Draco is hiding it from me—but the best way I can help Hawk is to do this.

So, I straighten in my chair, take a deep breath, and say, "Director, what I'm about to tell you could change everything."

Then the door flies open. A young man rushes in with a memo in hand, slams it onto the desk in front of Director Knox, and leans in close to whisper something as well. The director lets out a choice swear word. I don't think I've ever heard him swear. The news must be very bad. His eyes dart back and forth as he reads the memo. John and I wait on the edge of our seats waiting to hear what's happened.

"Go code whiteout across the board." He picks up the phone on his desk and starts dialing immediately while still talking to the messenger. "Find me Specialist Jaeger and round up the rest of Spartan Team Sierra at the hospital. Go."

The man runs out of the room as the blood drains out of my face. A code whiteout. I never dreamed it would get this far. It's a code I've never wanted to hear uttered. A code whiteout is the very last resort. It's the signal that the werewolf populace in general is no longer under control. It means every single werewolf goes into lockdown and surrenders themselves. It means they're treated like monsters again—

even killing could be authorized. And he wants the rest of our team rounded up. What's *happened?*

"You two stay put," Director Knox says sternly and then ignores us as if we aren't even in the room anymore. We wait and listen to what we can of his phone call.

"Director Dunham, this is Director Knox. I'm already rounding up Sierra per your request. What are we looking at?" There's a pause and I can barely hear someone talking on the other end but can't make out the words. Dunham . . . I know that name. She's the director of the Dreamland Division in Nevada. It's the United States' militarized IMS base. "Yes . . . that's right. I've just issued a code whiteout up here as well . . . What? Did you say *Merlin* did that?" He closes his eyes.

Wait, *Merlin*? I share a look with John and see my own confusion reflected there. John told me about Merlin before. A Blessed with amazing powers who is most likely the source of the bio-mech guns and possibly even the serum itself.

"Yes. I know." The director glances at John and me. "Of course. I'll get it setup."

He slams the receiver into its cradle. Whatever's happened, it sounds like Director Dunham has requested our team specifically. Maybe that means I'll get some answers then.

The director runs both hands down his face looking haggard. I don't fail to remember that his own brother is a werewolf. What does that mean for him? But then he straightens and becomes the commanding leader he normally is.

"A classified IMS facility has been attacked," he announces. "The werewolves have really forced our hand this time."

"What facility?" John asks calmly.

He temples his fingers together atop his desk. "The Fields."

I've heard the rumors of it. The place where the bad werewolves are sent. Werewolves like Jason.

"Are we being dispatched, sir?" John asks.

The director doesn't say anything to us. My stomach clenches. This isn't good. Moments later the door to his office opens and several field agents I recognize enter carrying bio-mech guns. John and I launch to our feet.

"I'm sorry but you and your team are going to be detained for the time being," the director says.

My heartbeat travels into my throat and my hands curl into fists as my body readies for a fight. What is this? Why are we being targeted? We've done nothing but put our lives on the line for the last several months. Heck, I was ready to turn myself over to the IMS to do whatever I could to aid the werewolves. Things aren't supposed to go like this.

John rests a hand on my forearm to keep me in check. He looks over his shoulder to the director. "We have a right to know what's going on."

"This is just a precaution. Cooperate for the time being. I'll be in to talk with you both shortly."

I really, *really* don't like this.

"We can't talk now?" I demand.

The barrels of the bio-mech guns turn slightly in my direction.

"*Go*, Mason."

John squeezes my arm. "Come on."

At his word, I sigh and gesture for our guards to lead the way. One takes point while the other two bring up the rear to box us in. They take us out of headquarters and follow a very familiar route to a sealed door. Dread washes through me as we enter the penitent cells. What on earth is going on? Our guards at least take us to the interrogation rooms and not the cells themselves. John and I share one last look—letting each other know we'll have one another's back no matter what—before we're put into separate rooms. The door locks behind me and I'm left alone to stew.

I stare at the white table and chairs with restraints before beginning to pace.

A breach at the Fields.

Jefferson and I sent Jason—the rogue werewolf from Moose Lake—off to a treatment facility for werewolves. It's quite possible he was sent to the Fields. And Ashley said he killed himself. Guilt weighs heavily on me. My hand was in that. Maybe if I hadn't been so afraid, if I had done more, it could have been prevented. Then there's the fact that Ashley knew about his death. Had Epsilon somehow found out about it? Have the lamia infiltrated that far into the IMS that they know about patients in a facility that even the rest of the IMS is unaware of? Or was it merely a lie? One to push Ashley completely over the edge?

And now something's happened with Hawk. Director Knox thought I'd be storming into his office full of wrath if I knew. Someone hurting Hawk would definitely do that. Also, someone caging Hawk would do it. Was Hawk shipped to the Fields without anyone telling me? But no . . . the director wanted to know if Hawk had contacted me. Then *what* happened? And who breached the Fields?

Could . . . could my brother have had a part in it?

No. That's not possible.

Is it?

I'm not sure how long I wait until the door opens and Director Knox walks in holding a laptop.

"Take a seat."

He gestures to the chair with the restraints. The one Dasc used to sit in. The director doesn't move until I finally take a seat. He assumes the spot I used to take in this room and sets up the laptop facing me on the table. At the click of a button, a video conference opens. A woman with blonde tresses, a severe expression, and crisp suit peers at me from the laptop screen.

"This is Director Dunham from Dreamland in Nevada," Director Knox explains. "She'll be joining me in this interrogation."

My face burns. "Interrogation? About *what*?"

Director Dunham clears her throat and starts to read off a piece of paper. "At 0400 hours this morning, the facility known as the Fields was breached. A transport van that had been carrying a prisoner to the facility was hijacked and its GPS used to locate the facility. A group infiltrated the base through a tertiary vent and accessed classified information. Five individuals involved in the attack have been identified including Genevieve Barnes, Rosalyn Graham, Aaron Wallowitz, and Hawk Mason."

My blood runs cold and I can't remember how to breathe. I feel the eyes of both directors pressing in on me. I gap like a fish but can't make a sound. *Hawk*. Hawk working with those traitors. I just . . . I can't. The ground is crumbling away beneath my feet.

"The fifth is a potent Blessed that goes by the name Merlin and until about six months ago worked at the facility.

All are deemed highly dangerous. Agents are given clearance to proceed with extreme prejudice if they are encountered."

Meaning kill them if they have to. Someone could kill Hawk. And Genna and Rosalyn and Witty. How—what—why—Hawk! I knew he was angry but *this*? There's no wiping the slate clean. There's no burying this secret in the woods. No matter what I do, I don't think I can save my brother. Not that it's going to stop me from trying.

Then there's Merlin. A "potent Blessed." I wonder if the reality is that he's a Magus, one of those who actually drank the blood of a dragon. If he's been the source of the biomech guns and the serum and whatever else, he has to be truly powerful.

My hands shake. I have no idea what to do.

And I realize something else. They've put me in an interrogation room because of what's happened. They think I'm involved somehow.

"Let's cut to the chase," I say quietly. "Why do you—better yet *how*—do you think I had a hand in this? That's why I'm in here, isn't it?"

Director Knox folds his hands together and bows his head.

The other director, however, gives me a shrewd look. "Your brother was involved in the assault," she says. "I've heard you two are close—very close. And you visited him in Seattle shortly before this attack."

I work my jaw before saying, "If I had known he was going to do something like this, I would have walloped him while I was in Seattle. I would have stopped him. Besides, one of my teammates was with me the entire time. There's no way I could have been conspiring with Hawk or whatever you think it is I did."

"And which one of your teammates was that?"

"Spartan Charlie Jaeger."

The director looks up and down at something and her eyes narrow. "It looks like he was severely injured and is in the hospital, unable to currently testify. How convenient."

I slam a fist down, jostling the computer and leaving a dent on the tabletop.

"Mason," Director Knox says sharply.

Ignoring him, I say, "This puts my brother in danger and I would *never* put my brother in danger. Anyone who knows me knows that."

The door to the room swings open abruptly and Draco steps inside in his human form. "I couldn't agree more."

My heart pounds painfully in my chest and I plant both hands on the table as if ready to spring into action. I haven't seen him in over a year but he hasn't changed in the slightest. Still overbearing, still intimidating, and of course, not aged since he's an immortal majestic class dragon.

He shuts the door behind him and rounds on me. "However, I must say the timing of your rendezvous was rather coincidental, don't you agree, Spartan?"

I'm not afraid of him but I'm afraid for my brother. Hawk's in a very bad position and there's little I can do from here to aid him. Had he been coerced by Genna and Rosalyn to help them? What pushed my brother to this breaking point? Why this attack?

"I was on leave," I say. "I hadn't seen my brother in months. Of course I went to see him."

"And did he act oddly in any manner?" Director Knox asks.

Yes. "No."

"Is that the truth?"

Not at all. "Yes."

"Did you know he was in contact with Genevieve Barnes?"

"Like I said, if I had, I would have done something about it," I growl. Everything about this boils my blood. Hawk was in cahoots with Genna? Impossible. It couldn't happen. "She shot me in the back. She let Dasc go. If I knew she was around, I would have found her. And I refuse to believe Hawk was working with her. If he was involved, he must have been blackmailed or—"

"Your brother was arrested last week," Director Dunham says. "He was caught attempting to access classified records using a co-worker's account. When he was found out, he tried to make a run for it. In the aftermath, we discovered discrepancies in his serum records that were covered up by one Aaron Wallowitz. Then another of his co-workers stepped forward with evidence that your brother was also involved in a conspiracy against several IMS directors. He was arrested and en route here, actually, when the transport was attacked by Barnes, Wallowitz, and Graham. They released him."

I can't take a full breath and become dizzy. "No, they . . . he wouldn't . . ."

"You honestly didn't know your brother was committing treason?" she demands.

I clamp a hand to my chest and dig my fingers into my skin as if I could reach my pounding heart.

"I don't believe she did," Draco says. "Questioning her further would be pointless."

Shock after shock—I don't understand Draco's willingness to let this go. He's never been this compassionate. And Hawk. No. I can't believe it. I won't. I won't believe a word of it until I can ask him face to face and demand the truth. If Hawk is in league with Genna, then that means he's in league with Dasc.

"Regardless, we need to secure this breach," Draco says. "The escapees disappeared from the facility and we need to locate them."

"I believe I have a lead on that front," Director Dunham says from the laptop. "It appears our assailants weren't only after our charges here. They were looking for someone in particular. A werewolf that was extradited to France from our facility."

"France is on lockdown," Director Knox says. "They're even barring contact from other IMS divisions. It's become a political nightmare."

"Their borders mean nothing to me," Draco snarls and makes to march away as if he's going to fly straight to France. If they were searching for this particular werewolf, then there's a very good chance that's where Hawk and the others are heading.

"The noble classes will disagree with that," Director Knox says before Draco can hustle out the door. "But there is another way in than by force. And I think you know it, too."

The majestic turns slowly about on Director Knox, his bright slit eyes boring into him. To his credit, the director doesn't cow under such a fierce glare.

"They might not let you or other IMS agents in," the director continues. "But they would let in a Benoit... and a Constantine."

Three seconds of silence tick by before I realize what he's saying.

"Who exactly are you suggesting?" Director Dunham says sharply.

"Spartan Theo Benoit—and Spartan Phoenix Mason who just so happens to be one of the last Constantines."

I swallow. Does everyone know about my history and decided not to tell me? At least this might be the first good thing to come out of my lineage. If the director is right and the Constantine name would have enough pull to get me into France...

"Absolutely not," Director Dunham objects and looks like she's ready to claw her way through the computer screen. "Mason is still under suspicion."

"I'd be happy to hear a better plan."

Neither Draco or Director Dunham say anything.

Knox sighs and leans back in his chair. "Unless you want the French to handle it, meaning they'll most likely execute Barnes and company as soon as they're found and we'll never find the hundreds of other werewolves they freed."

My throat closes up at the word *execute*.

"We don't even know if France will let them in," Draco says.

I can sense Director Dunham winding up to object as well.

"I'll go," I say quickly. "They'll let Theo and me in. They have to."

Draco narrows his eyes. "And then?"

"Then I'll bring them home."

31

Hawk

I don't know what to think when Genna shows me a long row of cages in the depths of the compound she's brought us to. This place she directed Merlin to—the Unknown—is a hidden base in the northern reaches beneath the surface of a Canadian forest. It's a complex series of tunnels stretching a good half mile. Some of the tunnels are in good condition with nice, smooth walls, but many have collapsed or have bits of roots hanging down that catch in my hair when I pass.

And according to Genna, this is where she grew up.

She stares at the long row of cages in this chamber near the center of the maze of tunnels. Her eyes are hard. Once before she told me that Draco and the adults would lock them up as children whenever they shifted. They would remain in these cages until they could shift back. It took Genna seven months to figure out how to do it.

"Are you okay?" I ask. It's a dumb question but I feel something needs to be said.

"I'm okay," she says quietly, arms crossed over her chest. "I just never thought I'd come back here. I thought I had left this place behind for good."

"And you're sure we won't be found here?"

She nods. "After this place was attacked and partially destroyed, the compound moved. I told the IMS about the newer one but not this place."

"And what about Dasc?"

"This is the last place he'd look for me." She turns away from the cages. "Come on. We don't have time for this."

She stalks away from the cages and down one of the crumbling tunnels. The place is packed with ragged werewolves in every corner. The place isn't big enough for them all, though, so some are in the surrounding woods and caves. Trying to organize everyone has been chaotic to say the least. But we can't stay here long. We walk past the new inhabitants of this abandoned place and to a small room with a single twin bed. Merlin is snuggled beneath the covers and a fire burns in a rocky hearth near his feet. He looks terrible. Every so often he coughs and speckles of blood coat his lips. His skin is far too pale and he somehow has two black eyes from handling the portal. He's been in and out of consciousness for the last hour since we arrived here but he explained a bit deliriously how he had to give of himself to make the portal work. He's in this condition because he sacrificed himself to save not only us but the werewolves currently housed in this bunker.

Witty and Rosalyn stand near his bedside as ever watchful guardians. Across from them sits a young man with bleach-blonde hair and a long pointed nose who checks Merlin's pulse and dabs at the poor wizard's lips with a wet cloth.

"How's he doing, Kelsey?" Genna asks and sits on the edge of the bed beside him.

"Not so good."

Kelsey's eyes flicker to me. He's not friendly to anyone except perhaps Genna. He was one of the children raised alongside Genna, whose family was butchered by vampires under Dasc's order when he attempted to escape in his youth. He's one of the werewolves that eventually rallied to Genna's cause and fled Dasc's influence. I don't know what to think of him but Genna trusts him and that's enough for me.

A long sputtering cough fills the silence and Kelsey dabs at Merlin's lips. The old wizard gestures weakly with one hand for Genna to come closer.

"I'm here," she says softly and leans in.

"I must . . ." He coughs again.

"Must what?"

"Must have . . ."

We lean forward with ears perked to catch his words. He must have what? Should we bring his magical staff to his bedside? Is there some healing remedy he knows of to help him?

"My music," he finishes on a wheezy breath.

Oh. I should have guessed.

Genna smiles and pats his aged hand. "Yup, you'll be better in no time." Out of her pocket she pulls his iPod. She must have been carrying it this entire time. I can't imagine why. She unwraps the earbud cords and he puts them in his ears, hands shaking. It's an odd sight as he squints at the screen and pages through his music until he finds what he's looking for. He sighs and settles into the bed as he closes his eyes.

"I guess we all heal in different ways," I muse quietly.

With Merlin set to take a nap, the rest of us stand and gather round the fire pit. We look to Genna, the one always with the plan.

"What's next?" Kelsey asks.

Her eyes hold to the flames as she ponders the question. "We have to get to Erebus before the IMS. I'm sure they know who we're after by now."

"Well, we can't take Merlin," I interject. "I don't think he's going anywhere for a while actually."

"It's dangerous," Rosalyn cuts in, "leaving him here with the others. If they figure out what he is—there's enough hatred for the serum that they might do something stupid."

"Then he needs guards to stay behind to protect him," Genna says.

She doesn't even have the chance to ask for volunteers before Rosalyn says, "I'll watch over him."

My eyebrows aren't the only ones that go up in surprise. Rosalyn rarely shows any sort of attachment let alone affection for anyone. Her act to volunteer first is out of character. She must gather as much from our expressions because she shrugs and says, "I've grown fond of the withered, old bat."

"Fair enough," Genna says.

Kelsey holds up a finger. "I can watch over him as well."

But Genna shakes her head. "The werewolves trust you, Kelsey. I need you to help keep them in line. Witty can stay to help Rosalyn." Which means— "Hawk and I will go to France and infiltrate the werewolf prison."

"Just the two of you?" Rosalyn says sharply. "You're going to need help."

"And we'll have it. I still have friends in the right places and with the right faces."

Rosalyn rolls her eyes. "Fine. Don't expect me to cry over your grave when you wind up dead."

"Oh, I expect crying from you but more likely tears of joy."

The two girls inch closer to each other, Rosalyn with a deep frown and Genna as stoic as ever. They size each other up. Really? Now isn't the time.

"At least you wouldn't have to worry about me stabbing you in the back," Rosalyn says. They're maybe two feet apart and I expect one of them to try strangling the other at any moment.

"Don't be ridiculous," Genna says. "You'd go for a frontal attack if anything."

"That's true. But I don't see much point in it."

The pair of them tense and my eyes jump between them waiting for someone to throw the first punch.

Instead, they wrap their arms around each other in a tight hug and pat one other heartily on the back.

"You better come back," Rosalyn growls but there's a soft edge to it like it's done only half-heartedly. "Don't die and leave me alone with these losers."

"Don't worry," Genna says with a glimmer of a smile. "I'll come back alive to give you a fighting chance of trying it yourself."

"You're the worst."

"I'll miss you too."

They pull apart and give each other a sharp nod. From that exchange, you might not think it but there is shared mutual respect in its own odd way—a way that tends to make me uncomfortable to be honest. I feel like I can count on Rosalyn until she decides to stab me or something.

Witty goes in to hug Genna next. Out of everyone, he looks the closest to tears. Genna whispers something to him and he nods before they pull apart. All of this saying goodbye stuff is making everything feel too final.

"Geez, guys," I say. "Next thing you know, we're going to be taking our last looks at family photos before going out in a ball of fire. This is too heavy for me."

The girls say in unison, "What?"

"Never mind." I move to Witty, shake his hand, then pull him into a hug all the same. "Thanks for helping me see the light, pal. I owe you, more than you know."

"Probably more than *you* know," Witty says and chuckles.

"Touché, computer whiz." We pull apart and I clap a hand on his shoulder. "Try not to let Rosalyn kill anyone while we're gone."

"No promises," Rosalyn mutters.

Genna clears her throat. "There's no point waiting any longer. Keep the place afloat while we're gone. With any luck, we'll return with the key to a cure. Dasc will never control us again."

"Good luck," Kelsey murmurs.

"You as well."

With the last of the goodbyes out of the way, we leave Merlin's healing chamber behind, stride through the tunnels, pass rooms filled by the werewolves we rescued, and into the cold outside. A chill wind whips my face and my gaze travels south. Phoenix is out there somewhere. I wonder if she's heard what's happened yet. I wonder what she thinks of me now.

"Are you ready?" Genna asks and passes over a pack Kelsey had prepared for our expedition.

"As I'll ever be."

We shift at the same time and our thick fur coats protect us against the chill as we sprint away from the Unknown and into the snow kissed expanse before us. It's already been a long day and it's about to become much longer but we don't have time to rest. Our only hope is the IMS will have just as much trouble getting into France as we will with the current lockdown. As a matter of fact, I don't even know how *we* are going to get in. I assume Genna has a plan. There's always something cooking in that brain of hers.

I have a lot of time to think about her as we run and run and run for what feels like endless miles through barren fields and pine forests. Before Genna freed Dasc from Underground, I felt a bond with her. We were kindred spirits. Then I assumed the worst of her when the attack on Underground happened. And now . . . I understand why Witty and Rosalyn follow her. She's made of stern stuff, I've always known that, but I've also come to see how much she believes in her cause and how much she's been willing to sacrifice for the people she's trying to save. Even now when we're both exhausted, she doesn't show any sign of slowing down. I keep pace knowing the stakes, even when my paws grow sore, my muscles ache, and I'm thirsty beyond belief.

Our unfaltering limbs carry us on until we reach a small outpost tucked away in the woods. There's not much except for a cabin and flat field beside it where a Jeep is parked. Genna shifts and gets to her feet out of breath. I follow her lead and she walks cautiously to the cabin.

"What is this place?" I whisper.

"An IMS listening post."

"*What?*"

A bright light shines out from the cabin window and a woman's voice booms. "Don't move! Hands where I can see them!"

I cast an angry glare in Genna's direction and raise my hands in compliance. Genna does the same but doesn't look the least bit surprised or wary.

"Let me whisper in your ear," she shouts at the window.

I sure hope that's a code or something, because otherwise I have no idea what's going on.

"And say what?" the woman shouts back.

"The pack survives."

The light flicks off and moments later the door opens to reveal a tall brunette wielding a high-powered hunting rifle. She rests the stock of it on her hip and cocks her head. Unlike us, she's dressed well for the cold climate in a fur-lined parka.

"I thought you were in the States," the woman says and is immediately friendly. I guess their conversation was a coded phrase. Does Genna have an IMS agent in her pocket up here?

"Change of plans," Genna says and walks forward to meet this mysterious agent out in the middle of nowhere. "We need a plane to France and fast."

Not surprisingly, the woman's eyebrows shoot up at our request. "You're joking, right?"

"Top priority mission, Zeredah. We're racing against time."

"Hmph." Zeredah's gaze turns to me. "And who's this?"

"A friend. Zeredah . . ."

"I get it, I get it. Wait here a second."

She disappears into the cabin and takes her sweet time doing whatever it is she's doing. I want to yell at her to hurry up. We've already wasted enough time running here.

Genna clears her throat. "So, about Zeredah…"

A different woman stalks out of the cabin but in the same parka and clothes as the one before. Instead of being brunette and pale, this woman has golden brown skin and sleek black hair.

"Alright, let's go," she says with an accent—I'd guess Mediterranean.

Then I realize—

"You're a shapeshifter?"

She pauses and looks confused. "Yes."

"But—"

Genna grabs my arm and hauls me towards the Jeep. "Not all monsters are monsters, remember?"

Zeredah gives me a sly smile and takes the driver's seat. I'm pushed into the back as Genna sits shotgun. I've got so many questions but realize they aren't truly important. We have a time sensitive mission to focus on.

"Buckle up," Zeredah says. "I drive like a crazy person."

I manage to click the buckle just before she guns it into the woods. Well, she certainly wasn't lying. We lurch every which way as we fly over roots and hills and plow through bushes. There's not really a path but this Zeredah—this shapeshifter—seems to know where she's going. Despite the lack of road, she seems alarmingly at ease and even rests an arm alongside the window leaving only one hand on the wheel.

"So. France," she says. "You *do* remember what happened the last time you went there, don't you?"

"I'm not likely to ever forget," Genna answers darkly.

"You're a different sort of crazy, you know that?"

"So I've been told."

The shifter clicks her tongue. "And yet . . . you always seem to pull off the impossible."

"It helps when you have an excellent smuggler on your side."

Zeredah preens at the compliment and we almost drive right into a tree.

"Okay. France," Zeredah says and doesn't appear concerned in the least that she's almost rammed a tree and barely skirted a sharp drop in the last five seconds. "Exactly what part of France are we talking about?"

Genna let's that question sit for a bit before she says, "Maison Bêtes de Gévaudan."

The shifter makes an odd sound and slams on the brakes so hard that my seatbelt almost strangles me. She gives Genna a sharp look before flooring it again.

"You really do have a death wish," the shifter mutters.

Silence lapses inside the Jeep before the women start discussing the specifics of our in and out strategy. Apparently they are very much aware of the conditions in France and the best routes to take. There's little I can offer for input apart from the obvious. I've never been to France but I've caught rumors every so often. None of them are good—well, from my point of view anyway. They say the country is relatively monster free. People just don't talk about how that came to be. I'd rather not think about it too much. My mind needs to stay focused on the things I can change and handle, like keeping a low profile and not attracting attention.

After an hour of driving, we finally reach an actual road but it takes us several more hours to reach a city. We keep on driving with our final destination the Toronto Pearson International Airport. I can't help but keep my eyes on the clock.

"How much of a lead do you think we have?" I ask.

Genna glances at the clock herself. "Not much of one at this rate. If they've figured out who we're after, then the French guards could already be in position waiting for us. But if the French are still keeping to their lockdown—which I suspect—that should buy us some time as the IMS deals with the political garbage."

"And what about *us* getting around the lockdown?"

"Don't worry," Zeredah says. "I've been doing this a long time. I'll get you through."

"How?"

"By lying very, very carefully."

That doesn't sound particularly comforting. There are security measures against shapeshifters in a lot of areas, including international airports, whether it be hidden sensors or IMS agents stationed in key areas. With new advancements in technology, the IMS has been closing the noose more and more tightly every year.

At long last we reach the sprawling complex of the international airport and Zeredah drops us off at the main entrance.

"Wait near the doors for about ten minutes," she instructs us. "Then I'll come find you."

Genna exits without question so I follow before the

shapeshifter drives away. I suddenly feel very exposed and vulnerable. Inside the doors I spot a legion of security guards and checkpoints.

"Do you really trust her?" I ask Genna in an undertone.

"I do," she says and walks casually to the doors.

I guess that's that, huh?

One of the most dangerous and complicated parts of this journey ends up being almost flawlessly easy. We wait by the front doors pretending to go over our paperwork and studying a map of the airport itself. Ten minutes later, a steward marches up to us, apologizes for the wait, and assures us we still have our seats for the one-way flight to France. She escorts us through the airport, bypassing certain areas of security, and then tells us to wait while she gets her superior to escort us in. She disappears and another woman appears with a wink to take us onto our waiting plane. At the boarding ramp there's a man hovering behind the flight attendant checking everyone in. Our hostess pauses and has us wait while she goes to "talk to a supervisor." Two minutes later, the man at the desk is paged away for some emergency and our escort reappears with a smile to let us know everything's been taken care of.

Within probably the shortest amount of time anyone has ever had to wait in an airport, we board our jet with tickets pressed into our hands by our escort, and take our seats. The steward disappears once more and a minute later, Zeredah, in what I assume is her home form, takes a seat next to Genna with a satisfied sigh. She gives me a winning smile.

"Told you she's good," Genna says under her breath.

"No kidding."

Well, I guess I can understand why Dasc likes working with them. They're immensely handy to have around. Though, I don't understand exactly why some shapeshifters work with the werewolves in the first place. What do they have to benefit from it? The question sits sour in my stomach as the jet finally starts to move and we take off.

It's a long flight with nothing to do except think about our next step. I'm used to exhausting thoughts but this is almost refreshing in a way. I'm at least doing something instead of sitting on the sidelines worrying about myself and my sister.

Phoenix.

I keep trying to picture her reaction to the news of what happened in the Fields. Will she even be told of it? Or will the IMS cover it up like the Kentucky riots that Spartan Knox told me about? If she does find out, will she think me a monster? Someone—or even something—worth hunting down?

I'm left unsettled the duration of the flight. There had been growing distance between my sister and me but now there's a gaping divide. I don't know how we'll ever find our way back to each other across it.

Genna lays a warm hand on my arm. "Are you all right?"

"Are you?"

"I've been down this road before," she admits quietly. "And I've already experienced the very worst thing that could happen."

"With . . . right." When she went to France with James years ago looking for Erebus before.

When she had to kill James in the end.

"I can't help feeling that . . ." She trails off and stares straight ahead. "That I'm coming full circle."

"Let's steer clear of déjà vu, okay?" I don't mean it in any joking manner. Repeating Genna's past is something we definitely don't want.

I turn my arm over so I can thread my fingers through hers and hold her hand.

Over the next hours of our very long flight, the three of us do our best to catch some shut eye. With my mind analyzing and determining all the ways things could go wrong, it's difficult to fall asleep but eventually I'm too exhausted to do anything else. A dead sleep takes me and I don't wake until Zeredah prods me in the shoulder.

"We're about to land. Hold onto your hats."

Not necessarily about the landing but what kind of reception we'll meet on the ground. Zeredah has done her part well but with France in lockdown, there's no telling what kind of security measures they'll have waiting for us.

My fear is answered when we walk out of the jet bridge and find a group of security guards checking everyone coming off the plane. While they look like normal security, I notice one of them discreetly holding a scanner like the ones used to collect data off probation rings.

"That's a problem," I say under my breath.

"Give me a second," Zeradah mutters and bends down facing Genna and me to retie her shoe. As she does, the hood of her jacket falls over her head. I can see the shade of her hand change skin color, her long hair turn bright blonde, and she shrinks inside her jacket. When she straightens once again as a different person, Genna tuts under her breath.

Zeredah is a bodacious blonde with pouty lips and squinty eyes.

"You know what agents hate?" she says in a voice much snootier sounding that her own. "Lots of attention. I'll catch up with you outside." She swings about her curtain of hair and saunters forward with one hand held daintily at her side and the other planted on her hip.

Genna and I hang back as other passengers disembarking gawk at her or flat out point.

"I don't get it," I say.

Genna sighs. "She went celebrity to draw everyone's attention and create a crowd."

"Oh. So . . . who is she now?"

"Paris Hilton."

"Oh. I have no idea who that is."

"That's probably a good thing. Let's go."

Sure enough, Zeredah—err, Paris Hilton—is certainly drawing eyes and getting the attention of the guards who realize there's a disturbance going on. Zeredah pauses in the middle of the exit and puts on a show, asks one of the guards about her luggage, and even signs an autograph. She's putting herself at risk getting so close to the agents but now's our chance. Genna and I skim by on the fringe of the crowd with the guards momentarily distracted and make a hasty exit into a nearby airport coffee shop.

We wait in line while keeping an eye on the people walking past the glass walls of the shop. I notice one of the guards from the group peel off and start searching the crowds. He must have spotted us slipping away.

"Genna."

"I see him." She sweeps the coffee shop. "Bathrooms."

"There's no exit that way."

"I know."

The guard sees us just as we turn to walk calmly to the back of the shop and enter the men's restroom together. Thankfully there's only one person in here. He gives us a shady look and leaves without even washing his hands. With him gone, Genna gestures wordlessly to me to stay where I am next to the sinks while she hides behind the door. I grab a wad of paper towel and ball it up in my hands.

Then we wait.

Three seconds later the guard slips into the bathroom and his hand immediately goes for the weapon at his waist when he sees me standing there.

"*Ne bouge pas!*" he shouts.

It's the only thing he gets to say. Genna flies into action, disarming him and putting him in a headlock. I jump in to shove the paper towel in his mouth before he gets the chance to shout anything else. Snatching his gun off the floor, I clock him hard in the head with it and he slumps in Genna's arms. Moving quickly, Genna gets her arms under his armpits while I lift his legs. Together we haul him to one of the stalls and hear the bathroom door swing open again. Genna immediately flips the unconscious agent over so he's facedown on the toilet seat and props one hand up on the other side as if he's holding the bowl. Footsteps turn the corner a second after I drop his legs and put a hand on his back. My face turned away, I making a retching sound.

The person stops directly behind us and we look back innocently at our onlooker. He's not a guard, just some tourist from the looks of him. Alarmed is too gentle a word for the look on his face.

"Doesn't handle flying well," I say for his benefit using my best British accent. Having an American accent could make us stand out and we don't need that.

Genna stares at the man to make him move away as I rub slow circles onto the agent's back. Once the man moves off, takes care of his business, and leaves again, Genna and I get to work. We strip the sorry sod of his badge, weapon, and jacket before propping him up on the toilet seat, locking the door, and slipping out from underneath. Hopefully that'll buy us some time.

We exit the bathroom and Genna slings the jacket over her arm. Thankfully none of the other guards have come looking for their companion yet but it's only a matter of time. We leave the coffee shop and make our way through the terminals. We only make it so far before we spot several airport security guards getting calls on their radios and immediately start scanning the crowds.

"Move," Genna breathes, and pulls me towards a baggage claim area to hide. I peek around the side of the bulky revolving belt and see three guards making directly for us. There are no exits close by. We'll have to run or fight our way out. Either way, we'll be drawing too much attention to ourselves and make it impossible to slip away.

A hand grabs the jacket on Genna's arm from behind.

"Give me that."

I spin about to find Zeredah in her home form again. She slings the jacket on and Genna presses the badge into the shifter's hand a second before the guards round the corner. Zeredah lays a hand on both our shoulders and jerks her head at the guards.

"*Est-ce que vous pourrez m'aider?*" she says. The guards nod and hurry to assist.

Genna and I are soon in cuffs and escorted out of the airport. Many eyes follow us pair of criminals but Zeredah remains in command, even waving off other agents that stop to help. Heck, she even gets one to bring a car around. Genna and I are put into the back seat—Zeredah has far too much fun pushing our heads down so we don't hit the car frame. She takes the driver's seat but unfortunately an agent remains in shotgun to ride with us.

The shifter and IMS agent exchange a conversation in French that goes right over my head. She laughs, he chuckles, he points something out to her, and she inputs an address in the GPS computer on the dashboard. They chat some more and we move through the narrow roads of Paris.

Zeredah eventually sighs and looks sadly at her side seat companion. "Sorry about this, love."

A bio-mech pulse rushes through the car and the agent slumps in his seat. When we stop at an intersection, she adjusts him so he looks like he might be taking a nap.

"I'm impressed," I say.

"As you should be." She digs out a pair of keys from her pocket and tosses them to us. "I got the location of this prison you're looking for."

"And?" Genna says as she scoots backwards to grab the keys and start undoing her cuffs.

"It's on an island off the northwestern coast. Pierre here—" She jerks her head towards the agent currently drooling with his face pressed against the window. "—even gave me directions to avoid construction. Oh, and we better hurry. From what he told me, there's a contingent of Spartans headed there now. We either get in and out before they get there or—"

"We wind up prisoners ourselves," Genna says. "Or dead."

32

Phoenix

When Theo gets the all clear from the French IMS branch to let our Spartan team into their country, the look on Draco's face could melt stone. Furious is such a small term for such a scary dragon. But Director Knox was right. The French IMS, despite being told about the possible infiltration into their country, refused to let any outsiders in. Yet when Theo laid his cards on the table, the French put up no resistance to our request to follow the werewolf lead. The Benoit family has a lot of pull in France, much more than I would have anticipated. They're famous. They're heroes. And the name Phoenix Constantine also got their generous attention.

"We'll send a contingent of *Spartiate* to meet you on the border," Director Chevalier says. "Follow them to base where you will be briefed. *Bonne chance.*"

"Roger, control," Theo says.

"*Bienvenue à la maison.*"

"Merci beaucoup."

It's a long flight and will require a pit stop on an aircraft carrier to refuel before we reach our destination. While en route, we watch video Director Dunham sent us so we have a better idea of what happened at the Fields as well as what they have on Merlin should we confront him.

And what we've seen is enough to turn my stomach.

The first thing we watch is the assault on the facility—Hawk and Witty hacking a computer, Witty *walking*, and getting surrounded. Thankfully there's audio. My eyes burn when I listen to Hawk explain his side to Knox, about setting the werewolves free, Jason Marsden's fate, his lack of faith in the IMS to do the right thing. I don't know how he found out about Jason, but his words ring in my head. A fight breaks out, the four of them are surrounded again, and it looks like the end of the line for them until a bright light blows out a wall and another figure emerges.

"Merlin," John informs me, clearly recognizing the Blessed—or Magus—he once encountered.

And when Merlin appears, the tide of the battle quickly turns. Eventually the camera feeds cut out from the explosions and gunfire but they escaped, we know that. Whether injured or not is anyone's guess. And we know Witty got into the system to find the location of a werewolf known only as Erebus. Why this werewolf? Why such a bold move? They must have known what was going to happen once they did this. The code whiteout wouldn't have happened otherwise.

After watching everything on the attack itself, I dig into the records on Merlin. Melody leans over my shoulder on one side as we watch surveillance video from his room. He's been there a long, long time. From what we figure, the facility was built at the same time he came in some thirty years ago. There's not much video from when he first arrived, just fragments here and there of when he went into the lab of the facility for tests. There are, however, reports about how they contained him by a careful balance of keeping him weak enough so he didn't have the power to escape and strong enough so he didn't die.

"Mercy above," Melody breathes beside me as we find a recent video from just before he escaped.

The Merlin here hardly looks anything like the one that burst into the Fields to save my brother and the others. This one is ragged, bone thin, and lies like a corpse on the table he's strapped to. I turn up the volume as he pleads with the orderlies.

"Please," he croaks. "*Please.*"

"It's okay, Merlin," one of the orderlies says while checking a monitor.

"You're killing me."

"We're not killing you."

"*Yes*, you are. Let me go. Please."

The orderly shakes his head as another one swaps out a full blood bag for an empty one to drain him. Merlin starts to weep and groan and fight uselessly against the restraints.

"You're saving lives," the orderly says before turning to one of the others. "Should we increase the sedative?"

"Last time we did that his heart stopped for two minutes. I'm not doing CPR again. Just leave him."

"Please!" Merlin howls. "Just kill me. Kill me."

"Shut up," the orderly says sharply. "Or I'll start talking about King Arthur again."

"Don't you dare!" Merlin shouts but his voice is thin, weak.

I'm staring at a broken man. I'm staring at my future. When I tell my secrets to Director Knox, I'll become the one strapped to a table with my blood being drained, too weak to escape but not enough to die. Scholar's and Jefferson's warnings are confirmed in a horrible way. This is what they wanted to protect me from.

Melody lays a hand on my shoulder and presses her lips into a thin line. She doesn't say anything but her pained expression tells me she's as distressed about this as I am.

This is the agency I've been fighting for. The one I put my faith and trust in. We're supposed to fight the monsters. We're not supposed to become the monsters along the way. And this . . . what I'm seeing them do to Merlin is monstrous. I don't care if he volunteered initially or not. It's clearly not what he signed up for.

When I look away from the screen, my eyes meet John's where he sits on the other side of the plane going through the same information.

"I didn't know," he says, a bleakness in his tone that makes him sound ashamed. "You told us you were warned but I . . . I didn't really believe it until now. I'm sorry."

"Don't be." I do my best not to worry my lower lip or look apprehensive even though that's exactly what I'm feeling. "It doesn't change anything anyway."

It doesn't, not really. As soon as I know Hawk is safe again, I'm going back to Director Knox. Sure, I don't want to end up like Merlin but . . . maybe I deserve it. I brace my forearms on my thighs and think about Ashley's fate, Jason's demise, and the werewolves with a target on their back. If only I had done more. I could have. I *should* have. It's my fault.

Charlie's face pops into my head with a scowl. He'd admonish me for thinking this way. He'd give me the kick in the butt I need. Now more than ever I can feel the void beside me where Charlie would usually be. I miss him. I miss him a lot. But it's also my fault why he's not here, isn't it?

I continue to watch the videos and try not to think of the pain Charlie's in or the pain I'll be in once I go to the labs. I watch one of the orderlies take pity on Merlin, sit with him, hold his hand, and even lessen the amount of blood taken to give him a break. But they want more. They always need more they say. This battle between monsters and slayers has been waging for thousands of years and there will never be an end to it. The good suffer, the evil thrive, and the world is lesser for it. But if the good don't suffer, if they don't battle day after day, then the world would be lesser still. There's always something worth fighting for but the fight takes its toll. I've learned that the hard way.

I sleep when I can but only manage brief stretches at a time. When I'm not asleep, I rewatch the video of Hawk at the Fields over and over again obsessively.

The Osprey shifts from its steady course and I listen as Theo talks with our escort that's arrived. They chatter back and forth in fast French and Theo relays the orders to Alona who shifts course to follow them to their base. Needing to better distract myself, I move into the cockpit to look out the windows over Alona's shoulder. Green fields, old roads, and buildings as small as pinpricks fill the land to the horizon.

"*Je suis à la maison*," Theo says and gives a heavy sigh as he stares out the windows as well over Alona's other shoulder. "I haven't been back here for a long time."

"Were you born in France?" I ask.

He shakes his head. "Born in Minnesota but we make trips to France almost every year. Haven't this year though. Been a bit busy, you know. Hydra and stuff."

"The usual."

"Yup."

He points to something far below out the window and Alona scowls at him as his arm cuts across her vision for a second. "My grand-mère helped kill Dracula right over there."

"Really?" I lean forward as the speck of a town flashes by out of sight.

"Earned national honors for that one."

"Why'd your family move to the States?"

He shrugs and smiles. "The vampires stopped coming to France. We cleared them out, then heard there was a big gathering in the States. The family figured they'd setup where they'd be the most useful."

"Well, that's dedication for you. So . . ." I angle my head towards him. "You ever hear of this werewolf prison we're heading to?"

His smile fades and face falls into shadow as he returns his gaze to the windows. "Rumors, none of them good. My family focused on the vampires, not the werewolves, but we heard things. Nasty things."

"I don't like the sound of that."

"France has a reputation," he says darkly. "The rougarous —err, werewolves—have never been given much opportunity for peaceful lives. They're usually either killed or shipped off to a prison."

"But the serum—"

"Didn't make much of a difference here. Not every country in the world treats monsters the same, Phoenix. France has been operating under a code whiteout since forever. They have some of the strictest laws regarding werewolves. But you know what France doesn't have?"

"A conscience?" I grumble.

"Werewolf attacks."

I don't respond. Theo sounds rather proud of his family's homeland even if I disagree with the country's policies. I also happen to remember that Dasc once said he had an investment in Paris so clearly this place hasn't been completely werewolf free if the alpha was strolling around. But considering the danger for werewolves, I wonder what on earth Dasc would even think worth it to come here for.

"Any other countries like this?" I ask.

"Romania's even worse. They have the Constantine Law there."

I raise an eyebrow at him at the same time my heart gives a painful ache. "I've never heard of it."

"Yeah, well . . . people don't really talk about it."

"What is it?"

He shifts on his feet as though uncomfortable. "Carrying the werewolf disease bears the death sentence, no matter what the circumstances."

I swallow and look away to the rolling green fields, a bright contrast to our dark conversation. So my ancestors have a law named after them under which werewolves are convicted for a crime they aren't even to blame for. Honestly, I wish Theo hadn't told me. The thought of it makes me feel unclean, as if that bloodshed is permanently affixed to my hands even though I had no part in it. That's my family's legacy. What other skeletons am I going to discover in that closet?

A deep voice comes over the radio. "Follow in, Sierra."

"Roger, following in."

"Keep on our tail. The fog is thick."

We continue on and the ocean opens up on our left. Ahead of us appears a wall of fog as our French comrades said. It seems oddly out of place with the sunshine but the closer we get, the darker it becomes. It's unnatural—or rather magical.

"Water sprites?" I ask quietly.

"That's my guess," Alona says. "Concealment fog for wherever we're heading." She switches her mic on again. "Control, are you going to tell us what we're heading into? I don't like flying blind."

"We're almost to our base," is all he says in reply. "The replacement for your sixth team member is waiting."

We share an apprehensive look and Alona turns off the mic.

"What replacement?" I ask.

Theo shrugs.

Alona looks sour. "I don't like the sound of that. They never said anything about a replacement."

John and Melody squeeze into the doorway behind us.

"What's our status?" John asks.

"We're about to get a mystery team member," Theo says

brightly. "Who probably isn't a Spartan or doesn't speak English. I just *love* surprises, don't you?"

I have a hard time considering anyone replacing Charlie. No one can truly replace him, but I'm sure the French want us to go in full strength, even if that means shoving an unknown onto us. I don't like it one bit.

"Prepare for descent," our French liaison says.

The aircraft ahead of us sinks into the fog and Alona follows. We eventually dip beneath the heaviest of the fog until it's a light misty gray over a lush landscape. The Osprey makes a slow descent as we crane our necks to look out the windows at the base we've come upon. There's a landing pad large enough to fit five Ospreys. A six-story building abuts the landing zone but the rest of the area is swallowed up by large trees with foliage already turning orange and red as the season heads into autumn. We touch down and the countryside is lost behind the dense copse of trees around the base.

"Let's move," John says in a solemn tone and Alona shuts down the Osprey.

We hoist our weapons and head out the lowered ramp to meet the French crew on the pad. They're a burly bunch in uniforms similar to ours except deep green in contrast to our stark black. Their leader wears a beret and steps forward to greet us. And trailing behind him is the last person I want to see.

"*Bonjour,*" the leader says and gestures to the man behind him. "This is your replacement to bring you to full strength."

Specialist Laurence Jaeger gives us a shady smile.

"You've got to be joking," I say under my breath—but not so discreetly as not to be heard. Theo and Melody nod in agreement beside me.

"They let you in?" John says flatly.

"You're not the only one who has contacts here," the specialist says and his gaze pauses briefly on Theo and me. "And you're going to need all the help you can get, so a little gratitude would be nice."

"I'm sure it would be," John says with no inflection.

The French leader holds his bio-mech rifle at ease in his arms but his brow scrunches up. "Is there a problem?"

"Not at all," Specialist Jaeger answers but then turns to us—eyes locked on me. "Is there?"

I don't trust myself to speak. John doesn't deign to give him a reply either and instead focuses on the French leader. "What's the plan?"

We're waved into the facility. Other agents move out of our way and clear room around a large operations table where a blueprint and map of France are spread out. I take note of the many men and women in the building looking haggard and a bit dead-eyed. I guess the situation has been taking its toll.

"We make for the Maison Bêtes de Gévaudan on an island off the coastline," the French commander says and points towards the northwest on the map. "It's a restricted rougarou facility. This is the first time outsiders have seen it. What you see does not leave here."

John nods. "Understood."

"We have been receiving strange reports from the prison since April and eventually lost contact. Every team we have sent to investigate has not returned. We suspect some of the shipments of prisoners were rerouted and used to transport other monsters—like hydra. If we are unable to secure the facility, we have orders to blow it."

"*Merde*," Theo says under his breath.

"Since April?" Melody asks. "Why are we only hearing about this now? It's been months."

The French soldiers shift on their feet and mutter vague words under their breath as the leader's eyes narrow.

Theo nudges Melody with his elbow. "This place isn't supposed to exist. And if anyone else knew that France couldn't contain its own facility . . ."

They'd be humiliated. Maybe even become a target for monsters sensing weakness.

"This is our mess," the French leader growls. "We'll clean it up."

I bite my tongue despite longing to throw a few choice words at these *Spartiate*. If they had asked for help sooner, we wouldn't be in this mess. If the hydra have been getting shipped out from their prison, their silence only made the situation so much worse. Of course, they wouldn't want to take the blame for the hydra fiasco. And they aren't cleaning up their own mess. We're here, aren't we? But it's the terms of this engagement that really worry me. I'm here to find and save Hawk. They're here to "secure it" or blow it up. Neither ends with Hawk getting out of here in one piece if he's managed to make it here already.

"We can't allow this to continue," the leader says.

"If you're so desperate to clean this up," Alona says, "why not blow it from a safe distance? You don't seem to have a problem killing werewolves here."

My blood boils imagining it.

"The prisoners are not our concern," he says. "But some guards might be alive as hostages. One of them is the director's son. We'd rather not destroy a facility if it can be helped, but if we cannot secure it, we will."

The *prisoners*. There's no plan to secure them, only the guards. I don't know if these werewolves have even committed a crime apart from being a werewolf. Either way, this isn't right. We can't just sentence those people to death. There has to be another way. I look desperately to John and the rest of my team. Each of them are stony faced and John spares me a single slow look. They know what's at stake. Not only the lives of the prisoners and any remaining guards, but my brother if he's come here.

"We have our own mission, I'll remind you," John says. "There's a prisoner that goes by the name Erebus. We have orders to locate and secure him along with other parties that may have reached the prison searching for him."

"We let you in on good faith. Your primary mission is our mission."

There's two beats of silence before John says, "Okay. Lead on."

The minutiae of the plan is explained, the briefing ends, and the French move out. John turns towards us and swipes at his nose with a stern expression. Got it. Our mission is still our primary goal. We'll back up the French but one way or another, we're going to find Erebus and secure the facility. No one's blowing up anything today.

It's a tense journey as we march through the thick trees to the beach where we find boats and diving gear waiting for us. Our teams take a boat each to infiltrate the facility.

We roll quietly over the open water and into the smothering fog. It's mid-afternoon but the sun isn't able to pierce or burn away the thick mist. It's definitely magical. After some time speeding along, I start to catch glimpses of the island. In the distance, over a series of large hills, I spot a decaying structure with turrets, ancient stone towers, and fencing lined with barbwire. The closer we get, the stronger the sense of foul, diseased magic becomes. The prison is rank with twisted yet powerful forces. I've never felt it so intense before, not even when that baby leviathan and its fellows came to attack Underground. Then I realize it's not only in the prison but in the waters beneath us. There's something—a lot of somethings—swimming in the dark water.

I tap John on the shoulder and gesture wordlessly to the bottom of our small boat. We're supposed to ride in through the fog out of sight of the beach but I can already sense those dark spots in the water slowly rising up to meet us. I think there's a good reason no one has returned from the island. I gesture in a fast circle to let my team know we have to move quickly. Specialist Jaeger's eyes are on me, suspicious as always, but I don't have time for him. My secrets are going to be revealed soon enough anyway. So let the specialist think what he wants. I don't care anymore.

After some silent gesturing, Alona steers the boat back towards land and we stick to the shallow waters, hunkering in the boat to keep a low profile.

"Sierra to Zulu and Bravo," John says quietly over the radio. "We've got hostiles in the water. Going for land side approach."

"Copy, Sierra. Identity?"

John looks to me but I shake my head. "Unknown." I hold up seven—no, eight—fingers. "Eight hostiles. Watch out for stealth attacks from below."

"Copy. Zulu is adjusting course."

"This is Bravo. We copy."

I keep my senses on high alert to monitor the threats below and the ones we're fast approaching. This whole thing feels like a trap and more than ever, I wish I had Charlie here to back me up. I trust him implicitly. If there's anyone I want watching my back, it's him. His uncle not so much.

We cut the motor on the boat and drift along silently through the wavering mist surrounding the island. Here and there it becomes clear enough to catch more glimpses of the fortress ahead of us once we pass around the bend and make a straight shot for the prison. The twisted presences I sense in the water continue to trail us like alligators waiting for the opportune moment to strike. They inch ever closer but I don't know what they are so I don't know if they have any ranged capabilities. Either way, they're getting much too close for comfort. I gesture to John to let him know the same. He nods, taps Alona on the shoulder, and we glide over to the shore.

Whatever's down there realizes that we plan to leave the water so they slingshot towards us. I motion for everyone to move their butts but whatever's down there is faster than we are. I leap out, splash into the water, and yank the whole boat onto the beach with Jaeger and Melody in the midst of clambering out as eight pairs of razor-sharp claws rise from the water. They manage to tear at the rubber edge before the water becomes a choppy mess with Theo, Alona, and

John firing bio-mech blasts into the beasts. I join them a second later.

Most of the monsters sink below the water, but one manages to rise up so we can see exactly what we're dealing with. Gray fish-like scales cover its abnormally thin arms and torso, webbing stretches beneath its upper arms and between its three, long claws that stretch towards us as if the thing desperately wants to tear us to shreds. Terrible, yellow eyes bulge from its sallow skin on its near humanoid face. The rest of it is hidden beneath the water's surface. I don't recognize it at all.

It ducks beneath our fire, moves like a lightning fast eel, and rushes Melody who's the closest to the water's edge. She fires point blank into its face with her bio-mech gun. It jerks backwards but manages to snag a claw on her sleeve. I'm only a step behind her so I grab Melody's shoulders and spin her out of harm's way. In the same movement, I twist on my heels and send my closed fist into the ugly thing's skull. It flies out over the water some twenty feet before landing with a noisy splash.

"What the hell was that?" Specialist Jaeger whispers.

None of us respond but we back up to the safety of land with our guns aimed at the water. I tug the boat up until it's completely out of the water and—hopefully—out of harm's way. As soon as we're into the tree line, we pause and Melody sinks to one knee to inspect her arm.

"I got nicked," she mutters and red blood trickles down her forearm.

"So, no one knows what that was?" the specialist says more urgently.

We shake our heads and Alona helps Melody bandage her wound.

"Just a cut?" John asks quietly.

"I think so," Melody says. She takes a sniff of her arm. "I don't think there's any poison from whatever that was but we can't be sure. John, that thing . . . that's a new breed of monster."

"I know." His jaw forms a hard line and he readjusts his bio-mech rifle tucked into his shoulder. "If you feel off at all, you tell us."

"I'm fine."

"Maybe right now, but we don't have a clue if that thing has special abilities. We're running into this blind."

A new monster. There hasn't been a new monster since—well, since the old days of Echidna's reign. This more than anything is proof of her return. Monsters don't just pop out of the ground. They're made. So we really don't have a clue what we're about to come up against. But why here? Why a French werewolf prison? I'm not afforded a chance to think on it as we move into the woods surrounding the prison.

There's an eerie silence across the island. No bird calls or buzzing insects break the silence. Only the soft sounds of our passage. Whatever's taken up residence here has scared away or killed everything. And somewhere in the depths of this nightmarish island is a prisoner Hawk and Genna are looking for. Why? What compelled them to do something so drastic to find this Erebus? I don't see any way this situation ends well, especially with Specialist Jaeger shadowing my footsteps. I wonder if that's the real reason he's here. I bet he'd like to capture Genna but maybe he's also here to make sure I do what I'm supposed to if Hawk shows up. How far am I willing to go to protect my brother? If I had asked myself that question a year ago, I know what my answer would be. But now . . . now I don't know. Maybe protecting my brother also means stopping him.

"Sierra is moving to secondary infil," John says over the radio.

"Copy. Bravo and Zulu approaching northern secondary infil. We'll meet you topside. Going radio silent in the tunnels."

We walk softly in a staggered line until we reach the secondary infiltration point we agreed to earlier. I sure wish we could have gone for our first plan of going over the south wall from the water. Now we're forced to take the storm sewer tunnels. Awesome. John makes a claw motion down his face and we pull on our breathing masks and goggles. I adjust mine into place and activate the breather before giving a thumbs up like the rest. Even Specialist Jaeger has his own pair. He must have borrowed a set from the French *Spartiate*. We don't have a clue what's in here and France has a couple monsters that can excrete poisonous gas. Best to be prepared.

I bend down to inspect the massive iron-wrought grate on the tunnel entrance. It's rusted and flaky but very solid. I dig my fingers around the edge, plant my feet and give it a good tug. It gives a loud groan. Once I've managed to prop it up enough, the rest of the team adds in their muscle and within short order we have it removed. We pause at the entrance and John slowly shifts into a crouch, flicks on the low beam light at the end of his bio-mech rifle, and steps carefully inside. Theo turns to me and shudders to convey his disgust before following after. Alona's next, followed by Specialist Jaeger, me, and Melody brings up the rear.

Our boots tread through an inch of stagnant water and even with my mask, the putrid odor of it makes me wrinkle my nose and take shallow breaths. We spread out enough so we don't bump into each other as we're forced to walk at a slight crouch to avoid hitting the ceiling. Water—and probably worse things—drip from the stone overhead and I feel it plop on my helmet or splatter on the back of my thick tactical gear. Nothing moves around us. No rats. No bugs. No nothing. But there are bones. Small ones that crunch under foot, the remains of mice and other critters eaten away with rot. Big bones I do my best to avoid but can't help but notice their shape and size. Wolf bones, human bones, and lots of them. Scraps of fur clump along the edges of the water and cling to the soles of my boots.

John halts and holds up a closed fist to signal us to do the same. We wait on high alert as he moves forward cautiously to something blocking half the tunnel ahead. At first it looks like part of the tunnel collapsed but then I see a face in the stone—what's left of one anyway. Half of it has been . . . well, *melted* away. It's the crumbled remnants of a gargoyle. Beneath its one intact claw of stone lies a broken and twisted skeleton of a wolf. This place must use gargoyles for additional protection and a werewolf made a run for it. Looks like things didn't end well for either of them.

Motioning with two fingers, John points to the ground next to the gargoyle's remains to alert us of danger. He skirts around what it is and when I come up to it, I realize there's a gaping hole in the bottom of the tunnel. Strings of greenish goo hang down into it—the same stuff we found on those hydra eggs. I guess the goo—along with the melted half of the gargoyle—confirms it. There are definitely hydra here. I can feel it. This place is saturated with the stench of foul magic. It's everywhere, covering everything, but ahead of us I can sense an even more powerful source like a core to this nightmare. It's massive and if I had to bet, I'd say it's a fully grown hydra waiting for us.

33

Hawk

The boat Zeredah procured for us moves smoothly across the fog blanketed waters surrounding our destination. It has the colors of the French military and Genna responds on the radio with all the right phrases to avoid suspicion. Having a shifter is very handy, even if she almost got caught getting us both the boat and codes. Now it's just Genna and me. Zeredah remained on the shore making arrangements for us to leave the country—if we can make it out of the prison first.

Our little patrol ship makes a wide loop for the island. The other patrols are staying far away from the island. That doesn't make sense. It's almost as if they're keeping a distant eye on their prison, too afraid to approach.

"I've got a bad feeling about this," I say quietly.

The eerie fog wraps around us and a shiver goes down my spine. No, I don't like this at all.

Genna eventually cuts the motor and we glide silently

along. Every now and then I get a glimpse of the island through the mist and stone towers amidst the distant trees. The boat slows to a crawl and we stay low waiting for the gentle current to bring us in.

The boat bobs oddly and we come to a complete halt. Then we start moving backwards.

"Something has us," Genna says sharply.

We pick up our guns and scan the water. The very top of long claws stick out of the surface and grasp the edge of the boat. Genna fires a bio-mech pulse. An angry hiss and splashing water answer in reply but we keep getting dragged backwards. She fires three more times and the boat drifts to a stall.

We remain tense and quiet on the lookout for more of those claws. I can't see a thing beneath the water's surface. There's no telling what could be swimming below us. The island's shore is in sight but still far enough away that this predicament makes me extremely uneasy.

There's a loud pop and I swivel around as the boat rocks. Air is leaking steadily from a puncture in the rubber lining somewhere and lets out a whistle as it escapes. I walk cautiously to the edge to find the leak and culprit when long, webbed claws come shooting out of the water from my left. I turn and fire but it's already upon me. I catch a glimpse of slimy gray scales and bulbous yellow eyes before I'm sent tumbling out of the boat and into the water. I can hardly see as the monstrous thing rakes its claws over me and drags me into the inky depths.

Survival instincts kick in and my inner wolf comes snarling to the surface. My limbs contort in a blinding flash of pain but then I'm paws, fur, and teeth. I thrash and claw at what has hold of me before I manage to sink my teeth into its scaly skin. Its shriek under the water puts my fur on end and it quickly lets go. I kick with all four limbs and break the surface. But there are more of those things. They slither around me in the dark water and grab at my paws. I do my best to kick them off while keeping my head above water.

A snarl sounds to my right and Genna's furry black head gets sucked under the surface.

I dive down through the wicked claws and bite at everything in reach. Their hisses bubble at me but their shredding claws disappear into the blackness. I breach the surface again and tread in a circle only to realize that Genna hasn't surfaced.

Sucking in a deep breath, I plunge below and pedal fast in the direction I last saw her. Movement in the water pushes me back but I swim on, clawing carefully forward with a paw until I brush scales. My teeth sink down and the creature thrashes away. My shoulder bumps into another shape. I prepare to take another chomp out of whatever's in front of me until wet fur brushes my nose.

It's awkward maneuvering under the surface when I can hardly tell which way is up. Somehow I manage to get myself positioned under Genna and doggy pedal as hard as I can for the surface. Cold air hits my face and I lap it in. Genna starts to sink again but I thrust my head under her foreleg, shift her partway onto my back, and make a bee line for the shore.

The water churns behind me but I keep my eyes straight ahead. Muscles straining, and cuts smarting ever so painfully in the salty ocean, the beach feels like miles away. Sharp claws and teeth nip at my back paws.

My forelegs catch sand and I pull myself up out of the water with Genna dangling off my back. I trot forward and she falls heavily to the ground.

Foul hisses follow us out of the water.

I spin about with fangs bared and a threatening snarl ripping out of my throat. Three pairs of yellow eyes glare at me and back away to sink slowly into the water.

What the heck are those things?

And more importantly—

Genna's not breathing.

I grab hold of my human self and shed my fur in a blaze of pain. My trembling hands roll Genna onto her side and water flows out of her jaws. I'm in the midst of adjusting her to perform CPR on a wolf when she sputters and coughs out the rest of the water in her lungs. I keep a hand on her back and my eyes on the waterline. Whatever creatures attacked us are keeping their distance. I guess they don't like werewolf bites. Good. I've finally found something useful for it.

Genna waves a paw at me and slowly sits up. She shivers and transforms into her human self, her black hair clinging to her face.

"Are you okay?" I ask, my hand still on her back.

She nods and coughs a bit more. "Unlucky hit to the head," she rasps. "I've never seen those things before."

"Me neither."

"Echidna's been busy."

New monsters. Now that's something I'd rather not consider. It's hard enough keeping the monsters in check that we know how to fight. New ones that we have to figure out? What a nightmare.

I scan the forest covering most of the island and the prison itself looming like a shadow in the near distance. No beach patrols, no signs of lookouts on the prison walls, and monsters in the waters surrounding this place.

"I'm pretty sure the French aren't in control of this place anymore," I say.

Genna gets to her feet. "I think you're right. It makes sense."

"How so?"

"That's why France is in lockdown, especially from other IMS branches. What sort of embarrassment do you think that would be for them if other people discovered they had a secret werewolf prison and then lost control of it?" She rolls her shoulders and coughs some more into her hand. "But then that begs the question, who's in control of this place now?"

"France has been on lockdown for a couple of months at least. If the French haven't been able to retake this place in that amount of time, I'm guessing something pretty nasty."

"If so, there's a good chance Erebus isn't actually here." Her dark eyes go cold. "They transferred him a few days ago. How could they bring him here if it's been overtaken?"

The pit of my stomach sinks. She's right. "We have to at least check. We have no idea what's going on."

"Let's watch our step."

Clearing her throat one last time, she begins the hike along the rocky beach. I shiver against the wind that blows through my wet clothes and follow after. There's no telling what could be waiting for us inside or if Erebus is even here or alive. I'm sick of hitting roadblock after roadblock. *Pixies*, he better be here.

We move quietly within the shadow of the trees and come to a cliff face supporting the northern wall of the prison. I pull off my pack that I managed to hang onto despite the attack on the water. I pass over a pair of climbing picks and line to Genna that she quickly ties around her waist. Despite the dangers of this approach, it's our best way to get in undetected. The prison is built up on a cliff for a reason—what idiot would think to climb it?

I guess we're a couple of idiots.

With my own climbing picks in hand, I scan the rock face and find the best hand holds I can. The ascent is slow and precarious with the wind, loose rocks, and unstable holds. Partway up, I stab a pick in the wall for an anchor and continue to climb. Genna trails me like a shadow up the vertical ascent. It takes a long time and the muscles in my arms and legs ache but I'd rather be slow than fast and slip. All the while I keep my ears and eyes open. Every now and then I think I hear something move in the prison beyond but it's mostly quiet—eerily so.

My fingers at last grip the edge of the stone parapet and I haul myself up to peer over at eye level. There's no sign of life anywhere along the walkways or in the courtyard beyond. I slip over the wall and land lightly, keeping an eye on my surroundings as Genna climbs over moments later. This place smells not only horrible but *wrong*. The hairs on the back of my neck stand on end.

Directly before us lies a courtyard in disrepair and full of what I think are piles of clothes and . . .

"Sweet majestics," I breathe.

Bones. Human bones.

"Shift and follow me," Genna whispers.

She shoots a frosty glare at the courtyard and transforms into a black wolf. I do the same and we trot light footed on the walkways overlooking the courtyard and to a door that leads into the prison itself. With my sense of smell heightened, it takes a lot of effort to fight the gag reflex. It smells absolutely wretched in here. Decaying flesh, vomit, blood, and a putrid mix of other undesirable things I'd rather not think about. We walk through a short hallway and find ourselves in some kind of horror room. There are more piles of bones and clothes in here next to three different tables covered in dried blood. I can't breathe. I don't want to imagine what happened here but scenarios run through my mind from torture to . . . worse things.

Footsteps pound our way.

Heartbeat drumming in my ears, I rush to hide behind one of the piles stacked high beside one of the tables. Genna does the same on the opposite side of the room. I curl up tight on myself until I'm little more than a ball of fur, hopefully blending in with the other remnants of fur in the pile in front of me. I lay my ears back and peer under the table to see four pairs of legs rush into the room.

"Where?" one of them asks. They sound human but that could be very misleading.

"South wing. Near the mother."

"And others at the west sewers."

Their conversation is only a snippet as they run by while talking. Whoever they are, it sounds like we're not the only ones sneaking into this hell hole. The Spartans must have arrived. Well, that equally helps and complicates things. If they keep these monsters distracted, it'll give us the opening we need to find Erebus. Or, the Spartans could find us first.

We wait another minute before getting up from our hiding places and continuing deeper into the prison. The stone hallway we enter looks like it could be the guard quarters. Doors line either side of the hall, some ajar to expose small rooms with single beds and dressers. I do my best to make sure my toenails don't click on the hard floor as we continue on, checking each room for signs of our target. The hallway ends at the melted remains of a heavy steel door. It sits open with the entire top half a lumpy mess like a candle that's been burning too long.

As if it had been hit with acid.

Or acid spit.

Hydra.

One look at Genna and I know she's deduced the same. Hydra have been cropping up everywhere. It's very possible there's one here. How or why, I don't know. Either way, it's something we definitely don't want to run into.

Moving even more cautiously now, we creep into the next hallway that branches off three ways. We don't split up but move as quickly as we dare down each section of what appear to be interrogation rooms. These aren't remotely like the ones in Underground with white walls and a pristine quality. No, these look more like I'd imagine medieval torture chambers looked like—splattered blood, claw marks on the walls and doors, smashed tables. No bodies though. I can imagine where those ended up if there's a hydra here.

Genna comes to an abrupt halt and I almost run into

her. She sniffs at the air and her head swivels to the final section we haven't checked yet. I sniff too but it's near impossible to pick up a single scent apart from the other nasty things I don't want to smell. But whatever has Genna's attention, she goes after it like a hound. Crouched low to the ground and nose sniffing away, she makes for the third door on the left. It's one of the few that isn't left open. She paws at the handle but it doesn't budge. Locked then.

I flap a paw at her and transform to get it open while she stays as a wolf just in case. We're lethal in any capacity but our jaws as wolves come in mighty handy. With some clever lock picking skills, I open the door slowly in case it creaks. Inside, a man is curled up in the corner in ragged clothes and smeared with dirt. At least I think it's dirt. He doesn't look up but shivers. Genna slips in behind me and gives a low huff.

The man snaps his head about and his eyes go immediately to her.

"Dasc," he breathes. "What are you doing here?"

Genna tucks in on herself and transforms within seconds into the woman I've come to truly admire.

"Not Dasc," the man mutters and turns his gaze back to the wall as if he couldn't care less.

She lets loose a relieved sigh. "Erebus. You're alive."

Genna motions to me and I stand guard at the door as she kneels before the broken shell that is Erebus and tries to capture his attention. My heart is hammering again. We found him. Now we have to keep him alive and get him out of here.

"Do you remember me?" she asks. He shakes his head,

eyes closed tight and a grimace on his face. Genna takes his chin in her hand and directs his face to hers. "Look at me."

He slowly opens his eyes and searches her face. Dawning lights in his eyes. "The Dark Whisper."

"I've come to rescue you."

"What?"

"We're getting you out of here. We need you."

His eyes narrow. "Why?"

He seems awfully reluctant and defensive despite the fact we're offering him a chance at escape from this place. I'd already be running out the door if I was him.

"You were entrusted to find the Magi. The pack needs you now more than ever." Genna's words are so sincere that no one could doubt her loyalty to Dasc—unless they were someone like me who knows the truth.

There's steel in his gaze. I realize something as he studies us. He doesn't look sickly or too thin or have sallow skin—the things I'd expect from someone whose been held prisoner in the Fields and now this place. There's nothing about him that says weak. In fact, I'd say just the opposite. I'd say he's dangerous and we've made a very serious misstep.

"Show me your backs," he says darkly.

I blink. "Excuse me?"

"Show me your backs," he says again with a snarl.

Genna and I exchange looks. Well, I certainly don't want to turn my back to this guy. But Genna nods to me and then spins around to pull up the back of her shirt while I keep my eyes on Erebus to make sure he doesn't try to stab her or something. He looks at Genna's bare skin then looks pointedly at me. Reluctantly, I turn around and show him my back as well. I'm not sure what he's expecting to find, but he doesn't attack us at any rate.

"What did that prove?" Genna asks.

Instead of answering, he licks the tip of his finger and begins tracing lines in the dirt on his exposed forearm. A straight line down, a capital C on one side and mirrored on the other. He holds it out to us.

"Have you ever seen this mark before?" he asks.

Are we supposed to have? Is that a sign he expects us to have from Dasc or something? What if we give the wrong response? What if he decides not to tell us anything or attack?

"Never," Genna says.

His eyes slip between us as if weighing our truthfulness. I have a bad vibe from this guy. Eventually he rubs the mark off his arm with the edge of his tattered sleeve.

"It's the sign of that witch. I needed to make sure you weren't one of hers."

"Witch?"

"Yes, the witch." He sighs and dusts off his filthy hands. "She's been trying to get to the Magi before me at every turn."

"Has she been successful in stopping you?" Genna asks calmly.

He gives a wicked smile. "Not even once. I have my ways. The Magi are in my pocket. But she's a clever devil. I thought perhaps the new breed of shapeshifter was hers. That's why I came here, trying to figure them out."

My mind is reeling from everything Erebus says. First there's some "witch" also on the hunt for the Magi—I can only assume it's Echidna. Now there's a new breed of shapeshifter and they're working with this witch? And Erebus decided to come here, he wasn't forcibly transferred. What on earth is going on?

"These shapeshifters," Genna says slowly. "Why do you think they're a new breed?"

Erebus rises and points to his face. "Their eyes go black and they somehow have the memories of the person they change into as far as I can tell. No shapeshifter before has been able to do that. They only steal appearances. These new ones steal identities."

That's a horrifying thought. But black eyes . . . like Doug. Stars above, he was a shapeshifter in the middle of the IMS?

"Is there any way to tell them apart from the people they're impersonating?" I ask.

"Not unless they show their black eyes."

Great. They could be anyone and we'd never know.

Genna takes a step backwards to the door. "We should get moving and warn the others about this new threat. We're going to need those Magi now more than ever. They may be able to help us against them."

"Yes, of course. We just need to get out of here. Help me up."

I try to catch Genna's eye but she ignores me and offers a hand to Erebus. He groans as he gets to his feet and mutters a thank you. He leans on Genna's arm even though I still think he looks far too capable.

"Where's Dasc now?" he asks quietly as we inch out of the cell and into the hallway. "I haven't been able to contact him for months."

"Working on his plan," Genna says vaguely. "Preparing for Echidna's forces. And the Magi are part of that plan."

"Hmm. That's interesting, because the last I heard he was searching for you, Dark Whisper. He's rather cross with you for betraying him."

Every hair on my body stands on end. How could he possibly know?

The three of us come to a sudden stop and Erebus moves faster than I can blink. He lashes out at Genna with a hidden dagger but she's fast too. She parries with her climbing pick just in time to avoid a blade to her ribs. I leap forward and grab his arm, twisting it until the blade drops from his hand. But he's clever. He manages to snatch up the blade with his other hand and drive it once more against Genna. The next several seconds consists of a very tangled brawl between the three of us, of twisting limbs and the keen clang of metal against metal. Eventually I get my arms around Erebus from behind and hold him in a headlock as Genna knocks the dagger out of his reach.

Erebus starts to laugh.

"It's over," Genna says slightly out of breath. "You're coming with us."

"I'll never tell you where the Magi are, little girl."

"I think you'll find I'm very persuasive."

I'm under the impression she means torture. I recoil internally at that. That's not what I signed up for. But if Erebus refuses to tell us about the Magi . . . what choice do we have?

"Hmm." He tries to wiggle out of my hold without success. "I can see it in your eyes. You'd do anything to find them, wouldn't you? What do you want with them, Dark Whisper? Weapons in your arsenal against Dasc? Or maybe—" He gasps and laughs again. "A cure, right? That's what this is about, isn't it? Because you found Merlin."

Just how much does this guy know? And in turn, how much does Dasc know?

Genna stares him down.

"Well, in that case," he says.

He bucks his hips and throws both me and him off balance. We fall sideways to the floor as he twists. In the midst of it, he throws his elbow into my face and I black out for a few seconds before coming back to lying on the filthy floor. Genna is on Erebus but he's reached his dagger. She makes to block him but he doesn't strike at her when his fingers curl around the handle. No, he turns the dagger about and stabs himself in the throat.

"No!" Genna gasps and grabs Erebus by his shoulder but it's already too late. His head rolls back and blood streams out of his neck with a gruesome gurgling sound as he dies laughing. Within five seconds he stops moving altogether and Genna lets him fall to the floor with his blood coating her hands.

He killed himself simply to deny us a way of finding the Magi. I lay stunned on the floor with my eyes glued to his unmoving body. The shock of it creates a ringing sound in my ears and the air leaves my lungs.

What do we do?

Genna presses two fingers to his neck, then his wrist, and neck again as if his pulse might be hiding somewhere even though he is clearly dead. She rises on shaky legs and looks to me, her face ashen. Then she looks to her hands and furiously starts wiping them off on her pants as her expression turns to that of agony.

"We have to get out of here," she says at last, her breathing harsh.

I stare at Erebus lying on the floor. It's over, just like that.

"Hawk." Genna staggers over to me and holds out a hand. "We have to go."

Once I remember how to breathe again, I take her sticky hand and she pulls me to my feet. Turning slowly away from the bloody scene, we move numbly down the hallway.

We failed. Everything we did was for nothing. Erebus is dead. Our link to the Magi is gone. And Dasc knows of Genna's betrayal. He'll be coming for us.

What do we do? The question echoes over and over again in my head.

We walk through the nightmare butcher room and to the walkway. When I hear voices, I shake out of my numb state, grab Genna, and get low behind the parapet. Someone is weeping below in the courtyard and another is whispering. I inch forward on my hands and knees until I find a crack in the wall to watch the scene. A team of Spartans in black tactical gear surround and help along a group of four wounded men all bent and haggard.

One of the sick men says something in French and points a shaking figure up towards the butcher room. The Spartans change direction and start coming up the walkway. Genna and I quickly shuffle towards where we first breached the prison. The group of haggard men and Spartans reach the room. One of the soldiers gasps when he takes in what's inside. At least that's what I think until I hear other gasps, some shouts, and bio-mech fire. I peer over the wall to find the haggard men the Spartans had been escorting suddenly turn on their protectors. With vicious jagged blades, they cut the men down from behind.

I want to rush to their aid and manage to make it a few feet before Genna grabs my arm to hold me back. We watch in horror as the team is murdered not twenty feet away.

Then the haggard men shift—not like melted wax as I'd expect from a shapeshifter—but like a ripple of water passing over their entire bodies. Even their clothes change.

Into the same team of Spartans they cut down.

They pick up the weapons from the fallen soldiers and take their headsets as well.

One of them taps his headset and says, "This is Bravo. We've found a small group of guards being held hostage. They passed the shifter test. We're leading them out through the atrium."

The fake gestures to the others and they march back down the steps, across the courtyard, and through a door below.

Now I understand why no one leaves this island. And also realize that Erebus was telling the truth about a new breed of shapeshifters more deadly than any that came before.

I look to Genna and her expression is stony. I can't imagine what's going through her mind. She placed all her bets on Erebus only for it to end like this. Our hope for a cure has slipped right through our fingers.

"I'm not leaving," she whispers and her blazing eyes connect with mine. "If there's a single werewolf left alive in this hell hole, I'm going to get them out. I'm not leaving here empty handed. Use the climbing picks. Get out of here and let the others know what happened in case I don't make it."

She tries to rise but I grab her arm.

"We do this together or not at all." And there's no way I'm letting her out of my sight in case she considers some stupid act of self-sacrifice. It sounds just like something Phoenix would do. My heart gives a painful twinge thinking of my sister and the last time we spoke. But she's a thousand miles away now. I can't afford to let my focus waver.

Genna doesn't argue against my joining up with her. Instead she holds out her hand and I grasp it with my own.

"Together," she says.

We let go at the same moment. As one we run at a crouch to the courtyard. Slipping past the gruesome piles, we make it to the door and pause outside its frame. After one final look of confirmation at each other—pack mates—we head into the gloom of the prison.

34

Phoenix

We step over more bones in the storm sewer until we come to a breach through the stone above our heads. John pauses at the entrance and gives Theo a boost so he can scan the next room for threats first. At his signal, the rest of us are boosted one at a time until I pull John up after us into the upper level of the prison.

I find myself in a very disgusting cell. Everywhere is human waste, filth, hanging spider webs, and more of that green goo oozing down the stone as if coming right through the walls. The same wretched stink remains and my eyes water from its potency. Directly ahead of us the barred gate of the cell has been melted through the center. Globs of green goo glisten on its bent and sharp edges. And framed almost perfectly in the ruined frame is an egg the size of a barrel. I look past its molten gray shell to the room beyond and catch my breath.

There are more eggs.

There are *hundreds* of eggs.

They fill every crevice with only the smallest of walkways between them—paths for whatever caretakers there must be. No wonder I could sense this place so far out. Here and there I make out pieces of shell already cracked open.

"This is Zulu," a soft voice comes over the radio. "Do you copy? Are you seeing this?"

"We read you," John says, ducking his head and covering his mouth even with his mask on to make as little sound as possible. "There are hydra eggs all over the place."

"Same here. Bravo?"

"No eggs but . . . bodies. I think we found their kitchen."

Oh sweet majestics. It didn't even occur to me. Growing babies need to eat. Maybe that's another reason why they set up in a werewolf prison. If Echidna has a grudge against Dasc and his kind, she wouldn't be averse to feeding them to her brood of nightmare. Mother of monsters indeed. I swallow and fight back my gag reflex.

"Any sign of captives?" Zulu leader asks.

"None here."

"Nor here," John answers. He glances to me and my eyes drift upwards. There's something in the upper levels. It's hard to tell with the fog of the hydra's sick magic surrounding me, but there could be werewolves being held up there. I nod to John and he presses the mic close to his masked face again. "We're going to head upstairs and scout the southeast watchtower."

"Stay alert."

As if we need telling.

John motions to me and I'm given the unsavory task of taking lead. If there are any magical traps ahead, I should be able to sense them. In the meanwhile, Alona takes flight and flies in steady circles overhead as another safeguard. Each step I take through the mass of eggs is carefully placed, every movement slow and precise. My breath is shallow, worried if I breathe too much the eggs nearby might crack open. I can imagine the terror of a hundred little heads emerging. That's something we definitely don't want to happen. I continue along a narrow path that goes from one row of cells to the other. Goo sticks to my boots and trails of it pull at my heels. There's a lingering stench that goes beyond feces or decay. I can't put it into words except to call it putrid.

I reach a stairwell—the one spot not covered in eggs—and head in the direction I sensed those other spots of magic. I pause at the top landing to take a better assessment of where exactly we are. The room is one long hallway with cells lining either side on two different levels. Rough stone makes up the place and iron bars sit ajar or closed at random. And everywhere there are hydra eggs—grayish, scaly things in goo wherever they can fit, stuffed in open cells, tucked into corners, jammed together, *everywhere*. If even a quarter of these things hatch ... there goes France.

John taps me twice on the shoulder so I keep moving. We make quick progress along the second floor walkway but have to step over large holes in the metal and stone where acid chewed through. Freakin' hydra acid spit.

"This is Bravo," a soft voice comes over the radio. "We've found a small group of guards being held hostage. They passed the shifter test. We're leading them out now through the atrium."

I'm amazed anyone's still alive in this place. There's no

telling what state they're in, though, if this place has been overrun for months. Pushing that sorry thought out of my mind, I turn left across a walkway and stand ready to breach the room where I sense those other unknown presences. Its massive wood door sits slightly ajar.

The rest of my team forms up on either side of the door, Alona shifts back into her human self to join us, and at John's signal we breach. I yank back the heavy door for Melody to slip in first followed closely by John and the others. Spread out on the floor are four men in filthy, tattered guard uniforms. They're chained to the walls and look like they haven't eaten in a week—cheeks sallow and pale, lifeless eyes, peeling lips. It looks like we've found another group of hostages. I'd be thrilled except for one thing.

They have tainted magic in their veins.

I hold out a hand towards John to warn him of danger. Something's not right.

Specialist Jaeger gives us a skeptical look as if wondering what the heck we're doing, then bends down to test the first man with a stun gun. The man winces away from the pain but nothing about him changes. He's not a shapeshifter. I don't think he's a werewolf either. There's no outward indication of monstrous traits—no fangs, bloodshot eyes, webbing, or fur. I don't know what he is.

"Help us," one of them says weakly.

Jaeger tests the rest of them and turns to John. "They're clean. Let's get them out of here."

Before John can respond, I step forward. "Of course."

If this is some kind of trap, then I plan on springing it to see exactly what's going on. They won't show their hand unless they think they have the advantage. I break apart the chains on the first man and the specialist and I help him to his feet.

"Thank you," he says weakly. "I think they were going to eat us."

"Are there any others?" John asks.

"I don't know. Maybe. I heard wailing sometimes."

"We'll take you to the landing pad," John says. "Our transport will be waiting for us there."

A lie. One to test this newcomer because John's no fool. Not when I've given him reason to suspect these men and we already came across unknown monsters here.

The man's eyes grow wide. "No, you can't go that way. They have a chimera hiding to take down any helicopters. We should go through the atrium, to the storm sewers."

"You sure?"

He nods and wobbles where he stands so the specialist puts a hand under his elbow to keep him upright.

John motions with the end of his bio-mech rifle. "Get him moving. We'll free the others."

The specialist looks confused and I don't blame him. He doesn't know I can sense the danger of these "hostages," and making him go off with an injured man on his own in this place is a tremendously stupid idea.

"I think we should go as a group," Jaeger says.

"Just stand outside and help him."

Specialist Jaeger looks like he wants to argue but does as he's told. The man clutches onto his arm and they walk stiffly out the door together. The others still chained stretch their hands out to us as if pleading to be set free. John motions to the team with the specialist out of sight to not make a move. I nod to our leader and walk silently behind the specialist and freed captive. I stretch out a hand and focus on the energy within the hobbling man. What's inside him is dark and twisted, like a slithering snake coiled and ready to spring. I curl my fingers around the strands of magic and clench my fist.

He jerks to a halt and spins around awfully fast for a man who looks dead on his feet. His eyes pin me where I stand as if he can feel me tugging at his foul magic. I tug again and he snarls at me. The specialist comes to a sharp stop and takes a step away, a hand going for his weapon as he realizes something is amiss. I squeeze my fist even more and—as if a ripple goes through the man's body—his appearance changes into that of a stout young man with the entirety of his eyes an eerie black. A shapeshifter, I think, but some kind of new breed. One we certainly aren't prepared for.

He moves surprisingly fast and manages to yank the specialist's weapon out of his hands. His fingers stretch for the specialist as if to wring his neck right then and there but the eerie silence is broken by the pulse of a bio-mech gun from Theo. The black-eyed shifter staggers back momentarily but recovers quickly to shoot at me. I snap my gloved hand up and the pulse is knocked aside by the dragon's barrier that pops up over my fingers and palm. Before he can try to shoot me again, there's a barrage of fire from my teammates. This new type of shapeshifter jerks at each hit and ends up falling over the railing to the trove of hydra eggs below.

Specialist Jaeger rushes to the railing to look down when chaos breaks out behind me. I spin about to find the other prisoners have slipped their chains and morphed neatly into versions of our team. There are two of Melody, Theo, and John complete with matching clothing. The pairs quickly engage each other in a confusing mess of limbs and bio-mech fire. Alona immediately shifts into a raven and swoops up out of harm's way and squawks at me. As of right now, I'm the only one that can tell who's who.

I rush into the fray with my sensors on high alert, latching onto the hollowness of Melody's true self and the three twisted beings mimicking the team. A bio-mech pulse goes my way but I swat it aside, grab fake Melody, and whip her out the door where the specialist helps out by stabbing her in the chest. The mimic smiles and rips the blade out to slash the specialist's arm with it. They struggle over the weapon while I try to get the others separated. It's a nasty scuffle and at some point retractable swords are drawn out. I eventually get my arms around fake John and squeeze so hard I feel bones snap. He lets out a gasp but continues to struggle. I keep my grip on him, freeing John and Melody to draw their bio-mech guns on the two Theos trapped in a haze of shared kicks and punches.

"It's me!" the Theo closest to me shouts.

"No, it's me!" the other shouts back.

"Fish sticks," John says—a pointed code word to see who answers correctly.

"Salmon!" they both say in unison.

Oh, sweet majestics. I shove fake John ahead of me and kick him so hard in the back that he goes flying over the railing past Jaeger and fake Melody still trading blows. Free to intervene, I make for fake Theo but he immediately backs up with his hands held towards me.

"Red, it's me! I poured you a glass of top-shelf milk at grand-mère's, remember?"

Which is true, but I can sense the dark magic within this mimic of the true Theo. Can these monsters not only copy appearances but memories as well? If so, we're well and truly screwed. But if he can copy Theo's memories, he must also know I can sense he's the imposter. The mimic's eyes shift uneasily between the four of us surrounding him and he backs up another step. The real Theo breathes heavily and runs the back of his hand under his bleeding nose.

"Take the fake," John says and swings about to help the specialist.

Melody and I aim our guns just as the mimic raises a knife to throw at the real Theo. Thankfully, the barrage we blast into his chest stops him and the blade falls to the floor. It takes a lot of hits to bring fake Theo down. These new monsters sure are resilient. As soon as he's on the floor and Theo gives him a swift kick to the head to make sure he's down, John and Specialist Jaeger appear in the doorway panting.

Alona lands on the floor, transforms, and presses a finger to her earpiece. "Bravo, Zulu, come in. We have a new breed of shapeshifters here. Electric checks don't work." There's no response. "Bravo, Zulu, come in."

"You're not coming through on my radio," John says. "I think we're being jammed."

Crap. Meaning we have no way to warn the other teams unless we find them—if it's not already too late.

"Someone mind telling me what's going on?" Specialist Jaeger says and jabs a finger in my direction.

In unison, the entire team including myself says, "*Shut up.*"

"We make for Bravo's last known position first," John says. "Let's move. Lock him in." He gestures to the unconscious version of Theo. We hustle out of the room and I jam the door in place behind us. I check over the railing but the mimics I had knocked off the walkway are nowhere to be found. However, I do notice something else.

"*Merde*," Theo says beside me.

Several of the eggs directly beneath us have begun to crack open and I can see glowing green eyes peering up at us out of the darkness within.

"Move," John breathes and we break into a run.

Our boots thunder on the metal walkway as a symphony of cracking eggs fills the air. John leads the way deeper into the prison in the direction Bravo said they were heading. They were making for the atrium—which is the same place the mimics wanted us to go. I'm guessing there's a trap waiting there. As we run, Alona swoops in and out of each cell along the way checking for any hostages or hostiles. From the glimpses I catch, the only thing left of what prisoners had been here are dried patches of blood, scratches on the walls, and scraps of clothing. A shiver goes down my spine. The massive presence I sensed earlier looms ahead, closer with every step we take towards the atrium. I can only assume that the kitchen and missing inmates have gone to feeding whatever it is waiting for us. And from the number of hydra eggs in this place, I can take a pretty good guess.

I run step in step just behind John. "It's waiting for us. The mother, I think."

"I figured," he pants. "And Bravo's walking right into it."

We slow as we come up to where the walkway splits, one going straight and the other turns left around a corner into another cell block. I'm so focused on the massive presence ahead of us that I don't notice the smaller one coming in from the left until it's too late.

"John, left!" I shout.

He comes to a sudden stop just before the corner, braces against the wall, and makes a sharp turn to fire at what's coming.

I come around behind him to help lay down fire.

There's a sharp hiss, a loud cry of "You!" and then I find Epsilon's bared fangs directly in front of my face. She tucks down so her shoulder goes into my gut and we crash through the railing—my back screaming from the contact with metal—and fall to the level below. The breath is knocked out of my lungs and I lay stunned between a nest of hydra eggs as Epsilon snarls and sinks her teeth into the front of my neck to rip out my throat. Still unable to breathe, I clamp one hand on her lower jaw and the other on the upper, wrenching those vicious shark teeth away from me. The dragon's barrier snaps into place to protect my fingers from her nasty bite. I keep on prying but she pulls away and hisses before I can tear her jaw clean off. I give her a good kick to the chest that sends her flying into the cement wall behind her.

I suck down air and press a hand gently to my bleeding throat. The magic of her bite tries to seep into my blood and drag me under but I snuff it out like stomping out a small fire. Alona swoops in and shifts midair as she extends a blade to take off Epsilon's head. But Epsilon isn't Iota. If their numbering system is any indication, Epsilon is on a higher level than the others I've faced. Epsilon catches the blade in her hand and snaps it before throwing Alona to the ground. Theo opens fire from above as John and Specialist Jaeger rush down the stairs to help us. Melody takes the faster route and leaps straight over the railing at an angle so she lands on top of the lamia, crushing her into the floor. Instead of trying to bite Melody or stab her with the bits of blade in her hand, Epsilon rolls out from under her and runs between the eggs across the atrium. We give pursuit with Melody in the lead. I sense the massive presence directly ahead like a deadly cloud of energy but don't see anything. Where is it?

"Did that boy Charlie die?" Epsilon taunts and laughs as she continues to run. "Too bad. His blood tasted so good."

"Blaigeard!" Melody shouts and hurdles over eggs in her rush to reach the lamia. Alona takes flight and zooms ahead. I, however, come to a halt, stretch out a hand, grasp onto the lamia's energy, and clench my fist around it. Epsilon stumbles and gasps as I peel away the energy inside that keeps her alive.

I'm going to *end* her.

Her magic is dwarfed as the other presence rises. Rises from below.

"Beneath us!" I shout.

The stone floor breaks apart in an explosive hail and I duck behind the hydra eggs to take cover. Chunks of floor pelt my back and I'm forced down to one knee as I take the heavy blows. A terrible roar magnified three times shakes the prison. I blink against the cloud of dust and debris as someone screams.

Three pairs of enormous green eyes glare at me. Through the haze, three monstrous heads of a full grown hydra rise out of the ruined floor, each the size of a small car. Its scales are the color of a pale corpse, its many rows of teeth stained red, and spikes for horns sprout all over the back of its three heads. I'm transfixed by its enormous bulk surging up out of the floor. One massive foot comes up to brace itself on the partially caved in stone like the mighty leg of an elephant—except four times bigger with deadly claws.

The head on the far left lashes forward and launches a glob of bright green, acid spit the size of my head at Theo and Jaeger on the walkway. They leap out of the way as the metal sizzles and almost immediately melts into a puddle on the floor below—before also melting through that too.

"Take cover!" John shouts somewhere in the destruction.

I take a deep breath and rush low between the eggs as the hydra heads seek targets and start a barrage of deadly acid. A scream rings out in the midst of its attack but I'm not sure from who or where.

"Phoenix! Here!" Alona calls from within the cloud of settling dust, close to the foot of the hydra.

I find her kneeling on the floor just as one of the hydra heads spots us and rears back. I grab the closest egg and hoist it up like a shield in front of Alona crouched on the ground. The hydra shrieks but still fires. Acid splatters across the egg and a speck sizzles through my left vambrace. I throw the egg away from me and quickly rip off the vambrace before the acid can eat through my sleeve to my skin. It's then that I realize what Alona is crouching over.

I drop to the floor as the skin on the side of Melody's face bubbles and melts away like hot wax. There's only one thing I can think to do. I activate the dragon's barriers in my gloves and scoop at the acid. Melody screams and I remove what I can, throwing it ten feet to the side. When I glance up, I find the middle hydra head a mere fifteen feet away with jaws open wide. I throw up both hands and the barriers in my gloves extend in a bubble around us. Acid falls upon it like rain. The shield holds—barely—but I don't know how long it'll last. If my magic is control, then this is devouring chaos. And it's stronger than I can handle.

"Get her out of here!" I shout at Alona.

She throws Melody over her shoulders and retreats to the back side of the bubble. I drop the barrier like a small doorway so she can rush away towards where John, Theo, and the specialist have raised a wall of shields and fire incessantly at the hydra heads trying to keep them at bay. It takes all of my concentration to keep the barrier in place against the seething rage and hate trying to burn its way past my defenses. Sweat forms on my brow and my arms shake as I give my abstract will a concrete thought to guide it. I think of an umbrella in a high wind when its contours snap in the wrong direction. The bubble around me snaps forward in an inverted concave shape that throws the acid back at the hydra's face. It flinches away, giving me the momentary window to turn heel and run to my team. Another volley of acid hisses around me as I slide across the rough floor through the goop and duck beneath a row of eggs, tucking in my limbs to avoid the spraying flecks. The others do the same next to me with makeshift shields of stone debris raised.

I lay there shaking on the ground trying to catch my breath as I hear the hydra slither ever closer. I can't pull many more stunts like that. Forcing the magic in my gloves into a shape they don't want to go is really taking it out of me, especially with the force I'm fighting against.

"What the hell was that?" Specialist Jaeger shouts over the roars and hisses of the angry hydra. He's staring at me with wide, deranged eyes.

"Our last ace in the hole," John says. "Phoenix?"

We duck under another volley and shuffle in a line down the eggs away from the melting floor.

"I can't do much more of that," I pant. "We have to fight smarter."

John glances up briefly and his eyes sweep the area before he's forced to duck again. The prison shakes as the hydra moves closer. We have to run at a crouch out of range again and hunker against the onslaught. Melody's screams have stopped from where Alona guards her in a cell further down the block. I can only hope she passed out. *Pixies*, I can't get the image of her dissolving skin out of my mind.

"We need to get close enough to impale that thing."

If only Charlie were here. Together, we could end this in a hurry. But he's not. Geez, he's probably in better shape than we're about to be.

Another volley launches and it seems the hydra has run out of patience. It stomps towards us—hindered somewhat by its own eggs—and we're forced to retreat again. If it keeps pushing us back, we're going to end up pinned at the rear of the cell block. Then it's game over.

"We can't get through that hide even if we do get close enough," the specialist points out. He flinches as a speck of acid lands on his pants. John takes his knife and quickly cuts the fabric off but there's a sizzling sound as the small drop goes through the specialist's skin. He lets out a cry of pain as it burns straight through and into the floor. Theo immediately tosses over a small applicator of medical foam and the specialist sprays it into his wound with a shaking hand. Although Theo doesn't say anything or hardly makes a sound, I notice a similar hole in the edge of his palm that he ignores until the specialist returns the medical foam for him to use too. We're all going to be peppered similarly soon enough. We have to end this now.

John motions for us to move and we run yet again until we reach the cell where Alona and Melody are hiding.

"Phoenix can get through that hide," he says without the slightest hint of worry. "It's getting her close enough that's the problem. We need to pin down those heads. Distraction won't be enough. It'll be too clever for that."

"Don't forget the lamia," I add. "And no sign of Bravo or Zulu."

"And we're down one," Theo adds.

"Then we better make this next shot count," John says.

We're forced back into the cell as the hydra comes ever closer. In the distance I can hear Epsilon laughing at us. We're cornered and we know it.

John motions to Theo. "Explosives?"

"I've got five C-4 sticky packs."

"It'll have to do."

Our specialist keeps his eyes on the doorway but says, "Throwing bombs at that thing is going to be useless. You know how fast they regenerate."

"Then it's a good thing we aren't going to be throwing them at it," John says coolly despite our situation. "Alona, take Theo's case and paint the main supports for the atrium.

We'll give you a bio-mech shield to get free. Keep moving. Don't let it get a bead on you."

She nods and takes the bandolier of explosives from Theo.

"Jaeger, Theo, and I will run distraction to split the heads. Jaeger go south, Theo north, I'll go west. Jaeger right head, Theo left, I'm middle. If we split the fire, we've got a chance." He turns back to Alona as the shadow of the hydra falls over the door and only exit. "The second it's in position and those explosives are up, blow the atrium. We're going to bury this bastard. Phoenix, that'll be your cue to end this. You stay hidden until then. We can't afford to lose you."

He points to the broken remnants of an iron cell gate and I get the message. The others, except for Melody unconscious on the floor, line up at the door with bio-mech rifles at the ready. I grab hold of one of the iron rods and wrench it free of the gate. Alona shifts into a raven and tucks the bandolier over herself between her wings. I make a small slice on my upper arm and wipe my magical blood on the jagged end of the iron rod for my makeshift spear. The magic is the key ingredient. It's the only way to kill this thing. Spear to the heart with a magical tip.

There's a chorus of "check" from our team moments before the hydra lowers a head to the gate.

"Now!" John shouts.

The team concentrates their fire into the nearest face of the hydra. It doesn't harm it but with that much firepower, it forces the hydra head back. Alona sweeps out in the small opening to lay the explosives while Theo, John, and Jaeger make a mad dash in different directions between the eggs. I hide in the shadow of the doorway's arch next to Melody's unconscious form.

Once the hydra thunders away from my hiding place, I peer out to wait for my moment. The men fire at their target head to keep the hydra's attention split in three directions. It must sense some kind of trap, though, because it starts glancing behind itself to make sure no one is sneaking up on it. It's so focused on the men and its blind spot that it doesn't take notice of Alona flying from pillar to pillar of the atrium slapping an explosive to each one that supports the high, rounded ceiling and steel beams. I can only hope it's enough to bring the place down. She's almost tagged each of them when a shot of green acid nearly hits her from the side. Epsilon slips out of the shadows and spits again using the power of hydra blood to give her a nasty ability. Alona squawks and falls from the air.

Curse it all!

I bolt from my hiding spot for the last pillar that hasn't been set to blow. I dodge around cracking eggs and have to fall flat on the floor to avoid the hydra's thrashing white tail before making it to the pillar. Alona flutters on the floor, one of her wings sizzling as Epsilon advances. Without a second to lose, I scoop the last explosive off Alona's back and stick it to the pillar just as Epsilon rears back her head to spit again. I duck and the acid splatters across the back of my uniform. I immediately begin ripping it off and feel the touch of heat before I manage to shred the material off me, leaving only the under layer to protect me.

The time I take to rid myself of the acid gives Epsilon the opportunity to slip in and wrap her hand around my throat. She lifts me off the ground so my toes just barely catch the broken floor.

"I'm going to rip you to shreds," she snarls.

"Go to hell." As she rears back to spit again, I grab her forearm and snap her bones. She chokes on her own acidic spit and loses her grip on me. I fall to the ground next to Alona's shaking raven form and find the detonator for the explosives a foot away. Epsilon towers over me and the shadow of the hydra falls across us having spotted the commotion.

Before either can put an end to Alona or me, I snag the detonator and hit the trigger.

I expand the dragon's barrier in my gloves at the same moment a shockwave hits me. The barrier I put in place over Alona and myself trembles as the explosion rocks the prison and deafens the world. I might not be able to precisely hear the crash but I can feel it, sense the shuddering thuds, the quaking of the building itself, as the atrium comes tumbling down on top of us. My body shakes and blood drips steadily from my nose as I put everything I have into the barrier to stop the explosion and falling debris from killing us. I can really feel it then—how little I've recovered from Epsilon draining my blood. I haven't had enough time to replenish. I strain so far that I feel the magic in Scholar's gloves blink out of existence. The barrier pops.

Dust, stone, and metal fall around us and something heavy lands across my back. The breath is knocked out of me and I'm flattened to the floor, unable to move. The iron rod I had lies useless beside me, the blood on its end collecting dust from the air. Silence falls in the gap after the explosion and a ringing fills my ears. The remnants of the atrium settle but I can already hear the hydra trying to move again. This is our one and only chance.

But I can't move. I can hardly breathe. I'm drained and I know it. I don't even know how much strength is left in me to escape the rubble let alone kill the hydra.

A hand stretches towards me and grasps my forearm.

"Don't you dare give up," Alona rasps. She's transformed into herself, her injured arm clutched to her chest and her face far too pale. "Get *angry*."

Get angry. I've *been* angry, I realize. I've been angry for a long, long time. I've been angry at how the world is. I've been angry at the things I can't change. I've been angry at the distance that's grown between Hawk and me.

And I've been furious about what happened to Charlie.

Thinking of him bleeding out at the hands of the lamia, something twisted inside me takes root. I set my hands against the floor and dig deep into that wellspring of fury and find it still has fuel that pushes past boundaries and ignores pain. It eats away at me yet gives me the one thing I need right now—a do or die drive. And one way or another, I'm ending this.

Alona adds her own muscle power to freeing me and with an almighty yell, I throw the beam off my back and stumble forward.

"Go!" Alona shouts and shoves the makeshift spear into my hand.

The floor beside us heaves and shakes as the hydra fights to free itself. It's almost got a head out of the rubble already. Tripping over my own feet, I stumble across the broken debris to the very top of the hydra's spiked spine where part of it is barely visible. My legs burn as I climb up over chunks of cement and stone, one hand lightly supporting me as the other hefts the iron rod. The breaths of the hydra shift my footing but eventually I fall onto the bare white scales at the top of its shoulders.

I hear Epsilon scream from wherever she's been buried.

The hydra shrieks and gets one head free.

My teammates shout to urge me on and warn me as the hydra's jaws open wide when it spots me.

Both hands grip the iron rod, raise it high above my head, and send it plunging down one, two, three, four, five feet deep until nothing but six inches remain sticking out of its hide. Black blood bubbles up and coats my hands and forearms, flecks of it on my face. Then deep within the hydra I can feel my magic on the end of the rod connect with the hydra's heart and explode. Its whole body gives one great shudder—causing me to fall to my knees and brace my hands to keep from falling—before it lets out a low, wheezing breath from each of its three heads before lying still.

"NOOOO!" Epsilon screams.

My eyes scan the wreckage until I find her partway out of the debris and gaping at me. Her broken limbs and shattered face realign themselves with the power of the hydra's regenerative magic coursing through her.

But that's not going to keep her alive for long.

She killed Ashley. She almost killed Charlie. She almost killed Hawk.

I pull the retractable blade from my belt and let the pieces fall one by one into place to form a singular sword as I advance on Epsilon. For the first time she looks afraid. I walk on jelly legs down the slope of the hydra's body as she manages to pull the rest of herself free.

"Phoenix!" I think it's John but I don't care.

The lamia turns tail and starts to flee now that her big hydra friend is dead. All around us more eggs are cracking open as if the babies have realized their mother is dead and they've woken for vengeance.

But so have I.

Epsilon moves at an awkward gait with her broken leg attempting to repair itself as I advance on her. She slips out of the ruins of the atrium and takes a stairwell that leads down into the prison. I follow after at a slow pace. I'm nearly spent but I have just enough for this. One last mission.

The lamia limps towards what might be an exit but I draw up my mother's loaded gun and fire into the back of her knee. She lets out a cry and falls onto her face. I fire again into her other leg. It'll only slow her down but that's all I need. Epsilon claws her way to a wall and pulls herself up regardless to face me with teeth bared. She looses a hiss but it's ragged. I fire again twice into her chest just because I can.

A dark hunger in my chest drowns out everything else. The girl that had nightmares of firing a gun no longer exists. The girl that vomited after beheading vampires is a fleeting memory. The woman that stands in my skin now is none of those things.

She is wrath. She is ruin.

When I reach Epsilon, she tries desperately to claw at me but I crush one hand in my fist and shoot the other. At last helpless, she flails like a trapped, panicked beast. I press the blade against her throat, gripping both the hilt and end of the sword.

"This is for Charlie and the rest," I snarl.

Then I shove with all my might.

Epsilon's head rolls past my feet and her body remains slumped against the wall. I stumble away and drop my sword as if burned. The white hot anger in my chest melts away leaving an empty void behind.

I did it. And yet it seems hollow somehow.

I blink and stare down the hallway as my subconscious feelers sense two presences slipping away down the tunnel.

The radio in my ear comes alive. "Sierra? Come in, Sierra!"

"This is Sierra, we read you," John answers over the line.

"This is Zulu. We managed to cut the jammer. Any sign of Bravo?"

"We just found them. They're dead. But we need to move. The whole nest is waking up. Phoenix, where are you?"

"I've got two runners," I say quietly as I make up my mind and draw my mother's gun up again. "I'm in pursuit."

"Sierra, we've called in an airstrike," Zulu leader says. "We've got ten minutes to clear the prison before they blow this place with spiked bombs."

"Damn it. Everyone move! Phoenix, get back here!"

I don't turn around but start a slow jog down the tunnel after those two spots of twisted magic making a run for it. "I'll be right there."

The others talk to each other about the fastest escape route, how they're getting their wounded out of here, and returning to the boats. It becomes background noise as I keep on moving. Within fifteen seconds I enter some kind of flooded power room. Water falls from a busted pipe above and sprays everything, including me as I sweep into the room with gun raised. Through the pipes, metal, cabinets, and fallen stones, I spot two figures running to another door at the back of the room.

"FREEZE!"

They don't stop. I halt and fire a shot at the doorway ahead of them that brings them to a sudden halt. I hurry down with my gun aimed at their backs, water dripping into my eyes.

"Hands where I can see them or I shoot," I warn.

The pair raises their hands level with their shoulders and slowly turn around to face me.

I almost drop my gun.

"Hawk," I breathe.

It's him. I know it's him. It's not some mimic or shapeshifter. I can feel him. He's actually here. *Here*, of all places. And the person beside him is none other than Genna Barnes. I don't want to believe it. I've been spinning stories and excuses in my head but seeing them together here in the belly of this nightmare prison . . .

Genna takes a step forward so I fire near her feet.

"That's far enough," I growl.

"Phoenix," Hawk says, almost pleading with me. "Phoenix, please. You have to listen to me."

"What are you doing?" I wheeze. The sight of them standing here together is too painful. After everything I just went through . . . I can't do this. I can't take it in.

"It's not what you think," he says and takes a single step forward while holding my gaze. He angles himself slightly with another step to put himself between me and Genna. He's *protecting* her. There's no blackmail here. There's no hold she has over him. He's chosen this. He's chosen her over his own family. The same Genna that betrayed us, that helped Dasc escape.

"Are you—" I lick my lips and readjust my grip on the gun as my palms go sweaty even though they're already slick with black blood. "Are you working for Dasc?"

"No," he says sharply. "Neither of us is. There's so much I need to tell you."

"You attacked the Fields."

He bobs his head. "We did."

He's not even going to deny it. The world starts to spin.

"You betrayed the IMS."

"The IMS betrayed us," he says hotly and throws an arm towards Genna to clarify who he means by *us*. Not me and him. Not the team we used to be.

"You lied to me."

"Phoenix, please—"

"You lied to *me*. I'm your twin. I'm your *family*. I could have helped you, Hawk. If only you had said something—"

"I did!" he shouts and goes red in the face.

John's voice over the radio startles me. "Phoenix, respond! We have eight minutes to get out of here!"

"Eight minutes . . ." I say vaguely. This is some bizarre dream. This can't be happening.

"What are you talking about?" Genna asks.

My eyes snap to her. "I'm not talking to you."

"Eight minutes to what?" Hawk asks.

His green eyes are wide. Angry or scared or surprised—I can't tell. I don't know who he is anymore. The brother I knew would never have done the things he has. The Hawk standing before me could very well be a mimic for all intents and purposes. He's a shadow of the brother I knew. But in those wide green eyes, I see myself reflected. I'm not who I used to be either.

"The French are going to blow this place back to hell," I say. "We have eight minutes to get clear. You're coming with me."

His eyes harden and he sets his jaw. "I'm not going back with you."

"Oh yes, you are."

"I can't ever go back," he says softly.

Genna grabs his arm. "We have to go."

"You aren't going anywhere," I snap. I raise my gun, very tempted indeed to shoot her, but Hawk shifts to the side and places himself fully in front of her.

"There's more to this than you know," he says quickly. "I can explain—this prison, the Fields, Erebus, the werewolves—everything. But not now. We have to run. You have to run."

"I can't." I shake my head and move a step closer but they take a step back. "I can't let you go."

"If we stay here, we're going to die," he says and holds out both hands palm first towards me. "Fifi. Please."

My hands shake with the barrel of my mother's gun pointed at my brother's chest.

How did it ever come to this?

Shame, anger, and confusion overwhelm me but there's no time to sort any of it out. French spike bombs are coming. We simply don't have any time.

I lower my gun to my side and Hawk exhales with relief.

"Meet us at the Pont des Arts Bridge tomorrow at

midnight. Come alone. We'll explain everything." He and Genna start to back track towards the door with hands still raised. "It was never supposed to come to this, Phoenix."

"Maybe. But it did."

With one last look of longing, Hawk turns on his heel and runs out the exit with Genna into darkness beyond.

35

Hawk

I run as hard and fast as I can through the ruined sewers beneath the prison. In my head I count down the seconds until this place is going to be turned into rubble.

Faster. We have to move faster.

I don't have the luxury of thinking about the confrontation I just had with Phoenix. I won't be able to think at all if we don't get out of here and fast.

"That way," Genna pants and points to our left.

Our shoes splash through two inches of watery filth and it drips from the ceiling in our faces.

Five minutes. If that.

The tunnel ahead is partially collapsed so we shift on the fly and squeeze through before sprinting full out in our wolf forms. We careen around corners and debris and ignore the hissing sounds we hear above our heads. Light draws us on ahead until we reach a barred grate that doesn't budge despite both of us ramming it with our shoulders.

Three minutes.

Turning away from the dead end, we fly back the way we came and take another side tunnel we passed before. Another minute is wasted as we hit yet another dead end. Knowing the next move will either kill us or free us, we turn desperate. Returning to the power plant room, we take the water ejection line out. I take a deep breath and plunge into the fast racing water. It rips at me and threatens to press the air right out of my lungs. I'm tossed and turned and snag on the walls. Just as my lungs are about to burst, I'm practically flung out of the pipe, hurled through the air and land in the deep water surrounding the island. Genna lands next to me with a big splash.

I break the surface again and gulp down air. We can't stay in the water but we can't go back to the island either.

Jet engines roar ever closer.

Genna barks at me and together we swim as fast as we can away from the island. The French jets come in low overhead and I watch as the first of the splinter bombs are dropped on the stone walls. I dive beneath the surface just as they hit. The force of the impact ripples through the water and would have been deafening above the surface.

Then another round hits. And another.

After four passes, I break the surface again to see the destruction left behind. The towering walls have become smoking piles of charred stone. The towers are gone and fires rage within the depths of the prison's scorched hall. I've never seen splinter bombs used before. When they hit, there's a bio-mech blast as well as an explosion that sends smaller bombs in every which direction that do the same thing but also contain bearings and spikes strapped with magical explosives. They're rarely if ever used because they're meant to take out large groups of monsters at once, but obviously they can't be used when there are innocents in the area, which is practically all the time.

I tread water and keep my head low as the jets make one final pass before veering off.

Phoenix and her team must have gotten out. They had to. If we made it, then they made it.

But now what?

Genna nudges me with her nose and starts pedaling for shore. Thankfully, none of the water monsters try to attack us this time. They're probably keeping well away from the prison after that show of force.

I find myself in a daze as we reach the rocky shore, transform and hunt for transportation away from here. The Spartans must have come in some way and I didn't see any aircraft on the landing pad back at the prison. By boat then. Indeed, after half an hour of scouring the coast, we find a single boat left behind that must have been from the Spartan team we saw get slaughtered. Genna takes the helm and we ride the bumpy waves away from the smoking island.

Phoenix. Hydra. Shapeshifters. Werewolves. Erebus. Magi.

Trying to sort out what it all means and how it links together makes my head spin.

But there are clues here and there that I begin to tie together. I sort through what Erebus told us and try to come to terms with his end. Despite that, I don't think he was lying about the shapeshifters. Maybe it was another test in his own way.

He said their eyes can turn black. Black eyes like Doug in Seattle.

A new breed of shapeshifters, ones that are clearly capable of bypassing IMS securities if Doug was able to work inside the IMS for months and never be discovered. New shifters protecting a brood of hydra and spreading them across the world. Echidna's certainly been busy. It turns my stomach and makes it difficult to think of any hope still out there I might cling to.

Then there's some "witch" Erebus mentioned also looking for the Magi—who we have no clue how to find.

And then . . . there's Phoenix.

A painful knot tightens in my chest and I press a hand to my heart as it aches. We're standing on opposite sides of a divide that I don't think either of us knows how to cross. I can't go back and it's clear where she stands. But she's a Blessed. Where else could she possibly be? This time apart has changed both of us. It doesn't take a genius to see that. I just never thought it would come to this.

To where I honestly don't know if Phoenix would have pulled the trigger or not.

"What do we . . . where do we even—how—" I can't put together a single sentence with the jumble of information running through my mind.

"We take it one step at a time," Genna says. "Right now that means reaching land. Then we take the next step."

"Which is?"

"Figuring out what on earth we're going to do."

I rise from my seat on the edge of the boat to stand beside her. "So the tally stands thus—we're on the run from Dasc and his loyal pack, the IMS has us on their most wanted list, Echidna has made a new and improved breed of shapeshifters, the Magi are in the wind, and there's some "witch" who sounds like she's another threat. Do we have *anything* going for us?"

"The hydra brood is dead or will be soon enough," Genna says. "Dasc doesn't know where we are. We've hidden hundreds of werewolves in sanctuaries away from both Dasc and the IMS. And in the end we have something they don't have."

"A positive attitude?"

"They don't know *we* know about the new shifters and their tell. Black eyes."

"That's not much to go on if they only show their black eyes when they want to. I was in a cubicle across from one for who knows how long and never knew."

"It's a starting point, Hawk. We build on what we have." She looks optimistic enough but it's hard to tell. She's always so stoic. "But I do have something to add to your list."

"By all means."

"If these new shifters were working hand in hand with spreading the hydra, then it's made me realize something."

"Don't leave me in suspense."

"The hydra got into the States without the IMS noticing. How many IMS personnel do you think have already been replaced by these new shifters? They could be anyone, anywhere. Maybe the point of the hydra wasn't just destruction, but distraction for the shapeshifters to infiltrate the IMS and take it down from the inside?

I run a hand through my hair. "Geez, this mess just got a lot more complicated."

At that we both look critically at each other as if unsure *we* are who we say we are.

Genna eventually shrugs. "We both saw each other shift into wolves. I'm assuming they can't mimic *that*."

"No, but Echidna could have agents in both the IMS and amongst our kind now. They could easily stir up a disaster simply by making it impossible to trust anyone."

"I think they already have." She raises an eyebrow. "All those IMS agents attacked by werewolf colleagues? I told you that Dasc wasn't behind it. And I have a feeling the sirens weren't the only ones playing the agents. Maybe these shifters were as well. Slipping in through the chaos."

I blow out a sharp breath. "How do we possibly fight something like that?"

She doesn't answer and I don't have a clue either. The choppy waves swallow up all sound as we make for the shore. I'm cold and tired and worried about what sort of trouble we'll find when we land. Zeredah was going to make arrangements for us, but after what happened at that prison, do we dare trust her? Shapeshifters were in command of that prison. I don't care if they're a new breed or not. If there's a chance the old and new are working together, it doesn't look so good for Zeredah.

We reach the coast under cover of darkness. A quiet town sits on the top of the cliffs where we land. Together we tug the boat up on shore—in case we need it later—and trudge through the shifting sand.

"Do you have a plan?" I ask quietly.

"We meet Zeredah as planned," she says. "If she has anything to do with those black-eyed freaks, she's going to regret it."

I believe it.

Unfortunately, we quickly discover the French are watching the shores to make sure nothing escaped the destruction of the prison. Patrols scour the beach and we're forced to hide in some bushes, then under a rocky alcove, ducking and moving as quickly as we can up to the village on the cliffs. It's a tense night of cat and mouse sneaking to the meeting point with Zeredah. Hunger gnaws at my stomach, sweat drips off my brow, and my feet are sore in wet socks. Neither of us dares to transform into our wolf half, not here, not in France.

But at last we see the light of the bed and breakfast Zeredah is to meet us at. The woman at the front desk looks shocked at our appearance. I'm sure we look awful but there's no helping it.

"It's about time."

Zeredah rises from the lounging chair next to the door and sets the book aside she had been reading. She's in what I consider her home form and bundled in a raincoat. She waves off the woman at the desk with the assurance that these are the other guests they had been waiting for. The shifter leads us up a flight of stairs and into a snug room with two twin beds. As soon as we're inside, she shuts the door behind us and advances on Genna.

"What happened out there?" she asks. "I could hear the explosions from here. And weren't you supposed to be bringing someone back with you?"

Genna holds up a hand. "Look, we've had a very long day. I'm going to get cleaned up first and then I'll answer your questions, okay? Where's the shower?"

The shifter scoffs and points towards the entryway. "Third door on the right."

"Thank you."

"And one for me?" I ask.

"Second on the left."

Genna and I walk out together and split our separate ways. We play it cool. I take a quick shower, rinsing off the mud, brine, sweat, and blood. When I return to the room, Zeredah passes over a set of clothes to me.

"Figured you could use something fresh," she says lightly and then prances out into the hallway so I can change in privacy. I'll admit, for someone we can't trust, she makes a good show of being a helpful friend. The jeans, shirt, jacket, and even underwear fit. It feels good to be in something clean again. Genna comes in next and we switch places as she puts on the clothes Zeredah also got for her.

I stand in the hallway with the shifter and pace outside the door.

"I hope someone's going to enlighten me soon," she grumbles with her arms crossed and leans against the wall.

"Inside," I say quietly. "This isn't something to talk about in the middle of a bed and breakfast."

She starts to pace as well and we cross paths again and again. I keep an eye on her without making it too obvious. I saw her shift the one time and it didn't look like the new breed of shifters at least. Still . . . she's a shapeshifter.

The door opens and Genna beckons us inside.

My eyes immediately go to the clock on the wall. It's 11:00 p.m.

"How long will it take us to sneak back into Paris?" I ask.

Zeredah gives me a look as if I'm crazy. "Why?"

"Because I made a promise to meet someone there at midnight tomorrow."

To try to fix this gaping divide between my sister and me. She needs to know about the new shifters, the Magi, everything. I don't want her to look at me as the enemy like she did in that wretched prison. We're on the same side. But another part of me tries to convince myself not to go. For all I know, Phoenix could show up with her Spartan team and arrest me. Do I dare take that chance?

"Are you sure you want to go through with this?" Genna asks and takes a seat on the closest bed. There are deep shadows beneath her eyes. I'm sure I look no better.

I swallow. "I think I have to."

Zeredah growls and rolls her eyes. "Fine, I'm coming with. You're going to need me. And on the way you're going to tell me what the heck happened out there. Give me a second."

She turns about and immediately strips off her shirt without warning to change into something else. I look away but then my eyes are drawn to the mark between her shoulder blades.

A straight line with a C on one side and mirrored on the other.

The mark of the witch Erebus mentioned.

The shifter throws on a sweater and grabs her raincoat.

"We should probably head out tonight," she says. "Ready?"

She marches to the door and flings it open.

A man stands in the doorway with a raised gun. "Hello there."

The pop of a silencer sounds and Zeredah crumples to the floor.

Genna and I launch to our feet as the man steps over the shifter's body and aims his gun at Genna next.

Sweet majestics.

"My dear, how far you've wandered away from home."

Dasc.

How? *How* did he find us?

"You're a brilliant yet disappointing child," he continues and stalks further into the room. In the shadow of the doorway I see another hooded man guarding the way in case we try to escape. "Don't move you two."

My heart thunders and a ringing fills my ears. Terror bleeds into my bones.

Genna doesn't say a word but there is fire in her eyes. I think she's been waiting for this confrontation for a long, long time. I just wish it had been on our terms. There's no way this doesn't end badly.

No compulsion comes over me to obey him or otherwise. I realize he's keeping to the bargain he made with Phoenix so long ago with the condition that he cannot hurt or go after me or his life debt with my sister is broken. That's the one hope I have in this mess.

But I see Genna start to fidget with her hands before going rigid. The same symptoms I witnessed when Dasc took control of the werewolves in Moose Lake.

"Genna, dear. Why don't you tell me why you came here?" Dasc casually walks over to the small desk and takes a seat on the edge while keeping the gun aimed at her.

"We came to find Erebus," she says stiffly.

"And why is that?"

"To . . . to protect the pack."

"Whose pack exactly?"

"Yours."

Genna once told me how hard it is to lie to Dasc when he's compelling you to tell the truth. She *is* telling the truth but from a certain perspective. All werewolves are technically Dasc's but that's not who she's been doing this for, not really.

"You're clever," he says and gives a dramatic sigh. "I've suspected your treason for some time but let you play your games. Tell me, where did you smuggle those werewolves to, the ones you rescued from the Fields?"

Oh no.

"To the unknown."

I almost want to laugh at how Genna has managed to play him. That's why they called the compound in Canada the Unknown—in case this ever happened.

Dasc's eyes flash yellow. "You're really starting to make me angry."

"Good."

When he smiles, my blood goes cold. "I gave you everything. A home, a community that loved you, a place as my right-hand warrior. You liked that, didn't you? You'd do anything for me?"

Her face goes blank before a benign smile settles on her face. "Yes."

I launch to my feet and plant myself between the barrel of Dasc's gun and Genna. "Stop it."

"Why?" He crosses one ankle over the other like he's at a dinner party. "Do you really think standing in front of her is going to shield her from me? Or that I can't touch you? You see, the funny thing about life debts is that you have to phrase them *very* carefully. The words make all the difference. Isn't that right, Genna?"

"Yes."

"That's my girl."

A shiver goes down my spine.

"Let her go," I snarl.

"Or what?"

I decide whatever happens next is going to end badly anyway so I make my move and damn the consequences. I rush at Dasc and knock his gun away. He doesn't even try to deflect or protect himself.

But he doesn't have to.

Genna's arms wrap around my throat from behind and stars appear in my eyes as she squeezes too tight.

"Stupid child," Dasc says and proceeds to walk around us as if inspecting a specimen. "I didn't go after you. I didn't tell Genna to do this, but I made her loyal again as she always should have been. The life debt remains intact and you—you stop interfering."

I try to gasp for air and wriggle out of her grip but she's strong. We struggle fiercely together and I hurl myself forward to try to fling her off. We fall hard to the floor in a tangle. She wraps one leg around my torso and the other around my arm to hold me in place as she suffocates me. All the while Dasc stands over me smiling.

"Just like your father, you know. He tried so hard but in the end it didn't matter."

Despite choking to death, my inner beast comes raging forth. Fur erupts over my skin and I change shape to snap my jaws towards the monster leering over me. Genna adjusts her grip and keeps me locked down.

"Like I said. Useless."

The world grows dim and darkness eddies into the room like a fog.

Is this what death feels like?

"Do stop choking the boy. I have need of him still."

Dasc sighs and Genna's grip slips away. I wheeze for breath through my raw throat and my head explodes into a pounding headache. My lungs fill and I can feel life returning to me. But the darkness remains. It floods the room like a supernatural cloud of inky black. It swirls around me and thickens to the point I can't even see the floor anymore. I can't feel it either.

And its source is none other than Erebus standing alive and well—Dasc's hooded guard. Blackness drips off his hands. His eyes glow red and when he twirls his fingers, the darkness coalesces, rising ever higher. What sort of monster —or demon—is he? I watched him die. Genna made sure he was dead. How is he alive?

"I really do hate it when you give me orders, little brother," Dasc says.

Little brother?

Dasc has a *brother*?

"Give them to me," Erebus says and stalks further into the room. He lifts a hand and darkness wraps around me like vines of night sky. I'm hoisted off the floor and hang suspended in the air—a fly in a web. "I'll make them tell me their secrets."

Black vines wrap around Genna too but she just stares blankly ahead as if she's already left her body. Dasc goes to stand beside his brother—and it's only then that I can see the small resemblances between the two. They have the same intensity in their eyes, the same cleft in their chin.

"This one—" Erebus gestures to me. "—could prove most useful in manipulating that Phoenix girl."

No. *No.*

"Yes, I suppose you're right." Dasc gives another dramatic sigh but his eyes remain ever on Genna. "Break them both if you have to. I want to know where my dear Genna took my wolves."

"Of course. The pack survives."

Dasc takes two steps closer until he's a foot away from Genna and peers into her lifeless face. He looks almost pained. "The pack survives," he murmurs.

I try to claw at the darkness holding me, to move, do *something*, but I'm stuck. It's difficult to draw breath and my head swims as Erebus stalks towards me.

"What are you?" I manage to choke out.

Eyes gleaming red, he says, "The start of the nightmare. It's time for you to sleep."

His smile is the last thing I see before the darkness swallows the room whole and the world disappears.

36

Phoenix

The call I make to Jefferson is both painful confession and hopeful reunion. He's relieved to hear from me after my last call. I explain how I found Genna and confess that I let her go a second time. At least I get to punctuate it with better news. I have a time and place where I know she'll be. Jefferson hangs up quickly afterwards to secure the first flight to France.

Left to wait and regain my strength, I wander the halls of the private facility Zulu team brought us to. It's a beautiful apartment complex in Paris with its own medical facilities, dining center, high security around the clock, and a secret underground tunnel for use by its residents. I pass an open door where two fauns dance to some kind of opera. They've been a noisy bunch but I don't mind the levity at the moment. So much has happened . . . it's nice to see that the entire world hasn't split in half yet. There are still those that can dance. I tried joining in with some elves practicing choreography one level down but found my heart wasn't in it at all. I keep walking and pass a large black cat I've discovered is a matagot. I've been warned to steer clear of it. The matagot's large green eyes follow me and its tail twitches. The thing apparently helps pay for this place, but if it's not kept fed, it might murder everyone living here. How charming. As the French keep reminding me, though, rent in Paris is killer enough so it's worth it.

I continue on until I reach a door second to the end and knock lightly. It opens a moment later and Theo waves me in with a bandaged hand. I follow him through the luxurious living room with velvet sofas and reclining chairs to the bedroom beyond. A huge four poster bed takes up much of the space. Several chairs have been crowded around the edges next to some medical equipment and a heart monitor that beeps in the background. John and Alona are already here. Specialist Jaeger is nowhere to be seen but that's expected. I've learned he rarely enjoys anyone's company but that's fine by me. Theo and I take up chairs next to our teammates and look to the person in the bed. Melody's asleep with a massive wad of white bandages covering half of her face. She's being heavily sedated to save her from the pain of her injuries until she's healed enough to wake. We've been camping out in this room since we got here the other day.

"Her vitals are good," John says before falling silent. He's never been much of a talker but he's been unusually quiet since the prison assault. He looks ragged around the edges—I mean, we all do but there's something more in his gaze as he watches over Melody.

"Any word from the hospital?" I ask.

Alona stretches her arms above her head, a long continuous bandage running from her shoulder to her elbow on her right arm. I'm pretty sure she's supposed to be keeping it in a sling but she never bothered to put it on. "Just that Charlie's still recovering and he's restless."

"Good. The recovering part, I mean."

We're silent for the next ten minutes until Theo says, "Shall I make some crème brûlée?"

"How many things have you cooked since we got here?" Alona says flatly. "You're going to make us fat."

He glowers at her and aimlessly massages his bandaged hand.

Someone walks into the room just then and I turn about in my seat to find Zulu leader, Tristan, standing behind us in a button-down shirt and jeans. He starts speaking rapid French with Theo. Guessing by Theo's angry face and gesture to Alona, they're discussing Theo's suggestion to make more food. The leader eventually chuckles and Theo heaves a sigh.

"So?" John prompts. "What's the word?"

"The island's been completely destroyed," Tristan says. "There hasn't been movement since the bombing. And what we gathered confirmed that the shipments originated from there. Now that we wiped out the nest, that should put an end to the threat."

"The hydra threat anyway. For now," John says quietly and goes to look out the window.

We here in this room know what the real threat is. It's those mimics—that's what we've decided to call them—and how far they might have spread. Even Tristan agreed with us not to tell anyone what we found over a long distance communication. If it's going to be reported, it has to be face to face and it has to be with me there in case the mimics have already infiltrated the IMS. It took some explaining to get Tristan on board with that part. He didn't understand and he certainly took some convincing to believe what I can do. I felt so vulnerable and exposed telling my secrets to a relative stranger—part of it anyway. Tristan doesn't know everything but he knows that I'm a magic detector now.

But even if I can detect a mimic, trying to persuade others that the person is a fake is going to be difficult to put it lightly. I've had time to think about it and worry that hydra eggs weren't the only things being smuggled across the ocean and over the continent. What if those hydra were a front to cover the real threat moving in? A double blind with the werewolves being thrown in the spotlight as the villains yet again? John had said it before. When there's a level five monster on the ground, all forces get diverted to it and nothing else matters. What if that call to arms became an exploited weakness?

I've discussed my concerns with the others and they've been thinking along the same lines. The IMS hasn't faced something new in a long time. We have to change our tactics if we're going to win this . . . this *war*. I hate even thinking the word. Because if this really is war, then this is only the beginning of even greater pain and loss.

So here we wait, gathering our strength and trying to make plans for facing any mimics that have managed to wiggle their way into the IMS. Heaven forbid if they've already secured spots of authority. We aren't ready to face them yet. We don't know their weaknesses or ways of detecting them without my assistance. We've all agreed on one thing, though—we need a live mimic to test. How we're going to do that, I've no idea.

And yet even with the looming battles ahead, I keep coming back to Hawk and Genna standing united against me in the bowels of the prison. The same thoughts go round and round in my head. Is Hawk being used and he doesn't know it? Why were he and Genna so interested in finding Erebus? Did they actually find Erebus in there somewhere? What happened to Merlin? Where's Dasc in all of this? What about Witty? And Rosalyn?

My head pounds and I massage my temples.

I find Alona's uninjured arm draped across my shoulders. Despite our sometimes tenuous relationship, she's become a steady guiding hand when I need one that's not afraid to be blunt. My eyes drift to Theo on my other side who's wringing his hands and probably aching to go bake something—the persistent optimist and bright spirit of our group. Then there's John, the rock that holds us together with soft words that can cut apart a man. And Melody—our heart and soul of compassion.

Although Charlie isn't here right now, his presence and absence are both felt. He's . . . well, he's turned into a best friend, a willing ear, and the first person I'd choose to have at my side to go into battle with. He can be the grump, sure, but he also puts one hundred and ten percent of himself into everything he does whether it be sarcasm or fighting. It's something I admire about him and feel a true connection to. His absence here is felt keenly indeed.

As for me, despite my jagged edges, I feel like a puzzle piece that's finally found where it fits in the grand scheme of things. These people around me are family. For good or ill, whatever comes next we'll face it together and it's with their support that I know I'll be able to face the days ahead. I take comfort in that, wrap my arm around Alona's shoulders, and she gives me a faint smile. I always wondered what it would be like to have a sister. Now I have two.

The day wears on and a nurse comes in to check on Melody. I have to look away when the bandages are swapped for fresh ones. Then before long, it's time for me to go.

I rise from my chair and face my team. "I need to pick up Jefferson. Alona, care to join me?"

"Spartans never go it alone," she says and rises to stretch.

"We'll keep watch here," John says. "Stay safe. Be careful."

"Molon labe," Alona and I say in unison before walking out of the room.

We stop in her room first to pick up our bio-mech guns and for Alona to throw a jacket on over her injured arm before we walk the streets of Paris to the airport. In the distance the Eiffel Tower peeks above the rooftops and a chill breeze nips at my nose as the first signs of autumn touch the country. It's a beautiful city with crazy, winding cobblestone streets, blossoming trees, and ancient architecture. Beneath the beauty are the bustling crowds, the smell of stale urine that seems to follow you wherever you go, and the knowledge I personally have that there are darker things afoot than most people know beneath the Parisian trees. As we walk, I don't feel the draw of dark magic around me. There are no spots of werewolf magic hiding in the crowds. They've been eradicated like a disease or sent to the prison that's now a pile of rubble. In fact, I hardly sense any foul magic here, only the bright lights from legendary creatures in their hidden sanctuaries. It's a miracle, to be honest, but I wonder what the price was.

We keep walking—avoiding the presents of poop left by the many little dogs. I notice Alona's eyes keep turning upwards to a murder of crows flying overhead. She won't be able to fly for a while, not until her arm—wing—heals.

"What's it feel like?" I ask, realizing that I've never asked before. "To fly."

She sighs and watches those crows with the utmost longing. "Freedom of the highest order." She cracks a grin and looks sideways at me. "Pun intended."

"I like the sound of that," I say quietly.

Alona raises her arms out to either side and closes her eyes as she keeps walking. "It's to be untethered. Some days I feel like I might never come down. To ride that blue sky and the clouds forever. What a life that would be."

"So why do you come back down to earth? Why not stay up there?"

She lowers her arms and kicks at a pebble under foot looking rather resigned. "Because you can't ignore your roots. And someone has to make sure you guys don't get yourselves killed."

"Oh, that's true."

We share a smirk and keep walking but Alona's words stir awake a deep-seated longing in me. To be untethered, to be free. I like the sound of that. I like the sound of that a lot.

Around the next corner we reach the bus stop, catch a ride using some rather hacked French learned from Theo, and figure out our destination. One long ride later, we arrive at the massive airport and walk some more until we find the right terminal. Thankfully, we don't have to wait long until the face I'm longing to see appears. Jefferson's beady eyes find me when I wave to get his attention and he quickens his pace to reach us. Once we're within five feet, he drops his single bag in order to wrap me up in a hug. I press my face into his canvas jacket and breathe in his familiar smell of coffee and pine needles.

"I thought I was never going to see you again," he says and cups the back of my head. "What were you thinking, Phoenix? Trying to hand yourself over like that."

I close my eyes and clutch onto his back. "I was thinking I've seen too much pain, Jefferson. Something had to give."

He's quiet for a long moment and we pull apart so we can get a good look at each other. He sets a hand on my shoulder and the crinkles around his eyes become more pronounced.

"Maybe," he says at last. "Maybe."

Then he slings an arm around my shoulders and the three of us leave together. We rent a taxi this time and talk about small unimportant things on the ride. How has Paris been? Tried any of the local cuisine? Come across anything interesting lately? Our driver doesn't pay us any mind.

Jefferson doesn't even bother dropping his bag off at the apartment complex. We head straight for the Pont des Arts Bridge. It's a popular tourist spot so there's heavy foot traffic. The bridge itself is probably the most unique bridge I've ever seen in my life. The sides are completely covered with locks of all shapes and sizes. Couples stroll around us now and then as they add new locks where there's hardly any room, throw the key into the river below, kiss, and walk away. It's still a long time until midnight but both Jefferson and I need to be here. Neither of us wants to risk somehow missing the loved ones we've been searching for.

When the crowds lessen, we sit on benches lining the bridge or stand side by side overlooking the river as I explain everything to Jefferson.

"So, these mimics could be anywhere," Jefferson says and rests his forearms on the stone railing of the bridge. "And we have no idea how many there are."

"Yup."

He runs a hand over his neatly trimmed beard and mutters something that sounds vaguely like a long string of curse words.

"And you're sure they weren't mimics?" he asks quietly.

I shake my head. "It was Genna and Hawk."

"I suppose I should be grateful that she's alive. I haven't had word of her in months. I was starting to think maybe—" He leaves his thought unfinished and we watch the river in silence for a time.

The day draws on and we're restless. Alona disappears at some point but hops back in her raven form with one wing somewhat mangled. She manages to flutter a little but gives a loud squawk and then sticks to strutting up and down the railing of the bridge much to the enjoyment of onlookers. Then the light wanes. The street lights come on. My stomach grumbles. We wait and count down the endless minutes until midnight.

I run through the things I want to say to Hawk in my head but there's a churning pit in my stomach I can't shake. We've both changed, that's obvious. I don't even know how to relate to my brother when he arrives. Has the rift between us grown so wide that we can't reach each other? I massage my forehead and watch Jefferson pace back and forth. I can't think like that and yet . . . that's all I can think about. Am I still the girl that would bury a dead dog's body in the woods to hide her brother's secrets? After what I've seen secrets can do and the devastation they cause, I don't know if I'm that person anymore. And my world has expanded beyond desires that only concern Hawk and myself. Sure, I've cared about others before but now it's something concrete I can hold onto. There are other people in my life that have taught me self-sacrifice and doing whatever it takes for the greater good.

The night grows and I join Jefferson in pacing back and forth across the bridge. Every other second I check the time. Midnight comes. I stand in one spot but my eyes go from one end of the bridge to the other in anticipation. Jefferson does the same but Alona remains perched with feathers ruffled and unmoving.

One minute past midnight. They're running a little late but we can wait. There must be security to dodge or IMS agents to skirt. They're both wanted after all. I shouldn't worry too much yet.

Five minutes past midnight. I start to pace again with arms crossed over my chest against the creeping chill of night.

Fifteen minutes past midnight. Something has to be wrong. Or did Hawk say he'd meet me because he thought it was the only way I'd let him go? Do I even know him well enough anymore to know if he was telling the truth? Or has something horrible happened?

Half an hour past midnight. I sit on the bench nearest

the middle of the bridge and tap one foot incessantly. Jefferson's pacing has turned more into storming back and forth across the bridge. Alona finally shifts into her human self to sit across from me with arms crossed and a scowl on her face.

An hour past midnight. Then two. Then three, and on and on we wait until the first hint of light appears on the edge of the horizon. The three of us stand side by side leaning back against the stone railing. Eyes drawn, eyelids drooping with fatigue, we struggle on despite hope dwindling into ash.

"I really thought they were going to come," I whisper.

"So did I," Jefferson says and faces the river with a sigh.

"I just have this feeling in my gut I can't shake that . . . the worst is just ahead. That I've missed something important, or there's something sneaking up behind me that I can't fight. And now this."

Neither of them says anything to reassure me that my thoughts are just a symptom of worry. Perhaps both of them are feeling the same way. Or perhaps that extrasensory ability I have is trying to tell me something that I can't put my finger on.

"How long do we stay?" I ask.

"As long as it takes," Jefferson says.

Alona gives us both a stony look. "You can't stay here forever."

Jefferson doesn't respond but walks away to the other side of the bridge. I'm inclined to agree with Jefferson but I also see Alona's point. We can stay longer, sure, but waiting isn't going to make them appear if they were never planning on appearing in the first place. My heart sinks and goes down, down, down into a dark abyss where there's not much feeling except despair and cold. As I stand there drowning in it, I sense a terribly dark presence drawing near. The sheer scope of it and power are on the same level as Draco—it's like the shadow of death. I shiver, my heartbeat quickens, and I look in the direction it's coming from.

"Phoenix?" Alona asks.

"Sweet majestics," I breathe as I spot the source.

A lone figure stands on the top of a nearby building, a ghostly white silhouette against the rising sun. Hair like lightning and in a pale dress that flutters in the morning breeze, for a moment I think the woman looks like Iota, but that lamia is dead and this woman is far more powerful than any of the lamia I've encountered. It's more powerful than any monster I've faced, even that full grown hydra. And with power of that magnitude, I can only think of one monster that fits the bill of the woman currently watching us from afar.

A creature of alabaster and bone with the burning red eyes of the devil. And as the wind shifts her dress, I see two tails curling around her right leg, the true tell that she's no woman at all but a dragon in disguise.

The Mother of Monsters.

"Echidna."

She's here.

We aren't ready. I'm not ready.

Alona and Jefferson stiffen. I'm sure she's going to swoop down and end us in a matter of seconds. She could if she wanted. But she just stands there and watches. Does she know who we are? Does she know what I can do? Or that Alona and I were part of the team that destroyed the hydra nest? Why come here now? I'm so distracted by nightmare incarnate on top of the building that I hardly notice the men and women converging on the bridge. I don't pay them any heed until Echidna stalks away out of sight as if we aren't worth her time.

Then I notice the guns pointed at us, at the agents stationed on either end of the bridge and the boat in the water below. They shout at us in French but I think I get the general gist. I put my hands up in the air along with Alona and Jefferson. The streets nearby quickly empty and any stragglers are herded off by agents and soldiers. I can't imagine what on earth is going on until I sense the two spots of twisted magic amongst the agents boxing us in. I hone in on who they are and discover one appears to be leading the agents shouting at us. The other is just another one of the men.

I chance a slow glance back at my companions and mouth, *mimics*.

"*Aller sur le terrain!*" the leader—the mimic—says sharply.

"We don't speak French!" Jefferson says loudly in reply.

"Get on the ground!"

I refuse to budge. "What's going on?"

"Get on the ground!"

"Not until you tell me what's going on!"

The mimic leader scowls at me. "You are under arrest for conspiracy, treason, and colluding with the criminal known as Lycaon. Now, get on the ground!"

Oh, no.

With the hydra threat over, we thought we had more time to plan for the next big threat but we've moved too slowly. We didn't consider that the mimics would strike first, not when they hadn't been exposed yet. I may know the leader is a fake, but his comrades don't. He'll pass any shapeshifter check, he'll have the memories or at least some grasp of them of the man he's impersonating, and there's no reason for them to take my word over his. And if I just take him out now, they'll probably kill me before I have a chance to try to explain.

The hydra posed a great threat but they were a known entity, monsters in obvious fashion. A war with mimics will create an even greater challenge that could very well rattle the IMS to its core—who can you trust when anyone can be a monster in disguise?

I look to Alona and Jefferson. There is no easy way out of this predicament. We're trapped between loyalty and lies. As I slowly get down to my knees as a sign of compliance, I can tell the mimic knows just as well as I that we're truly trapped. The edges of a smile creep onto his face as if they've already won.

But they forget something.

We Spartans have a motto. Molon labe. It's a taunt, really, to our enemies. *Come and take them.* No matter the challenge, no matter the cost, we will always fight and will never be alone in our struggle. Because some sacrifices are worth it.

The mimics are about to discover how very wrong they were if they thought Phoenix Mason would go down without a fight.

I am wrath. I am ruin. And they should fear me.

THE ADVENTURE CONTINUES...

Get news about the next book in the series at:
brightway-books.com

Find exclusive content at:
bethanyhelwig.com

ABOUT THE AUTHOR

Bethany Helwig is the author of the successful International Monster Slayers series. She enjoys writing fantasy novels, composing music, creating art, and participating in various fandoms. She lives in a small town in Minnesota with her dog.

Made in the USA
Columbia, SC
14 November 2018